Praise for Vince Flynn's bestselling thrillers

'Vince Flynn is Tom Clancy on speed. He grabs you by the scruff of the neck on page one and doesn't let you go until the end'
Stephen Leather

A fast-paced political rollercoaster with a razor-sharp edge, featuring a CIA superhero that George Bush would no doubt give his right arm to have at his disposal' *Lads Mag*

A thriller with deadly aim . . . moves at the speed of a stinger missile'
People

'A Rambo perfectly suited for the war on terror' *Washington Times*

'Flynn perfectly measures all the ingredients for a fast and furious read' *Publishers Weekly*

Vince Flynn is the *New York Times* bestselling author of eleven thrillers, including most recently *Extreme Measures* and *Protect & Defend.* He lives in Minneapolis with his wife and three children. Visit www.vinceflynn.com

Also by Vince Flynn

Extreme Measures
Protect and Defend
Act of Treason
Consent to Kill
Memorial Day
Executive Power
Separation of Power
The Third Option
Transfer of Power
Term Limits

VINCE FLYNN

PURSUIT OF HONOUR

POCKET BOOKS

LONDON • SYDNEY • NEW YORK • TORONTO

First published in the USA by Atria Books, 2009
A division of Simon & Schuster, Inc.
First published in Great Britain by Simon & Schuster UK Ltd, 2010
This edition published by Pocket Books, 2010
An imprint of Simon & Schuster UK Ltd
A CBS COMPANY

1 3 5 7 9 10 8 6 4 2

Simon & Schuster UK Ltd
1st Floor
222 Gray's Inn Road
London WC1X 8HB

Simon & Schuster Australia
Sydney

www.simonandschuster.co.uk

A CIP catalogue record for this book is available from the British Library

A Format ISBN 978-1-47111-278-2
B Format ISBN 978-1-84983-033-1

Printed and bound by CPI Group (UK) Ltd, Croydon, CR0 4YY

To my publishers, past and present—

Carolyn Reidy, Judith Curr, Louise Burke, Jack Romanos

and

In memory of Kent Mosher

ACKNOWLEDGMENTS

As always, to the two people who guide me through this process every year—Emily Bestler and Sloan Harris, my editor and my agent. To David Brown, the best publicist in the business. To Sarah Branham and Laura Stern, for polishing things up and making sure the trains run on time. To Jeanne Lee and the Art Department, for once again patiently listening to everyone's opinion. To Al Madocs, sorry I did it to you again this year. To Michael Selleck and the S&S sales force, for doing an amazing job in a tough market. Kristyn Keene, Niki Castle, and Molly Rosenbaum, for all of your hard work and much-needed levity.

To Rob Richer, a good friend and someone to whom this country owes a great debt. To Edward Shoppman and Dennis Finnegan, for the new hardware. To Larry Nevin, Tim Flynn, and Bill Beaudette, for setting things up. To Dr. Jodi Bakkegard—we are lucky to have you in our lives. To all those who choose to remain in the shadows, thank you. To all those whom I may have forgotten, my sincere apologies.

To my amazing wife, Lysa, after ten years, you still take my breath away.

PURSUIT OF HONOUR

CHAPTER 1

NEW YORK CITY

IT was nearing ten o'clock in the evening when Mitch Rapp decided it was time to move. He stepped from the sedan into the April night, popped his umbrella, clutched the collar of his black trench coat, and set out across a rain-soaked East Twentieth Street. He navigated the puddles and swollen gutter without complaint. The weather was a blessing. Not only did it clear the streets of potential witnesses, it also gave him a reasonable excuse to hide his face from the city's ever-increasing array of security cameras.

Rapp had traveled to New York City to decide the fate of a man. At an earlier point, he had debated the wisdom of handling the situation himself. In addition to the inherent risk of getting caught, there was another, more pressing problem. Just six days earlier a series of explosions had torn through Washington, D.C., killing 185 and wounding hundreds. Three of the terrorists were still at large, and Rapp had been ordered, unofficially, to find them by any means necessary. So far, however, the investigation had been painfully complicated and had yet to yield a single solid lead. The three men had up and disappeared, which suggested a level of sophistication that few of them had thought the enemy capable of. The last thing Rapp expected, though, was that he would still be dealing with this other issue. In light of the attacks in Washington, he thought the fool would have come to his senses.

Beyond the significance of deciding if the man should live or die, there was the aftermath to consider. Killing him had the very real potential to cause more problems than it would solve. If the guy failed to show up for work there would be a lot of questions, and the majority of them would be directed at Rapp and his boss, Irene Kennedy, the director of the Central Intelligence Agency. One tiny misstep, and the shit storm of all shit storms would be brought down on them.

The head of the surveillance team had tried to talk him out of it, but Rapp wasn't the kind of man who was going to start pulling the trigger from a climate-controlled office a couple hundred miles away. He needed to see with his own eyes if they were missing something—if there wasn't some unseen or unpredictable factor that had caused the bureaucrat to jump the tracks. Rapp was keenly aware of the universal disdain for the man he had followed to New York. There were plenty of people on the clandestine side of the business who had cause to wish the prick dead, and that was another reason Rapp needed to be absolutely certain he was guilty of what they suspected. His dislike for the man would make it all that much easier to pull the trigger, and Rapp knew he had to fight that urge. He needed to give this idiot every last chance to save himself before they did something that could never be undone.

It would be a mistake to read too deeply into Rapp's cautious attitude, though. If he found the proof he was looking for, there would be no hand-wringing or queasiness. He'd killed too many people to begin acting like an amateur, and although the man was a fellow American, he was also very likely a traitor. And not some low-level, paper-pushing traitor, this guy had one of the highest security clearances in the federal government and his hypocrisy had likely gotten one of Rapp's agents killed.

Rapp moved down the sidewalk toward Park Avenue at a casual pace. He was dressed in a fashion similar to that of the thousand-plus executive car drivers who were shuffling their clients around the city on this rain-soaked evening—black shoes, black suit, white shirt, black tie, and a black trench coat. To anyone who happened to notice him, he would look like just another driver out stretching his legs, trying to kill a little time before his client finished his meal and was ready to head someplace else or call it a night.

As Rapp took up a position across the street and one door down from the Gramercy Tavern, he reached into his pocket and fished out a pack of Marlboros. Standing in the rain in New York City doing nothing might get you noticed, but throw in a cigarette and you looked like all the other addicts battling the elements to get their fix. Rapp turned away from the street and faced the blank façade of the building behind him. He tilted the umbrella so it looked as if he was trying to block the wind and flicked his lighter. He was not worried about the wind, but he was worried about one of the other drivers' catching a glimpse of his face in the glow of the flame.

After a deep pull off the cigarette, Rapp casually looked out from under the rain-soaked umbrella and across the street. The target was sitting in one of the restaurant's big windows sharing a meal, a lot of booze, and too much conversation with a man Rapp had never met, and hoped to keep that way. The other man was a concern, to be sure, but Rapp was not in the habit of killing private citizens simply because they were witnesses to the ramblings of a bitter man who was past his prime.

Despite every effort to find a different solution, Rapp's mood was decidedly fatalistic. The surveillance team had the restaurant wired for sound, and for the last two hours he had been sitting in a parked Lincoln Town Car listening to his coworker trash-talk the Agency. As Rapp watched him take a drink of wine, he wasn't sure what bothered him more, the man's self-serving criticism, or his reckless behavior.

One would think that anyone who worked at the CIA would be a little more careful about when and where he decided to commit treason.

So far his associate had done little more than espouse his political and philosophical views. Bad form, to be sure, but nothing that had risen to the level of outright sedition. Rapp, however, could sense that it was coming. The man had been drinking heavily. He'd downed two gin martinis and four glasses of red wine, and that wasn't counting the bump or two he'd probably had on the flight up from D.C. and possibly at the hotel bar. Rapp had ordered his surveillance people to steer clear of the airports. There were too many cameras and trained law enforcement types who would eventually be interviewed by the FBI. If the night went the way it was looking, every moment of this guy's life would be rewound and scrutinized, and they'd start with that U.S. Airways commuter flight he'd taken out of Reagan National up to LaGuardia earlier in the day.

Rapp casually took another drag from the cigarette and watched as the waiter placed two snifters of cognac in front of the men. A few minutes earlier, Rapp had listened as the other man tried to pass on the after-dinner drink. Rapp got the feeling the man was starting to think the dinner meeting had been a waste of his time. Rapp's coworker, however, insisted that they both have a drink. He told the other man he was going to need it after he heard what he was about to tell him.

Now, with the rain softly pelting his umbrella, Rapp watched the waiter place two snifters on the table. The waiter was still within earshot when the man from Langley leaned in and began to tell his story. Rapp heard every word via a wireless earpiece. For the first few minutes it was all innuendo. Rapp's coworker put his information on the table in a series of hypotheticals, and while Rapp had no doubt that the lawyers at the Justice Department would have found wiggle room in the statements, Rapp saw them as further proof of the man's reckless intent. Anyone who had been read in at this level of national security knew what could be discussed and what was strictly off limits.

Rapp was in the midst of lighting his second cigarette when the conversation moved from the abstract to the concrete. It started with the specific mention of an operation that was known to only a handful of people, including the president. *This is it,* he thought to himself. *The idiot is really going to do it.*

As casually as he could, Rapp brought his eyes back to the big window of the restaurant. There, the two men sat, hunched over the table, their faces no more than a foot apart, one speaking in hushed tones, the other looking more horrified with each word. The classified designations came pouring out in a rapid-fire staccato of dates and targets. One secret after another was tossed onto the pile as if they were inconsequential nuggets of gossip. The breadth of the damage was even worse than Rapp had dared imagine. So bad, in fact, that he began wondering if he shouldn't simply march across the street, pull out his gun, and execute the idiot on the spot.

As quickly as things had heated up, though, they came to an abrupt halt. Like some belligerent drunk who'd consumed one ounce too much of alcohol, the man from Langley put away his wares and announced that he'd divulged only a fraction of what he knew and that before he said anything further they needed to come to an agreement.

Up until now, Rapp had thought his coworker's rigid principles had driven him to take this risky step, but as he listened to the two men discuss the financial details of their new relationship, that last shred of grudging respect vanished. Rapp looked through the rain at the traitor and realized that like the hundreds of miscreants who had gone before him, his coworker's often-flaunted idealism came with a price, just as with all the other bastards.

Rapp flicked his cigarette into the gutter and watched it bob and swirl its way into the sewer. As he turned toward Park Avenue he felt not even the tiniest bit of remorse over what he had just set in motion.

Without having to look, he knew that a man bearing a striking resemblance to the traitor was now climbing into the back of a Lincoln Town Car. Every detail had been arranged from the eyeglasses, to the tie, to the hair color—even the black and orange umbrella from the hotel. All that was left for Rapp to do was walk a block and a half and wait for the idiot to come to him.

CHAPTER 2

NEW YORK CITY

GLEN Adams drained the last precious drop of Remy Martin from the bulbous snifter and immediately felt cheated that he wasn't going to get a second glass of the smooth, warm cognac. His dinner partner and former law school classmate, while brilliant, was also a bit of a bore, and had insisted on the tab. They'd graduated from NYU's School of Law twenty-six years earlier and since then they'd run into each other about once or twice a year, either at alumni events or at various professional functions. Every so often they'd grab lunch and catch up, but there was no doubt they had drifted apart. It was neither man's fault, of course. Between careers and family, there was little time left for old friendships.

The two men had chosen drastically different paths after law school. Urness scored a coveted job with the Public Defender's Office in New York City. After putting in three years of utter servitude, he bolted for the private sector and quickly earned a reputation as a fearsome trial attorney. By his midthirties he'd already argued two cases before the U.S. Supreme Court. At thirty-nine, he started his own law firm and quickly grew it into one of most well known and successful in a city filled with high-priced law firms.

Adams, while not nearly as successful, was proud of what he'd accomplished. Following in the footsteps of his father, he went to work for the CIA. His first two years, while enlightening, were worse than anything he could have imagined. Since childhood he'd dreamed of becoming a spook. Unfortunately, it didn't turn out to be anything even remotely close to what he thought it would be. Adams had grown up in the house of a father who had fought in World War II and then gone on to work for the CIA in its Special Activities Division. His dad was rarely around, and that left a lot of time for a young, impressionable boy to dream about unseen heroism and daring exploits. Even in his absence the man managed to cast his huge presence over the house and the aspirations of his only son.

In the real world Adams found the Directorate of Operations at Langley to be staffed by crude, rude, and dimwitted ex-military types, who were challenged to think of the world in any colors other than black and white. Having graduated from one of the world's top law schools, Adams found it unbearable to work around so many simpletons. After two years of service, and despite strong protest from his father, Adams left the CIA and went to work for the Justice Department. It was a decision that ended up causing irreparable damage to their relationship. It took the younger Adams years to come to grips with the rift it had caused, and in many ways this evening was a major step in putting the entire thing behind him.

Despite the problems it had caused with his father, Adams always felt he'd made the right decision in leaving the CIA. While at DOJ he'd tackled a series of increasingly tough jobs, and his career steadily advanced. Then 9/11 hit and everything changed. That first year or two after the attacks, Adams found himself caught up in the patriotic fervor just like everyone else. Eventually, though, he regained his senses and realized elements of his own government were every bit as big a threat as the terrorists. A vocal minority on the Hill had been screaming for increased oversight at the CIA, and before Adams knew it his name had been thrown into the hopper. His reputation as a tough federal prosecutor pleased the politicians, and his family history with Langley, and brief employment there, made him what many thought to be the perfect choice for inspector general of America's premier spy agency.

Adams experienced a glimmer of hope that the new post would help mend the rift between him and his father. His dad, now in his eighties, didn't have many years in front of him, and Adams knew there wouldn't be many opportunities like this. He couldn't have been more misguided in his optimistic assessment. The afternoon that he told his father of the prodigal son's return ended up being the last time they spoke. Unknown to Adams was his father's deep-seated disdain for the office of the CIA's top watchdog. What was supposed to be a moment of healing ended up being a catastrophe that destroyed any hope of repairing their relationship. Four short months later the elder Adams passed away.

The surviving son took to his new job with ministerial zeal. Like a missionary converting the heathens to Christianity, Adams would bring a passion for justice and the rule of law to the wild and uncouth. And like the missionaries who had worked the backwaters of South America, Adams would use force if need be—conversion by the sword. He would use his considerable talents to usher in a new era at Langley. An era they could all be proud of.

At least that was what he had told himself at the time. What he'd told his wife and his law school classmates like Urness. His fellow alums had been a great source of strength. They saw the CIA for what it was: a rotten, outdated organization. If he had known then what he knew now, he wondered if he would have taken the job. Had he been too idealistic? *No,* he'd told himself on many occasions, *they were just too corrupt.* The Constitution and the rule of law were more important than a thousand careers. A million careers.

Adams gazed into his glass in hopes that there was a drop to be found in the little indentation at the bottom, but there wasn't. "All is not wasted," he mumbled to himself. Tonight was proof of that. His plan was good, better than good—it was perfect. None of them would expect it. Besides, they had their hands full at the moment, trying to figure out how they'd fucked up and allowed nearly two hundred of their fellow citizens to get killed in broad daylight. They were nothing more than a bunch of goons, and these attacks were proof that their methods had served only to hearten the enemy.

"This is a big step," Urness said as he slid his black American Express card back in his wallet. "Are you sure you want to go through with it?"

"Come on, Kenny," Adams said to the other attorney, "I've never doubted your determination."

"I just want to make sure," Urness said with a toothy grin. "There's going to be some very powerful people who are going to be really pissed off."

"No doubt. Are you sure *you're* up to it?"

The attorney took a moment and then said, "I'm ready for a new challenge. A cause I can believe in. I've made a shitload of money. Now I'd like to make a difference."

With a raised brow, Adams said, "Like Woodward and Bernstein?"

"Yeah, except you'll be Deep Throat."

"Let's hope I don't have to wait until I'm ninety to admit my role in all of this."

"If I'm reading this right," Urness said, "and I usually do, I don't think you'll have to wait more than two years. I'll have it all gamed by then, and you'll be treated as a hero."

"By some."

Urness pushed his chair back and started to stand. "Fuck 'em . . ."

Adams laughed and stood, oblivious that his white dinner napkin had just slid from his lap to the floor.

"I'm serious. Fuck 'em. You're never going to get those fascists on the right to understand what we're doing, so I'm telling you right now fuck 'em and forget 'em."

"You're right," Adams said with an impish grin. As Urness came around the table Adams put his arm around him. He was almost a head taller than his friend. "You're a good shit, Kenny. I really appreciate this."

"I'm more than happy to help, Glen. These are strange times. If we don't take a stand, I'm afraid what kind of country will be left for our kids."

The two men moved from the restaurant into the bar and toward the front door. Adams looked at the booze behind the bar, and like one of Pavlov's dogs, began to salivate. He slowed his pace and rubbed his right hand over his belly. "What do you say we have one more bump before we call it a night?"

Urness abruptly stopped, looked up at his friend with a seriousness that he usually saved for his clients, and blurted out, "I think you drink too much."

Adams looked away nervously and chuckled. "Come on, Kenny," he said with forced levity, "a guy's in New York for the night. What's wrong with wanting to get a little lit up?"

"Nothing if you're some tire salesman from Akron in town for a convention, but you, my friend, are no salesman. You have wandered out onto a very dangerous cliff. One tiny misstep, and splat." Urness clapped his hands together to emphasize the point.

"I am well aware of what I'm doing."

"I'm not so sure. If we're going to do this, I want you to keep your drinking under control."

"Hey," Adams said in an easy tone, "I'm not going to tell you that I don't like to drink, but I'm not driving. I'm just trying to blow off a little steam."

"Yes, you are, and as your friend I'm telling you to tone it down.

This shit is serious. If you fuck this up, Glen, and don't handle it perfectly, you could end up in jail or worse."

"Message received." Adams put up his hands, feeling a bit embarrassed.

"Good, because I'm going to keep an eye on you. Now let's get you in your car. I need to get home and review a case before I go to bed."

CHAPTER 3

ADAMS and Urness found themselves huddled under the small awning outside the restaurant with their umbrellas in hand. Each man scanned the rain-splattered windows of the closest executive cars in search of a white placard with his name. Adams was lucky. His car was only twenty feet away. Urness said a rushed good-bye and then hurried away, darting between the puddles. At each passing sedan he stopped to search for his name. Adams plotted his own course and bolted for the rear passenger door of his Lincoln Town Car. He opened the door, closed the umbrella, and ducked into the backseat.

The driver gave him a polite nod and a soft "Hello," followed by a "Back to the hotel, sir?"

Adams was half tempted to ask him if he knew of any good bars and then thought better of it. Urness's admonition about his drinking had wounded his pride. "Yes, my hotel, please." Adams was already looking out the window, his mind trying to justify the joy he received from a good glass of booze or bottle of wine. A guy like Urness didn't understand. He was too focused on his career to enjoy the other things life had to offer. Come to think of it, the man didn't have a single hobby or passion other than the law.

Besides, Adams thought to himself, *I'd like to see Urness walk in my shoes for a month, let alone six years.* Adams felt like General Custer at times—surrounded by savages, trying to fight the good fight. Every day brought a new level of duplicity and treachery. The entire clandestine service and most of the leadership at Langley was staffed by professional liars and manipulators, men and women who had not an ounce of respect for the Constitution and the coequal branches of the Republic. There was nothing wrong with the occasional drink, he decided. He would just have to be a little more discreet about it.

Adams looked out the window as they rolled through a busy intersection. Despite the concern over his drinking, he was pleased with the pact he'd made with Urness. Considering how complicated it was, he felt the night couldn't have gone better. Adams smiled at his bold step, allowed himself to think how sweet victory would feel when the rotten house of Langley came tumbling down on itself.

Adams realized he hadn't felt this good in months. It was as if a massive yoke had been lifted from his exhausted shoulders. This was going to be fun—turning it around on them. He loved the irony. He was going to use one of their own ploys to take them down. He'd come to think of it as his own little covert operation. He would have to continue in his role as inspector general and look, with feigned zeal, for the leaker. He'd have to be careful, though, to not seem too eager. The operatives, while not bright, were at least instinctive. If he changed his behavior too much they would sense it, so he would have to do his job, while letting it be known that he had warned all of them this day would come. Adams couldn't wait to see the looks on their faces when the news broke.

The car hit a pothole and began to slow. He looked up and was about to ask the driver why he was pulling over, when suddenly the driver's-side rear door opened. A dark figure dripping with water glided into the vehicle and took a seat next him. Before Adams had the chance to figure out who it was, the door was closed and the car was moving again. Somewhere in a seemingly distant part of his brain he heard the automatic locks slam into place with an ominous thud. His mind was suddenly racing to understand what was going on. Why was this strange man in his car? Adams was about to ask him just that, when the man turned to face him.

The alcohol caused a slight delay in connecting the dots, but Adams knew instantly who he was looking at. The jet-black hair with a touch of gray at the temples, the olive skin and eyes so dark they looked like two pools of oil—they all belonged to none other than the CIA's chief thug—Mitch Rapp. But what in the hell was Rapp doing in New York City, let alone his car?

"What?" Adams stammered. "What in the hell are you doing?"

"How was your dinner?" Rapp asked in a casual tone.

"My dinner? What in the hell are you doing? Get out of my car right now!" Panic crept into his voice as his inhibited brain began to comprehend the gravity of the situation.

"Easy, Glen," Rapp spoke in a deep, calm voice. "You're in no position to be handing out orders."

"The hell I'm not!" Adams reached inside his jacket.

Rapp made no effort to stop him. "What do you think you're doing?"

"I'm calling the attorney general, is what I'm doing!"

Rapp let out a protracted sigh, followed by, "Put your phone down." He'd figured this was how Adams would react. Rapp took his gloved right hand, brought it up by his left shoulder, and unleashed a backhanded slap that caught Adams square in the nose. The blow was just enough to stun. Rapp did not want him bleeding—at least not yet.

Adams yelped like a dog and dropped the phone at the same time. He instinctively brought both hands up to cover his face and began complaining loudly.

Rapp grabbed the phone and started patting Adams down; sliding his hands around his waist to make sure there wasn't another phone or pager that he didn't know about.

"Take your hands off me!" Adams demanded.

"Stop moving," Rapp ordered as he quickly searched the jacket pockets.

"This time you've gone too far!" Adams shouted. "There is no way you're going to be able to weasel your way out of this. Kidnapping, assault . . ."

Rapp ignored the list of charges and told the driver, "It's just the one phone."

The driver nodded and put out his hand. Rapp gave him the phone and a second later the driver pulled over, rolled down his window six inches, and handed the phone to a man standing on the street corner.

Rapp turned his attention back to Adams, who, while done listing the potential charges, had now moved on to expressing the joy and satisfaction he would receive from watching Rapp brought to justice.

"Glen," Rapp said, "that's not going to happen."

"The hell it isn't!" Adams said emphatically.

Rapp sighed. "The chance of your ever seeing me brought to justice is zero."

"You don't know me very well, if you think for a minute I'm somehow going to be talked out of going to the attorney general with this."

"I know you all too well, Glen, but apparently you don't know me very well, if you think I'm going to let you live."

"Live?" Adams asked incredulously. "You wouldn't dare!"

"I've dared more times than I can count, and for far less than this. You're a traitor, and unless you can somehow explain to me why in the hell you've been leaking classified information, I'm going to kill you." Rapp looked into the eyes of the man sitting next to him and said, "It's really not that complicated, and if you really believe I'm the monster you claim, you should know I'm serious."

The seriousness of his predicament finally sank in. Adams, his jaw slack, stared at Rapp for a long moment and then, blinking, looked to the driver and shouted, "Pull over right now!" The driver ignored him, so Adams repeated himself, but even louder.

Rapp twisted in his seat, took a good look at Adams, picked his spot, and then let loose a left jab that caught the inspector general square on the chin. Adams's head bounced off the window and then his entire body went slack.

CHAPTER 4

TOOLESBORO, IOWA

THE old farmhouse sat nestled in a cusp of trees a few hundred yards from the banks of the Mississippi River. A creek flowing from the northwest forked and flowed around the rise of land before joining up again and draining into the big river that divided America roughly in half. The eighty-acre parcel was mostly wooded, with some rolling open land to the west. Most important, it offered concealment.

Hakim had found it on his drive north from Hannibal, Missouri, the previous fall. It had been advertised in the West Burlington newspaper as the perfect retreat for solitude, and Hakim decided it was worth a look. After a brief phone call with the local realtor he learned that the family had been selling off parcels of land for over a decade. The kids were all gone—one in Chicago, two on the East Coast, and one on the West Coast, Dad was dead, and Mom had just been moved into a nursing home. All that was left to sell was the old house and two barns that sat on the heavily wooded eighty acres by the river. The realtor warned him that the land around the house flooded most springs and the driveway sometimes washed out, so it wasn't good for much of anything except hunting.

Hakim told the woman it didn't sound like it would work, thanked her for her time, and hung up. He then drove north on Highway 99 until he found the place, which proved to be more difficult than he had thought, which in the end of course was a good thing. From a tactical standpoint the place had a lot of positives. There wasn't another house in sight and the local road dead-ended at the property's driveway, which meant there would be minimal traffic, if any. Hakim took a few photos and then called the lawyer in New York and instructed him to buy the property through a game and wildlife conservancy trust that had already been set up. The lawyer handled the closing. Hakim then directed him to hire someone to put up a gate along with a lock box, and some No Trespassing signs. Since then he had been back to the property just twice, both times to lay down provisions and make sure everything would be ready for them.

As it turned out, the house ended up being one of the rare parts of the plan he and Karim had agreed on. They had labored over the best route of escape after the attacks. The airports were out of the question, as was private aviation. The Americans were well rehearsed in closing those two avenues. Next they looked at the seaports on the East Coast and then the Gulf of Mexico. During normal times, stowing away on a container ship would not be difficult, but the Americans would be at a heightened state not seen since the Towers had been taken down. Every port would have hundreds of eyes and countless security cameras looking for them.

They looked at crossing the border into Canada or Mexico. Driving through a border-controlled checkpoint seemed far too risky, so they decided they would have to make the journey on foot, hiking through rugged wilderness. Karim was confident that they could handle the physical aspect of the trip. The real problem would be finding someone they could trust on the other side. Their resources were stretched too thin already. They would have to turn outside the group to find help. Hakim, knowing the depth of his friend's paranoia, offered his counterintuitive suggestion of driving to America's heartland and lying low.

Like Saudi Arabia, America was an immense country with large cities as well as vast open spaces that were sparsely populated. While it was true that America was a melting pot, especially compared to a closed society like that of Saudi Arabia, it was not exactly as open as it looked on paper. All those various groups tended to cluster together, which nullified much of the potential for concealment. Karim had originally thought his friend meant driving to a city like Chicago. With over ten million people in the metropolitan area, they would be the proverbial needles in a haystack. Having actually spent some time in America, Hakim had to explain why going to Chicago was a bad idea. There were too many eyes and ears in a big city and there would surely be reward money offered. If everyone was looking for them, the best solution was to find someplace where they could let the storm blow over in absolute privacy. Karim loved the idea and gave his best friend the approval to find such a place.

Hakim stared out the small kitchen window toward the river and the rising sun, and watched a single wild turkey strut across the yard toward the woods. He looked to his right in search of the others. Five mornings in a row he'd seen the seven turkeys strut along their little trail and into the woods. Had the others been killed, was this one kicked out of the herd, or flock, or whatever it was that you called a group of turkeys? Whatever it was, Hakim could identify with him. Every morning for the past week he'd thought of going it alone. Just walk down the hill to the river and get into the little boat he'd stashed in the underbrush. He'd fire up the twenty-five-horsepower outboard and push off from the bank. Head south like Huck Finn. Take the big river all the way to the Gulf.

Had there been a single incident that had caused the rift, or was it a culmination of events? Hakim had been searching for the answer all week. Was it when he left his best friend in the mountains of Pakistan almost a year ago? Was it the jungles of South America that had warped his friend's brain, or had it happened much earlier? Like most childhood friendships, theirs had progressed without question or challenge. Karim was the student with the best marks. He was a naturally gifted athlete with a competitive streak unmatched by any of the other kids in the neighborhood, and he had always been the most diligent when it came to prayer. He had been intense even then, while Hakim was far more laid back. They had always complemented each other.

As Hakim took a sip of tea he wondered if it had been an illusion of sorts. Had they ever really been that close? Hakim wanted to believe they had been the best of friends, but it was possible that the relationship had always been one-sided. It was hard to tell the difference between a driven individual and a self-centered ass—maybe they went hand in hand. Whatever the case, there had been a change, although it was possible that it was more of a progression. His old friend was proving to be every bit as narcissistic as the rest of the al Qaeda leadership. With each passing day he was increasingly obsessed with the coverage of the attacks and the aftermath. The prophet had warned against such self-love.

Hakim was attempting to reconcile the thorny theological aspects of their struggle when he heard the voice of his friend.

"Good morning."

Hakim was not surprised. He had long ago grown used to Karim's ability to move about silently. He looked over his shoulder and nodded. Glancing at the nearby clock he noticed it was 6:00 A.M. His shift was over and he wouldn't be back on again for eight hours.

"Anything interesting happen on your watch?" Karim asked.

"No," Hakim said honestly.

"Any news?" Karim asked, pointing at the small TV on the table.

"I did not turn it on."

"Reading again?"

"Yes."

"Those same blasphemous American books you read when we were kids?" Karim asked with an edge of disapproval.

"I would hardly call *For Whom the Bell Tolls* a blasphemous novel."

"Do you think Imam bin Abdullah would approve?" Karim asked as he grabbed the remote and turned on the TV.

Hakim thought of the imam of their local mosque back in Makkah, Saudi Arabia. The man was perhaps the most unenlightened cleric he had encountered in all of his travels. As much as he wanted to tell his friend just that, and then some, he decided to bite his tongue. The week had been peppered with these little fights. They were both on edge and Hakim was too tired to engage.

"Look at this," Karim announced, as he pointed the remote control at the TV and began pressing the volume button.

Hakim looked at the screen. It was turned to one of the American news channels. It seemed that his friend could not get enough of the coverage of the attacks they had perpetrated the previous week. He took an almost perverse joy in keeping track of the death count and the names of those who had been killed. He kept a running tally in a small spiral-bound notebook. Two cabinet members and seven senators had perished in the initial explosions. The first part of the mission had gone with clocklike precision. Three car bombs in front of three of Washington's most celebrated haunts all detonated at the height of the lunchtime rush. Those bombs alone had killed nearly 125 people. A fourth bomb was then detonated several hours later, during the height of the rescue operation, killing many more and dealing a devastating psychological blow to the satanic people of America.

At least that's how Karim chose to describe it. Hakim, however, was not so exuberant. The secondary explosion had killed dozens of firefighters, rescue workers, law enforcement officers, and civilians who happened to be standing nearby. Hakim had argued against the tactic. He saw no honor in the use of such underhanded moves, and that was only the beginning. One of his greatest struggles within al Qaeda was trying to get his fellow members to take a less myopic view of the world. Very few of his fellow jihadists were widely traveled, and even fewer had spent any real time in America. They had no understanding of America's sense of fair play. An explosion that was designed to target and kill rescue workers would enrage the American people. Karim and the others who thought such tactics would weaken the American resolve to fight couldn't have been more wrong. Dastardly tactics like this would only drive young men to the military recruiting centers. This would prolong the war and hurt their cause in the eyes of the international community. Hakim had stated his case as forcefully as he dared, and once again he'd lost.

"Look," Karim said almost gleefully. "This is why they will never win this war. I have been telling you this for years."

"What are you talking about?" Hakim was more irritated than interested. As he stepped closer to the TV, he saw a picture of a man in his late twenties. The screen suddenly changed to a still photo of a smiling woman and a baby girl.

"He was supposed to meet them for lunch," Karim said. "He works for their Treasury Department. Or I should say worked," he added with a chuckle. "He was more than thirty minutes late for the lunch last week. The mother and daughter were killed in the explosion. He survived."

"And why are you so happy?" Hakim asked.

"He just committed suicide." Karim started laughing. "Can you imagine such a thing? They are so feeble."

Hakim watched him take out his spiral-bound notebook. He scratched off the previous number, and with a self-satisfied smile, wrote down the new tally.

In a tired voice, Hakim said, "And you worry about what I'm reading."

Karim, having not really heard his friend, closed the notebook and looked up. "Excuse me?"

"What do you think Imam bin Abdullah would think of your merriment over the pain of others?"

With a dismissive grunt, Karim said, "He would thank me for killing another infidel."

Too tired to get into another heated debate with perhaps the most obstinate person he knew, Hakim ignored his friend and headed down the short hall to a warm bed and what he hoped would be a long and undisturbed sleep.

CHAPTER 5

LAKE ANNA, VIRGINIA

MITCH Rapp looked down at the calm, glassy lake as a bright orange sun began climbing over the trees on the eastern shore. Pockets of fog clung to the inlets, but the middle of the lake was clear. Somewhere around the bend he could make out the whine of an outboard engine, more than likely carrying a fisherman to his favorite early morning spot. Rapp had been to this place often since the murder of his wife. It was always a bit conflicting in the sense that it reminded him of the good times they had shared but also of the harsh reality that she was gone.

The setting reminded him of both his place on the Chesapeake, where they had fallen in love, and her family's place back in northern Wisconsin. He'd only been there a few times while she was alive and would not go back now that she was gone. He'd made the one trip to Chicago to apologize in person to her parents and brothers. He'd dreaded every minute of that conversation, but knew he would never be able to live with himself if he didn't face them. Rapp hadn't been the one who killed her, but he was the selfish idiot who had pulled her into his shitty little world where, all too often, innocent people got caught in the crossfire. He'd been a fool to ever think he could have a normal life.

He remembered, as he looked down at the smooth morning water, how she and her brothers liked to ski first thing in the morning. He thought of all those family photos that hung on the knotty pine walls of the cozy family cabin. Shots of Anna as a little kid, all legs, like a fawn, skiing knock-kneed on two old boards—her golden brown skin and the freckles around her nose. Those amazing green eyes that still haunted him every night. He'd never known anyone as beautiful, and would have bet everything he had that he never would again. He had decided after several years of mourning that it was hopeless to think otherwise. There'd been a couple brief relationships, but he still wasn't over her, so each woman was doomed from the start.

The squeak of a screen door caught his attention and Rapp looked over at the main house. It was a story and a half with three big dormers on the second floor and a wraparound porch that covered three sides. The four-inch siding was painted white, and the trim around the windows and the doors matched the green asphalt shingles on the roof. The owner stepped out onto the porch and struggled with the zipper on his khaki jacket. After a moment he got it started and then stepped forward with the help of a cane. His name was Stan Hurley, a seventy-eight-year-old veteran of the CIA. He'd been officially retired for nineteen years, but unofficially he was still very involved. The irascible Hurley had handled much of Rapp's training those first few years after he graduated from Syracuse University. On more than one occasion Rapp had wondered if the bastard was trying to kill him. Most of that training had taken place right here on the banks of Lake Anna.

Rapp had been an experiment of sorts. The clandestine men and women at Langley all went through the CIA training facility near Williamsburg, Virginia, known as the Farm. A group of veterans at Langley, however, felt the changing political winds and decided they would have to begin hiding things from the opportunists on Capitol Hill. That was when Hurley left the Agency and set up shop an hour south of Washington, D.C. Rapp didn't know how many others they had auditioned, but he gathered that Hurley had chewed up and spat out at least three guys before he arrived on that hot, humid summer day almost two decades ago. He knew because Hurley referred to them as Idiot One, Idiot Two, and Idiot Three. He'd say things like, "I spent two days trying to teach Idiot Three how to do this, and then the jackass nearly killed himself."

Watching the old prick hobble across the asphalt driveway, Rapp had to admit that he was still a bit intimidated by the man. There weren't many guys who could give him that kind of feeling. Rapp remembered showing up for training as if it were yesterday. He was in his early twenties, and he thought the best shape of his life after finishing a near-perfect season captaining the Orangemen lacrosse team. There was nothing as humbling as getting your ass kicked by a chain-smoking, bourbon-drinking, sixty-some-year-old man who was all cock and bones. It had happened only a few feet from where Rapp was standing. In the big barn, on the old stinky wrestling mat that Rapp had been forced to manhandle seven days a week for nearly four months.

Looking back on the situation now, Rapp could see Hurley had been in complete control, but back then, he seriously wondered if he was going to survive. Hurley woke him up at 4:00 A.M. with a cigarette dangling from his lips. When Rapp didn't get out of bed fast enough, Hurley flipped his military-issue cot and dumped him onto the hard, dusty floor of the barn. He was told that the barn was where he'd be sleeping until he proved himself worthy to sleep in the house. The real trouble started when Rapp came up swinging. In hindsight it had been an extremely stupid move. The geezer was far more agile than he looked. Rapp threw the punch and then next thing he knew he was back on the floor, the wind knocked from his lungs, gasping for air like a fish flopping around on a dock.

Hurley had announced while standing over him, "A fighter! Idiot One was a fighter. He only lasted a week, but at least he was a fighter!"

Rapp made it through that first week despite being knocked to the ground on average probably eight times a day. He was also called every dirty name in the book and ordered at least once an hour to quit. Hurley would tell him over and over in the foulest possible language that Rapp was wasting his time. Rapp had seen enough movies to know what was going on. He'd also run enough captains' practices to understand that Hurley was trying to figure out if he had what it took to make the cut. Knowing it, and experiencing it, however, are two very different things. Rapp had never quit anything in his life, and he sure as hell wasn't going to start now, but Hurley and his sadomasochistic trials tested him.

As the tough old spy hobbled along the drive with the help of his cane, Rapp couldn't help but smile over the fact that the guy used to kick his ass six ways from Sunday.

"What's so funny, dickhead?" Hurley asked in his throaty three-pack-a-day voice.

"Nothing." Rapp's smile got bigger.

"Bullshit. You think this cane is funny?" He picked it up and shook it at Rapp. "I'd like to see how you get along when you're my age. Doc says most guys are all whacked up on drugs for the first week after they get their hip replaced. I haven't taken shit."

"That's if you don't count the fifth of bourbon you drink every day."

Hurley stopped, his dark eyes zeroing in on Rapp. "Are you trying to ruin my life?"

"No," Rapp replied with a grin and threw one of Hurley's favorite lines back at him, "just trying to keep it real, Stan."

Hurley looked toward the barn with his baggy eyes and stuffed his right hand into his jacket pocket. After digging around for a moment he retrieved a soft pack of unfiltered Camels. "Yeah . . . well things are about to get as real as they can get."

"You sure you're up for this?" Rapp asked, wanting to give him another chance to skip it. "I can handle it."

Hurley cupped his left hand around the tip of the cigarette and spun the wheel on the old Zippo. The flame shot up, and after a long, deep pull he exhaled a cloud of smoke and said, "I know you can, but I need to do this."

Rapp would have preferred to handle it himself, but he knew there would be no changing Hurley's mind. "Well . . . let's get started. I have to be back up at Langley by nine."

CHAPTER 6

THE big double doors to the barn were closed, so Rapp and Hurley used the smaller service door around the corner. A medium-sized tractor, a couple of ATVs, and a Ford F-150 pickup truck were parked on the side closest to the big doors. The other side of the floor was dominated by what looked like a large safe but was actually an industrial kiln that Hurley used for his incongruous hobby of pottery and a few other things.

The two men walked to the opposite wall and approached a large oak card catalog cabinet. The brown wood was scuffed and dusty and a few of the old brass pulls on the drawers were missing. Even without all the various screws, nuts, bolts, nails, and assorted knickknacks that filled the eighty drawers, the thing looked as if it weighed a thousand pounds. Hurley reached around the back, pressed a button, and the cabinet began to swing away from the wall, revealing a concrete staircase. Rapp went down first, and once Hurley's head was clear, he punched a code into a keypad. The cabinet began sliding back into place.

Once the cabinet was back in place, Rapp punched in another

code. When the light turned green, and he heard the electric motor release the lock, he turned the knob and stepped into a rectangular room with poured-concrete walls. There were two battleship-gray metal desks, a couch, and a round table with four chairs. One man was sitting behind the closest desk. He stood when Hurley and Rapp entered. The second man was on the couch, lying on his back, his feet up, a Baltimore Orioles hat covering his face. He was either sleeping or didn't care to look and see who had just arrived.

The room had the heavy, sour smell of nicotine. When Rapp had gone through his training this place didn't exist. Hurley used a discreet contracting firm that was run by a former operative and had it built after 9/11. The floor of the barn was excavated and the foundation underpinned, to make room for the basement. The walls were poured and Spancrete sections were placed on top to create the roof for the new rooms and the floor of the barn. Within a two-hour drive of Washington there were three similar facilities, all of them built with private funding, and each one known by only a handful of individuals. Necessity was, after all, the mother of invention. In order to fulfill its mission the CIA needed to be able to conduct most of what it did away from prying eyes and in secret. Hurley had explained on many occasions that during the Cold War they had more than a dozen such places that they would use to debrief defectors as well as the occasional traitor.

"Where's the doc?" Hurley asked the big man who had been sitting behind the desk.

The muscular man pointed toward the steel door at the far end of the room and said, "Talking to Adams. Been in there almost two hours."

The big man's name was Joe Maslick. He was a native of Chicago, and a former Airborne Ranger, who'd done three tours, one in Iraq and two in Afghanistan. He was wearing a black Under Armour T-shirt and a pair of jeans.

Hurley looked at Rapp and asked, "Is he drunk?"

Rapp nodded. "He was pretty much on his way when we picked him up last night."

"And since then?"

"I gave him a few drinks on the plane ride down."

"No problems at the airport?"

Rapp shook his head. "Loaded him in the hangar right there at Teterboro."

"The pilots?" Hurley asked.

"Cockpit door was closed the whole time."

Hurley mumbled something under his breath and then said, "Why didn't you just drive him down?"

Hurley's words were less a question than a criticism, and Rapp did not do well with either. If it were anyone other than his old instructor, Rapp would have asked him why he hadn't gotten his lazy ass out of bed and handled the job himself, but it was Hurley, so he gave him a pass. "Stan, these pilots have flown me all over the world. They've seen a lot of shit."

"And if they're asked at some point who was on that plane . . . ?"

"They'll say they deadheaded it down to Richmond because they had an early hop the next morning."

"And when the feds want to talk to the exec who chartered the plane?"

Rapp glanced at his watch. It was 6:58 A.M. "The plane is on its way to Mobile as we speak. And the man on board has no idea I even exist."

"I still don't like it," Hurley grumbled as he began digging for a pack of cigarettes.

Rapp almost said, tough shit, but didn't, because he knew this was harder on Hurley than he'd ever admit. He had been best friends with Adams's father. Had served all over the world with him. Wanting to get off the subject, Rapp asked, "Did you listen to the audio from last night?"

"Yeah." Hurley exhaled a fresh cloud of smoke.

"And?"

Hurley stepped behind the desk and looked at the flat-screen monitor on the left. It showed Adams sitting in the next room talking to a fiftyish man with curly blond hair. His name was Thomas Lewis, and he was a clinical psychologist. Hurley wasn't sure who he was more upset with, himself or the little turd sitting in the other room. "He's a fucking traitor . . . an embarrassment to his family name."

Rapp didn't know what to say, so he kept his mouth shut, and since Maslick wasn't much for conversation the three of them stood there in silence watching the screen. Across the room, though, the man napping on the couch decided to make himself heard. From under his baseball cap he announced, "Embarrassing the family name is no reason to kill a man."

Rapp wasn't surprised by the comment, but it still pissed him off. He'd been arguing with Mike Nash about this entire mess for the last few hours.

"How about committing treason, boy genius?" Hurley asked.

"Definitely a capital offense, but then again it doesn't exactly fall under our jurisdiction."

Hurley's eyes scanned the surface of the desk, his hands beginning to tremble with rage. He skipped the stapler, grabbed a ceramic coffee mug, and whipped it across the room. The mug hit the concrete wall just above the leather couch and shattered into a thousand pieces, shards raining down on Nash.

Nash jumped off the couch shouting, "What the hell?"

"You wanna argue with me, sport, you do me the courtesy of getting off your ass and looking me in the eye!" Hurley turned to Rapp and snarled, "What kinda shit show are you running? If I wanted personal opinions I'd join a fucking book club." Hurley set out across the room, growling and cursing under his breath. When he reached the steel door he banged on it several times with his cane and then punched in the code to release the lock.

Rapp looked at Nash and mouthed the words, *What in the hell is wrong with you?*

Nash didn't bother to reply. He was too steamed at Hurley to deal with Rapp.

A moment later Dr. Lewis joined them and the door to the interrogation room was closed and locked. No one took a seat. Rapp and Hurley faced Lewis while Maslick stayed behind the desk to keep an eye on the monitors and Nash stayed on the other side of the room, still stewing about his rebuke.

"Give it to me straight," Hurley said to the shrink.

Lewis started to speak and then paused as if deciding where to begin. He ran a hand through his curly blond hair and said, "Classic narcissistic personality disorder."

"That's it?"

"No, it's quite a bit more complicated than that." Lewis hesitated and then asked, "You knew his parents?"

"Yep."

"Dad not around much?"

"None of us were. That's how it was back then."

Lewis nodded in understanding and studied Hurley with his blue eyes. "He was in the clandestine service with you?"

"Yep."

"So he was around even less than the average dad?"

"I suppose so."

"Was his mother detached?"

"Marge," Hurley said, as his eyes became unfocused, as if trying to remember some distant memory. "She wasn't exactly the warmest person."

"Not very affectionate?"

"About as affectionate as that desk over there."

Lewis nodded. "It all fits the profile. Adams has an overinflated sense of worth and that carries over into a sense of entitlement. The flip side is that his self-esteem is very fragile. It would be extremely difficult for him to take criticism. To deepen the problem, he lacks empathy, which enables him to be extremely exploitative of others. He feels that he is special . . . and can only be understood by brilliant people. That he should only associate with others whom he deems talented enough, while at the same time he needs their real talent to validate his underlying insecurities."

"Martyr complex? Always thinks he's getting screwed by someone and needs to let everyone know it?"

"Very common. When he comes across someone like Mitch, for instance," Lewis gestured to Rapp, "someone who is strong-minded, independent, results-oriented, not prone to handing out compliments, someone who is acknowledged as being at the top of their game. When that happens," Lewis winced, "he feels that person is the enemy and has to be knocked down to size. It is not uncommon for people with this disorder to become lawyers. It makes them feel smarter than most other people, and they can use their knowledge of the law to bully those who do not validate their imagined genius."

Hurley thought back to some of the family trips they'd taken some forty years ago. He remembered his friend Mark getting mad as hell at the way his son would pout if he didn't get his way. "Suicidal?"

"No . . . virtually unheard of. He's too in love with himself. Might fake it or threaten it, but most certainly would not follow through."

"Anything else?" Hurley asked.

"He's asked for you."

"He knows I'm here?" Hurley asked in surprise.

"No, he has no idea you're involved in this. He claims you'll understand what is going on."

Hurley frowned. "Understand? How could he possibly think that of all people out there, I would understand what he's doing?"

"I wouldn't read too much into it. As I said, he has an overinflated sense of his own importance. Also . . . remember, it is extremely difficult for someone with this disorder to ever accept responsibility for his actions. There is always a rationalization." Lewis looked at Rapp and added, "He's scared to death of Mitch because he knows nothing that he can say or do will change his mind. With you," he looked at Hurley and shrugged his shoulders, "he's hoping that he'll find some empathy from an old family friend."

Rapp could see that Hurley was having a hard time with this new twist. He took no joy in seeing the tough old bastard like this, so he touched his arm and said, "Let me take care of it."

"No." Hurley shook his head and stood up as straight as his seventy-eight-year-old frame would allow. "I need to do this."

CHAPTER 7

WAPELLO, IOWA

TED White slid out of bed and grabbed the pile of clothes sitting on the chair in the corner. Through the gap in the shades he glimpsed the gray predawn morning. He picked up the bundle, looked over his shoulder at his wife, and began to carefully tiptoe out of the room. As he walked past the open door he grabbed the handle and slowly pulled it until the door closed with a soft click. Safely in the hallway, he allowed himself to breathe. He waited for a moment to make sure she didn't stir, and then he took two steps and entered his son Hayden's room.

The seventeen-year-old lay there twisted up in his sheets and blankets, two of his four pillows on the floor, one trapped under his body, and the last one on top of his head. He was due to graduate from high school in one month. White grabbed him by the shoulder and gently shook him. Nothing. He waited five seconds and tried again. This continued for another thirty seconds with increasing force until Hayden's eyes snapped open with a dazed, crazy look.

"What?" he asked, still delirious with sleep. "What's wrong?"

"Shhhh," his dad said. "If you wake your mother up, there's no way she'll let you come with me."

The kid didn't reply, he just looked around the room and tried to figure out what was going on.

"Grab your hunting gear."

"But Mom said I couldn't go. I have an English test third period, and I have a game tonight."

Hayden was headed to the University of Northern Iowa on a baseball scholarship. "You've worked hard enough over the past four years. I think you're entitled to a little turkey shoot with your dad."

"But Mom . . ."

"I know," his father cautioned, shushing him with his hand. "As long as I have you back in school in time to take that test everything will be fine."

"Coach doesn't like it if . . ."

"I already talked to your coach. He likes to turkey hunt just like me, and he knows they're randy as hell this week. He said it was fine just so long as I have you back in school in time for the test. We'll head out to my uncle's old place. Fifteen minutes out and fifteen back. If you get your butt in gear we should have no problem getting in a few good hours."

Hayden untwisted himself and put his feet on the floor. He raised both arms above his head and groaned. "Mom's going to be pissed."

In a hushed yet forceful voice, White said, "I'm going to be pissed if you wake her up. Now get moving. I'll make us a couple of fried egg sandwiches. We can eat them in the truck." With that, White left his only child's room and made it down the hallway to the kitchen. He started the coffee and warmed up the frying pan. Next came the hard part. He found a notepad and a pen and leaned over, placing his right elbow on the counter, and wondered how best to admit to the crime. Like most things in life he decided it would be best to be brief and hold his ground.

Honey,

I checked with Coach last night. He says it's fine if I take Hayden hunting. I will make sure I have him back in school for third period. This is probably our last spring shoot. Next year he'll be away at college. Where did all the years go?

Love,

Ted

CHAPTER 8

TOOLESBORO, IOWA

HAKIM closed the door to the bedroom, and despite wanting to clear his mind, he began to think of the attacks. The lunchtime explosions, the bomb that had decimated the emergency personnel who were sifting through the rubble of the Monocle—a restaurant that was a favorite haunt of U.S. senators and lobbyists—and then the final bold move. Hakim considered it a stroke of genius. For all his recent disagreements with Karim, he had to admit that the audacity of the plan was impossible to ignore. Karim had asked Hakim to locate America's National Counterterrorism Center—the nerve center for the Great Satan's illegitimate war on terror, as he called it. Without telling any of the senior al Qaeda commanders, they put together a daring plan to assault the building. Karim wanted to turn the hunters into the hunted. They would hit the National Counterterrorism Center while the Americans were in disarray and focused on the initial attacks and the secondary explosion.

Hakim had been there with Karim when their six comrades, dressed in SWAT gear, burst into the building. Having spent a decent amount of time in Washington, Hakim knew it was not uncommon to see big black SUVs driving down the street loaded with menacing men armed to the teeth. With the confusion created by the initial blasts, they would drive right up to the gate of the counterterrorism facility and easily dispatch the light security.

The men had been trained for months in every detail of the plan, and from what they saw it had worked perfectly. The Suburban drove over the curb and right up to the front door with its emergency lights flashing. The men poured out of the vehicle, formed up in a single-file line, and entered the building engaging targets as they went. They were to avoid the elevators and take the stairs to the top floor where the nerve center was located. In addition to the M-4 rifles and Glock pistols, each man wore a custom-made suicide vest that was packed with C-4 plastic explosives and half-inch ball bearings.

Karim had predicted that the attack on the facility would cripple America's ability to effectively attack al Qaeda for years to come. And it couldn't happen soon enough. The hunter-killer teams and the unmanned aerial vehicles with their missiles had decimated the upper ranks of their group. They expected casualties to exceed one hundred, but something had gone wrong. Either that or the Americans were lying. So far only eighteen individuals had been reported dead in the assault on the counterterrorism facility. Six days later, Karim still refused to believe the reports. He was convinced the Americans, in an effort to save face and reassure the public, were covering up the true damage.

Hakim had noticed one little problem with that theory, though. News crews had been able to get shots of the building's upper floors from outside the security fence, and they were still intact. If the suicide vests had gone off as planned, every window would have been blown out and there was a better than fifty-fifty chance that the roof would be nothing more than a jagged hole. He had mentioned this to his old friend and had suffered a harsh rebuke. He was told he was naïve in the ways of the world and the West's ability to manipulate the media.

Hakim was growing tired of his friend's inflexibility. He was the one who had traveled the world, while Karim had done little more than hang out at cafés and mosques surrounded by like-minded men. He had done almost no traveling outside Saudi Arabia. There were things Hakim would like to say to his friend, but he knew the timing was not right. They needed to find a safe way out of the country and then, when things had settled down, he could confront him.

When Hakim was done washing his face and brushing his teeth, he faced east, knelt on the floor, and began to pray. For most of his life he had prayed the required five times a day, often spending a total of two hours prostrate in an attempt to prove himself a good Muslim. It had been several years since he'd been that devoted, however. To accomplish his mission he'd been forced to abandon many of his habits and rituals. His travels to America and other countries required that he draw as little attention to his faith as possible.

Even now, in the secrecy of his room, in the middle of America, with not a person in sight, he rushed through his prayers. He offered himself up to Allah and asked for his guidance on this dangerous journey, and then, as was increasingly the case, his mind began to wander. He was still talking to Allah, but instead of asking for guidance he was asking questions. He was trying to reconcile the irreconcilable. He stumbled through it, as he did so often lately—asking the question, giving half the answer, and then moving on to the next thing before completing the thought. Doing so prevented him from having to face the truth. These shortened prayers were turning into bleak sessions. Almost as if he were jotting down notes with Allah and saying, when I get through the hardest part of this journey, you and I will sit down and sort our way through this mess.

Hakim still believed in Allah. That was not the problem. His lack of confidence had more to do with his followers—the men who claimed to know exactly what Allah wanted. As he slid under the covers, he tried to clear his mind. His faith, he realized, was not in crisis. It was his faith in his friend that was causing the problem. Hakim thought back to the day they had met, but quickly stopped himself. He had spent too much time wrestling with this of late. He was tired, and if he was ever going to sit down and discuss his concerns with Karim he would need to be rested. Using an old trick, he picked one of his best memories and began to replay it in his mind.

The sun was glistening off the familiar cool blue water of the Florida Keys. Hakim leaned back in the chair and then let himself come forward almost as if he were praying to Allah, but he wasn't. His right hand went round and round in tiny circles on the reel, drawing in as much line as he could in the few seconds he had, and then he leaned all the way back. Despite the strain of wrestling with the great big marlin for the better part of an hour, he had a look of childlike elation on his face.

The trip to Cuba had been inspired by his reading *The Old Man and the Sea*, by Ernest Hemingway. For Hakim, it had been the single greatest experience of his life. A day didn't pass without that beautiful marlin jumping into his thoughts, and rarely did he fall asleep without a glimpse of it. He knew it was a coping mechanism. There had been a lot of death and dismemberment—bullets and bombs that did horrific things to friends, strangers, and enemies alike. He'd seen men literally shredded by the shrapnel of an artillery shell. So bloody and fleshy and cut to pieces that you'd swear there was no way on earth they would ever survive, but by God's mercy some of them did, and if they'd had the medical facilities that the enemy had, even more would have lived. And then there were other times where you would find a comrade after an air strike and you would swear he was simply knocked unconscious, because he had not a blemish on his body. You would nudge him, even splash some water on his face, and there was no bringing him back. Hakim learned later it was the concussive blasts of the big two-thousand-pound American bombs. The shock wave from the explosions would cause blunt trauma to the internal organs of individuals without leaving any outward mark of death.

These were just some of the images Hakim tried to suppress every time he attempted to sleep. Like the six well-trained men assaulting the counterterrorism facility. Hakim did not like the casual way they convinced other followers to throw their lives away. That was why he clung to the memory of his trip to Cuba and the unforgettable day he spent chasing the marlin, fighting and eventually landing the huge fish. The chasm between the two worlds, however, created a paradox. He had either been halfheartedly trying to reconcile the issue, or trying very hard to avoid it. Whichever was the case, Hakim knew he couldn't put it off much longer.

Now is not the time, he told himself. He quieted his mind by thinking of the warm sun on his face. He remembered the humid salt air and the soft breeze, the balletic dance of the big blue fish as it sailed through the air. Hakim began drifting off to sleep, hopeful that he would someday return to Cuba. That familiar voice in his head was calling him a fool.

He had no idea if he had been asleep for two minutes or two hours. He was still on his back, his eyes closed, when he heard the heavy footsteps of someone running in the house. The door to the bedroom burst open with a thud, and Hakim, startled, sat up in complete shock. His mind, numb from its deep state of REM, couldn't quite place the face of the burly man standing in the open doorway.

"They are coming," the man said with genuine fear in his voice.

Hakim realized it was Ahmed, the lethargic Moroccan.

"Hurry, they are here," he said in heavily accented English. "Grab your gun and get to your post."

"Who is here?" Hakim asked, suddenly very alert.

"Two men with orange . . . like they put on their vehicles."

Hakim was used to trying to translate the mangled sentences that the men often concocted, but this was a new one. "What are you trying to say?"

"Get up," the Moroccan said with genuine panic. "Karim wants you now! Hurry!"

CHAPTER 9

LAKE ANNA, VIRGINIA

ADAMS couldn't figure out where in the hell things had gone wrong. His plan had been perfect. He'd seen what happened to whistle-blowers. They ended up celebrated by one party and trashed by the other. Legal bills bankrupted the poor bastards while the slow workings of justice placed their life in a near-permanent state of limbo. No matter how just their accusations, they ended up pummeled. Politics in D.C. was a blood sport and whistle-blowers were cannon fodder. Adams had thought about it long and hard. It would have been like being the first guy off the very first landing barge at Omaha Beach on D-Day. They would have slaughtered him.

No, he was convinced he had plotted the right course. He knew with every fiber of his body that Rapp, and Nash and Kennedy and a bunch of others, were trampling all over the Constitution. He had been working feverishly behind the scenes to try to get the right people at Justice to stand up and take notice. Most of the deputy AGs wanted nothing to do with Rapp and Kennedy. There was a long list of people in Washington who had tried to tangle with them and so far they had proven themselves untouchable. More and more, people saw it as a career-ender. Adams thought he had finally found an ally in Senator Lonsdale. The senior senator from Missouri chaired the Judiciary Committee and shared Adams's dislike of the CIA and its cowboy ways.

Then the bombs had shattered the civility of the capital and the mood changed yet again. Adams had gone to see Lonsdale only a few days ago, and the meeting had been a disaster. After months of working with each other, and finally finding an aggressive attorney at Justice who was brave enough to go after the criminals at Langley, she had now lost her nerve. She suggested Adams drop the issue and focus his energy on tracking down the millions in unaccounted funds the CIA had squandered in Iraq and Afghanistan. He desperately tried to get her to see that now was not the time to quit. They were so close. All Adams needed was the political clout and subpoena power of the Judiciary Committee and they could finally put Rapp and the rest of them behind bars.

Adams could not do it by himself. Despite their overall lack of brainpower, Rapp and the others were survivors and had gone to great lengths to cover their tracks. With Lonsdale abandoning him, and the rest of the Senate and the House too morally bankrupt to lift a finger, Adams saw no hope in dragging them out of the shadows and into the bright light of court. With no support from Justice or the Hill, and the whistle-blower option deemed suicidal, Adams had to find a third way. His source of inspiration was none other than Mark Felt, the now deceased assistant deputy FBI director who had brought down President Richard Nixon by selectively feeding information to Bob Woodward and Carl Bernstein.

While Felt was the template, Adams was not going to be so foolish as to allow some reporter to make millions off his bravery while he retired on his meager federal pension. He would publish a scathing exposé of the CIA, its illegal programs, and the men who ran them. He had already picked out a title—*A Quest for Justice.* He would write it under the pen name Jefferson. No first name, just the last. Adams had told Kenny Urness that a CIA black ops agent had come to him and was asking for help. The fictional agent wanted to shop a tell-all manuscript that would expose the CIA and its myriad illegal programs. Urness would set up a blind trust to hold the millions the novel would make, and then when things finally settled down five or seven years from now, Adams would step forward as the brave man who had brought down the fascist wing of the American government.

There would be uproar for sure, but Adams knew how to hide his tracks. He'd already purchased, with cash, a used laptop that would be destroyed once the book was finished. He'd even found a software program that would allow him to change his prose to avoid identification by writing experts. Polygraphs would be administered far and wide, but he would pass them as he always did. The lie detectors were useless against someone with his IQ. He'd had it all figured out, but despite all of the careful planning, he'd missed something.

Adams fingered the empty glass sitting on the table and silently wished they would get him another drink. The vodka was starting to wear off and that was the last thing he needed right now. Staying calm was no easy thing when you knew a man like Mitch Rapp was loitering on the other side of a steel door, and you had no way of calling for help. Despite being caught off guard, Adams had already vowed that he would make Rapp pay. He would say what he needed to say to win his release, and then he would raise hell.

No sane person would ever kill him. At least that's what he kept telling himself. He was the inspector general of the CIA, for God's sake. The media would dig. The Hill would demand answers. It would simply be too difficult to cover up. That's what his highly rational brain kept telling him, but there was another voice in his head. One that was far less confident. One that had been warning him with increasing seriousness that Mitch Rapp was a man capable of extreme violence.

Adams was again trying to reassure himself that all would be fine, despite his deep forebodings, when the door opened. He recognized the lined, worn face immediately, and notwithstanding the fact that he didn't care much for the man, he felt a huge sense of relief that he was here. Regardless of their differences, Stan Hurley was an old family friend, a covert ops legend, and maybe the only man Rapp would listen to. Adams was confident he could get the old man to sympathize with him.

"Uncle Stan," Adams said in a hope-filled voice, "thank God you're here." He stood and moved forward, his arms open, ready to embrace one of the meanest cusses he'd ever known, but before he could get close enough, something hard poked him in the stomach. He froze.

"Sit down," Hurley ordered.

Adams looked down to see the rubber tip of a cane pressed into his belly. "What happened to you?"

"Nothing . . . sit." Hurley nudged him back and pointed at the chair.

Adams slowly retreated and took his seat. "Uncle Stan, there'd better be a hell of a good explanation for this."

"Really?" Hurley said with skepticism. "I was about to say the same thing."

"This is crazy; I'm the inspector general of the CIA. I can't be kidnapped in the middle of the night and interrogated like this."

"The fact that you're sitting here is proof that you're wrong on both counts."

Adams frowned and said, "This isn't Prague circa 1968. Neither Mitch Rapp nor anyone at the CIA, for that matter, has any right to abduct me."

"I suppose from a purely legal standpoint you are correct."

Hurley's admission gave Adams a shot of confidence. "You're damn right I am. Everyone makes mistakes, but this one is a whopper."

"It sure is."

"Well," Adams studied the face of his father's best friend in a vain attempt to gauge his true intention, "as a favor to you . . . I'd be willing to look the other way on most of this, but I'm going to need some reassurances."

"Such as?"

"For starters . . . Rapp and his band of goons need to promise that nothing like this will ever happen again."

Hurley gripped the back of the chair with his free hand. He didn't say anything for a long moment. His mind flashed through a movie reel of Glen Adams's life. He hadn't put much thought into whether he liked the kid until he was in high school, and then only because his friend was worried that his boy didn't quite get it. As Hurley looked at the younger Adams he thought how right his friend had been to worry.

Hurley finally spoke. "And you think all of this is a mistake. You're here through no fault of your own?"

Adams knew this was where he needed to be careful. "I know you've been out for a while, so I don't expect that you've kept up on everything that's been going on, but let's just say, Rapp stuck his nose into something that doesn't concern him."

Hurley almost laughed, but managed to keep a straight face. "Really?" Hurley said as if he were intrigued. "Why don't you enlighten me?"

CHAPTER 10

ADAMS'S mind was moving at light speed trying to plot the correct course that would allow him to sucker this old codger into thinking Rapp had made a monumental mistake. He couldn't remember the exact date, but as best he could recall Hurley had been out for at least fifteen years. There was no doubt he kept tabs on certain things, but most of his old sources would have dried up. The key, he decided, was to stay as vague as possible and keep things current.

Adams averted his eyes and seemed to study the dented and scratched surface of the metal desk. "This thing I'm working on . . . I'm afraid I can't talk about it."

Hurley looked at him with his bloodshot but shrewd eyes. "So if I call Director Kennedy right now, she'll tell me you were on official CIA business?"

Shaking his head, Adams replied, "She wasn't involved in this."

"Tell me who to call then. Give me a name." Hurley folded his arms across his chest as if he were settling in for a long wait.

"Stan, you're not read in on this." Adams shifted in his chair. "Hell, you don't work for Langley anymore. I can't discuss this with you."

Hurley snorted. "I know more shit about our black ops than the president, so stop wasting my time and start answering my questions, or we're going to test that little *euphorian* theory of yours."

"And what theory would that be?"

"The one about torture . . . how you like to tell all your buddies in the press that it doesn't work. That it's nothing more than a recruiting tool for al Qaeda."

Adams looked dumbfounded. "Well, that's true."

"And how in the hell would you know?" Hurley leaned over the chair. "Have you ever interrogated someone? Had to get rough with him to save lives?"

"You know the answer to that. I'm the inspector general of the CIA."

"What about those twenty-three months you spent in the clandestine service that you like to brag about? A whole five of them in the field. And even then the only time you left the embassy compound was to play golf or try to get laid."

"I'm not going to relive all that with you," Adams said with a forced smile. "Let's just agree that there are two sides to every story."

"Yeah . . . like the truth and then the stuff that isn't the truth. Like your little dinner date last night."

"What about it?"

"According to Mitch you were in the process of committing treason."

"Mitch Rapp is a professional liar."

"It might be a good idea if you didn't try to make this about Mitch. You either start answering me honestly, or I'm going to bring him in here, and you know as well as I do that he cares even less about your feelings than I do."

"Fine . . . fine," Adams said, backpedaling. "But there's only so much I can say."

"What were you doing in New York last night?"

"Having dinner with an old college friend."

"Discussing?"

Adams hesitated. He had to be careful not to catch himself in a lie. "I respect you, Stan. I always have, so I'm going to say this as politely as I can. I don't answer to you. I don't answer to Mitch Rapp. I answer to the president and the oversight committees on the Hill. That's it."

Hurley exhaled a sigh of frustration. "I don't seem to be getting through to you."

"I feel the same way," Adams said in disappointment. "I understand how difficult this business is, so I'm willing to look the other way this one time, but this offer is not going to last very long. I'm tired and I have a busy day of appointments. I'll give Rapp one chance to let me walk out of here. And I mean right now. One chance." Adams held up his index finger.

Hurley started to laugh. "You don't understand what's going on, do you?"

"I understand that in about two hours people are going to start wondering where I am, and once that happens it is going to be very hard for me to look the other way on this. So, for the last time, let me go and I'll forget all this, but I tell you," Adams's face flushed with anger, "if Rapp so much as looks at me the wrong way, I will bury him."

Hurley wouldn't have believed the man's arrogance if he hadn't been here to witness it. "I don't think you're going to be going anywhere for quite a while."

"I'd better," Adams felt his heart begin to race, "because what little understanding I have is quickly wasting away."

"You're an idiot," Hurley said as if he were telling him his shoes were untied. "I tried my best to help you early in your career, but you really are one dumb son of a bitch."

Adams acted as if he'd been slapped in the face. "Uncle Stan, I have done nothing wrong. I am the one trying to do the right thing."

"If you think you've done nothing wrong, then I might as well shoot you in the head and get this over with."

Adams's mouth was agape. Here was a man he had known since

birth—his father's best friend, for Christ's sake. Adams blurted out, "I've served my country. I don't understand . . . I signed up just like you and Dad."

"Do yourself a favor and don't start comparing your clandestine service career to your father's."

"I . . ." Adams stammered, "I wasn't about to go down with that ship of rats. They were the most corrupt bastards I'd ever met."

"Corrupt? You talking about our fine boys down in Bogotá back in the eighties?"

"Of course I am. They should have all been thrown in jail."

Hurley considered slapping him, but he didn't want to make this any more personal than it already was. "This is all my fault. The other instructors at the Farm wanted to wash your ass out, but I protected you. They knew you didn't have what it would take, and I knew it, too, but I thought I owed it to your father, so I talked you up and let you graduate." Shaking his head in self-loathing, he added, "It was one of the biggest mistakes of my life."

"Didn't have what it would take?" Adams asked, some anger finally seeping into his voice. "You mean like a frontal lobotomy? You mean the ability to ignore every ethical standard I'd ever learned? Ignore everything Congress says about what I should or shouldn't be doing?"

"The problem with you, Glen, is that you always thought you were special, and the truth is you're not. You were a dogshit operative. The only thing you were good for was wining and dining at the embassy parties. Anything that involved getting your hands dirty, you pissed and moaned like a little girl."

"By getting my hands dirty you mean breaking the law?"

"You're damn right I do. What in the hell do you think it is that the CIA is supposed to do? You think we're supposed to obey everyone's laws? Go ask the International Court and the U.N. and the fucking State Department for permission to find out which Colombian military officers are on the drug cartel's payroll?"

"Oh . . . I think you're simplifying it a bit."

"You want me to simplify things? Here it is. You were a complete failure as an operative, you were a mediocre prosecutor who kissed all the right asses and managed to land an empty-suit job as the chief watchdog at the CIA where your entire mission is to get in the way of people who are actually trying to keep us safe. Is that simple enough for you?"

"Get in the way!" Adams shouted. "You think things like the rule of law and the Constitution simply get in the way?"

"No, but neither have I deluded myself into thinking that the men who wrote it ever intended for a second that it be used to protect our enemies."

"So guys like Mitch Rapp should be able to do whatever they'd like without any oversight? Kill whomever they deem a threat without answering to any higher authority?"

"If I have to choose between Mitch and those menstruating partisan hacks on Capitol Hill, I'll put my money on Mitch."

Adams, his fists clenched, stood and demanded, "Do you know why they hate us?"

"Who?"

"The terrorists? Who do you think? They hate us because of men like you and my father and Rapp and Nash and rest of you knuckle-dragging goons."

"Those goons," Hurley said in a quiet angry voice, "have done more to protect this country than the entire House and Senate put together, and they've done it without an ounce of recognition or thanks from all the intellectually arrogant fucks like you." Hurley stepped back and swung his cane around, smacking Adams in the elbow.

Adams yelped and grabbed himself. "What in the hell is wrong with you?"

"I was your only chance, you dumb ass. All I wanted was the slightest sign of remorse, and instead I got more of your pompous defiance." He turned for the door.

"Where are you going?" Adams asked in a voice that had suddenly lost its command.

"To get the man you think so little of."

"Wait!" Adams said in a voice that finally betrayed a bit of fear.

Hurley didn't bother to turn around. "You blew it. Now you get to find out firsthand if torture works."

CHAPTER 11

RAPP checked his watch. He had thirty minutes at the most and then he would have to hightail it up to Langley. He wasn't worried about his alibi. Should the feds come knocking, he'd send them to Hurley, and as long as the tough bastard kept breathing, he'd tell them that Rapp had arrived shortly before seven the previous evening and stayed the night. As to what they'd discussed and done during the roughly twelve hours since, they could confidently tell the feds to pound sand. The agents might not like it, but the men and women of the clandestine service had good reason for being tight-lipped with them and the good ones knew it.

What bothered Rapp was the fact that there were more important things for him to be dealing with—like trying to find the three terrorists who had vanished. They had launched a manhunt like nothing he'd witnessed in his nearly twenty years of service. Every law enforcement officer in the country was on high alert, and so far they'd only come up with thousands of false leads. Seven days postattack they finally started looking at different scenarios. At first they'd concentrated on the airports, the borders, and the big ports. The Navy had boarded and searched twenty vessels that were deemed suspicious. Not a single person had been able to explain to Rapp what intelligence had landed those ships in the suspicious category, but he'd learned enough over the years to not try to swim against the current. The Navy was simply doing what they were ordered, and those orders were coming from men and women who would rather look busy and earnest than get thoughtful.

Now they'd moved on to the smaller marinas, airstrips, and remote border crossings. In Rapp's opinion, and he'd voiced it rather loudly, this should have been the area of focus from the beginning. The men who were behind the attacks had shown a discipline and level of sophistication that he was sure would lead them to be every bit as creative and careful in their escape. Despite all the hard-working and devoted individuals who work for it, the federal government is not a precise instrument. In the post–9/11 world the training was better, the equipment was superior, and the ability to share information in real time had improved dramatically, but the alphabet soup of government agencies had also grown. As only Washington could do, layer after layer of bureaucracy was added, all in the name of streamlining the federal government's ability to prevent and respond to a terrorist attack.

Rapp, and a handful of others, had predicted how the politicians would react. The very room he was standing in was proof that they had been right, and that they'd managed to stay one step ahead of the lemmings as they continued to do what they thought would be least offensive to the very men they were fighting. And now, on top of trying to find out where the terrorists were, he had to deal with this sideshow—this little drama with Glen Adams. It was adding undue stress to an already difficult situation. Rapp hadn't liked it when Hurley asked him to bring Adams down to the lake house, but knowing the family history he conceded. Looking back on it now, Rapp wished he'd flown out over the Atlantic and dumped Adams out the rear luggage hatch of the G500 at about five thousand feet. It would have been a lot easier.

Now Rapp and the others had to stand around and watch this painfully slow tragedy unfold in real time. Rapp had been through this enough times to know that once you decided a man had to be killed there was no sense putting it off. The hand-wringing and moral debate had to take place up front. In Adams's case, that meant before they even picked him up. Once that was done there was no turning back. You couldn't undo the fact that they'd already broken a number of laws. Yet here Nash was making waves. No doubt it had something to do with the strain they'd been under lately, but even so, Rapp expected more from him.

Rapp had seen it before, usually in the military, where despite amazing effort, the use of force was not always as precise as they would like. One too many innocent bystanders blown up by a bomb or killed by an errant bullet, and you were likely to have the occasional foot soldier check out. It wasn't always easy to detect. Everyone acted different in the days immediately following an engagement with the enemy. Especially the first twenty-four hours after combat. It was not unusual, for instance, for one of the men to become quiet. The noncommissioned officers put up with it to a point, but if that brooding turned into questions about the morality of the mission, the noncoms stepped on it quick and hard. If a trooper or Marine couldn't snap out of it, they were gone. Effective fighting units were not the place to debate the ethics of urban warfare. The integrity and effectiveness of the unit could not tolerate it, so the men either snapped to, or were dumped.

Rapp was beginning to question if he would have to do the same thing with some of his men. He would not have guessed that Nash would be one of the problems. He looked across the room at the retired Marine officer who was giving Lewis an earful, and thought it must be the stress of the past week. None of them had slept much, and Nash knew the men and women who worked at the Counterterrorism Center much better than he did. Watching tough men in full combat gear die on a mountain range was hard enough, but was not incongruous with the mission or the surroundings. Watching civilians blown away at point-blank range in an office setting was an entirely different matter, though. Rapp had begun moving toward Nash and the doctor, when he heard his name called from the overhead speaker.

"Mitch, get in here and bring the file."

Rapp stopped. It was Hurley. He would have to wait and talk to Nash in the car on their way back to D.C.

CHAPTER 12

TOOLESBORO, IOWA

DESPITE the urging of the mentally challenged Moroccan, Hakim took his time. He put on his pants and a shirt before grabbing his pistol and gas mask. He'd thought about this exact moment many times since purchasing the safe house. Escape was an illusion. Yes, they might make it to the river, but America was a country with vast resources. In the aftermath of the attacks on the Towers and the Pentagon every county and city in the country had received federal dollars to bolster law enforcement and critical response to terrorist attacks.

Local law enforcement went on a spending spree, snatching up state-of-the-art communications gear, biohazard suits, and weapons that rivaled those used by elite Special Forces units. Budgets for training increased in some cases by a thousand percent. Planes and helicopters with night vision equipment were added to the arsenal as well as boats and specialized vehicles of all shapes and sizes. And that was just at the local level. Chicago was less than an hour away by air, and the FBI Field Office there had a SWAT team that was considered every bit as good as their venerable Hostage Rescue Team that they kept in Quantico, Virginia.

Hakim, in general, was equal parts optimistic and pragmatic, but on this issue it was hard to be optimistic. He knew from the moment he found this place that they would be dead if the Americans ever found them. They went through the motions of discussing escape routes, and the provisions had been put in place, but both he and Karim knew it would do them little good. Ahmed, on the other hand, was probably naïve enough to think they could get away.

Hakim started down the hallway at an almost casual pace, his pistol in his right hand and his gas mask in the other. He made no attempt to stay low to the ground. The Americans would not fire first. They would try to contact them, ascertain the situation, negotiate their surrender, and if all of that failed they would strike or they might simply wait them out. That last point concerned Karim more than any other. If they were going to go down, he wanted to do it in one final, glorious battle, taking as many Americans with him as possible. The idea of being surrounded and forced to choose between suicide and surrender was extremely unappealing.

A few steps before Hakim reached the front of the house he heard the squawk of a radio. It was Ahmed calling out the distance to his targets. Hakim walked past the center staircase and reached the front portion of the house. A small dining room was on his left and a living room on his right. Karim was in the living room, kneeling at the window ledge, peering through the lace curtain.

Karim looked at Hakim and ordered, "Get down."

Hakim ignored him and walked straight to the front door, where he looked through the small twelve-by-twelve-inch window. Two men were coming up the gravel driveway and they were definitely dressed in orange—orange hats and orange vests. Hakim was slack-jawed for a moment, and then began to snicker as he thought of Ahmed's confusion. In Afghanistan the Americans would drape their vehicles and positions in orange panels to reduce the chances of their own planes bombing them. Ahmed assumed these men were wearing orange for the same reason—that they were federal agents and they did not want their own men shooting them.

"Get down," Karim hollered.

"Relax," Hakim said. "They are hunters."

"How do you know?"

Hakim often grew tired of having to explain the obvious to his friend. "Hunting is very popular in this part of America. Animals are color-blind. They wear orange so they don't get shot by another hunter."

Ahmed's voice crackled over the radio. "I have the shot. Do I have your permission?"

Hakim looked up the staircase and yelled, "No. Do not shoot."

Anger flashed across Karim's face. "It is not your place to give such orders."

"They are hunters."

Karim's eyes narrowed. "What if they are agents posing as hunters?"

Hakim hadn't thought of that, but he wasn't about to admit it to Karim, so he looked out the window and studied the two men. They were now just fifty yards away. They'd made it up the long, straight stretch of the driveway and were now entering the large gravel square that sat between the house and the barn. The man on the left was half a head taller and quite a bit heavier than the other man. A few seconds later Hakim realized the shorter man was a teenager.

"They are not agents," Hakim said assuredly. "One of them is a boy."

"It could be a trick."

Hakim didn't even have to think about this one. The Americans would never try such a stunt. In a voice loud enough to carry up the stairs he said, "Both of you stay calm and keep out of sight. I will see what they want." He bent over and set his gas mask on the floor.

"No," Karim ordered.

"Trust me for once, you fool." He slid his gun into the back waistband of his pants and covered it with the tail of his black long-sleeved T-shirt. As he started to open the door he heard Karim hissing obscenities at him. Hakim stepped onto the front porch and put a warm smile on his face. Holding his right hand up in a casual, friendly gesture, he said, "Good morning. Can I help you?" His English was near perfect, with only the slightest accent. If a stranger had to guess, he was more likely to think he was Indian or Pakistani than Saudi.

"Sorry to bother you," the older of the two said. "My name is Ted White . . . this is my son, Hayden."

"Hello, my name is Harry. How can I help you?"

The two men stopped about twenty feet from the front porch. "Well . . . I'm sorry to intrude, especially this early. I saw the No Trespassing signs." The father looked over his shoulder back down the long drive. "But I didn't know what else to do . . . you see, I'm a cousin of the Terwilligers . . . the family who used to own this place. I assume you're the new owner."

"That is correct."

The man smiled a bit awkwardly. "Do you like to hunt?"

Hakim smiled back and said, "No . . . but I have nothing against it."

"That's nice to hear." The man looked at the ground for a moment and shifted his weight from one foot to the other.

Hakim was extremely calm. He looked down the driveway and saw nothing but open gravel road. These two were not the advance element of some larger force. It was obvious the man had a question on his mind. "So what brings you out here at this early hour?"

"Well, I was wondering if you would give us permission to hunt down by the river. You see, I've been hunting turkey on this land ever since I was a little kid, and so has Hayden here. I promise you we won't disturb you. We'll just be using little .22s. Nothing more than a little pop really."

Hakim nodded. Things were beginning to make sense. "How early do you like to start?"

"Well, that depends." He gestured at his clothes. "We were hoping to get some in this morning. Got the rifles back in the truck. But if now's not a good time I don't want to disturb you."

"I suppose now would work," Hakim offered, already thinking the best way to handle this was to be nice. They had monitored the media closely, and while Karim's photograph had been everywhere, Hakim's involvement had yet to be reported.

"Thank you," the father said and then pointed at him and asked, "You a Hawkeye?"

Hakim looked down at his black University of Iowa T-shirt and its bright yellow lettering. "Yes. I went there for graduate school. Their writing program."

"You an author?"

"Yes. That's why I bought this place. Nice and quiet."

"I understand," the man said, holding up an apologetic hand. He seemed to sense this would be a good time to leave. "Well, we really appreciate you letting us use the land. We'll just skirt the creek down there and make our way down to the river. You'll never see us. Really appreciate it. It means a lot."

Hakim waved and said, "No worries. Be safe." Right as he said it, he heard the door open behind him. Hoping he had imagined it, he kept his eyes on the father and son. They were turning to leave but then they suddenly stopped. Hakim watched the expression on the father's face turn friendly before his entire demeanor changed. Hakim felt the old porch boards sway under the weight of an additional person. He pulse began to quicken.

"Hello," the man said in a nervous voice.

Hakim turned his head slowly to see Karim standing beside and just behind him. His gun was clearly visible in his right hand. Casually he raised the weapon and pointed it at the two men. "Why are you really here?"

Hakim whispered in an angry voice, "I had this under control."

Without taking his eyes off the two visitors, Karim said, "You are a fool."

CHAPTER 13

LAKE ANNA, VIRGINIA

RAPP walked over to the closest metal desk and picked up a plain manila file. Being asked to come into the room at this juncture was either a good or a bad thing depending on your perspective. Rapp's guess was that it was a bad sign for Adams. He punched in the code and opened the door. Maslick was right behind him. Adams was seated where Rapp had left him and despite looking tired, he still managed a smug look of defiance.

"Glen here thinks you're the problem," Hurley announced.

"Really?"

"That's right. He doesn't want to talk about what he was doing last night." Hurley rolled his eyes. Turning to Maslick he said, "Grab the cart."

Maslick wheeled a three-level cart into the room and left it in the corner. Then, dragging the table away from Adams, he pointed at the nearest chair and said, "Sit."

"Listen," Adams said while holding his hands up in an affable manner, "I don't know who you are, and I don't have to know who you are, but trust me when I say you don't want to be involved in this."

Rapp stood in the doorway, his hands on his hips, a determined expression on his face. "You're wasting your breath, Glen. He'd just as soon kill you, but he's a good soldier, so he'll wait until I tell him. In the meantime, sit down and do what you're told."

Adams hesitated so Maslick helped him back into his chair. Then the big man grabbed some flex cuffs from one of the cargo pockets on his khaki pants. Adams complained while his wrists were pulled behind the back of the chair and bound. Next came his ankles to each of the chair's front legs. Rapp wheeled the cart over. On the top sat a polygraph machine.

Hurley stood in front of Adams and asked, "Glen, since you're so smart, I'm wondering if you could tell me what makes a guy like Mitch here get out of bed and bust his ass for people like you?"

"I don't pretend to know the criminal mind, but if I had to guess, I would say it's a perverse thrill that he derives out of inflicting pain on others."

"That's the best you can do?" Hurley asked. "No other reasons?"

"None."

"Well, I trained him, you dumb ass. If I thought for a moment that he was some sadistic brute who was two ticks away from being a career criminal, I'd a bounced his ass right out of the program, and trust me I know the difference, because I got rid of plenty of them over the years. The only thing that a guy like Mitch gets out of climbing down in the gutter with these religious nut jobs is the knowledge that he is fighting the good fight. That he's doing the honorable thing, while all the overeducated assholes like you sit in your nice leather chairs and criticize his every move."

"And you would have me . . . what? Let him defy the rule of law? Let him kill whoever his pea-sized brain thinks deserves killing?"

"No, but at a bare minimum I expect you to resist the urge to delude yourself into thinking our enemies would like us if only we were nicer to them."

Adams exhaled a tired sigh as if to say they were wasting his time.

"Do you want to wait until the poly is hooked up so you're sure I'm giving you the right answer?"

"We're not going to bother with the poly," Hurley said half laughing. "Any clandestine officer with half a brain knows how to fool that thing."

Rapp stepped forward, grabbed Adams's shirt, and tore it open. "Normally, I'd try to stay detached while interrogating someone, but this is going to be tough."

"You are making a huge mistake," Adams warned.

"The only mistake I've made in the last twenty-four hours was not killing you sooner."

Adams laughed nervously. "I know all about your methods."

"As usual, I think you're talking out of your ass."

"You're going to scream at me, you'll keep me up for seventy-two hours . . . you'll raise and lower the temperature in this room, you'll probably give me more vodka." He shook his head and added, "In the end you'll learn nothing and you'll have to let me go. After that I will march straight into the attorney general's office and demand that you be brought up on kidnapping charges, and that's just for starters. So . . . if the three of you can scrape together enough brain cells to see that the only rational course is to let me go while I'm still in the mood to forgive this lack of judgment, you might be able to avoid some serious jail time."

"There's one big problem with your plan," Hurley said as he leaned against the wall and lit a cigarette. "When we're done wringing the truth out of you, I'm going shoot you in the head with this." Hurley pulled back his jacket and drew a pistol from a shoulder harness.

Adams was suddenly transfixed by the gun.

"It's a Kimber Stainless Gold Match Two, .45 caliber pistol. Finest production pistol in the world."

Adams blew off the threat as theatrics. "You wouldn't dare. The Intelligence Committees, the DOJ, the FBI . . . they all know I'm close to exposing this cancer in the clandestine service. They know I'm on to Rapp, and if I turn up dead, they'll be all over you guys."

"Who said you're going to turn up dead?" Hurley looked at Rapp and said, "Show him the file."

Rapp held a photograph in front of Adams. "We got this off the surveillance cameras at JFK. It was taken last night. Does the guy in the bottom right corner look familiar?"

Adams studied the grainy black-and-white surveillance photo and after a second saw the mirror image of himself.

"Here's the flight manifest." Rapp placed another sheet in front of him with Adams's name highlighted in yellow. "Your flight will land in Caracas in one hour. You will be seen leaving the airport, and then you will simply vanish."

Adams swallowed hard. Feeling real nerves for the first time, his mind scrambled to find a way out. "You don't think I've taken precautions?"

"You mean like the safety deposit box you have at the First Bank of Bethesda?" Rapp asked.

"And the used Dell laptop you have stashed behind the workbench in your garage," Hurley added. "The one you're using to write your book." He took a big puff from his cigarette and then pointed the hot end at Adams. "You have a lot of problems, Glen. Chief among them is the fact that you're insecure. It's not unusual . . . in fact, most of the assholes I've come across suffer from the same affliction. It's the reason you could never cut it in this line of work. Not because you're not smart enough—you're far from retarded. The problem is . . . when you're as insecure as you are, the only way you can make yourself feel good is to convince yourself that your enemies are stupid. And in this line of work, you can never underestimate your enemies."

"It'll never work." Adams forced a smile onto his face and some confidence into his voice. "There are too many people in Washington who know I was about to blow this thing open."

Rapp could see he was going to have to jump-start things if he was going to make it back to Langley by nine. He held up his right hand and said, "You see this?" Rapp watched Adams's eyes zero in on his right hand, and then with his left hand, he unleashed an open-handed slap that cracked Adams flush across the face.

Adams yelped like a wounded pup, and then in a panicked voice yelled, "That's it. You've crossed the line. I am going to make sure you spend the rest of your days in a jail cell. I'm going to—"

He never finished the threat because Rapp whacked him again, this time with his right hand. He then grabbed him by his thin silver hair and forced him to look at the sheaf of documents in his left hand. "Do you think those defenders of yours know you've been going through two bottles of vodka and another six to eight bottles of wine a week?"

"That's a lie!"

"It's the truth! You're a frickin' drunk! We have your bank statements, credit card receipts, ATM withdrawals . . . we even have video of you buying booze at three different liquor stores, and they're the only three we checked. We found vodka in your trunk, your desk drawer. We even have video of you stopping at a park to dump your extra bottles."

"Marty and Mary are out of the house," Hurley chimed in, mentioning Adams's two children. "Off to college and calling home once every couple weeks. You and Gretchen don't even sleep in the same room anymore. Hell . . . we've had your house bugged for a week . . . you don't even talk. You're the classic bitter narcissist who's pissed at the world because everyone has failed to recognize his genius. The biggest laugh of all is that we don't even have to plant evidence. It's all right there for them to see, and trust me they'll find it. Your wife . . . your kids . . . your friends . . . they're all going to get put through the wringer."

"The curtain's going to get pulled back," Rapp said in a dire tone.

"You really want your kids to find out their old man is just a bitter alcoholic? A failed fucking bureaucrat, who committed treason?"

"It won't work," Adams said with sweat cascading down his forehead. "Kenny Urness will know you guys killed me, and he's not the only one. They won't rest until you're brought to justice."

"Who," Hurley growled, "other than some fucking looney, anti-American, CIA-hating scumbag is going to A, care that you've disappeared and B, spend the next five years of his life trying to find out what really happened?"

"You have no idea how powerful my contacts are!"

"Really?" Hurley said skeptically. "Is that why you had to fly up to New York and meet with an ambulance chaser last night? So you could hatch a plot to write a tell-all book and line your pockets?"

"That's not why I went to New York."

"Almost two hundred of your countrymen were killed last week, and you're out trying to get rich off it."

"That's a lie and you know it," Adams spat. "You two are the problem . . . not me. You are why they hate us, not me."

Hurley smacked him across the head and yelled, "You're a fucking embarrassment to your family."

Adams felt his options slipping away. Felt really for the first time that they might actually kill him. "You don't know Kenny Urness if you think he'll just drop this whole thing when I don't show up for work."

"What Kenny Urness saw last night was a drunk," Rapp said in a flat voice. "A delusional drunk, and when he finds out that you flew to South America and disappeared, he won't waste more than two minutes trying to figure out if it's true."

"And if he comes after us," Hurley said, "tough shit. He can look all he wants. We've been through your shit. If you had any real evidence you would have already taken it to the feds."

"That's not true!" Adams pleaded.

Hurley stepped forward and extended the big .45 caliber pistol. "Any last words before I blow your head off."

With tear-filled eyes, Adams shook his head and cried, "You can't do this, Uncle Stan. You and my father were best friends."

"I can, and I will."

"But my father?"

"You were a disgrace to your father," Hurley growled. "You broke his heart."

"But . . . I didn't know," Adams pleaded, tears now rolling down his cheeks.

"You didn't know because you're a narcissistic fuck. The only person you've ever cared about is yourself."

"That's not true," Adams half yelled. "I *have* sacrificed. I *have* done what I thought was right."

"Well, you were wrong." Hurley placed the muzzle of the pistol against Adams's forehead and squeezed the trigger.

CHAPTER 14

THE report of the big .45 Kimber was deafening. Rapp didn't have time to cover his ears. He'd barely had enough time to grab Hurley's wrist and deflect the shot. Just barely, as was evidenced by the red powder burn that was now painted in a cone shape across the top of Adams's forehead. The slug was now lodged in the concrete wall beyond Adams's head. A crater the size of a fist marked the spot.

Rapp couldn't hear a thing but he could see just fine. Hurley was screaming at him and Adams was sobbing—his eyes closed, his head down, his chin bouncing off his chest every few seconds as he gasped for air, snot pouring out of his nose. Hurley pointed his Kimber at Rapp and began to use it to punctuate whatever point he was trying to make. Rapp, none too fond of having a gun pointed at him, almost snapped the older man's wrist, but caught himself in time. He slowly brought his hand up and gently moved the muzzle of the gun to a less threatening direction.

After pointing at his left ear, Rapp mouthed that he couldn't hear what Hurley was saying. He walked over to the door and gestured for Hurley to follow him. Rapp hit the intercom button and asked for the door to be opened. As he stepped into the outer room, he found Nash, Lewis, and Maslick all standing there with shocked expressions on their faces. Rapp placed both palms over his ears and pressed down for a good five seconds while he swallowed several times and flexed his jaw. The first words he began to recognize belonged to Hurley. He was still cursing up a storm.

Rapp looked at him still waving his gun around and yelled, "Put that damn thing away before you shoot someone."

Hurley pointed the gun at Rapp again and barked, "Someone! You're the only one I'm thinking about shooting!"

Rapp's entire posture was instantly transformed. Like a big black panther who had been stirred from a lazy nap, his muscles flexed and his weight was transferred onto the balls of his feet. His eyes narrowed and his brow furrowed and he half shouted, "Stan, put that gun away right now, or I'll break your wrist."

Hurley, having trained Rapp, knew not only that he meant it, but that there was a good chance that at this close distance, Rapp could do it before he got off a shot. Slowly, and with a not-too-happy look, he shouldered his pistol and asked, "Why in the hell did you stop me?"

The answer was complicated, although there was one really good reason and several decent ones. Rapp decided to go with the big one—the one they all should have thought of to begin with. "Where in the hell is he getting his information?"

"We've already gone over that," Hurley said in an irritated voice. "He's filling in the gaps. If he had anything real, he would have taken it to the Justice Department."

Rapp shook his head. "He still had to start somewhere. Someone is talking to him."

"He's the Gestapo. We've already found dozens of bugs. He has half the offices on the seventh floor wired."

The inspector general's office at Langley was often called the Gestapo by the front-line troops at Langley. This was exactly what Rapp had feared—that they would let their dislike of Adams cloud their judgment. He took a deep breath and asked, "What's our rush?"

"You know as well as I do, you can't let shit like this fester. The best can lose their courage, and besides, we have bigger fish to fry."

"And we also have one shot at finding out what he knows."

"We've gone over this," Hurley snarled. "We have what we need. We kill him and whoever he was talking to won't know if he's dead or if he's disappeared. Either way the effect is the same. We send a clear signal that we're done fucking around."

"By we," Nash jumped in, "I assume you mean the royal we, because no one knows you're involved in this. Mitch and I are the two guys with the targets on our backs."

"Why you little . . ." Hurley reached for his gun.

Rapp stepped forward and grabbed Hurley's wrist. He looked at Nash and his bloodshot, tired eyes and instantly knew he was strung out. Hell, they were all strung out. Sleep was a luxury they had experienced far too little of in the past week. "Head up to the house," Rapp said to Nash, "and get cleaned up. We need to be on the road in less than thirty minutes."

"But, I don't—"

"I don't give a shit what you think!" Rapp barked. "It's an order. Stan's right . . . this isn't a frickin' book club. Now get your ass up to the house and get cleaned up."

It was obvious by the constipated look on his face that Nash wanted to say something, but he managed to keep his mouth shut and head for the door. After he left, Rapp turned his attention back to the group and said, "Something Doc said earlier got me thinking." Rapp looked at Lewis. "You said he'd never commit suicide."

"I said it was highly unlikely."

"Good enough. So his desire for self-preservation is pretty high?"

"Absolutely."

Looking back at Hurley, Rapp said, "I think we can turn him."

"And I think you're nuts. Doc, tell him why we can't?"

"Once we turn him loose," Lewis said, "and he feels safe, he will turn on you."

"What if he never truly feels safe? I could check in on him from time to time and remind him that I'm looking over his shoulder."

"And why take the chance?" Hurley asked.

"Because he might be useful."

"Doc?" Hurley said as if he wanted him to explain the obvious to Rapp.

"It's risky, Mitch. With someone like this, there is never any real loyalty."

"What if we co-opt him," Maslick suggested.

They all turned, a bit shocked, and looked at the linebacker of a man, who was known for his quiet demeanor. "What exactly do you mean?" Lewis asked.

"What if we get him to take ownership?" Maslick asked in a soft voice. "Get him to help us out." Looking directly at Hurley, he said, "Like flipping a foreign agent. You've said so yourself many times, Stan. All you need is a little money, a little time, and a cause worth fighting for."

CHAPTER 15

IF the words had come from anyone else, Rapp felt confident that they would have elicited a rather strong response from Hurley, but they'd come from the gentle giant, so the old spymaster stood there and quietly chewed on them. Rapp took the time to figure out his next move. As he did so, he saw the tension leave the old man, and it occurred to him there was a heavy emotional toll attached to this untidy situation. No matter how tough he was, there was no accounting for the burden of almost killing your best friend's son, a boy you had cradled in your arms as an infant and bounced on your knee as a toddler.

Hurley hobbled over to the closest desk and sat on the edge. Rapp looked at Lewis, who was watching the old man with legitimate concern. Thinking the silence was only making things worse, Rapp said, "Stan, this could work. You may have just scared him straight."

"That is a valid point," Lewis added. "He expected you to save him from Mitch . . . not the other way around. And that was a pretty close call. I doubt you could have faked it any better."

"I wanna go back in there and throw him a life line," Rapp said. "Doc?"

Lewis shrugged. "You know the routine. To start, don't ask him anything you don't already know the answer to."

"And don't try to turn him," Hurley offered in a detached voice. He'd swiveled the monitor on the desk around so he could look at Adams. Faint sobs could be heard on the small desktop speakers. "That comes later. After he's proven he really wants it. Go ahead and hold out a glimmer of hope, but that's it."

"Understood." Rapp nodded. He grabbed a bottle of water from the fridge and a bottle of vodka and a glass. "Buzz me if anything comes to mind."

Rapp knew all he had was twenty minutes, but he was probably never going to get another shot at Adams when he'd be this fragile. Rapp punched in the code and opened the door. There Adams sat, with his crimson forehead peppered with a hundred little droplets of blood from the muzzle blast, his eyes closed and his chin down. His pants were damp and there was a puddle of urine at his feet. Hurley was right about one thing—this was a nasty business, and it was easy to lose your nerve if you didn't operate under tight constraints. Put a bullet in a guy's head, dispose of the body, and move on. No sense slowing down to peruse the carnage, and don't bother to look in the rearview mirror either. You start doing stuff like that and you're inviting trouble.

Even so, Rapp saw an opportunity. It wouldn't be long before people began to wonder where Adams had gone. The office didn't expect him back until this afternoon, and unless they'd missed something, he had no breakfast meetings in New York. His staff would probably start to get nervous around midafternoon. They'd try his cell phone and get nothing. Then they'd try the house, and if they got hold of his wife she'd tell them she had not spoken to him and, while that might be strange for some couples, it was not strange for them. The staff would alert the appropriate people at Langley, who would more than likely sit on it overnight. But if he didn't show up for work the next morning, the feds would be brought in, and not long after that they would discover he had left the country. Rapp had no illusions that he could roll Adams and have him back at the office by tomorrow morning. That simply was not going to happen. But there was another option—one that would buy them more than enough time.

With one hand Rapp dragged the table back over and placed it in front of Adams. He set the water bottle, vodka, and glass down on the table and then withdrew a small tactical knife from his belt. He then walked behind Adams, cut the flex ties from his wrists, and said, "I think you probably need a drink."

Rapp circled back around the room and stood facing Adams. He wanted to have a good view of what would happen next. Adams slowly lifted his head and looked at the objects sitting on the table. He hesitated and then reached out. His right hand went straight for the bottle of vodka, which Rapp had expected.

Adams clutched the bottle and spun the silver cap off, not caring that it fell to the floor. With a shaky hand he clanged the neck of the bottle against the rim of the glass and let the clear alcohol come splashing out, a good portion missing the glass. Adams set the bottle down and drew the glass to his lips, downing about three ounces of vodka in two gulps. For a moment he looked as if he was going to pour another glass, but instead he started to shake uncontrollably, and then he was sobbing again, his head on the table, cradled in his arms.

Rapp could only make out every fifth word or so. It was a complete meltdown. He'd seen it before and knew there was no stopping it, short of smacking him, but that would be a mistake. The die had been cast five minutes earlier, and Rapp was now going to have to play the good cop. After a few minutes the sobs softened and the breathing stabilized. Eventually Adams looked up at him with pleading eyes and spoke.

"Why?"

It was a pretty open-ended question, so Rapp said nothing. He just stood there and stared back at Adams's puffy, bloodshot eyes. The guy was a mess.

"I don't understand," Adams sniffled. "I've lived an honorable life. I don't deserve this."

Rapp wanted to refute the comment, but managed to stop himself. Playing good cop didn't come easy to him. His instinct was to smack the fool across the head a few times and make it really clear if he didn't do everything he was told, he'd get Hurley back in the room and have him finish the job. Instead, he sighed and said, "Glen, a lot of people have lost their bearings during this mess."

"Not me."

"I know you think you've done the right thing," Rapp said carefully, "but you haven't. You've been suckered into this partisan game that everyone wants to play in Washington. Republican versus Democrat . . . liberal versus conservative . . . none of that matters. At Langley, the only thing we're supposed to concern ourselves with is national security. That's our mission, and the day the ACLU starts driving our national security policy is the day America is really fucked."

"But you guys don't see what you're doing," Adams pleaded. "We are becoming the very monsters we are trying to defeat."

Rapp had heard this bullshit line too many times. "Give me one example."

Adams held out his hands and looked around the room. "What would you call this?"

Rapp laughed and said, "If you worked for al Qaeda, and they caught you divulging their secrets to the media, they wouldn't simply kill you, they'd kill your wife and kids and make you watch, and then if you were lucky they would put you out of your misery quickly, but they probably wouldn't. They'd toy with you for months and use you as an example to anyone else who was less than resolute in his faith."

"We're not them. I was left with no other options. I couldn't just sit there and watch you guys operate with such reckless disregard for the law."

"Really." Rapp looked at the door again. "Maybe I made a mistake."

"You're damn right you did. You should have never brought me here." Adams grabbed the bottle of vodka.

"I'm talking about stopping him from blowing your head all over that wall."

Adams looked up while he was pouring another drink. "I am not the enemy."

"Actually you are, Glen, and if you can't see that you've fucked up, there's no hope of saving you. Stan would just as soon tear your head off and piss down your throat. He despises you. He sees you as the bright shining example of how the baby boomers have fucked up this country."

"That's a good one," Adams sneered, "coming from the most racist, bigoted generation this country has ever seen." He took another drink.

"You can bring it up with Stan." Rapp checked his watch. "I have to get back to Langley for a meeting." He took a step toward the door and stopped. "I thought you might be worth saving, but I guess I was wrong."

"Wait!" Adams said desperately. "You can't leave me here with him."

"Why's that?"

"Because he'll kill me!" Adams yelled.

"And how would that affect me?"

"It would." Adams's eyes darted around the room as his brain tried to come up with something. "It would make you an accessory to murder."

"You're kidding, right? That's the best you can come up with?"

"I have powerful allies," Adams warned.

Rapp rubbed his forehead and decided to write off the man's lame excuses to the vodka. "Glen, I don't think you're a bad person. I just think you're confused. You've gotten yourself wrapped up in the legal aspect of this. You're focused on 2 percent of the issue and you're ignoring the other 98 percent. You've lost all sense of proportion, and if you can't open your eyes to that, there is nothing I can do to help you."

"I have done nothing wrong."

"Last chance, Glen. I'm going to walk out this door and Stan's going to come back in here and blow your head off. Then they'll cut you up into six pieces and incinerate you limb by limb. By lunch the only sign that you ever existed will be a pile of ash that'll fit into a coffee can. By dinner that ash will be spread far and wide. All evidence destroyed. The only thing the feds will have to go on is the fact that you left the country . . . that and the fact that you're a drunk. They'll look for a few weeks and then they'll write your ass off."

Adams shook his head defiantly. "They will know something is wrong and they won't stop until they get to the bottom of it."

Rapp shrugged as if he'd given it his best shot. "I wish I could say it was nice knowing you, Glen, but I'd be lying. You're a self-serving prick, and you won't be missed . . . not even by your own family." Rapp hit the intercom button. "I'm done in here. He's all yours."

CHAPTER 16

TOOLESBORO, IOWA

HAKIM learned to play chess when he was seven years old. His grandfather had taught him the game, and for the next six years until the kind old man died, they played every week. One of the first things his grandfather had taught him was that a chess match was often decided because of one bad move. A move that, once made, set the game on an almost certain path. And in chess, as in life, a move like that could never be taken back. So the moral of the story, according to his grandfather, was to think long and hard before deciding something difficult. Look at it from every angle. See what you see and then ask yourself if there's something you can't see.

Hakim didn't know if it was all that chess, or a God-given abundance of common sense combined with an easy attitude, but whatever it was, he had been able to avoid a lot of trouble over the years by staying patient and making prudent decisions. The same could not be said for Karim. His daring, brash behavior had led him to great success on the battlefield in Afghanistan, and his plan to attack America, despite his own criticism, had been a huge success. In the more subtle arena of daily life, though, his ability to pick up on the moods and currents of a foreign land was almost nonexistent.

The gun came up and before Hakim could react it was fired. It was as if the entire thing painfully played out before him in slow motion. The father went down with a wound to the gut and the kid turned in panic and began to run. He made it three steps and then collapsed with a bullet to the lower back.

Karim lowered his weapon and turned to Hakim, "Now let's find out why they were really here." He walked down the porch steps and onto the gravel.

With the loud cracks of the 9mm pistol still echoing down the river valley, Hakim's brain took off headlong in an attempt to assess the damage. In the first millisecond he knew it was bad. Extremely bad. He had had the situation under control and then Karim's massive, paranoid ego led him to step in when there was so clearly no need for him to do so. It was as if all the frustrations of the last week came pouring out at once. He followed his friend down the steps and said, "I already know why they are here, you idiot."

Karim spun to face his friend. "What did you just call me?"

"I called you an idiot! An unbelievable idiot!"

"You will show me the proper respect," Karim commanded, "or you will be punished."

"I'd like to see you try." Hakim took a step toward his old friend and pushed his sleeves up. "Do you have any idea what you have done?"

An incredulous look on his face, Karim answered, "I stopped these two men from walking away and telling the authorities that we are here. I did what you should have done."

"Should have done? You are an utter fool. You have ruined everything and for nothing. These two weren't going to tell anyone anything other than what I told them. They were going to go hunt down by the river and leave us alone." Hakim looked at the father and son. Both of them were writhing on the ground in pain. *Now what the hell were they going to do with them?* "They believed me, you arrogant ass."

"You are the fool," Karim spat back. "They only acted like they believed you. They are probably police."

"You have never been to this country before. You have no idea how to read these people. They are not police." Hakim motioned at the house, the barn, and the surrounding land. "Where are we to go?"

Karim was obviously irritated by the question. "Well . . . if they are hunters as you say, we will bury the bodies and be done with them."

"And when they don't make it home for dinner tonight, and the wife calls the police and tells them they were coming out here to hunt. What do we do then? Because the police will come and look for them."

Karim saw that the boy had pulled a cell phone from his jacket and was trying to make a call. He raised his gun, took aim, and squeezed the trigger. The orange hat flew off the boy's head in a puff of dust and his foot twitched a few times before he went completely still. Looking back at Hakim as if nothing had happened, he said, "Then we will have to leave."

The father howled in agony and started to frantically crawl toward his son. Hakim was sickened by the entire scene. None of it had to happen. These two men had done nothing wrong. "I explained to you what would happen if we had to leave. I told you in detail that our best chance for survival was to stay here for at least a month. To wait them out. Then we would be able to slip out of the country."

"I am sick of your complaining," Karim announced. "I question your devotion."

"And I question *your* devotion. You are a coward. No different than the rest of the lazy rich men who claim to lead us."

Genuine anger flashed across Karim's face. "How dare you question me?"

"I am not one of your brainwashed robots. I have known you for too long. If you were a real warrior you would have gone into that building with your men and martyred yourself. But you are too obsessed with your own fame. The Lion of al Qaeda . . . Ha!" Hakim spoke in reference to the name that Karim had given himself in the videos he released after the attacks. "You should be called the coward of al Qaeda." He looked back to the father, who had reached his son and was sobbing uncontrollably.

Karim could not take another word. The insolence of his friend should have been checked a long time ago. "Prove to me that you are not a coward. Kill the father now. I order you." Karim tossed his gun to his friend.

The gun sailed through the air, but Hakim made no effort to catch it. The gun landed at his feet and skidded a few inches along the gravel. Hakim looked down at the gun and shook his head. "There is no honor in this. No bravery in killing an unarmed father and son who have done nothing to offend you, or Allah."

"I order you!"

"We are the infidels in this land. This is wrong. If you want him dead, then you should finish what you started."

"For the last time I order you to pick up the gun and shoot the father."

"I don't take orders from you," Hakim said with a derisive scowl.

"Yes, you do."

Hakim turned and started back for the house.

"Do not turn your back on me," Karim yelled, but Hakim paid him no attention. Karim had finally had enough. He broke into a run and caught his friend just as he reached the steps. He delivered a quick rabbit punch to Hakim's kidney and then kicked through the back of his right knee, collapsing him to the ground. Karim then grabbed him by the shirt, threw him onto his back, and dropped on top of him, delivering a flurry of punches to his friend's face. "This," he said in between his third and fourth punches, "is a lesson I should have taught you a long time ago."

CHAPTER 17

LAKE ANNA, VIRGINIA

ADAMS pleaded, then cried, and in between the sniffles and tears he began mumbling to himself. The door buzzed and Rapp opened it to find Hurley standing on the other side, looking none too pleased that he was going to have to shoot his best friend's son in the head for the second time.

"I should have never stopped you," Rapp said in an apologetic tone.

"Damn right you shouldn't have." Hurley pushed past him, his cane in one hand and his gun in the other.

Adams snapped out of his mumbling trance and began screaming for Rapp to stop. Upon seeing Hurley and the gun, he tried to stand, and forgetting that his ankles were still tied to the chair, toppled over. He caught the edge of the table and brought it down with him, sending the glass and bottle of vodka crashing to the floor at the same time.

Hurley moved into position over him and took aim.

"Don't shoot!" Adams screamed. "Mitch, wait! I know things! I can help!"

Rapp shared a quick look with Hurley as he walked back to Adams.

He squatted and said, "You get one shot at this, Glen. Tell me something worth knowing, and it better be good."

Adams was lying on his side, the toppled chair still attached to his legs. He looked at the puddle of urine and then at Rapp. "Help me up first."

"Fuck you!" Hurley growled as he jabbed the gun into Adams's face.

Rapp stood and again started for the door. Adams began screaming frantically for him to stop and Hurley let loose a litany of profanity that described in very colorful terms exactly what he thought of Adams. To further punctuate each word he stabbed his gun closer and closer to Adams's face until he had it pressed into his temple.

Rapp was halfway out the door when he heard a name. It was repeated three times in quick succession. Rapp stopped, his interest finally piqued, and turned. "What did you say?"

"Kathy O'Brien!" Adams said with his face pressed into the floor.

Rapp's eyes narrowed. He wasn't sure exactly what he had expected to get out of Adams, but the name Kathy O'Brien wasn't anywhere on the horizon. She was the wife of Chuck O'Brien, the director of the CIA's National Clandestine Service. "What about her?" Rapp asked cautiously.

"That's how I knew about the operation you were running."

One of the keys to a successful interrogation, at least early on, was to keep the subject off balance. No matter how shocking or strange a piece of information might be, you never let it show. "Which operation," Rapp asked, "would that be?"

"The mosques."

"Go on," Rapp ordered.

"The undercover guys you sent into the mosques."

Rapp walked back and looked down at Adams. "You mean the operation that was leaked to the *Post* last week."

"Yeah . . . Yeah . . . that's the one."

"The story you leaked, you mean?" Rapp asked.

Adams didn't answer fast enough, so Hurley gave him a little love tap with the tip of the barrel—just hard enough to draw a drop of blood.

"Yes," Adams screamed. "Yes . . . I was the one who told Barreiro."

"The leak," Rapp said, "that ended up getting one of my agents killed."

"I . . . I . . . I," Adams stammered, "wouldn't know anything about that."

Rapp glanced at his watch. He might have to be late for the meeting. "And just what does Kathy O'Brien have to do with this?"

"She's . . . how I found out."

"You already said that. I want specifics." Rapp saw Adams's eyes begin to dart around again, which was a sign that his brain was scrambling to find the right lie. "Don't do it."

"Do what?"

"Lie to me."

"I'm not . . . I mean I wasn't going to."

"Anything you say to me I'll have verified within the hour, and if I find out you've lied to me . . . well, let's just say I'm going keep you alive as long as it takes to make you feel some real pain."

"She . . ." Adams's eyes started darting again, until suddenly, a knife tip appeared an inch in front of the left one.

Rapp held the blade perfectly still. "I can tell when a man is lying to me. So one more time, what does Kathy have to do with this?"

Adams closed his eyes and said, "She's been seeing a therapist."

"And?"

"We had the office bugged."

With great effort to conceal his surprise Rapp asked, "The therapist's office?"

"Yes."

Rapp's mind was flooded with a half-dozen questions, but for now he needed to keep Adams focused on the most immediate facts. They could squeeze the rest out of him later. "So if I call my source at Justice, she'll tell me that you had warrants to wiretap the therapist's office?"

Adams took a long time to answer, which in itself was an answer.

Rapp cocked his head to the side. "You didn't have a warrant?"

"Not exactly," Adams admitted.

Rapp pulled the knife back and shared a quick look with Hurley. Things suddenly began to fall into place for Rapp. Why Adams knew the broad brushstrokes of what they had been up to, but could not pass the threshold needed to refer a case to Justice. "You wiretapped the office of a doctor and recorded the private therapy sessions of the wife of the director of the National Clandestine Service. And you did it illegally."

"I was only trying to do my job."

"And you lecture me about breaking the fucking law," Rapp snapped.

"I was just trying to stop you. You were out of control."

"Out of control . . . I break those laws to keep people safe. Real people. You break 'em to protect some piece of paper you don't even understand."

"I am trying to protect the world from animals like you."

Rapp stuck the tip of the knife into Adams's left nostril and said, "I should—"

"Mitch," Dr. Lewis announced from the door, "I'd like to have a word with you and Stan."

Rapp resisted the urge to slice the traitor's nose clean off his face. They had a standard policy during interrogations that whenever Lewis asked anyone for a private word, they were to drop everything and leave the room. Rapp stood and left the cell with Hurley. They closed the door and found Lewis pacing nervously. Nash was back from the house, shaved and in a dark blue suit, while Maslick was sitting behind the desk keeping an eye on the monitors.

Lewis held up a couple of fingers and said, "Two things . . . the first

. . . I don't think you can ever allow him to go free. There is a chance that his illegalities were driven by a lack of judgment precipitated by the onset of alcoholism, but I think the odds of it are small. It's more likely that in addition to suffering from narcissistic personality disorder, he is also a sociopath."

"And this changes things . . . how?"

"He uses rules as a weapon. He gets extremely upset when he thinks anyone has acted inappropriately, or has broken the law, yet he sees nothing wrong when he decides to break those very same laws. I'm not even sure he's aware of it. He's so narcissistic, so in love with himself, that he thinks he's privileged. Rules are for the commoner, not someone like him, who is destined to make a difference in the world."

"I could have told you that," Hurley said, "and I didn't even go to med school."

Lewis ignored Hurley and said, "The narcissistic sociopathic combination is extremely dangerous . . . almost impossible to treat and never in a situation with this much pressure. He will say and do whatever he needs to stay alive and then after you let him go, the first chance he gets he will bolt. He would turn to anyone who he thought had the power to take you down."

"Your second point?" Rapp asked.

"Normally, I would never admit this, but considering the situation, I think it would be best." Lewis hesitated, wrestling with how best to word his admission.

"Doc," Rapp said, "I don't have all day. Spit it out."

Lewis cleared his throat and nervously announced, "I am Kathy O'Brien's therapist."

CHAPTER 18

RAPP was out of time. If he and Nash were to have any chance of making the powwow at Langley, they had to be on the road in the next few minutes, and even then they would have to drive at least eighty miles an hour to give themselves a chance. Normally, Rapp didn't concern himself with getting to meetings on time, but this was not your average run-of-the-mill bureaucratic black hole of a meeting. Kennedy had made it very clear the president had requested the presence of both her senior counterterrorism operatives, and while Rapp really didn't care much for politicians, he'd dealt with a few presidents over his career, and found them tolerable in the sense that they understood it wasn't a bad idea to have a man like Rapp around to deal with some of the stickier situations that popped up.

"Mike and I have to go." Rapp looked at Hurley and said, "I wanna know who he used to bug Doc's office. I wanna know where the originals are and I wanna know how many copies he made. And I want to move on this ASAP."

"My money's on Max Johnson," Hurley said.

"Yeah," Rapp replied. He was thinking the same thing. Max Johnson had been the second in charge of Security at Langley until he retired a few years earlier. He now had his own consulting firm, which coincidentally did a lot of work for Langley. Rapp didn't know him personally, but had heard a few things over the years that would lead him to believe the guy would have no problem stooping this low. "I want a list of everybody Adams has talked to about Kathy O'Brien."

"I want those tapes handed over to me immediately, so I can destroy them," Lewis said.

"Doc, I don't like this any more than you do, but someone is going to have to listen to those tapes." Rapp thought of Chuck O'Brien. It would kill him to know that Kathy's private sessions with her therapist had been recorded.

"I think you can trust me, Mitch."

"It has nothing to do with trust," Rapp said impatiently. "I need to listen to them so I can assess the damage."

"I don't think Kathy would approve." Lewis shook his head and added, "and I don't think Chuck will be too pleased either."

Nash entered the fray. "Well, maybe he should have thought about that before he started sharing classified information with his wife."

"She worked in Ops for twenty-three years," Lewis said defensively. "Her record is unassailable." Looking back to Rapp, he said in a very forceful manner, "I want the tapes. They are private and they belong to me."

"It ain't going to happen, Doc," Hurley said matter-of-factly. "Kathy was read in on a lot of serious shit, but that doesn't give Charlie the right to start sharing stuff with her, and it sure as hell doesn't give her the right to spill her guts to you. That's why we have these rules."

"But . . . I think we can all agree that you trust me." Lewis looked around the room. "I mean let's get real. What we have going on here is far more serious than anything that might be on those tapes."

Rapp was about to speak, but Hurley beat him to it. "Doc, your office isn't secure. Fuck . . . the Russkies . . . the Chicoms . . . anyone could have the place bugged. In fact I bet Mossad has had it bugged for years." Hurley looked at Rapp. "You better send a team in there tonight and have them give it the once-over."

Rapp was nodding as Hurley spoke. "I was thinking the same thing. I'll make it a priority."

"I need to be there," Hurley said, in a voice that made it clear this point was nonnegotiable.

"Fine," Rapp said, knowing he was out of time. "As far as the rest of this goes . . . we'll have to sort it out later. Mike and I have to go. In the meantime, start to peel him open. I want you to wring him dry."

"I don't think it will be a problem," said Lewis, "but I would discourage ever releasing him. He would betray us the first chance he got."

"I agree," Hurley said.

Rapp simply shrugged and said, "I don't give a shit."

"It might be useful, however, for us to make him think we are trying to turn him. Someone with an ego this fragile needs to have a carrot constantly dangled in front of him. Along those lines I think we should have him write a note to Kennedy and his wife saying that he has checked himself into a rehab clinic. It's something he needs to do . . . has been thinking about for some time. Only way to do it was to go cold turkey before he lost the courage. The important thing is to give him some hope."

"Fine," Rapp said.

"And if he proves uncooperative?" Hurley asked.

Rapp shrugged. "Do whatever it takes."

"And Chuck?" Lewis asked.

Rapp thought about Chuck O'Brien, the current director of the National Clandestine Service. "What about him?"

"He knows Kathy was seeing me. Who's going to tell him that our sessions were recorded?"

That was one conversation Rapp did not want to have. He could only imagine what had been discussed in those sessions. They'd been married for over thirty years. If Max Johnson were in fact the guy who had bugged the office, Chuck would want to kill him. And while Rapp wouldn't raise a hand to stop him, he at least needed to talk to Johnson first. "I don't want anyone saying anything to Chuck until we know who made the recordings, and I've had a chance to talk to them."

"When the time is right," Hurley announced, "I'll do it."

"Are you sure?" Rapp asked.

"It would kill him to hear it from you young pups. He's still your boss. I'll handle it."

"All right . . . it's settled." Looking to Nash, Rapp said, "Let's go."

"Mitch?"

Rapp turned and looked at Maslick, who was now standing. "Yeah?"

"I want you to promise me something."

Rapp got an ominous feeling. "What?"

"When it's time to punch his ticket," Maslick nodded toward the cell door, "I've got dibs."

Rapp understood immediately. Chris Johnson, Rapp's agent who had been killed a week earlier, had been Maslick's best friend. They'd served in the 101st Airborne Division and had done three combat tours together. "If it comes to that and you still want to do it, I won't stand in your way."

CHAPTER 19

LANGLEY, VIRGINIA

RAPP blew past the Georgetown Pike exit at eighty-plus miles an hour and continued north on the Beltway. As expected, traffic had been rough. Rapp had hoped to catch a little sleep on the drive up, but had given up on the idea as soon as he'd found out where Adams was getting his information. Rapp would never go as far as to say it didn't bother him that the CIA's inspector general was a colossal hypocrite. It surely did, but it was pretty small stuff compared to the other glitch they had just uncovered.

Kathy O'Brien was not the only client of Dr. Lewis who had ties to Langley. Rapp didn't know specifics, because Lewis never talked about his clients and the CIA wasn't the kind of place where people ran around talking about their feelings, let alone divulging that they were seeing a shrink, but it was known among the professionals that Lewis was a man you could trust if you needed a little help getting your head screwed back on. Rapp wasn't sure, but he got the distinct impression CIA Director Kennedy had spent some time on Lewis's couch trying to sort through some of her personal issues. Rapp knew this because

Kennedy herself had tried to get Rapp to sit down and talk with Lewis after his wife had been killed.

Even with the near-crippling pain he was experiencing after Anna's death, Rapp never considered consulting Lewis. He wasn't wired that way. Rapp knew he had to work his way through it on his own. He had nothing against therapy. He was sure that there were plenty of good docs out there who could help people get through a rough patch. And while he would never deny that he had a lot of issues, they weren't exactly the kind of things he could share. Doctor-patient privilege was a nice legal protection for the average person, who might someday end up in a courtroom, but intelligence agencies were instituted to not play by the rules. Bugging offices and eavesdropping on important conversations were standard operating procedure.

"I can't believe we're going to be late," Nash said in a tired voice.

Rapp looked over at his friend, who was clean-shaven and dressed in a crisp white shirt, blue suit, and yellow tie. Rapp glanced at his own reflection in the mirror. He had thick black stubble on his tan face and was not wearing a tie. If he had had time he probably would have shaved, but not necessarily. This was not his first meeting with this president, or the previous one, but it occurred to him this was probably Nash's first dance. He glanced at the clock. It was three minutes past nine, and they were still a few miles out. Rapp hit the blinker, cut across two lanes of traffic, and took the George Washington Parkway exit without slowing down. By the time they cleared security and parked, they'd be about ten minutes late, and while Rapp didn't like to keep the president of the United States waiting, he knew from experience that presidents weren't exactly the most punctual people.

Staring out the side window at the passing trees, Nash asked, "What in the hell are we doing?"

Rapp merged onto the parkway and said, "You're going to have to be a bit more specific, sport."

"This." Nash made groping gestures with his hands, "This crap . . . last night and this morning."

After glancing at him Rapp returned his attention to the road. They were 99 percent sure the car was clean, but they had their work phones on them, and although they were encrypted, the technology existed for an outfit like the National Security Agency to turn the phones into listening devices. Rapp chose his words carefully. "Maybe we can carve out a little time this afternoon to talk about it."

Nash wasn't so easily deterred. "I didn't sign up for this." Under his breath he mumbled, "I'm not a cold-blooded killer."

Rapp thought he'd heard him, but wasn't sure. "What was that?"

"You heard me," Nash said.

"It's hard to understand someone when he's slouched over like a teenager and mumbling to himself."

"I said," Nash spoke with exaggerated clarity, "that I'm not a cold-blooded killer."

"That's interesting . . . because I'd swear I saw you pop a few guys when we were over in the Kush." Rapp was referring to the operations they'd run in Afghanistan.

"That's different."

"How so?"

"They were the enemy."

"And what would you call this guy . . . our ally?"

"How about a fellow American?"

Rapp sighed. He did not want to talk about this right now, but he needed to figure out what in the hell was wrong with Nash and he had to do it before he put him in the same room as the president and God only knew who else. "Threats both foreign and domestic," Rapp said, quoting the oath they'd both taken. "Everyone likes to forget about the domestic part. Just because you're an American doesn't automatically make you one of the good guys."

"Well . . . just because he disagrees with us doesn't make him an enemy."

"So he can break whatever law he wants?"

"We're not exactly angels."

Rapp's patience was fading. "I think you're tired. This conversation is over."

Nash chuckled and said, "This has nothing to do with me being tired, and everything to do with the fact that you don't want to face the truth."

"Mike, I've been doing this shit since I was twenty-two. I've been accused of a lot of things but sticking my head in the sand is not one of them."

"Well . . . there's a first time for everything."

"Is this how you ran your command in Corps? Was it a debate club?"

"Don't compare this to the Corps. I would have never considered kidnapping a fellow Marine."

Rapp had heard about enough. He didn't like the fact that they were veering into specifics. He glanced over at Nash's bloodshot eyes, shook his head, and said, "I don't think you're going to attend this meeting."

"I don't think that's your decision to make."

"The hell it isn't."

Nash scoffed. "Oh . . . you're never the problem . . . not Mitch Rapp. It's always someone else's fault. You wanna write my attitude off to a lack of sleep, but it's a lot more complicated than that. I can tell you right now being tired has nothing to do with it. What we're doing back there . . . to one of our own . . . it's just wrong."

Rapp checked his rearview mirror and then yanked the steering wheel to the right. The car moved onto the shoulder.

"What are you doing?"

"Pulling over."

"We don't have time," Nash said with alarm. "We're late."

"Well, you should have thought of that before you decided you wanted to have a bitch session." Rapp brought the black Charger to a sudden stop and threw the gearshift into park. As he unbuckled his seat belt, he said, "Leave your phone in the car." Rapp checked the mirror, waited for a car to whiz by, and then got out and circled around the trunk. He had a .45 caliber Glock on his left hip in a paddle holster and as he stepped onto the grass he rested his left hand on the butt of the weapon.

Nash reluctantly got out of the vehicle and said, "Come on, Mitch, this is bullshit."

"What would be bullshit, would be putting you in front of the president and whoever else he's bringing to this meeting."

"I'm not the problem here, Mitch." Nash pointed at himself and then, turning his finger on Rapp added, "I think you need to take a long hard look at yourself."

"You are so fucking out of line right now, I don't even know where to begin."

"Why . . . because I have a conscience . . . unlike you and Stan, who pretty much do whatever the hell you want, whenever you want, to whoever you want?"

"You're cracking up, Major," Rapp said, using Nash's Marine Corps rank. "Combat fatigue. You haven't slept, you look like shit, and you've lost all discipline."

"Discipline," Nash spat the word back at Rapp. "Coming from you that's just ripe. Your entire career has been one insubordinate move after another."

"You used to talk to your battalion commander like this?"

"Stop with the Marine Corps analogies, all right. This is nothing like the Corps."

Rapp took in a deep breath. What little patience he had was gone. "I'm giving you two options. You either take two personal days . . . five days . . . I don't care how many days you need to sort this mess out, but you take 'em, and don't come back until you get your head screwed back on."

"What's my second choice?"

"You resign right now."

"And if I choose neither?" Nash asked with a forced lack of interest.

"Then I'll fire your ass," Rapp responded without hesitation.

"This is bullshit. I'm not the one with the problems. Maybe you should be the one taking a few days off."

Rapp was on the verge of snapping. He'd seen this type of behavior before. Perfectly healthy guys who succumb to the stress of a job that can grind up and spit out the most hardened warrior. Hurley had warned him a week ago that Nash had been showing signs of fatigue. Nash's wife had called Hurley and shared some things that she probably should have kept to herself. Rapp thought of that conversation and asked Nash, "Tell me, when was the last time you had a hard-on?"

Nash frowned. "What the hell are you talking about?"

Rapp stared at him. "You know exactly what I'm talking about."

"Fuck you."

Rapp shook his head. "You can try to make this about me and what happened down at the lake, but you know that's a lie. The only reason your plumbing doesn't work when you're thirty-eight is because you got some shit going on in your head."

Nash's face flushed with anger and he took a step toward Rapp and clenched his fists. "Don't make this about me. I didn't sign up for this shit. No one told me I'd be involved in kidnapping and murder . . . least of all of a fellow American. I don't care how much you hate—"

Rapp was already alert to the fact that Nash might take an ill-advised swing at him, so when he heard him getting a little too close to divulging what had gone down the night before, he took a quick step forward, and his left hand shot out like a battering ram. The palm strike landed in the center of Nash's chest, rolling his shoulders forward and nearly breaking his sternum. The blow sent Nash backpedaling for a few feet and onto his butt.

Rapp closed the distance and remained in a combat stance. "If you're dumb enough to get up, I swear I'll put you in the hospital."

Nash was clutching his chest and had the look of a feral animal on his face.

Rapp could tell he was calculating odds. "You're so damn tired you look like a strung-out junkie. I don't wanna see your face for at least two days. I want you to go home and sleep . . . and spend some time with your family, and if after two days you still can't get your emotions under control . . . then I want your resignation."

"And if I don't do what I'm told," Nash said clutching his chest, "what are you going to do, kill me? Hurt my family?"

Rapp was in a state of semidisbelief. "You know damn well I'd never touch your family."

"I'm not so sure."

"Let's be clear on one thing." Rapp stepped closer. "If you break that oath you took . . . I wouldn't dream of hurting your family." He lowered his voice and added, "But I will kill you. It won't be easy, and it'll probably haunt me for the rest of my life, but this is bigger than our friendship."

CHAPTER 20

CIA HEADQUARTERS

RAPP parked in the underground garage and proceeded to the director's private elevator. Kennedy had made arrangements for him to use it when he wanted to get into and out of the building without being seen and stopped, which was often. Rapp wasn't a big fan of headquarters and stayed away as much as possible. Due to the unique nature of his job, however, he couldn't always pick up the phone and tell Kennedy what he was up to. They had both been trained by Thomas Stansfield, a World War II icon, to never assume that a secure phone was secure just because a technician announced it was. The history of espionage was riddled with stories of great nations' assuming their communications were safe only to find out after being trounced by their enemy that they had been compromised. There were times, however, when logistics, distance, and operational constraints necessitated a phone call. The key at that point was to keep things vague, but if you were in the process of doing something that might land your hide in jail, then you'd better sit down and have the talk in person.

Rapp entered the elevator, pressed the top button, and as the doors began to close, he thought of Nash. Decking him hadn't bothered

Rapp a bit. They were not analysts; they were front-line operatives who lived in a physical world of sparring and training. Judo, karate, wrestling, kickboxing, they practiced it all. Rapp himself was a devotee of the Gracie style of jujitsu and Nash, having been a state high school wrestling champ, was no pushover. Rapp knew more tricks and had never been bested by the slightly younger Nash, but the fact that Rapp had been able to knock him on his ass with one well-delivered palm strike said more about Nash's mental state than one might imagine. If Nash ever came to his senses, he'd probably thank Rapp for knocking him on his ass. That's the way Marines were wired. They could get pissed as all hell in the middle of a fight, but after things had calmed down, they would laugh at their own stupidity. They weren't the type to be obsessed with the past. What was eating away at Rapp was the fact that he never saw it coming. Nash had been his recruit. The guy was a natural. Tough as nails, yet relaxed enough that he wouldn't look like a robot the way a lot of the military guys did when they tried to transition into other careers.

Not more than two weeks ago Nash would have been the first guy in line to punch Adams's ticket, and now he was wringing his hands like one of those blowing-in-the-wind politicians on the Hill. Rapp had seen a few guys burn out and crash land. Their line of work wasn't exactly stress-free. More often than not they would bounce back after a little R&R, but occasionally a guy would end up in a free fall like some druggy who'd taken a bad acid trip. Rapp could only think of one time when that had happened and the guy had to be put down like a rabid dog. He didn't even want to think they might end up there with Nash. Rapp knew his wife and kids well. Nash was a good family man and a friend, and unfortunately he also knew too much.

The elevator stopped and the second the doors opened, Rapp sensed something was up. Two of the director's bodyguards were standing post, both of her assistants were on the phone, and there wasn't a single Secret Service agent in sight. Even if the president were running late, a couple of the advance guys should already be here keeping an eye on things. Rapp was about to ask Steven, one of Kennedy's personal assistants, what was going on when the young man pointed toward the office door and gave Rapp the signal to go in. Rapp banged his fist on it a few times and then entered.

The corner suite ran from right to left, with a sitting area straight ahead, then the director's desk, and beyond that a large conference table. To the right were the director's private bathroom and the door to the deputy director's office. Instead of the six to eight people Rapp expected, there were only two—his boss and a man he had never met but knew by reputation. He was handsome as hell. Short-cropped hair that was equal parts black and white and walnut-colored skin that didn't have a blemish or wrinkle.

Rapp had never much cared for the seventh floor at Langley. In fact he couldn't think of a single time where he had looked forward to making the trip up to the rarified top floor of the Old Headquarters Building. It wasn't that he disliked the people. Irene Kennedy was like family, and her predecessor, Thomas Stansfield, was one of the finest men he'd ever known. The clandestine guys were all good and the intel people were sharp as hell, but this floor more than any other in the business served as a portal to politics, and a whole host of issues that had nothing to do with running an effective intelligence agency.

The man sitting in Kennedy's office was proof of that. Gabriel Dickerson placed his coffee cup on the saucer that was sitting on the glass table and stood. He extended his right hand and with a warm smile said, "Young man, it is an honor to finally meet you."

Rapp could not match the sentiment, so he simply nodded. His first impression was that Dickerson was taller than he would have thought, especially since he had to be close to eighty. Rapp was six feet tall and Dickerson was every bit that plus a couple of inches. The second thing Rapp noticed wasn't the least bit surprising. Dickerson had a smile and charisma that could charm the lollypop out of the sticky mitts of a five-year-old. Whether he'd been born with all this charisma or had learned it on a used-car lot, Rapp didn't know and didn't really care, but he knew he'd better damn well be careful, because Gabe Dickerson was to politics what Rapp was to the intelligence business. Their tools were different, of course, but they were both experts at getting things done behind the scenes. While Rapp dealt with problems in an often unpleasant and violent way, Dickerson was known to be every bit as ruthless. The big difference was that while Rapp used his fists and a gun, Dickerson used his Rolodex and a small cadre of litigators, publicists, and political operatives to destroy his enemies or curry favor for his clients.

"Where is Mr. Nash?" Dickerson asked.

"He couldn't make it," Rapp said as he glanced at Kennedy, who was still sitting on the couch.

"That's a shame," Dickerson continued in his deep basso voice, "I was very much looking forward to meeting both of you. I heard about what you did last week and wanted to thank you personally."

Rapp's right eyebrow shot up a notch. "Last week?"

"The attack on the Counterterrorism Center. I heard if it weren't for the quick thinking and heroics of you and Mr. Nash, things would have been significantly worse."

It's already starting, Rapp thought to himself. *No one in this damn town can keep a secret.* "Don't believe everything you hear, sir. You know how rumors get rolling around here . . . take a little truth, exaggerate it to suit your needs, and then spin the hell out of it."

Dickerson let loose a deep, infectious laugh. "You have it all figured out. You could work for me."

Before Rapp knew it he was smiling and he thought to himself, *Damn, this guy is good.*

"You're a brave man, Mr. Rapp . . . charging a group of men like that." Dickerson shook his head in semidisbelief, "I don't think too many men could have pulled that off."

"Like I said, you can't believe everything you hear in this town." Rapp's desire to keep his name out of the press was paramount, and a guy like Dickerson got a great deal of his power and influence by whispering juicy secrets in people's ears.

"I didn't hear anything," Dickerson said in defense. "I read it in the FBI's official report. Six terrorists entered the Operations Center in a single-file line and began systematically executing personnel. Mr. Nash engaged the terrorists from a balcony that overlooks the Ops Center, striking the first man in the line once in the helmet and three more times in the side . . . all .40 caliber rounds. You then proceeded to charge the line of men while Mr. Nash kept the first man distracted. You shot the second man in the throat, the third man in the nose, the fourth man twice in the neck, the fifth man once in the face, and then the last man twice in the small of his back . . . all with a 9mm Glock.

"Then you discovered they were all wearing suicide vests and you had the presence of mind not to flee." Dickerson shook his head in a manner that said this was the part that most impressed him. "You and Mr. Nash, with the aid of several agents, then proceeded to throw all six terrorists out a window, where they landed at the base of the concrete ramp that led to the underground parking structure. Each vest then exploded and caused severe damage to the parking garage, but not another person was lost."

It had all gone down pretty fast, but from what Rapp could recall, the man had pretty much nailed the high points.

Dickerson continued, "Now, there's a fair number of people who would consider what you did to be either stupid or crazy, but I see things a little differently. You see, Mr. Rapp, much of my job depends on sizing people up. Not all that different from a good tailor who has the ability to look at a man from across the room and know exactly what jacket size the man wears. Although I'm not worried about jacket size." Dickerson tapped his temple with one of his long, manicured fingers and then patted his chest. "I'm worried about what's up here and what's in a man's heart. I can usually size up a prospective client in thirty seconds." Dickerson looked Rapp over from head to toe and said, "There was nothing stupid or crazy about what you did last week. You are at your best when things are most chaotic. While others panic and react without thought, things slow down for you. You tune out all the noise . . . your brain begins looking for avenues of action first and avenues of retreat second. You size up an enemy the way a lumberjack surveys a tree and then you move efficiently and effectively." Dickerson shook his head. "Nothing crazy or stupid about it."

CHAPTER 21

RAPP didn't like any of this. Didn't like the fact that the damn FBI had to put everything in writing, or triplicate or whatever in hell it was that they did now with all the damn forms they had to fill out. It was one of his big bitches about this war on terror—too many lawyers created too many cover-your-ass bureaucrats who in turn demanded that everything be put in writing. Assuming it took a few days to put the report together, it couldn't have been in circulation for more than three or four days, yet here was a private citizen who had already read it. Rapp was pissed, not because of Dickerson really, but because he had failed to have the damn report sanitized, or at least have his role in the affair minimized to a footnote and have someone else given the credit. Things were happening too fast, and he was making mistakes.

Everyone took a seat and then Dickerson said, "You don't look too pleased."

"I'm not used to discussing classified information with civilians."

"Ah . . . I see. You're bothered that a man like me, who does not work for the federal government, and has no security clearance that you know of . . . ended up with the official FBI report of what happened at the National Counterterrorism Center last week."

"That's a pretty accurate assessment."

Dickerson nodded in a thoughtful manner and said, "The president showed me the report this morning."

Rapp looked at Kennedy, who appeared to be taking the news much better than he was. "And why would he do that?" Rapp asked Dickerson.

"He trusts me, Mr. Rapp."

Rapp looked around the room. "I assume he's not showing up?"

"That would be correct."

Rapp looked to Kennedy.

The CIA director said, "It's politics, Mitch."

"What does this have to do with politics?" Rapp knew it was a stupid question the second it left his lips. The factions in D.C. could turn anything into a partisan issue. Much of it he ignored, but when it came to National Security it really got his blood boiling.

Kennedy said, "That FBI report that Gabe is referring to contained mention of an incident between you and Mr. Abad bin Baaz."

"You're talking about the Saudi terrorists that I apprehended the day of the attacks?"

"Yes," Kennedy replied.

"So?"

Dickerson answered, "He has dual citizenship."

Rapp was afraid some Dudley Do-Right would make an issue of this. "He's a Saudi terrorist who applied for dual citizenship so we couldn't put the screws to him. If we had any common sense left in this town, you'd take his citizenship away and hand him over to me so I can finish interrogating him."

"The president," Dickerson sighed, "actually agrees with you, but there is a rather vocal group in his party that, to put it mildly, disagrees with him."

"Don't tell me they're going to come after me for this?" Rapp asked Kennedy. "There is too much going on right now. Too many things that I need to take care of. I can't be dealing with these idiots right now."

Kennedy said, "Fortunately, it looks like they have run into an obstacle."

"What kind of obstacle?"

Dickerson said, "A fellow senator who has vouched for you."

"Lonsdale?"

"Yes. The FBI report has a section that outlines Mr. bin Baaz's claim that you dislocated his shoulder and a doctor's report that backs up his claim that the injury was caused by you while he was in your custody. Before he was turned over to the feds."

Rapp knew it had been caused while in his custody. He remembered vividly dislocating the little pecker's arm and twisting it to the point where he thought he might actually rip it off. "And Lonsdale?"

"She has filed an affidavit stating that Mr. bin Baaz was in perfectly good condition when she arrived at the National Counterterrorism Center and that he was hurt during the attack when he was thrown to the floor by none other than herself."

Rapp concealed his surprise. The fact that the senator had lied for him was an interesting development, to say the least. Rapp kept a straight face and asked, "So what's the problem?"

"Things in Washington are very rarely open and shut. This group of senators and representatives has retreated for the moment, but they have very powerful lobbying groups that give them piles of cash, and in return they expect them to take the fight to the enemy. Those groups will demand that they open a new front."

With evident sarcasm Rapp said, "I thought we were all on the same team."

"They despise you, Mr. Rapp." Dickerson looked around the office. "They despise this entire Agency."

Rapp was somewhat alarmed to hear he was on their radar screen, but he wasn't about to let on. "I would imagine some of those powerful lobbying groups are clients of yours."

"They are."

"And you make a lot of money from them."

"I do."

"So why do I get the feeling you're not here on their behalf this morning?"

Dickerson smiled, "You are a quick study, Mr. Rapp. I am not here on their behalf."

"Conflict of interest?"

"Don't confuse lobbying with the legal system. It's the first thing I tell my new associates, who are almost always fresh out of law school and full of ideals. I'm a pragmatic man, Mr. Rapp. I've been a lot of places . . . seen a lot of things, and if I'm lucky I've got another ten years before I meet my maker. I take money from these groups because I'm a capitalist, and I earn every penny of it trying to moderate their crazy demands. I know who they are, and I don't particularly sympathize with their view of the world, but they are a force to be reckoned with."

"So whose meter are you on right now?"

"Let's just say I'm here because I feel it's my patriotic duty . . . that and because the president asked me to take his place."

"And why would the president do that?"

"Because I advised him to cancel this meeting."

Rapp asked the obvious question, "Why?"

"He was briefed by the FBI late last night about the ongoing manhunt, and let's just say it didn't go well."

"How so?"

"They don't have a single lead and the suspects that you took into custody the day of the attacks have all lawyered up and are refusing to talk."

"And this surprised the president?"

"Not entirely, but he is a man who expects results. He thought some progress would be made, but these three men have simply vanished. The FBI doesn't have a single solid lead."

"Well . . . when you fight with both hands tied behind your back it's hard to win."

"The president is starting to see things your way, but I'm getting ahead of myself. There was another development at the meeting. One of the deputy attorneys general also pointed out this sticky issue between you and Mr. bin Baaz. He went so far as to say he felt Senator Lonsdale had filed a false affidavit and that you in fact had abused the prisoner."

Rapp groaned, "I bet the president loved hearing that."

"It did not please him in the least." Dickerson turned even more serious. "He told the briefers that the only two people who seemed to have gotten anything done in the past week were you and Mr. Nash, and that in his honest and very important opinion, if men like you didn't have to spend so much time answering the Justice Department's inquiries, you might have been able to prevent the attack that occurred last week. He then went on to suggest that it might be a good idea if we stopped persecuting our own people and focused a little more on the terrorists who attacked us."

Kennedy said to Rapp, "The president called me after the meeting. He said he wanted to talk to you and Mike first thing. Thank you for the sacrifices you've made and ask you for a favor."

Rapp turned to Dickerson. "And you talked him out of coming?"

"Yes."

"Why?"

"Please don't take this the wrong way, Mr. Rapp, but I think it would be best if the president kept his distance from you."

CHAPTER 22

RAPP really wasn't the insecure type, so rather than taking offense at Dickerson's comment, he began to laugh. He didn't need to ask for clarification. Any fool could see why a gamer like Dickerson would advise the president to steer clear of a man of Rapp's ilk. His curiosity, however, was piqued by the revelation that the president had suddenly taken an interest in his unique skill set. It was funny how that worked in Washington. Guys like Rapp were often viewed as the problem until the politicians themselves were threatened.

Rapp looked at Dickerson and with a slight grin said, "As you may have already guessed . . . it's pretty hard to offend me."

"No . . . I wouldn't imagine you care too much about other people's opinions. Probably not even the president's."

"I don't want to sound disrespectful," Rapp said. "He is our president after all . . . it's just that I've been at this a while. I'm a little jaded."

"So am I. I've worked in this town for fifty-five years. I've seen a lot of administrations come and go and while each one has its strengths and weaknesses, the good ones all have something in common."

"What's that?" Rapp asked.

"Deniability."

Rapp's face showed his surprise. There were a lot of words he could have anticipated, but this was not one of them. "How so?"

"This is a shitty business and the chief executive needs to stay out of the shit. I served in the Navy after college. Learned a lot about a lot of things, but the thing that impressed me most about the Navy was the way they thought everything through to the tenth . . . twentieth . . . sometimes hundredth degree. The way they design those ships is amazing. The training . . . everything is geared toward not just putting out a fire, but putting out the fire while still taking the fight to the enemy. You take a torpedo, up front below the water line, you close the watertight doors and keep fighting. You seal off that part of the ship and there more than likely are going to be some guys who aren't going to make it out . . . but you seal the doors anyway."

"Your point?"

"I'm that watertight door between you and the president."

Rapp thought about it for a moment and then said, "So in other words you expect me to put my neck on the line, but if things start going bad . . . water starts flooding the compartment, to use your analogy, and I try to get out, you're going to slam that door in my face and let me drown."

Now it was Dickerson's turn to put a frown on. "No, that's not what I'm saying."

Rapp's version of the sinking-ship analogy was more accurate than Dickerson would allow himself to see. The only problem was, the political operative, mostly due to his station in life, viewed the scenario from the top down. Not an unusual thing for a wealthy, successful person. Dickerson naturally saw himself on the bridge of the ship with the captain. To save the ship others would have to die. Conveniently, however, they would also be saving themselves. Rapp understood the draconian necessity in the military application, but in the political arena it was tinged with selfishness and arrogance. Especially when bracketed in the context of national security. The number of politicians in

Washington who were willing to stand on principle and put the security of the country before their beloved party was quickly becoming a pathetically small group. They'd all spent too much time on the bridge and not enough time in the engine room.

Rapp leaned back and crossed his legs. "I think that's pretty much exactly what you're saying."

"No." Dickerson shook his head vehemently. "And trust me on this, the president is a big supporter of yours. I have advised him, however, that due to the way things work in this town it would be best if he kept a few people between himself and you. Especially in light of what he wanted to talk to you about today."

Here it is, Rapp thought to himself. He bet a guy like Dickerson billed between five hundred and seven hundred dollars an hour, and while it was unlikely that he would be charging the president for this slice of time, he was nonetheless an extremely busy man who wouldn't bother coming out to Langley unless it was something serious.

"As I already stated, the president is not happy about the FBI's lack of progress."

"I know some of those guys, and to be fair to them, the Justice Department isn't doing them any favors."

"I wouldn't disagree with you, but we are a nation of laws."

Rapp leaned forward and put out his hand, giving Dickerson the stop sign. "You know you're the second person today who has used that line on me and I gotta tell you I think it's a copout."

Dickerson was not used to people speaking to him so bluntly. "Really?"

"A throwaway line that means everything and nothing at the same time."

"You don't think we're a nation of laws?" Dickerson asked.

"No . . . I agree we're a nation of laws, but there are a lot of people running around parroting that statement without any sense of history."

"I think I have a very good sense of history."

"Then help me with this . . . when did we get so hell bent on affording our legal protections to our enemies?"

Dickerson paused a beat and then said, "That's a complicated answer, Mr. Rapp."

"No, it isn't," Rapp replied bluntly. "You don't want to answer it because you're going to ask me in a very coded way to put my neck on the line and break these very laws you and the president pretend to hold so dear, and if I'm right about that, I'd appreciate a little honesty from you on this issue." Rapp paused for a beat and then added, "And don't worry, I won't be running to the press. Not my style. The only people I dislike more than politicians are reporters. I just want to make sure we're on the same page, before you send me down to the engine room to plug the leak."

Dickerson nodded as if to say, fair enough.

Kennedy held up a finger, looked at Rapp, and said, "If I may?"

Rapp said, "Go right ahead."

"This country of *laws*," Kennedy said in a slightly sarcastic tone, "has a long history of curtailing its citizens' rights during times of war and national emergency. The Civil War is the most obvious example. Lincoln suspended what many would argue is the most sacred law of all . . . habeas corpus. During World War II, the FBI opened any piece of mail they wanted. They listened in on phone calls, intercepted cable traffic, and they did it all without a single warrant. And anyone who is naïve enough to think we treated every POW to the exact standards of the Geneva Conventions has never spoken to a Marine who served in the Pacific. Not every Japanese POW was treated as well as we'd like to believe. FDR, a man who is considered by many to be one of our greatest presidents, interned thousands of Japanese Americans as well as German and Italian Americans. We simply rounded these people up based solely on their ethnicity and stuck them in prisoner of war camps until the war was over.

"Then the Cold War came along, and despite all the people who have tried to rewrite history, the Soviet Union had a massive intelligence operation here in the United States. Joe McCarthy may have been a drunk and an ass, but that didn't make him wrong on the big issue. It is an undeniable fact that the Soviet Union was engaged in espionage on a colossal scale. They were recruiting agents, stealing our vital national secrets, and attempting to undermine our political process by funding communist and socialist political parties in this country. This little chapter in our nation's history was not simply cooked up by the alcohol-soaked brain of the junior senator from Wisconsin. So while there are a lot of people in America who would love to embrace compassion and tolerance, and they have correctly labeled Joe McCarthy a bully, they do so by conveniently ignoring the fact that the Soviet Union was doing everything that Joe McCarthy and J. Edgar Hoover and JFK and a whole host of political figures accused them of doing."

Dickerson's expression soured. "I think on this point we will have to agree to disagree."

"No . . . I don't think so," Kennedy said firmly.

Even Rapp was surprised by how forcefully his boss had responded to Dickerson.

"I don't want to sound disrespectful, Gabe, but I'm pretty sure I know why you're here, so I think you might want to hear our concerns before you ask us to risk our careers and possibly our freedom."

"Fair enough."

"Fifteen years ago, do you know what we used to do when we'd close in on a suspected Soviet spy? And I'm talking about the ones who had U.S. citizenship."

"I'm sure you would refer the matter to the FBI," Dickerson said, showing the hint of a grin.

"No," Kennedy answered seriously. "We'd grab them . . . usually in the middle of the night, and we'd take them to any number of undisclosed locations, and we'd use every form of interrogation you could imagine."

"And you weren't always right, were you?"

"Of the nearly one hundred cases I'm familiar with, there was only one instance where the individual turned out to be innocent."

Dickerson scoffed at Kennedy's claim. "How could you be sure?"

"Those groups you referred to earlier. The ones you represent."

"Yes."

"You know how they like to say torture doesn't work?"

"Yes."

Kennedy tapped her leg with her reading glasses and said, "Well . . . trust me, it does."

CHAPTER 23

RAPP looked at his watch. He had a mental list two pages long of stuff he needed to get to, and sitting in his boss's office trying to persuade one of the president's closest advisors that torture worked seemed like it might be a waste of time. Rapp had found in his various appearances before the intelligence committees that you were wasting your breath if you tried to convince people in thousand-dollar suits who had Ivy League law degrees that torture was an effective and necessary tool against an enemy who refused to put on a uniform and intentionally targeted civilians. Given the right team and enough time to work on the individual, there wasn't a person out there who didn't break, but Rapp had learned the hard way that most politicians preferred an issue and a ready-made talking point to reality.

Rapp had tired of trying to convince people that it worked. He'd come to the conclusion it would be like a major league slugger arguing with fans over why he swung or didn't swing at a certain pitch. If you've never been in that batter's box, with some freak of nature perched a little more than sixty feet away on an elevated mound of dirt, who was about to whip a hard white ball at you in excess of ninety miles an hour that might or might not hit you in the head, you really couldn't understand what it was like to decide in a split second to swing or not swing. It's easy to sit in the stands with a hot dog and cold beer and criticize, and it's every bit as easy to sit in a federal office building in Washington, D.C., and do the same thing.

In response to Kennedy's admission that they not only used torture but it worked nearly 100 percent of the time, Dickerson said, "There are certain things I don't need to know." He smiled uncomfortably and added, "This is why I advised the president not to attend this meeting. This type of discussion is way off the reservation. Having said that, I sympathize with your position. Does it bother me that I am surrounded by people who want so badly to be liked . . . want so desperately to be thought of as enlightened that they are willing to tear this country apart? Yes, it bothers me. Does it drive me to the brink of madness that there are people in this town who think the way to peace is to afford tolerance to an intolerant group of bigoted Muslim men? People who should know better, by the way . . . Yes, it drives me mad."

Rapp felt a glimmer of hope. He couldn't recall the last time he had heard someone this well connected speak so frankly.

"It is utter insanity," Dickerson said, "that the Justice Department has four men in their custody who we know for a fact helped plan and prepare for attacks that killed nearly two hundred of our fellow citizens. All four of those men were born in Saudi Arabia. Two of them have dual citizenship. Those men know things that could help us find the three men who are at large and possibly information that could help us prevent further attacks. And what are we doing?"

"Nothing," Kennedy said.

"They all have lawyers," Dickerson said while making a hopeless gesture with his hands.

"And," Kennedy said, "I was told the ACLU will be filing a brief this morning fighting any extradition to Saudi Arabia."

"Why am I not surprised?" Dickerson answered.

"They think that we will hand them over to the Saudis so they can torture them for us."

Dickerson thought about it for a second and said, "Not a bad idea."

Rapp shook his head. "Actually, it's not such a good idea. The Saudis like to say they'll share information with us, but they rarely give us the whole story. They suck them dry, and then they kill them, and we only get what they want us to know, which never includes anything that might connect them to certain wealthy subjects as well as high-placed government officials."

"So what do we do?"

"With the four men in custody?" Rapp asked.

"Yes."

"Nothing," Kennedy answered for him, "unless the president wants to sign an executive order that authorizes us to use extreme measures."

"And a blanket pardon would be nice," Rapp added with a smile.

Dickerson suddenly looked less than enthusiastic about the new direction of the discussion. "The president was hoping you would take a more active role in the search for the three men who are still at large. This Lion of al Qaeda character has really got under the president's skin."

He was under Rapp's skin as well. "So, I'm not going to get the blanket pardon?"

"I don't think so, but there is something else I think I can help you with. I'm not sure if you are aware of this, but there are certain elements on the Hill who are already maneuvering to make this Agency and you, Director Kennedy, the scapegoat for what happened last week."

Kennedy said, "I was not aware of that, but it doesn't surprise me."

"Well . . . you have a PR battle that you have been losing for some time."

Both Rapp and Kennedy nodded. It was universally agreed that when the CIA did something well, it was never discussed, but when they screwed up, it was plastered across every media outlet for weeks, if not months.

"I think I can help you more effectively defend yourselves. Get out in front of these other groups before they strike. I can help shape your message. Get it told in the right way over the best outlets."

"And just how are you going to do that?" Rapp asked in a skeptical tone. "The media elite in this country don't exactly like us."

"I've got something they won't be able to resist."

"What's that?" Rapp asked.

"You, Mr. Rapp."

"Come again?" Rapp asked, looking more pissed off than confused.

"You're a hero. What you and Mike Nash did last week is the type of thing legends are made of, and I don't even have to exaggerate your accomplishments. The media will eat it up and you and Mr. Nash will become untouchable. There won't be a politician in this town dumb enough to try and take you on. You will become this generation's Audie Murphy."

"You're nuts!"

"Mitch," Kennedy cautioned.

"No way in hell am I—"

"Mitch," Kennedy cut him off, "just calm down for a minute. I want to hear what else he has to say."

"Well, I sure as hell don't."

Kennedy gave him the look of a mother about to cuff her teenager across the head, and after he'd backed down a bit, she looked at Dickerson and asked, "In exchange for what?"

"He . . ." Dickerson said, referring to the president but not wanting to use his name, "thinks it would be best if you found these three men first."

"Why?" Rapp asked.

Dickerson took a long moment to answer. "Let's just say that he thinks you might be able to cut through some of the red tape."

"So you mean he wants me to put the screws to them before the FBI reads them their rights and they hire a lawyer?"

Dickerson shrugged. He didn't dare open his mouth, for fear that his words might be recorded.

"Boy," Rapp said in near disgust, "you guys are a real profile in courage."

"You know darn well the president can't endorse something like this."

"It sounds like he wanted to, but you got in front of him and convinced him it was a bad idea. You somehow persuaded him that you could barter a trade with us. A couple hundred billable hours of PR from your firm in exchange for me putting my nuts on the chopping block."

Dickerson had a pained look on his face. "I know it doesn't seem like a fair trade, but I think you're minimizing the potential upside. This PR offensive could get a lot of these politicians to back down. Some of them might even turn into supporters of yours."

Rapp placed his face in his hands and shook his head. After a long moment, he looked up at Dickerson and said, "Somewhere in this building there's a safe filled with a bunch of medals and commendations for guys just like me who've put their asses on the line over the years. We don't do this job for public recognition. We don't want public recognition, and we can't effectively do our job if people know who we are. So I will not be participating in your PR offensive, and if my name somehow ends up leaked to the press, I will find out who did it and I will hurt them."

Dickerson looked at Kennedy to see if she would overrule Rapp.

Rapp didn't give her the chance. "I call my own shots on something like this. Going over my head won't work. So . . . sorry to disappoint, but I won't be going on *Oprah* to talk about my top five favorite movies."

"So, I should tell the president your answer is no."

Rapp thought about it for a second and with a deep frown said,

"I'm going to keep doing what I've always done. You can tell the president that I'm going to find these three guys. I don't know if it's going to take a week or a year, but I'm going to find them and when I do, I don't give a shit what the ACLU or the Justice Department or anybody else thinks about how they should be treated. I'm going to find out everything there is to know about their organization . . . who supported them . . . where they got their money . . . where they got the explosives . . . how they got into this country, and if they got out who helped them. And then I'm going to track all of these people down, and I'm going to kill them."

Dickerson was more than a little surprised by the frank admission. "The president will be very, ah . . . happy to hear that you will be taking an active role in the case."

Rapp stood. He'd already wasted enough time. "Yeah . . . well, tell him if the shit hits the fan, I'll scream from the rooftops that we had this little powwow and you asked me on his behalf to disregard the law and do whatever it takes to bring these men to justice."

Dickerson looked as if he might vomit. In a deliberate, cautious tone he said, "I would . . . advise . . . against . . ."

"Don't worry," Rapp said casually. Pointing at Kennedy, he added, "I think she and I are the only two people left in this town who know how to keep their mouths shut."

CHAPTER 24

WHILE Kennedy said good-bye to Dickerson, Rapp grabbed his BlackBerry, walked to the far end of the office, and began listening to the nine messages that had been left during the meeting. Rapp saw no sense in thanking Dickerson for a meeting at which, at least from his perspective, nothing had been gained. As usual, Rapp and his people were going to shoulder the risk, while the political elites inoculated themselves against any fallout. Rapp took a bit of joy in the fact that Dickerson left looking none too pleased. Rapp figured he made the man nervous.

Dickerson was a professional handicapper and Rapp was a wild card—the aberration that his formula couldn't account for. Dickerson was used to assessing his chances for success in a game where people played by a certain set of unwritten rules. The players all moved along a path where their incentives were money, power, and notoriety. Rapp had more than enough money, and as far as power was concerned, it could be easily argued that he represented the very essence of physical supremacy, at least in the individual sense. Put him up against pretty much any guy in town, and you'd be a fool not to put your money on Rapp.

The thing that had really thrown Dickerson, though, was Rapp's outright refusal to become a national hero. Dickerson's substantial fees were generated by ambitious men and women who couldn't compute turning down such an offer. Many of them wouldn't bat an eye at manufacturing tales of bravado, if they knew they could get away with it, and more than a few had done just that over the years. Passing on an opportunity to bask in the lights, cameras, and microphones of the national media was unthinkable. It would be like a sex addict saying no to a weekend in bed with a *Playboy* centerfold.

There was another reason, Rapp knew, that Dickerson didn't look too happy. He had recognized Rapp for what he was—a Molotov cocktail that could ignite a conflagration that would bring down a presidency and put a party on a course for a few decades of permanent minority status. It was why Dickerson had argued against the president's attending the meeting in the first place. Even so, Dickerson was acutely aware of both the risks and rewards that were circling the president. An attack had gone down on his watch, and he hadn't raised a finger in protest of the very people Dickerson represented. Apparently being nice to the terrorists wasn't working out so well.

"And you wonder why I don't like coming in here," Rapp said as Kennedy closed the office door on her guest.

Kennedy began walking across the office toward her desk. "Should I be offended?"

"Has nothing to do with you, boss. You know that. It's just that I've got a few things that need my attention, and I just wasted the better part of the morning sitting here listening to I'm not sure what."

"Gabe is a good person to have on your side."

Rapp shrugged. "Maybe if you want to get booked on *Oprah*, but from where I'm standing, he doesn't appear to offer a lot."

"You could have been a little more subtle. Maybe a simple thanks but no thanks."

"A guy like that would see that as a yellow light. He'd hit the gas. The only way to stop him is to make your intentions crystal clear. Maybe even make him think you might come unhinged."

"Well, you accomplished that." Kennedy looked at the blinking message light on her phone and decided it could wait. She needed to go over a few things with Rapp first and she could tell by his fidgeting that he didn't plan on staying long. Lifting her gaze she focused on Rapp's face and asked, "Where were you last night?"

Rapp didn't waver. He looked her straight in the eye and said, "I was down at Stan's place. We had a few things to go over."

Kennedy nodded. "And you didn't bring your cell phone?"

"I had it with me."

"But you turned it off and took out the battery."

Rapp shrugged as if to say, what do you expect. "Call me paranoid."

"No doubt . . . and if I need to get hold of you?" Kennedy asked.

"You'd leave me a message, and I'd call you back, or try Stan's number next time."

"He's no better than you are. He never answers his phone. I'm not even sure he has a phone, now that I think of it."

"I call him all the time."

Kennedy eyed him. "I'm never going to get anywhere with you on this, am I?"

Rapp shook his head. "Listen, before we get too far off track, did you know that this meeting was going to be about a big PR offensive?"

"Of course not," Kennedy answered. "I know better than to waste your time."

"So, if he's as smart a guy as you say he is, how could he possibly think I'd go along with something like this?"

Kennedy picked up a small tube of hand lotion. "I think he was a bit desperate." She squirted a dollop the size of a quarter into her palm and began rubbing her hands together. "The president has good instincts. He can see where this is all headed. We haven't even finished burying all the dead from last week and in certain circles he's being labeled as weak on terror. You have to remember, he ran on a rule-of-law platform, and now we've been hit."

"And so the brave thing to do is launch a PR offensive."

"Theirs is a different world, Mitch." Kennedy shrugged. "The president told me himself that he is really frustrated with the FBI."

"Why?"

"Because they have come up with nothing. They know very little about the men who carried out the attack. And the three men who are still at large. They've vanished."

"Well, don't get mad at the FBI. They're operating within the very constraints the president campaigned on."

"And that," Kennedy said, "I suspect is why he wanted to sit down with you and Mike."

"But Dickerson waved him off," Rapp said.

"Correct, and to be honest, I'm not sure it wasn't wise counsel."

"God forbid the president get a little dose of reality. Maybe sign an executive order that allows us to really go after these guys."

"Be careful what you wish for, Mitchell."

"If I could wish for anything it would be some damn support from the White House and the Hill."

"As foreign as it seems, that's what Gabe was trying to offer you, but for reasons that I completely understand you would prefer to not have your image splashed across the world media outlets." Kennedy hit the space bar on her computer to take it out of sleep mode. "The PR offensive isn't a bad idea. You're just the wrong guy for it. You know as well as anyone that it would be nice to get some of our esteemed senators and representatives to back us a bit more. It has been a long time since . . ."

Rapp stopped listening. His mind was wondering off down a path that involved a bird in his hand and two in the bush, or was it a stone and two birds? Whichever it was he saw an opportunity.

"Are you listening to a word I'm saying?" Kennedy asked.

Rapp shook the dazed look from his eyes and said, "Sorry, I was just thinking of something else."

"Were you guys drinking last night?" Kennedy thought of Hurley and his colorful history and said, "That was a stupid question. You were at Stan Hurley's lake house . . . of course you were drinking. Where is Mike, by the way?"

Rapp thought about his roadside confrontation with Nash and wondered how he would explain to his boss that one of her most valued operatives was experiencing a mental collapse.

"Don't tell me he was too hung over to see the president."

It sounded like as good a story as any, so Rapp gave it the nondenial denial and shrugged his shoulders.

Kennedy shook her head in disappointment. "Do I even want to know what goes on down there?"

Rapp thought of Adams and said, "Probably not."

"How bad can it be?"

Rapp was tempted to tell her it involved hookers and a bunch of drugs, but he didn't want to push her over the edge. "Some cards, some drinking, some harmless talk. That's all it ever is."

Kennedy gave him her schoolmarm frown.

"Hey . . . this isn't exactly the easiest job in the world," Rapp said defensively. "There's nothing wrong with blowing off a little steam."

"I agree. Just make sure that's all it is." She maneuvered her mouse and opened up her email. "Speaking of PR . . . the last thing we need right now is some TV news crew to catch you guys doing God only knows what you do down there."

Rapp found the idea preposterous. Hurley had more damn security than some federal buildings. If any reporters were dumb enough to ignore all the signs and wander onto the property they would end up running for their lives from Hurley's pack of dogs. "The last person you need to worry about is Stan Hurley. He's smarter than all of us and he's been doing this for a hell of a lot longer." Rapp thought of the inevitable confrontation between Hurley and Nash. If Nash didn't snap back 100 percent, and do it quickly, Hurley would want him gone. Not killed necessarily, but he would want him transferred out of the clandestine service and probably out of the CIA entirely. Rapp looked a few days into the future and saw a way that he might be able to defuse the conflict. "Speaking of PR . . . maybe Gabe's idea wasn't so bad after all."

Kennedy looked surprised. "Really?"

"Not for me," Rapp added quickly. "I'm thinking of Mike."

Kennedy thought about it for a second. "Why Mike?"

"He's perfect. Former Marine officer, gorgeous wife, four cute kids. Dickerson could do wonders with something like that."

Kennedy's hazel eyes narrowed. "What are you up to?"

"What do you mean?"

"You know exactly what I mean. Fifteen minutes ago you thought it was the craziest thing you'd ever heard, and now all of the sudden you're offering up Mike."

"You're always telling me I need to be more open-minded . . . that's all this is."

Kennedy studied him for a long moment. She wasn't buying it. "You're up to something. I know it."

CHAPTER 25

RAPP was thinking on the fly. He wasn't about to explain to Kennedy that Nash had come unhinged in the last twelve hours. She was too perceptive, and she would want to know what the catalyst had been. She would also assume it was something that had taken place at Hurley's lake house and she would be right. Rapp could fabricate a hell of a lie that would stand up to a lot of digging, but there was one weak point. Sometime in the next three days she would have Nash standing in front of her desk just as he was now. She would begin to probe, and if Nash was still in his volatile state and mad at Rapp, he was likely to say a few things that would cause a lot of trouble. Rapp would have to get to him in the meantime and prepare him, but for now, he had to give Kennedy a plausible reason for his newfound respect for Dickerson's plan.

There wasn't a cover story worth a damn that wasn't somehow grounded in truth, and Kennedy knew him too well, as was evidenced by her suspicion. Rapp started speaking and before he knew it, the answer was on his lips. "I think Mike is having a hard time with what happened last week."

"So your answer is to thrust him into the spotlight and end his career as a clandestine operative."

Rapp shrugged and tried to play down the obvious. "It wouldn't be ended. There's still plenty of work for him to do around here. He just wouldn't be involved in some of the more risky operations." Rapp watched her eyes burrow through him as if she were trying to read his soul.

"Something happened last night," Kennedy said.

This time it was a statement, as if she knew for certain something had gone on. Rapp sighed and said, "He's burnt out, Irene. This shit has really gotten to him. I'm not sure he ever fully recovered from the injuries he suffered over in the Kush." Rapp was referring to an operation they had run in Afghanistan nearly a year ago. The intel had been solid. A high-value target was staying in a village on the border. They had gone in with a Special Forces team right at dawn. Everything was looking good and then the house they were about to raid blew up, killing two troopers and nearly killing Nash. "The docs are still picking shrapnel from him, and his wife tells me he wakes up every morning with an ear-splitting headache. Then last week he sees his secretary and a bunch of his coworkers gunned down by some gun-toting jihadists. Considering what he's been through, it's a wonder he can get out of bed in the morning and face the world."

"And you?" Kennedy asked with a bit of amusement in her voice.

"What about me?"

"It could be argued that you've suffered through the same events."

"I wasn't wounded on that operation in the Kush, and I didn't know those people at the NCTC like he did."

"But you've been wounded before."

"And I've always bounced back."

"That's debatable."

Rapp knew she was referring to his lengthy absence after his wife had been killed. "Listen . . . I think it would be a mistake for you to try to compare Mike and me. For starters I've been at this a lot longer, and I think I have proved beyond a shadow of a doubt that I'm committed. I—"

"You don't think Mike is committed?" Kennedy asked, cutting him off.

Rapp's frustration was apparent. "Are you going to let me talk or are you going to keep interrupting me?"

Kennedy put on a pleasant smile and said, "By all means, continue."

"I'm not saying Mike isn't committed. I'm saying his life is a little more complicated than mine. He has certain obligations that I don't have."

"His family?"

"Yes. I think this job is really taking its toll on his personal life."

"We are all aware of the pressures that go with this job."

"It's deeper than that, Irene. It's not just the job . . . it's the way the job has crept into his life." Rapp paused for a beat and tried to honestly put his finger on what was going on with Nash. Shaking his head he said, "I think maybe I scare the hell out of him."

Kennedy was surprised by Rapp's statement. "Why would Mike have reason to be afraid of you? Has he done something you're not telling me?"

"No . . . it's not that. He hasn't done anything that I know of. I think he's afraid he's going to become me."

"Interesting."

"He has a family to go home to at night, and he has to somehow shut down this portion of his brain that deals with all this crap. He has to be a father and a husband. Try to teach those kids the difference between right and wrong. Live up to the ideals of Maggie and reassure all of them that everything is all right and will be all right . . . when he knows damn well the world is a scary place. At some point it creeps into your head that you might not make it home." Rapp paused as he thought of an image he had blocked from his mind. "Just last week he looked down and found his secretary lying on the floor with her brains blown all over the carpeting. Something like that is going to haunt a man for a long time."

Kennedy made a steeple with her hands and asked, "And how do you cope with it?"

Rapp sighed. She'd been trying to get him to discuss his wife's murder for years. "I don't know. I just do."

"I think it's a little more involved than that."

Rapp shrugged. "I'm not normal. I'm wired different."

"So you say," she said in an accusatory tone.

Rapp saw his chance to counterattack. "How do you deal with it?"

"With what?"

"The pressures of the job. You ever sit down and talk to a therapist?"

Kennedy inclined her head and took on a stern look. "That is none of your business."

It wasn't easy to read Kennedy, but Rapp thought he saw something in her eyes. A flash of anger and a look that told him to back off. It was probably as close as he would get to an admission that she had seen a therapist, and in all likelihood it was Lewis. "It's interesting how at this juncture everything becomes a one-way street. As my boss and my friend," Rapp stressed, "you've been very vocal about the fact that I need to sit down with a professional and talk about my pain over the loss of Anna."

"Yes, I have, but don't try to change the subject. This isn't about me. It's about you and Mike."

Rapp was willing to let her off the hook for now. This was about Nash. "It's apples and oranges. For starters . . . I go home to an empty house. I don't have to confront the lie every time I walk through the door."

"The lie?"

"Telling your kids to be good . . . don't cheat in school . . . play life by the rules . . . and, oh, by the way, I just broke five federal laws today and killed a man. That kind of shit weighs on a guy after a while."

"It doesn't weigh on you," Kennedy focused her gaze more intently, "just a little bit?"

Rapp was surprised that he actually paused to think about it. As crazy as it was, no one had asked him this question in a long time. "Which part of the job?"

"All of it, but let's start with the part that most people would have a hard time with. The killing."

Rapp shook his head. "It's never bothered me. The guys I'm whacking aren't exactly upstanding citizens."

Kennedy had read every after-action report he'd written and verbally debriefed him on the ones that were too sensitive to put in writing. She knew Rapp wasn't big on detail or blowing his own horn, so more often than not she got a very abbreviated version of what had gone down. "You've never accidentally killed an innocent bystander?"

"Define innocent . . . if you're talking some rent-a-bodyguard who's hired to protect some piece of shit, he's not exactly innocent in my book. You wanna play tough guy mercenary, you'd better understand the bullets are real."

Kennedy nodded. They'd covered some of this territory before.

Rapp considered it further, took a kernel of an emotion and decided to blow it up. Turn it into something Kennedy would get. "The only thing that weighs on me is not having his life."

"What do you mean, 'his life'?"

"I'd leave this shit in a heartbeat if I could turn back the clock and have Anna back. When he's in town, he goes home to that family and they're his. Those kids love him and the dumb shit takes it for granted. When you don't have something," Rapp caught himself and added, "when you've had something that meant more than anything in the world to you, and it was taken away . . . it's hard to imagine why anyone would want to do this shit when the price is that high."

Kennedy didn't speak for a long time, and then she said, "You know it's not too late for you, Mitch? You're in your early forties."

"You mean to find someone else. Settle down, have a bunch of kids." Rapp shook his head. "Not so sure it's for me. Besides, someone has to do this job, and I don't see too many guys with my skill set ready to step into the breach."

"I'm sure I could find someone else."

With a confident grin, Rapp asked, "And do you think they could do it as well?"

"I doubt it." Kennedy reflected on the subject and began to see that maybe Rapp was coming at it from the right place. "So your solution, as far as Mike is concerned, is to let Dickerson turn him into the CIA's poster boy?"

"I haven't worked out the details yet, but, yeah . . . that's pretty much the plan."

"And you think he'll go along with this?"

"Not sure, but we don't have to give him a choice in the matter."

Kennedy shook her head. "I don't think he'll like it."

"He probably won't at first, but I think he'll come around pretty quick."

Kennedy winced. "I don't know, Mitch . . . He's not as stubborn as you, but he's pretty close."

"When he sees how proud Maggie and the kids are . . ." Rapp smiled, "all will be forgiven."

"I'll think about."

"Good." Rapp checked his watch. "I gotta get going. I need to—"

Kennedy stopped him. "Yes, you do. You need to get out to Dulles. Your friends have requested a meeting."

"Which friends?"

"Your counterparts from across the pond."

"Oh." These neutral-site, face-to-face meetings were a recent development. "How much time do I have?"

"If you don't want to keep them waiting, you need to be wheels up in fifty minutes."

Rapp swore to himself. He always kept a go bag packed in his car, so that wasn't a concern, but he needed to talk to Scott Coleman and get him to sweep Lewis's office.

"Anything I can help with?" Kennedy offered.

Rapp almost laughed at the question but before he could reply there was a muted knock on the door and then it opened. Rapp looked over to see six-foot-three Chuck O'Brien enter the room. The ruddy-faced director of the National Clandestine Service had been with Langley for thirty-three years, and if Rapp was reading his clenched jaw and austere expression right, they were about to get some bad news.

"Sorry to intrude," O'Brien covered the distance in a few long strides and pulled up next to Rapp, "but some info just got kicked up to me."

"What's that?" Kennedy asked.

"Apparently, Glen Adams decided to take a little unauthorized trip."

"Huh?" Rapp asked, more than a little surprised that the alarm bells were already being sounded that the CIA's inspector general had gone missing.

Kennedy asked, "Where to?"

"Venezuela," O'Brien answered. "He landed in Caracas about an hour and a half ago. Left JFK late last night."

"Caracas?" Kennedy asked with a puzzled look on her face. "Why Caracas? Does he have any relatives down there?"

"Not that I know of."

Kennedy slowly turned her gaze to Rapp. "Any idea why Glen Adams would take an unannounced trip to Venezuela?"

Rapp unflinchingly returned his boss's stare, shook his head twice, and said, "How the hell would I know? We're not exactly drinking buddies."

CHAPTER 26

FORTUNATELY for Rapp, Scott Coleman wasn't big on sleep. The retired Navy SEAL had returned home from the operation in New York at 4:00 A.M. and after three short hours of sack time he'd gotten up and started his day. By the time Rapp called, Coleman had already hit the gym and gotten in a five-mile run. Coleman confirmed that he could meet Rapp at one of their usual spots in twenty minutes. Rapp grabbed his go bag from the trunk of his sedan and took a quick shower in the men's locker room of Langley's fitness center. Ten minutes after leaving Kennedy's office he was in his car and heading west.

Rapp exited the main gate, got onto Dolley Madison Boulevard, and grabbed his phone. After searching his address book he found the mobile number for Maggie Nash and punched the call button. Through his Bluetooth earpiece he listened to the line ring.

On the fifth chime a familiar upbeat voice answered, "Maggie Nash."

"Hi, Maggie . . . it's Mitch. How are you?"

"Fine," she answered in a cautious voice.

Maggie was a great person and Rapp had always gotten along with her. He knew immediately by the uncertainty in her voice that she had talked with her husband. "You spoke with Mike?"

"Yes."

Rapp had to multitask. He had to get Maggie to see things from his perspective and he had to make sure he made it to his next meeting without the wrong person or group following him. Fortunately, he had grown up only a few miles from Langley and knew the winding residential streets as if he'd laid them out himself. It was the ideal terrain to detect surveillance. With all the parks and creeks there were a lot of dead-ends and if it turned out the FBI was following him he could always fall back on the fact that there were hundreds of foreign spies in Washington who would love to know what he was up to. Being security conscious, and aware of America's enemies, was a big part of his job. That was both his reality and his cover, but the sad fact was that he was now more worried about his own government following him than the Chinese or the Russians.

"Did he tell you we had a little problem this morning?"

"Yes."

"Maggie, I don't expect you to take any side other than your husband's, but I'd like you to hear me out on a few things."

"I'm listening."

"I care a great deal about you and the kids. I think of Mike as a brother. I'd risk my life to save him and he'd do the same for me." Rapp cut down Vincent Place and turned onto Elm Street two short blocks later. The truth was he had already risked his life to save him and Maggie knew it. "I'm worried about him."

Maggie sighed and emotion flooded her voice, "I don't know what happened between you two this morning . . . he wouldn't talk about it, but I do know he is extremely upset and because you guys live such a screwed-up life, and can't talk about anything that you do, I don't have the slightest idea how to help him."

Rapp turned on to Chain Bridge Road, relieved that Nash had at least informed her that there was a problem. "Maggie, I need you to listen to me and I need you to understand that this comes from the heart. I'm damaged goods. I'm good at my job and that's about it. I've given up on ever having a normal life. But—"

She cut him off, "Don't say that, Mitch."

"Please let me speak. If I don't say this right now I don't think I ever will. I see you and Mike and your kids and I see the life I could have had with Anna. I blew it. I thought I could do both. I thought I could keep the two lives separate. Continue to do all the stuff I'd done for a decade and half. All the nasty shit I can't talk about."

"Mitch, you can't blame yourself."

"Anna knew it, Maggie. She begged me to get out of the field, let a new crop of guys take the fight to the bad guys, and I told her I would, but I never did. I kept telling myself, one more operation. One more bad guy to take down. I made excuse after excuse. I even lied to her about the crap I was involved in because I knew she'd freak. I thought I could keep the two lives separate, and it was all a bunch of bullshit. And you know it, Maggie. I saw what you and the kids went through last year when he almost died, and then this crap last week . . ." Rapp's voice trailed off as he thought of their dead colleagues. In a remorseful tone, he said, "This is no business for a family man."

Maggie sighed. "You don't have to convince me."

"Good. Then here's what we're going to do."

"We . . . as in you and I?"

"Yes." Rapp checked his mirrors.

"Mitch, I love you and I respect what you do. I admire your courage. I admire Michael's courage and commitment to what he believes in, but I hate your jobs and Michael knows it. I have tried to get him to quit, and he has yet to listen to me. What makes you think this time is going to be different?"

"Because we're not going to give him a choice in the matter."

"So . . . what are you saying? Are you going to fire him?"

"No. The opposite. I'm going to promote him."

"To what? For all I know you've been promoted a dozen times and it hasn't changed a thing."

"This is going to be different. I'm going to do you a favor, Maggie. I'm going to give you and your kids the life you deserve."

"That sounds great, Mitch, but I still don't get how you're going to pull it off. He's not a quitter. You try to promote him out of the clandestine side of the business and he'll turn you down."

"I might need your help on this, but in the end he's not going to have any choice in the matter. You're just going to have to trust me. You know Gabriel Dickerson?"

"Of course I do. Everyone in D.C. knows who Gabriel Dickerson is." Maggie worked for a prominent PR firm in town.

"Did Mike by chance tell you anything about last week . . . what happened at the office?"

"You mean the attack?"

"Yes."

"Yeah . . . I mean we know Jessica died. We went to the funeral."

She was referring to Nash's assistant. "He didn't talk about any heroics?"

"No. He never talks about that stuff."

Rapp was relieved. At least Nash still knew how to keep his mouth shut. He began telling her a little bit about what her husband had done, leaving out his own part in the heroics and focusing on Nash. Then, in broad strokes, he told her about Dickerson's plan. That the CIA needed a hero. That America needed a hero. And then he fudged a bit and told her the president wanted to give Mike a medal. That he wanted to do it at a public ceremony at the White House and they wanted Maggie and the kids there. Her husband would finally be rewarded for his sacrifices and Maggie would no longer have to live the lie, because he would be outed. Rapp made her promise not to tell anyone, especially her husband.

"You know how these politicians work," Rapp warned her. "This morning they think this is a great idea. Dickerson is championing it for the president, but it's never a done deal until it actually happens."

"You don't have to tell me. I've been burned plenty of times."

Rapp could hear the hope in her voice. "Maggie, there's a lot of fucked-up guys like me out there who don't have a family to take care of. Let them take their turn stepping into the breach. Mike's done his part. Go home . . . support him . . . make sure he gets some rest and don't breathe a word of this to him. You know him . . . if he gets wind of this he'll stop it dead in its tracks."

CHAPTER 27

RAPP took a quick left and then a quick right. He backed into a private drive halfway down Pathfinder Lane and stopped under a massive elm tree. The leafy canopy of the tree would frustrate any airborne surveillance. One of Rapp's high school buddies had lived on the street, and he knew the driveway serviced only a couple of houses. The street jogged at both ends so it wasn't used to cut through the neighborhood like some of the other side streets. Rapp checked the clock on the dashboard and settled in to see if any American-made four-door sedans came skidding around the corner.

He thought about his conversation with Maggie and stared at his phone for a long moment. A sliver of guilt crept in as he wondered if he could deliver on the promises he'd just made. After a beat he knew he could. He knew he had to. He would call Dickerson and make it happen. Feeling better about it, Rapp punched in Stan Hurley's number on his secure BlackBerry to get an update. After three rings the scratchy voice of Hurley answered. Rapp didn't bother to say hello. "So . . . were you right?" Rapp asked in reference to Hurley's prediction that Adams had used Max Johnson to bug Lewis's office.

"About who he was using?"

"Yeah."

"Yep," Hurley answered. "He's been on the payroll for about two months."

Rapp wanted to ask him how he was paying him, but was hesitant to get into too much detail over the phone. "Motive?"

"Another member of the Mitch Rapp fan club."

Rapp looked north and then south. No cars so far. "How so?"

"Can't say if there was any personal animosity, but my guess is he was intrigued by the idea of taking down a real gunfighter."

Rapp thought about that. Hurley liked to refer to the clandestine folks as gunfighters. Everyone else was a limp dick or a desk jockey. Theirs was an entirely separate culture from that of the other folks at Langley, and it was not unusual for other groups to harbor acrimony against the spooks in the building. Johnson had spent his entire career within the secure perimeter of Langley. There were probably a handful of times that he'd gone overseas to do a security review of an embassy and the CIA's personnel, but he'd never participated in a real op. The entire focus of his career had been to protect Langley's secrets and bust those who didn't play strictly by the rules. "Any idea what he was using to listen in on the sessions?"

"He's not certain, but it sounds like it might have been off-site."

"All right, I'm on it. I gotta go. I'll call you later." Rapp hit the end button and thought about the task he was going to give Coleman. Max Johnson, while not exactly an A Team field guy, was nonetheless someone they should not take lightly. What concerned Rapp was that Johnson would be dumb enough to get involved with a guy like Adams. Hurley's assessment of the situation was as good as any, but they weren't talking about an impulsive twenty-year-old. Johnson was a thirty-plus-year veteran of the business. He should have known better than to get mixed up in something like this.

Rapp checked the street again. No Crown Vics, Caprices, or LTDs came sliding around the corner on two wheels, so he put the car back in drive and drove over to Lewinsville Park. Rapp had spent countless hours here as kid. He and his neighborhood buddies played every sport there was, and if they weren't at the park they were down at the pool and tennis club off of Great Falls. Rapp was smiling to himself and thinking about the summer his brother had gotten them banned from the pool when he saw Coleman pulling into the parking lot in his big black SUV. Without saying a word they both left their vehicles and traveled down the path between the bleachers to the synthetic-turf lacrosse field.

It was a typical late April morning for the area. The temp was in the midseventies and the skies were partly cloudy, with the threat of storms off in the distance. Rapp had changed into a pair of comfortable jeans and a long-sleeved shirt for his flight. Coleman had on a pair of khakis, a button-down shirt, and a blue sport coat. The two men faced each other but didn't look at each other. They were more concerned with their surroundings than making eye contact.

Coleman looked over at the basketball courts. There were four kids playing hoops, young enough that they should probably be in school, and definitely too young to be on the payroll of the FBI or any other organization. He ran a hand through his blond hair and asked, "Don't tell me we already have a problem."

Rapp kept his eyes on the parking lot. "Not with the thing you're thinking of," he said, referring to the op they'd run in New York, "at least not in the way you might be thinking. Although," he said, glancing at Colemen, "I did hear something interesting this morning."

"What's that?"

"Charlie O'Brien told me that little prick Glen Adams took off for Caracas without letting anyone at Langley know he was leaving the country."

"You don't say. I thought you guys had rules about that."

"Most definitely. You have to notify senior management as well as security."

"And he did neither?"

"That's right. He's stepped in some real shit."

"Do they have a line on him?" Coleman asked, already wondering if his guy had been able to disappear. They had agreed that it would be best to have no communication unless there was an emergency.

"You mean Langley?"

"Yeah."

"No," Rapp said. "Not so far."

"Is the FBI in on it?"

Rapp shook his head. "Irene wants to keep it in the family . . . at least for the next six hours. We have some people looking at the hotels, and we're quietly talking to a few of our contacts in the Venezuelan DIS. If we don't get some answers quick she's going to have to bring in FBI and State."

Coleman nodded. "Do you think he defected?"

"Who knows . . . as long as the guy doesn't give away any of our secrets I'd just as soon he hung himself." Rapp checked out the boys on the court and then finally looked at Coleman. "The name Max Johnson ring a bell?"

Coleman's blue eyes closed a touch as he tried to remember where he'd heard the name. After a moment he said, "Yeah. He's one of you guys, or I should say was."

Rapp frowned. "He was never one of my guys. That would be like me telling you an Investigative Services guy was on the Teams."

Coleman thought about it for a second and said, "Point taken. But he did work at Langley, right?"

"Yeah. For a long time."

"Does he know where all the bodies are buried?"

Rapp shrugged. "Hard to say with a guy like him. He's not the bubbliest fella, but then again those security guys are supposed to make people nervous."

"You ever have a beef with him?"

"Not that I can recall," Rapp paused a beat and then added, "but I've pissed off so many people over the years I can't keep track."

"Irene?"

Rapp thought about his boss. He couldn't imagine her running afoul of her own security service, but then again Johnson had been passed over twice for the top job. "Not directly, but you know how it is . . . it's the rare bird who gets passed over for a promotion who doesn't hold some kind of a grudge."

"So what exactly has he done?" Coleman asked.

"He runs his own consulting company now."

Coleman said, "I know. That's how I heard of him. The word is he's pretty hot shit on the new technology. Specializes in surveillance."

Rapp nodded. The War on Terror had been a boon to private security and consulting firms. Outsourcing was the new hot trend. "You'd better grab Marcus then," Rapp said, referring to his resident computer genius.

"Can you tell me what this is all about?"

"You got a pen and a piece of paper?"

Coleman dug in his jacket pocket and pulled out both.

Rapp flipped open the small notebook and clicked the plunger on the pen. He hesitated for a brief moment while he decided on the best way to relay the information while still being cryptic. Pressing lightly, he began to scrawl the pertinent information on the lined paper. When he was done he handed the notebook over.

Coleman glanced down at the words and read Rapp's blocky print: *Last night . . . Found out where he's been getting info . . . hired Johnson to bug Doc's office . . . know of at least one person who spilled the beans . . . assume there are more . . . find out how he was doing it and get me a full scouting report on him.* "Holy shit," Coleman said out loud as he thought of Dr. Lewis and the number of people he worked with. "This could be a real mess. Information like this could be sold over and over."

Rapp took the notebook back and tore out the top five sheets. He grabbed a lighter from his pocket and lit the bottom corner of the pages. He watched the flames lick their way up and then he flipped them over so they had to work their way down to his fingers. When there was a square inch left, he waved the paper back and forth until the flame was out. "Be careful with this guy. Don't tip him off. I don't want him getting spooked and running off with the goods."

Coleman thought of Adams. The news that he had supposedly left the country for Venezuela would spread like a dry autumn wild fire through the intelligence community. "He'll hear about this other thing sooner rather than later."

"No doubt."

"And he'll probably get a little skittish."

"That's why I want you on this right away."

"ROE?" Coleman asked.

ROE was military jargon for Rules of Engagement. Rapp thought about it for a moment. He didn't know Johnson anywhere near well enough to predict any of it. Coleman would have to use his instincts. "Do what you have to do. Just make sure we know what our exposure is. If he has recordings, I want them all back."

"If I have to get rough?"

Rapp shrugged. "I should be back late tonight. If it can wait till then, I'd appreciate it, but you're going to have to play it by ear."

"Where you off to?"

"Can't talk about it. It'll be a short trip. I'll shoot you an email and let you know when I'll be back." Rapp started walking back to the car and Coleman fell in beside him. "Send me some updates, and make sure they're as obscure as possible. Assume everything you write or say will be intercepted."

"Got it. Anything else?"

"Yeah . . . be careful. I got a bad feeling about this Johnson character."

CHAPTER 28

WHEN Hakim finally woke up he made no attempt to open his eyes. His head hurt too much. His body hurt too much. It seemed that everything hurt too much. Slowly, his senses started to send reports back to his brain. There were bruises and cuts and scrapes and maybe some breaks. He kept his eyes closed, not because he didn't want to see where he was, but he thought it would hurt too much to open them. Without forethought his brain decided to take inventory. He wiggled his toes and was pleased to see they worked. His left foot rolled outward and everything felt as it should. When he tried the same thing with his right leg his knee sent back signals of sharp pain. He couldn't tell the extent of the injury but nothing felt broken. His torso ached, but it was nothing compared to the pain he suddenly noticed in his arms and face.

Hakim tried to open his eyes, but nothing happened. It was if his eyelids were glued shut. He tried again, and with a little more effort he was able to get his left one open a sliver. It felt as if something was weighing down his eyelids. He was surrounded by a soft natural light.

Somewhere in the distance he heard a throbbing hum that was faintly familiar. His sense of smell slowly came back and he picked up the weak scent of a campfire.

Hakim managed to get his left eye open a bit more and after staring at the strange wood grain pattern for a while, he realized he was in the back of the RV lying on the bed. He tried to roll onto his side, but didn't get far. He let out a small gasp. It felt as if he had been stabbed. Things slowly started coming back to him. He had no idea how long he'd been out, but the last thing he remembered was Karim on top of him, his fists rising and falling with crazed rage.

Remember those punches, it suddenly occurred to Hakim why he couldn't open his eyes. With dread, he brought his hands up to touch his face. It was one of those things you never thought of. What your own face felt like. Mostly, because you didn't have to. You touched it so frequently throughout the day, for so many reasons and over so many years that every centimeter of it was imprinted on your brain. You could feel your way to the slightest blemish or new wrinkle. Hakim gently touched the area around his left eye. Everything was foreign. It felt like a ripe tomato, plump and smooth. His fingers continued their search. His lips were even worse, and his right eye felt twice as bad as his left.

Then, as if a switch had been thrown, the pain started. It was both specific and everywhere at the same time. As if his brain were stuck in a circular loop of agony moving from one area to the next and then back again, running faster and faster, until he felt like a thousand fire ants were feasting on his face. He started to moan and after a good five seconds he stopped himself. The thought of Karim hung above him like some awful nightmare. He did not want to feed the man's arrogance any more than he already had.

How could one friend do this to another? Hakim lay there and asked himself the question over and over. The answer was so obvious that he was no longer able to ignore it. The truth was now staring back at him like an old, wise parent telling him he had been warned long ago but had been either too stubborn or too immature to heed the advice. Hakim felt his puffy face again. Was it true? Had he been so blind for so many years, or was he suddenly in full martyr mode—casting himself as the ultimate victim and his friend as the archvillain?

Hakim knew he wasn't exactly in the best frame of mind to be dealing with such a question, but it was no longer possible to ignore the obvious. Had he been the one who had changed or was it Karim? Was it both, or had he simply drifted away from their radical worldview—the myopic one the Wahhabi clerics had brainwashed them with? It was so foolish, Hakim thought as he looked back on his testosterone-laden late teens and early twenties. They had been indoctrinated like brainless fools.

Even so, there was another question that was more troubling. Was Karim a monster? Hakim thought of the father and son who had showed up at the farmhouse and asked permission to hunt by the river. He had had the situation handled. They were not federal agents or local law enforcement. They were just a father and a son such as you would find anywhere in the world, and if Karim had been able to keep his ego and anger in check everything would have been fine.

The sinking feeling he'd had when he heard the screen door open came back. Hakim replayed it all in his mind, but without any sound. For some reason the audio wouldn't play. It was just the cold, harsh visual of bullets hitting flesh and bodies falling in slow motion to the gravel. The agony on the father's face. The fear on the son's. And all for what? What had they gained? What had Karim gained with his obtuse, inflexible methods? They were now on the run—foreigners in a land where everyone was looking for them.

Hakim had calculated their chances of escape many times, and he was convinced that nothing offered more hope than the house in Iowa. It was the last place anyone would look. He had even told Karim not to worry if someone should stumble upon them. He and Ahmed were to stay out of sight. Hakim's cover story was solid. He would be able to deal with anyone, possibly even law enforcement. It had all been discussed and rehearsed many times.

Hakim was in the midst of asking himself why his friend would be so reckless when the floral curtain that separated the rear sleeping area from the rest of the RV slid back a half foot. Hakim looked up to see a pair of large, almost childlike eyes staring down at him. It was Ahmed. The Moroccan pulled the curtain back a little more and then stepped into the sleeping area and let the curtain close behind him. He had a damp washcloth in one hand and a bottle of water in the other.

Ahmed placed the washcloth on Hakim's forehead and then, holding the water in front of him, asked, "Thirsty?"

Hakim began to shake his head but it hurt too much. He winced in pain and tried to speak but that hurt as well. He moved his tongue around in his mouth and realized he was missing at least two teeth.

Ahmed leaned in close and softly said, "I am sorry for what happened."

It was obvious by the way he spoke that he was afraid of being heard by Karim. Hakim saw fear in his eyes, the kind of fear a man shows when he is in over his head. Through puffed lips caked with dried blood and a swollen and possibly broken jaw he managed to ask, "Where are we?"

"I am not sure. I think still in Iowa."

"How long have I been unconscious?"

"I'm not sure. But it was a long time. I was afraid you might be dead."

"What time is it now?"

Ahmed held up his black digital watch. It was twelve-fifty-six in the afternoon.

Hakim worked his way backward and figured he'd been out for over five hours. "How long have we been on the road?"

The Moroccan shrugged.

Hakim suddenly noticed a familiar, but much stronger odor on Ahmed. "You smell like a fire."

After looking over his shoulder, Ahmed nervously said, "Karim had me put the father and son in the house. The basement. I then set fire to it."

"Why?" Hakim asked in near disbelief.

"He said it would destroy the evidence."

"And bring the police. What did you do with all the supplies in the barn?" Hakim watched Ahmed shrug and then flinch as he heard Karim call his name from the front of the RV. He was obviously driving.

"I will come back and check on you later."

"What about their vehicle?"

Ahmed didn't understand.

"The car that the hunters drove?"

Ahmed shrugged his big shoulders and said, "I don't know." Then he was gone.

Hakim slowly rolled his head back to his left. As he closed his eye and tried to rest, he wondered how long it would take before the police figured out who had been staying at the house. He doubted they would remain at large very long, and part of him was fine with that.

CHAPTER 29

EASTERN ATLANTIC

RAPP woke up on descent, about an hour out, as he almost always did. Takeoffs put him to sleep and landings woke him up. He'd never figured out exactly why, but he guessed it had something to do with the way takeoffs kind of pinned him back in his seat. The end of the flight was easier to understand. When the pilots eased back on the throttles and started their descent it was as good as a flight attendant placing a gentle hand on his shoulder.

On this flight, however, there was no flight attendant. Just two sixty-plus-year-old former Air Force jocks at the controls, and Rapp riding in back. All three men knew how to keep their mouths shut. That left fifteen open seats. Rapp had logged countless miles in the service of his country, and at least early in his career, they were rarely in such comfort. The Gulfstream 550 was a beautiful bird from top to bottom and a far cry from the noisy C-130s he used to fly around in. The old military transport had been in service for over fifty years, and while it was robust and dependable it was not designed for comfort. Zero noise suppression, minimal insulation, web seats along the sides, a latrine that consisted of a curtain on a wire and a funnel on the side of the plane, plus four of the loudest turboprop engines known to man. Rapp had flown all over the damn world on the things and the end result was always the same. The thing vibrated so much it shook your senses right out of you. It was a wonder units could deploy on them and still shoot straight.

It was all those darn C-130 hops that had enabled him to take this new development in stride. In the days after 9/11 Rapp understood almost immediately the full extent of what had happened, and where it was all headed. He knew the public outcry of his countrymen would be nearly uniform, and for that delusional 5 to 10 percent who wanted to blame America for the attacks there was nothing he or anybody else could do to convince their illogical brains otherwise. But Rapp had read enough history that he could see part of the future. The population's support for the War on Terror would wane over time, and it had, but the one thing he never fully expected was just how low the politicians would stoop. This little trip to the middle of the Atlantic was proof that their actions had far-reaching and unintended consequences.

Just a few years ago all of this could have been handled with a secure conference call or an encrypted message. Those sanctimonious politicians, however, with their chant that the people deserve to know the truth, had turned the intelligence community on its ear. The British and French had been crucial in the war against Islamic extremism, far more so than the American people and most politicians in Washington understood. In many ways they had done the heavy lifting. They had more experience in dealing with some of these characters, and at least in the case of the British courts, they took a more pragmatic view of what the people deserved to know.

With the politicians in America and their various left-wing special-interest groups demanding investigations, hearings, and trials, the British and French, and a good number of other allies, began to reassess what they were willing to share. They had participated in many of the same terrorist interrogations. The far left was now screaming to see the tapes and notes of those not-so-pretty sessions. It is a fundamental tenet of any intelligence organization to keep its means and methods a secret, so when federal judges starting ruling in favor of the ACLU and other groups' requests for the release of information under the Freedom of Information Act, some very important allies in Paris and London got nervous.

Kennedy and Rapp flew to both cities and met with their counterparts. Each group of professionals was worried about the same thing. The stuff the ACLU was asking for was damaging enough, but it paled in comparison to the mountains of highly sensitive encrypted data that had been sent back and forth between the three intelligence agencies—stuff that was hidden or destroyed with the understanding that the information could start a world war if ever leaked. They all trusted each other, but there was one glaring problem. America's National Security Administration captured almost unimaginable amounts of signal traffic. As with one of those big commercial fishing trawlers, it looked as if their nets might bust at any second. They might be looking for tuna, but they caught everything else, big and small. They all knew that somewhere in the NSA's vast files, their own highly sensitive and encrypted traffic sat like an ancient cipher waiting to be solved.

So the flow of daily information slowed to a trickle and a handful of trusted men and women who had earned their spurs in the field began meeting face to face. Rapp dreaded the trips at first. It seemed there was always something else that needed his attention, but after a few of them, he realized they were a bit of a blessing in disguise. For starters, they allowed him to unplug. The planes always had a secure comm package, and he would usually take an hour or two to catch up on the more mundane stuff, but in general he turned everything off and used the silence of the long flights to crack some of the more stressful problems they were dealing with.

With all of the damn technology around today, strategizing was in danger of becoming extinct. The other bonus was that he no longer felt the need to plod through twenty-plus pages a day of cable traffic that was rarely germane to what he was most concerned with. Now, they'd meet face to face two or three times a month and go over the most important information.

Rapp put on a fresh pot of coffee in the galley and then brushed his teeth and washed his face. Since his hair was only a quarter inch of black stubble there was no need for a comb. When the coffee was ready, he poured himself a cup, took a few sips, and then changed back into his dark suit and a fresh light blue dress shirt. The closest in-flight screen told him they would be landing in approximately ten minutes. Rapp turned on his laptop and used it to skim forty-one emails. Thirty-nine of them were pretty much useless chatter, but two jumped out at him as things he would need to deal with.

Rapp slid back a wood compartment and retrieved the handset for a secure satellite phone. He punched in the number for Kennedy's direct line and thought about the best way to convince her that his plan was sound. After six rings Rapp knew the call was rolling over to one of her assistants.

"Director Kennedy's office." The woman's voice was neither polite nor rude—just efficient.

"Kristen, It's Mitch. Is she around?"

"She's on the phone."

"Can you interrupt her?"

"Let me see."

There was a click as he was put on hold and then a few moments later Kennedy was on the line. Rapp said, "You know that meeting we had this morning?"

"Yes."

"I'm on board."

"You sure you're up for all the attention?"

"No . . ." Rapp said, making no attempt to hide his lack of patience. "I'm talking about Mike."

"I know," she said. "I was just jerking your chain."

"Can you get it done?"

"Do you care what your boss thinks, or are you calling the shots now?"

Rapp groaned. "Why are you doing this?"

"Doing what?"

"Torturing me. You told me this morning that you thought it was a good idea."

"That was when I thought you would accept the medal as well. I've had the visual in my head all day of you sitting on Oprah's couch talking about skin-care products."

Rapp pulled the phone away from his head and looked at it as if he might snap it in half. "Are you done?"

"Yes, but I want you to at least recognize the fact that you are giving Mike no say in the matter while you have threatened me or anyone else with extreme violence if we dare recognize your achievements, which were even more remarkable than Mike's."

"We've been through this so many times . . . Do we have to go over it again?"

"No, we don't have to go over it again," Kennedy said in slightly playful tone. "I just want you to recognize that you're not being entirely fair."

"Fine . . . I'm happy to admit it. Life isn't fair. Mike has four kids and a wife who need him. My wife and unborn child are dead, because of what I do for a living. Maybe I don't want to see that happen to him. Maybe I don't want to have to knock on Maggie's door some night and explain to her and the kids that their dad is dead. We're different people. I'm damaged goods. He still has a shot at a seminormal life, and that's why he's going to be the face of this thing. Not me."

Kennedy didn't answer for a long time. Rapp rarely talked about his deceased wife and it had caught her off guard. "I think I understand."

Rapp felt like an ass for coming down so hard on her. "Sorry, boss."

"For what?"

"For snapping at you like that. You know I'm no good at this stuff. I just . . . he's not doing well," Rapp said, changing gears. "I've seen it before. The lie is tearing him up."

"I don't think seeing his assistant and another dozen and a half coworkers killed did him any favors."

"No, it didn't." Rapp thought about Nash's fragile state. "Just please do this for me, and do it quick. Before he does something stupid."

"What do you mean something stupid?" Kennedy asked with trepidation.

"Nothing," Rapp lied. "It's just a feeling. Tell Dickerson it's a go. Get it set up for tomorrow if you can."

"Aren't you forgetting something?"

"What?"

"Mike. You know he'll never go for this."

"Don't worry about him. You tell me what time you need him at the White House, and I'll have him there. Just make sure everyone keeps their mouth shut."

CHAPTER 30

SANTA MARIA ISLAND, AZORES

THE landing gear thudded into the down position and the plane banked to port. Out of the nearest window Rapp caught a glimpse of the western edge of Santa Maria Island and her big ten-thousand-foot runway, courtesy of the U.S. taxpayers. The place had been a busy hub during World War II and in the decade after but was now nothing more than a tourist destination and convenient meeting place for three spooks who didn't want to be noticed.

The plane landed so softly Rapp wasn't sure they were down until the pilots began to brake, but with ten thousand feet of concrete there was no rush. He looked out the window and saw the other two private jets parked in the distance at the refueling station. That was the other thing Santa Maria Island was known for—fuel. Roughly a thousand miles from the European mainland, the big airstrip offered a convenient place to stop for fuel or repairs on transatlantic flights.

The other beauty of the island was that it only had five thousand residents, who were more or less uninterested in the tail numbers on the planes that came and went. Even so, Rapp grabbed a pair of sunglasses and a newspaper as he prepared to exit. When the plane stopped he disengaged the safety lock and lowered the steps. He moved stiffly down the stairs and pretended to read the newspaper as he proceeded around the nose of a Bombardier Global Express. He hesitated for a moment at the base of the Bombardier's stairs and looked around. Not a person in sight. Rapp bounded up the steps two at a time. Once inside, he glanced to his left. The door to the flight deck was closed. Rapp hit the close button on the hatch and the stairs began to fold back into the closed position. He then walked through the well-appointed galley to the rear of the long-haul private jet. All of the shades were down on the windows, and there, sitting side by side at a table near the back of the plane, were two familiar people.

They were both facing the front, but only one of them stood. At six foot four, George Butler had to tilt his head a few inches to the right to avoid hitting the ceiling. The forty-eight-year-old Brit offered his hand and said, "Hello, Mitch. Good of you to come."

Rapp grabbed the hand of MI-6's counterterrorism chief. "Good to see you, too." Rapp turned to look at the woman who had remained seated. She was petite, just under five and a half feet tall and weighing no more than 120 pounds. Rapp had known her for nearly fifteen years. Her name was Catherine Cheval and she worked for France's Directorate General for Security External, or DGSE. She gave Rapp a faint smile and offered her cheek. Rapp leaned over the desk and kissed her first on her right cheek and then the left. "Always good to see you, Catherine."

"The feeling is mutual," she said in perfect English. Cheval sat back and brushed a strand of her raven black hair behind her right ear. She looked a decade younger than her fifty years.

Rapp took one of the two seats across from them. Cheval leaned forward and gestured toward the coffee cup sitting in front of Rapp. "Please." As Cheval poured Rapp a fresh cup, he apologized for being late.

Butler nodded and said, "Frankly, I'm surprised you could make it on such short notice."

"Irene didn't give me an option. She said it was important."

Butler and Cheval shared a look and then nodded in unison. Cheval said, "We have discovered some information that you might find useful."

"But before we begin," Butler added cautiously, "we would like to revisit the ground rules."

Rapp could have been offended by the comment, but wasn't. In many ways, these two, and the people who worked for them, were better allies than the people in his own government. The fact that Butler had brought it up, though, told Rapp two things: first, that they had some good intel, and second, that they had come by it through means that the Department of Justice and U.S. Congress would not approve of. "If you need to modify the rules I completely understand, but remember when it comes to certain elements of my government, few have more motivation than I do to lie to them."

"True," Cheval said, "and we trust you. It is just that certain nosy people in your country will begin to walk the dog back. They will want to know how this information fell into your possession."

"They might even make assumptions," Butler added. "If they begin to stir the bleeding hearts in our own governments it could create a rather unhealthy environment for us."

"Understood. As far as I'm concerned, none of what I hear today has to be shared."

"That would be nice," Cheval said, "but not realistic. What we have to tell you, you will most certainly want to share."

Cheval reached under the table and grabbed a manila file. It was simple enough looking, and intentionally so. She placed it in the center of the table and hesitated for a long moment. Her light brown eyes slowly drifted away from the file and settled on Rapp. She looked as if she still hadn't figured out precisely how she was going to handle the exchange of intel.

Rapp had seen the file before, and it had always carried information that was far more valuable than its worn, simple appearance would lead one to believe. Ingenious on Cheval's part, Rapp had always thought. The files at Langley were made of sturdy, heavy stock. The important ones were red, although Rapp had known a few people over the years who had used Cheval's method of misdirection. Typically, though, the really important stuff was in red files with letters strewn across the label. Some designations were easy enough to figure out, like Top Secret, but most were covered with phrases like Eyes Only and a string of letters that were nonsensical to the uninitiated. All of it was Compartmentalized Intel. Some had locks and most had twine clasps—the kind you had to twirl around a little disk to secure and unwind to open. The twine wasn't there to defeat prying eyes. It was there to give a person pause, one more step to go through to get the thing open, and hence an extra few seconds to consider just what the hell you were doing.

The CIA was funny about that. They liked their people to keep their attention focused on their particular area of expertise. During Rapp's tenure he'd seen two complete overhauls of the system and a bunch of little modifications. At the end of the day, one of the quickest ways to land yourself in serious trouble was to get caught opening a file that was none of your business. The French and the Brits operated with similar constraints, so Rapp had guessed long ago that Cheval's worn file had likely never been carried through the security checkpoints at the DGSE headquarters in Paris.

Cheval asked, "Have your services made any headway on the identity of the men who carried out the attacks?"

"Very little." Talking to two colleagues like this, Rapp was slightly embarrassed to admit that they had made zero progress. The race to find out what had happened had been going on for a week, and they were still wandering around the starting line looking for clues.

"Nothing?" Butler asked, looking surprised.

"As far as the six guys who raided the CTC are concerned . . . there isn't really anything left to identify. The surveillance footage doesn't give us anything useful. They were dressed in full SWAT gear, complete with balaclavas, goggles, helmets, gloves, heavy vests . . ." Rapp shrugged, "There's nothing to see."

"Physical evidence?" Cheval asked.

Rapp thought about the stew of body parts that had been created when all six suicide vests were detonated at the same time. They were still finding bits and pieces in the woods a couple of hundred yards away. The men had ended up at the base of the twenty-foot-wide parking ramp. The smooth, poured-concrete walls looked like an old subway car that had accumulated five years of graffiti, but instead of spray paint it was chunks of bone and flesh and lots of blood, and instead of a half decade, it had happened in the blink of an eye. "They've been able to identify six separate sets of DNA, but that's about it."

"Surely, there's a fingertip or two to be found," Butler said.

"I've seen a lot of nasty shit over the years, George, but this one was disgusting." Rapp thought about it for a second and then corrected himself, saying, "I take that back. It wasn't disgusting . . . it was bizarre. There was nothing left, except chunks of indistinguishable goo."

"But you did manage to get six separate sets of DNA?" Cheval asked.

"That's what I was told."

She asked, "FBI?"

"Yes."

"We might," Cheval said guardedly, "have a relative in our possession."

"Can you get me a DNA sample?" Rapp asked.

Cheval and Butler glanced at each other.

Rapp picked up on it and asked, "What?"

"It would be best if you gave me what you have. I will see if I can get a match."

Rapp gestured with his hands as if to say, no big deal. "I think I can take care of that. This relative," he continued, "sister, mother, father?"

"Brother," Cheval answered.

"Where'd you find him?"

"This stays here."

"Of course," Rapp said.

"One of my teams picked him up in Casablanca."

"Moroccan?"

"Yes."

"Active investigation?"

Cheval shrugged her slender shoulders as if to say, "who knows?"

Rapp gave her a disbelieving frown. Cheval ran the DGSE's Directorate of Intelligence. Anything on the covert side of the business fell into her purview. "How can that be?"

"My operative who brought this to my attention," she paused, "how do I say this?" After a moment of searching for the right description, she smiled at Rapp and said, "He reminds me a lot of you."

Rapp grinned. "Tall, dark, and handsome . . . highly intelligent. Women hanging on his every move."

"Don't forget delusional," Butler added with a wry smile.

Rapp chuckled.

Cheval smiled and said, "He does not follow directions well."

"Ahhh," Butler said while nodding at Rapp. "He has authority issues. I think I know the type."

"Yes, that is the phrase. He has authority issues. Very difficult to manage. Unnerving at times." Cheval smiled at Butler and he nodded as if to say, "I share your pain."

Rapp laughed at both of them. "Well, if he's so difficult, why do you put up with him?"

The question had a solemn effect on Cheval. "You know why I put up with him?"

"Because he gets things done," Rapp said with a bit of pride in his voice.

"That is correct. He is extremely effective, but . . ." Her voice trailed off.

"What?"

"Let's just say I know how Irene feels."

Rapp was well aware that Kennedy and Cheval shared a history that went all the way back to Beirut nearly thirty years ago. "You're afraid he's going to land you in jail one day."

"No." Cheval shook her head.

"Then what?"

"Every time he leaves the country, I wonder if he will return."

Rapp lowered his eyes and felt like a bit of a moron. "Sorry." He'd been through this with Kennedy on many occasions. He didn't spend a lot of time worrying about his fate, but apparently she did.

"No need to apologize. It is the business we are in. This man spends a fair amount of time in Algeria and Morocco, and he has very good contacts. He picked up a rumor that some of the men involved in the attack were Moroccan. After some diligent work he found a man who was bragging that his brother had participated in the attacks on America."

Rapp frowned. "There are probably a million young Muslim men who are claiming that they had a relative involved in the attacks." Rapp knew he sounded slightly ungrateful, but it was the truth.

"Trust me when I say my man verified the information."

Rapp looked at Butler for confirmation.

The Brit nodded and said, "I think you will want to hear the rest of the story."

It was Rapp's nature to be skeptical. The craft of espionage was filled with half truths and guesswork, lies and deception, so much so that it was often impossible to unravel all the layers of misdirection, but this was not Cheval's or Butler's first dance. They were every bit as suspicious as Rapp, and maybe more. And both had a look that said they had solved a very important piece of a complex puzzle. Rapp had seen this same look on their faces a few weeks earlier sitting at this very table on this same little island in the middle of the Atlantic Ocean. It was when they had informed Rapp that a third terrorist cell was at large and headed to America. Rapp reached for his cup of coffee and settled into the plush leather seat. He braced himself for what was to come and said, "Let's hear it."

CHAPTER 31

THE original plan had called for three cells to hit America. In typical al Qaeda fashion they had picked New York, Los Angeles, and Washington, D.C. Ninety percent of the intel they collected pointed toward attacks on those three cities. Occasionally Chicago or another major city popped up, but al Qaeda was especially obsessed with New York and Washington, D.C., for obvious reasons. Al Qaeda was acutely aware of the role media could play in amplifying their message. Infidels were infidels, but killing a couple of hundred people in Toledo, Ohio, simply wasn't as good a story in the media's eyes as hitting a big, glitzy city.

The Brits had nabbed one terrorist cell while it was transiting through Hong Kong and the French had picked up the second cell in West Africa. Much better at keeping secrets from their elected officials, MI-6 and the DGSE took the men to black sites and proceeded to peel back the onion on what was to be a very lethal operation of three coordinated attacks. The one thing they couldn't do, however, was glean the whereabouts and identity of the third cell. The various groups had never met. The only thing they knew about each other was that they existed, and that they each had been assigned one of the three major cities. No specific targets were known to anyone other than the individual cell leaders.

Rapp wondered if they had managed to squeeze a little more information out of the men in their possession and asked Cheval, "Have you had more success with the cell you intercepted?"

"My man," Cheval said without pretext, "was heavily involved in those interrogations. Like you, he is not afraid to get his hands dirty. So I have absolute confidence in what I am about to tell you. We originally told you that these three groups didn't know each other. No crossover whatsoever. While that is still true, the men all belong to the same organization in the broad sense."

"And the majority of them earned their stripes fighting in Afghanistan," Butler added.

"Terrorists talk the same as everyone else," Cheval continued. "They were tight-lipped about operational details but there is gossip about the more trivial aspects of their lives. They looked at their best men to create these three teams. There were quite a few rivalries. The Saudis, with their usual arrogance, demanded to be in charge of all three units and fill the ranks with their own people. That, however, presented a problem."

"Let me guess," Rapp said, "they found out it was a one-way trip and the courageous sons of Arabia decided they'd pass."

"That was part of it. The other problem lay in the fact that the Saudi ranks are bloated with wealthy men who rarely see combat. They are there to provide funds and then go home and thump their chests. For this operation they needed real shooters . . . real veterans of combat. The best without question are the Afghan and Pakistani tribesmen, but these men didn't like the idea of dying in a strange country thousands of miles from their homes."

Rapp said, "So they looked to the Moroccans, Algerians, Syrians, Jordanians . . ."

"Precisely," Cheval said, "and these men talk. There is a rivalry that is not different from that in our own military services. They like to brag and inflate their successes, and of course taunt the other groups."

"And they all hate the Saudis," Butler said, "but tolerate them because they have the money."

"Yes. At any rate, my man picked up in one of his interrogations that the Moroccan contingent was very proud that three of their men had been chosen to serve on one of the teams. I checked with George," Cheval said, glancing at Butler, "and he confirmed that none of the men in his possession were Moroccan."

"So you guessed that the three men were in the third and unknown group."

"Yes. So my man went to Rabat and then Casablanca and began to beat the bushes. It took him a week, and then he found what he was looking for."

"The sibling."

"Yes." Cheval gave Rapp an uneasy look and added, "It was slow work at first."

"You mean the brother was not cooperative," Rapp said.

"That is correct. It took a little longer than my man would have liked, but you know how such things work. Eventually, even the toughest decide to cooperate."

Rapp thought of asking if the sibling was still alive, but thought better of it.

"We now know the identities of all three Moroccans who participated in the attack."

"Let me guess . . . they were all part of the suicide crew?"

Cheval shook her head. "Not according to my man. One of the men is still alive."

Rapp leaned in a bit. "One of the three we are looking for."

"Yes." Cheval ran her ring finger along the edge of the file and flipped it open, revealing a photograph. She spun it toward Rapp and said, "Look, but do not touch. No reason to put your fingerprints on any of this."

Rapp nodded. "Who is he?"

"Ahmed Abdel Lah. Twenty-four, born in Casablanca, spent the last three years in Afghanistan and Pakistan."

"And you're sure he's still alive?"

"As sure as one could be considering the situation."

"How?"

"He sent his brother an email yesterday."

Rapp lifted his eyes from the photograph of Ahmed. He had a you-have-to-be-kidding-me expression on his face. "What did he say?"

"He told his brother not to worry. That he is alive and well and that his mission was a total success."

"Did you get a fix on it?"

She shook her head. "Only that it originated from a server in America."

"What about the other two?"

"We have some ideas, but I think George should fill you in on what he has found out first."

Butler cleared his throat and said, "We think we know how they funded their operation."

"Saudis." Rapp had found over the years that nine out of ten times the money trail led back to Saudi Arabia.

"No. Surprisingly enough, we think it was South American drug money."

This piece of information caught Rapp off guard. "Are you sure?"

"Yes," Butler continued. "I've been able to piece together a strange string of events which I think will explain how this cell managed to get into your country."

"South American drug money?" Rapp repeated himself, still not quite buying the idea. They had looked into the possibility years ago due to the opium trade coming out of Afghanistan and Southeast Asia. The rationale was that if the cartels could run drugs and sneak them into the country, they could easily do the same with terrorists. "They're all Catholic down there," Rapp said, referring to South and Central

America. "And I mean old-school Catholic. The Church has made it very clear that it's their continent, and the Muslims aren't welcome. As strange as it sounds, the cartels are very loyal to the Church on this issue. Plus it would be bad for their business if we found out they aided a terrorist group. The leaders know it'd be a good way to get a two-thousand-pound bomb dropped on their heads."

"I've seen the same reports, and I agree with your assessment," Butler said, "but this is something different. This third cell," Butler said in an admiring tone, "they're smart. They decided to do something none of them have tried before."

"What's that?"

"They unplugged."

"Unplugged?" Rapp asked with a puzzled look. "What in the hell is that supposed to mean?"

"They cut all ties to al Qaeda. Strict operational security."

CHAPTER 32

BUTLER went on to explain what they'd discovered. The other two cells had stayed in contact with al Qaeda's senior leadership during their training. They sent back regular reports and received orders from their commanders. Targets were adjusted and modified based on the success of the training and the ability to smuggle explosives and weapons into America. "But this third cell," Butler said, "they went dark. No one had heard from them in months. That is, until the bombs started going off last week."

Rapp wasn't here to punch holes in his colleague's stories, but on this point he couldn't resist. "That's normal operational security."

"For us, yes, but there is always a failsafe. We always keep in place a way to contact each other in case the mission needs to be modified or scrubbed."

"We verified," Cheval said, "that they had such protocols in place. We also verified this past week that they feared the third cell had been intercepted months ago."

"Why?" Rapp asked.

"Because no one had heard from them," Butler said. "They went completely dark. No communication whatsoever."

"What about finances?" Rapp asked.

"We found the account. It hasn't been touched in five months."

Rapp shook his head with a bit of skepticism. "We all know how expensive it is to run an operation like this. To move men and materials into position . . . to bribe people to look the other way . . . we're talking a significant amount of cash."

"I agree," Butler said as he reached under the table and retrieved a file of his own. Instead of manila this one was brown, but every bit as worn as the one Cheval had on the table. "And I think I know where they got it."

"South American drug money," Rapp said, still not buying it.

"Yes." Butler tapped the file and with a dire expression said, "Mitch, I can't stress this enough. I trust you. If I didn't, I wouldn't have boarded a plane this afternoon and flown down here."

"But?"

"What I have in this file is extremely sensitive. It is information that you need to see, but how it came into my possession is one of my government's most closely guarded secrets."

Rapp thought he knew the cause of Butler's cautiousness and nodded. "You're worried about exposing your source."

"Yes."

"Tell me how you want me to handle it?"

"For starters, nothing gets put in writing. At least nothing truthful."

Rapp smiled. "Create a false source—Cuban, perhaps?"

Butler hadn't considered going that far. He was thinking more of a misdirection play, but he instantly liked the idea of creating a ghost. It would unnerve the Cuban intelligence service and force them to dump resources into chasing a mole. "We can talk about that later, but let's go over the background material first. I've checked on this first part. You can confirm this information with your Drug Enforcement Agency. This past week, while the world has been focused on the attacks in Washington, a minor drug war has erupted in South America. It started in a remote jungle region of the Triple Frontier and has spread to a half dozen cities. The estimates of those murdered is in excess of one hundred people and while they can't seem to agree on who started it, they all agree on the single event that caused the spark."

Butler retrieved a pair of black-rimmed reading glasses and put them on. He opened the file, withdrew a satellite photograph, and then closed it. He slid the image to the middle of the table so Rapp could see better and pointed at a line of brown in a photo that was filled with green. "Jungle landing strip operated by the Red Command Cartel out of São Paulo. It serves as regional distribution center for their cocaine-manufacturing operation. Local peasants cultivate the coca crops, make the cocaine, and then they bring it to this strip where it is gathered and shipped out once a week.

"Three days before the attack on Washington, the facility was hit. It hasn't been easy to get exact numbers, but we think approximately eight of the cartel's men were killed and the entire week's shipment was stolen. Again, there's all kinds of rumors floating around, but the estimated street value of the stolen merchandise is somewhere between ten and twenty million dollars."

"That's a lot of cocaine," Rapp said.

"The Red Command agrees. They have offered massive rewards. They want their drugs back, and they want the guilty party punished. They played nice for a few days last week and then when no useful information turned up they began hitting the rival cartels and all hell broke loose."

"You don't think it was a rival cartel?" Rapp asked.

"No. I think it was the third cell."

Rapp nodded. "I'm listening."

"This is where it gets tricky. What I'm about to tell you is for your ears and Irene's only."

"Understood," Rapp said. They could figure out the best way to disburse the information later.

"The same day that the distribution center got hit a plane showed up in Cuba, with nine men and two pallets of cocaine. They were met by a colonel in the Cuban army and a small contingent of soldiers who helped them off-load the cocaine and transfer it onto two speedboats. This particular colonel was given 10 percent of the shipment in exchange for his help. Somewhere between one and two million dollars in product."

Rapp digested the information and said, "Cuba isn't exactly my area of expertise, but from what I've heard this isn't an uncommon thing."

"It happens to be one of my areas of expertise, and there's more." Butler withdrew another satellite photo. It was another shot of the jungle but instead of a rectangular clearing this one was square. An analyst had taken the time to label the various features. "We've all seen this before. Barracks over here, obstacle course here, this square area here used for PT, and a firing range here."

"Training camp?"

"Yes."

"Where is it located?" Rapp asked

"Next valley over from the airstrip. About ten kilometers away as the crow flies."

"So you think these guys hit the distribution center, loaded up a plane, flew it out of there, and landed in Cuba?"

"That is precisely what I think."

Rapp was skeptical. "I know a little bit about the Red Command. They're some of the most ruthless bastards on the planet. I find it hard to believe they haven't already figured this out. This is their backyard, after all."

Butler looked over the top of his black reading glasses and said, "Yesterday afternoon . . . in the Triple Frontier town of Ciudad del Este, a mosque was firebombed and burned to the ground, killing eighteen people."

Rapp swallowed hard. "What else?"

"My source in Cuba tells me that the nine men who came in on the plane looked more Mediterranean than South American. And then there's this last part that you are probably aware of. The day after this plane landed in Cuba, two speedboats approached your Florida Keys. Your Coast Guard scrambled a helicopter to intercept. It crashed at sea. Your rescue divers located the wreckage and discovered fifty caliber bullet holes in the engine."

Rapp was slightly embarrassed that he hadn't already made the connection. Thousands of data points had passed in front of him in the last week alone. Emails, text messages, voicemails, briefings, internet searches, off-the-record conversations with his counterparts at a half dozen foreign intelligence agencies, FBI reports, and of course, the not-so-little side show with Glen Adams. Rapp was suffering from sleep deprivation and information overload at the same time. It was time to strip it all away and start over.

He rubbed his eyes for a moment and then said, "All right, you've convinced me. What else do you have?"

Butler slid another sheet from the file. This one was white and had a sketch of a man's face on the front. "This was the advance man who set everything up in Cuba."

Rapp studied the drawing. The man was handsome. He looked to be in his late twenties. His hair was wavy and a little long but not mangy. "This was done off a photo?" Rapp said, referring to the sketch.

"Yes."

"You really are sure about this source?" Surveillance photos could be analyzed by experts who could tell you with amazing accuracy where the photo had been taken. By having an artist sketch the image one ensured that all those background clues were no longer a concern.

"Again, this is between the three of us. Nothing gets put in a file. My source in Cuba . . . I recruited him myself a long time ago. I would do anything to protect him."

Rapp and Cheval nodded. They had both been in similar situations before.

"Do we have a name to go with this face?" Rapp asked as he looked at the artist's sketch.

Cheval smiled and said, "Have you ever known us to waste your time?"

"No."

Cheval tapped the artist's sketch and said, "George sent this to me and I had my man show it to a few of the prisoners. Two of them recognized him. Would you like to guess his nationality?"

Rapp looked at the drawing. It was black and white so it was impossible to pick up any skin tone. The nose and the cheekbones offered some clues, though. "If I had to guess I'd say Saudi or Yemeni."

Cheval nodded and said, "Saudi. We don't have precise dates but we think he fought in Afghanistan for at least a year. They said he was very cosmopolitan."

Rapp frowned. Cosmopolitan was not often a word used to describe jihadists fighting in the mountains of Afghanistan. "How so?"

"He liked to read . . . especially American authors. He had traveled to your country before. And Cuba as well. His favorite writer was Ernest Hemingway. He talked of going to his house in Key West and in Cuba as well. As far as we can gather, he left the fighting a few months before the teams had been assembled. It was rumored later that he had been sent ahead to scout out potential targets."

Rapp's doubt was quickly dissipating. "Name?"

"Hakim al Harbi. Grew up in the town of Makkah, Saudi Arabia.

And here is the really interesting part. As you know, most of these fighters sign up in groups. Hakim joined with his best friend, a man named Karim, who in a very short period gained a reputation as a fierce and capable fighter."

Butler said, "One source says that he was barely one week in the fight when the Taliban mixed it up with an American hunter-killer team that had staked out a mountaintop position. The local Taliban commander ordered three assaults on the position . . . each one a complete disaster. This Karim and his fresh group of Saudi fighters were ordered to lead the fourth assault. Rather than lead his men on a suicide mission he shot the Taliban commander on the spot and took over."

"Nice way to receive a battlefield promotion."

"And that's exactly what happened," Butler continued. "Apparently this Taliban commander was a bit dim. The al Qaeda leadership was looking for an excuse to get rid of him and without their lifting a finger Karim took care of their problem. The Taliban didn't make a stink, because this particular commander had made a habit of burning through fresh conscripts."

"Anything after this incident?" Rapp asked.

"We're working on compiling and checking the stories, but he was known to be a tough and disciplined commander with a wicked temper."

Cheval said, "And apparently wasn't afraid to engage in a little self-promotion."

"How so?" Rapp asked.

"He gave himself a nickname."

Butler asked, "Care to hazard a guess?"

Rapp was used to connecting the dots, and this was something he should have picked up on several minutes ago. With a shake of the head he said, "The Lion of al Qaeda."

"Exactly," Cheval answered.

Rapp looked at Butler's file and then Cheval's. "Please tell me you have one more photo to show me. We've been after the Saudis but they haven't given us shit. They're denying that he's even one of them."

"That does not surprise me," Butler said. "Sorry to disappoint, but we have no photo at the moment. I promise you, though, we are throwing a lot of resources at the problem."

CHAPTER 33

MIDWEST, U.S.A.

HAKIM came to, and the first thing he noticed was a lack of movement. There was no gentle swaying back and forth and the occasional bounce. They were either on a very smooth road or they had stopped. His head moved to the right and then the left. He felt fluid sloshing around inside somewhere and then a stabbing sensation in his ear. He knew instantly his left eardrum had been burst. After clenching his jaw for a long moment he opened his eyes and looked around the bedroom in the back of the RV. The shades were still drawn on the two windows, but a bit of light still managed to make it through.

Something felt oddly different this time. To say that he had been a bit out of it would be a huge understatement. Hakim had no real sense of time, but it felt as if he had slept on and off for most of the day. Occasionally something would hurt so badly he'd come to for a moment, and then things would get hazy again. His memory was foggy, but at one point he seemed to remember Ahmed sticking something in his arm. That image jogged a few things loose and he suddenly realized he was really thirsty. He tried to sit up, but it was too painful. A few ribs were surely broken.

Reaching out, he managed to get hold of the curtain that separated the bedroom from the kitchen area. He moved it a few inches and saw Karim sitting in the booth talking to Ahmed. Maps were spread out on the table and they were talking in hushed tones. Karim sensed he was being watched. He lifted his dark eyes and looked through the gap at the man he had pummeled earlier in the day.

Hakim did not look away. He stared back at his friend with his sliver of a left eye, the right one still puffy and closed. He wanted Karim to have to look at his battered face. He wanted Karim to know exactly what he had done to his supposed friend.

Ahmed realized Hakim was awake and quickly slid out of the booth. He yanked open the door to the half-sized refrigerator and grabbed a bottle of water. He quickly brought it over to Hakim and after gently cradling his head, he pressed the bottle to his swollen lips.

Hakim took several sips and after a long pause a few more. When he felt he could speak without his voice cracking he asked, "Where are we?"

Ahmed looked over his shoulder and Karim reluctantly nodded for him to go ahead. He looked back at Hakim and said, "We are not sure."

"Not sure. You mean we are lost?"

"Yes."

Hakim didn't know if he should laugh or cry. "How could you be lost? Where is the GPS device?"

Ahmed did not answer. From behind, Karim announced in a quiet but noticeably angry voice, "It was left in the house."

Hakim looked up at the ceiling and laughed silently. He had taken so many precautions. How could they have screwed it up? He wasn't worried for a second that they would remain lost. He had driven all over this part of America. He had spent more nights than he could ever recall sitting in lonely roadside motels poring over maps, so many that he imagined he could win nearly any geography competition in the country. "What time is it?"

Ahmed looked at his watch. "Almost five in the evening."

"When did we leave the farm?"

"Around nine." Ahmed added, "I think."

"It was eight-forty-seven," Karim announced with confidence.

"Do you know what state we are in?"

Ahmed sheepishly said, "I thought I knew, but now I am not sure."

Hakim was dumbstruck. The states in the middle of America were huge. "How can that be?"

"The river," he said as if that would explain everything. "It turns like a snake."

Now Hakim understood the confusion. The Mississippi River acted as a state line for almost all of its twenty-three hundred miles. The RV had two gas tanks, which Karim knew held seventy-five gallons. He also knew the tanks were full because he had topped them off with the reserves he had stashed at the farm. If they'd been on the federal interstate highway system and had driven at the posted speeds they could have traveled as far as seven hundred miles without refueling. That was almost ten hours of driving, and they had been on the road just eight. "How much fuel do we have left?"

"We are low."

"How low?"

"Barely above empty."

Hakim was hit by a pang of fear. How could that be? He had gone over the escape plans with both men. He had drilled it into their thick heads that if anything should happen to him, they should follow one of two escape plans, either to Chicago or Houston, and stick with whichever one they chose. Both involved getting on the interstate and blending in, getting as far away as possible, as quickly as possible, with the least chance of something going wrong. Like getting lost. "What happened to the escape routes I gave you? They were simple to follow. Even without the GPS."

Ahmed made a gesture with his eyes as if he was looking over his shoulder while not wanting to turn his neck.

Hakim understood. "Karim, why did you not follow my plans?" He wished Ahmed would move so he could see the pained expression on Karim's face.

"I made a tactical decision. When I looked at recent developments I decided we must adapt."

"And how did that work for you . . . deviating from the plan?" Hakim asked, not caring if he upset him again.

After a long pause, Karim said, "I do not need your help. I can figure this out without you."

"Is that why we are stopped? We should be halfway to Houston or safely parked under a bridge in Chicago if that were the case. You chose to ignore all of my hard work and once again, look where it has gotten you."

"Ahmed, move!" Karim ordered.

The big man got up and walked to the front of the RV.

Karim gave his old friend a long, hard look and said, "I will not hesitate to beat you again. I do not have the time or the patience to deal with your hurt feelings."

"And I no longer have the time or inclination to condone your arrogance and stupidity."

Anger flashed across Karim's face. He pulled back his untucked shirt, showing the handle of a pistol.

Hakim smiled, his once-perfect set of teeth now ruined. "You talk of mission and faith and doing what is best for the jihad, but you can't humble yourself for even a second."

"I am your commander. It is not my place to humble myself before you."

Hakim said, "Who gave you the rank of commander?"

Karim started to draw the gun.

"You gave it to yourself. I was never part of your little group that you trained in the jungle. You may have deluded yourself into thinking that I was, but deep down in your heart you know I am speaking the truth."

"I am sick of all your talking," Karim shouted as he stood.

Hakim remained calm. "And you think that justifies killing me."

"On the battlefield it certainly does. Discipline must be kept."

Hakim started to laugh, but it hurt too much and quickly turned to coughing. He spat up some blood that dribbled down his chin. His face was so bruised and numb, though, that he didn't even feel it. He asked, "What would Allah think of this? You say that everything you do is to please Allah. How will your murdering me please Allah?"

Karim held on to the gun so tightly he began to shake. "Allah wants this mission to succeed. That is what will please him. You and all of your Western ways disgust him. Allah cares nothing for you. He would award me for ending your life and sending you to hell."

"Now you claim to know what Allah thinks. I am truly in the presence of greatness. Maybe you could ask him where we are."

"I have heard enough." Karim raised his pistol and pointed it at Hakim.

From the front of the RV, Ahmed called, "Sir, please, may I have a word with you?"

Karim turned to find Ahmed standing ramrod straight, his hands at his sides, his chin pointed slightly up and his eyes looking straight ahead as if he was on the parade grounds waiting inspection. "What?"

"In private, please, sir."

Hakim lay there on the bed wondering briefly if he had lost his senses. Why provoke an unstable man who had killed and would gladly do it again rather than admit he was wrong? The answer, he guessed, was that he didn't care. He watched Karim hesitate and then yield to

Ahmed's request. The two men stepped outside and closed the door, leaving Hakim alone in the RV wondering if he would have the courage to leave these two on their own. Let them fend for themselves. That would be poetic justice. Let the egomaniac rely on his inflated opinion of his own skills. He wouldn't last more than a few days.

Ahmed came back into the RV by himself and closed the door. He moved carefully to the back and sat on the edge of the bed. In a quiet tone he said, "I know this hasn't been easy for you. That jungle changed him. It changed all of us."

"That is no excuse."

"No, but it is a cause."

Hakim thought for the first time that Ahmed might not be as dimwitted as he seemed. "Be that as it may, he is not my commander."

"You may think that, but you will have a hard time convincing him."

"Then there is nothing to talk about."

Ahmed made a calming gesture with his hands. "I think you need some time away from each other."

"Please, by all means . . . drop me off at the next town."

Ahmed ignored him. Lowering his voice to a mere whisper he said, "I have offered to deal with you."

"Are you my superior officer now? We must keep the chain of command in place," Hakim said in a mocking tone.

"No. I want to save your life. I think you are a good man. And I think we need you. Please help us."

Hakim thought about it for a long moment and then said, "In the rear luggage compartment on this side," Hakim pointed over his head to the starboard side of the vehicle, "you will find a black Oakley backpack. Bring it to me."

Ahmed left and a minute later returned with the backpack. Karim came back into the RV and stood just behind Ahmed, his gun still in his hand. It occurred to Hakim that he was keeping an eye on him in case he drew his own weapon from the backpack. Instead he unzipped one of the pockets and withdrew a Garmin hand-held GPS device. He fumbled with the device for a second and then pressed the power button. As the unit powered up, Hakim looked at Karim with his one squinty eye and said, "All you had to do was ask. I have a backup for nearly everything."

CHAPTER 34

HAKIM held the small device in his bruised and battered hands, waiting for the inner workings to reach out to the nearest satellite, or mobile phone tower, or whatever it was that allowed it to be so precise. It took a total of forty seconds for the device to power up, run through a bunch of graphics, and deliver the information he was looking for. Hakim would have laughed, but the pain from his previous attempt was still fresh on his mind, so he kept his composure.

Squinting at Karim, he announced, "Congratulations, we are in Mexico!"

Karim frowned, "How can that be?"

"Mexico, Missouri." Hakim wanted to throw in a *you idiot,* but knew it would likely elicit a further beating or maybe even a bullet. "It is a town west of St. Louis."

"I knew we were near St. Louis."

Hakim didn't believe him. He looked at Ahmed and said, "There is a laptop in the bag. Would you please hand it to me." After he was given the laptop, he said, "And in the outer pocket, on the side, you will find a small USB device with Verizon printed on it. Please find it for me."

Hakim turned on the computer, and while he waited for Ahmed to give him the USB modem he asked Karim, "Do you have any idea where you have been?"

"Not precisely."

"I didn't ask precisely. I asked if you have any idea."

"I know we were in Illinois at one point."

"Several times," Ahmed said while he kept digging through the pockets. He came up with something and said, "It this it?"

"Yes." Hakim took it and stuck it into the USB port. "And what was wrong with the route I had laid out for you?"

Karim looked at his watch and said, "I did not want to be seen, so I decided to stay off the main roads."

The man was a stubborn idiot. "And you got lost. Did it ever occur to you that the big roads have more traffic? That it is easier to blend in?"

"And they have more police," Karim said boastfully. "That is why we got lost. I wanted to avoid St. Louis. Too many police and there was construction."

"You left the farm more than eight hours ago. If you had followed my plan you would already be in Oklahoma, and well on your way to Houston. Now you are barely in the next state."

"Everything is fine," Karim said dismissively.

"Three minutes ago you were lost."

"I knew we were near St. Louis."

Hakim didn't believe him. He glanced at the laptop screen and saw that he had a connection. He logged onto Google Maps and double-clicked on the middle of America. Using the track pad, he began to zero in on the area north of St. Louis. He eyed the distance between the Iowa farmhouse and Mexico, Missouri. "You have traveled approximately 150 miles in eight hours."

"That is a good distance."

Hakim realized the idiot was still thinking as if he were in the mountains of Afghanistan, where traveling twenty miles in a day was considered a huge success. "If you had trusted me, you would have traveled more than five hundred miles in that time."

"It does not matter. We are safe and we know where we are."

"Doesn't matter? Three Arab men in America's heartland. A town like Mexico is probably 90 percent Caucasian. The other ten percent is divided up between Hispanics, blacks, and some Asians. They have probably never seen an Arab before."

"It doesn't matter. No one will be looking for us in this part of the country."

"And when they find the father and son in the house?"

"It will be days before they find them," Karim said with confidence. "If they find them at all."

"I would be willing to bet that they have already found them."

Karim shook his head. "Not possible. We are fine. All we need to do is wait for nightfall and then fill up on fuel. With your device we will no longer be lost."

"Why wait until nightfall?"

"We only have cash and that means we must go into a store to pay. They will see our faces."

The man was an idiot. Hakim asked Ahmed for the backpack, and after digging through a pocket for a second he pulled out a small billfold. It had a Texas driver's license, cash, and a few other things. Hakim held up a credit card. "We can get gas now."

"Where did you get that?" Karim asked with derision. "How do I know it is safe?"

Rather than answer the question, Hakim began tapping away on the keyboard. A moment later he'd pulled up the website of the *Iowa City Press Citizen.* It was the closest big city to the farmhouse. He found what he was looking for at the very top. "Double homicide," he announced and turned the screen so Karim could see. "The bodies have already been discovered and it has been ruled a murder."

"I don't believe you."

"You are a stubborn fool," Hakim said without passion. "The Americans work fast. I'm sure somebody will recall seeing an RV driving away from the farm at about the time of the fire. The police will call other departments and ask them if they've seen an RV that fits this description. Before you know it they will receive dozens of calls that it was seen wandering back and forth between Illinois and Missouri for most of the day."

"You give them too much credit."

"And you obviously don't give them enough. They will alert all of the law enforcement in the region. It is standard procedure. Did you burn the barn down as well?"

Karim and Ahmed shared a quick look. Ahmed said, "We think so."

"You think so?"

"It burned down," Karim said with forced confidence.

Hakim could tell there was some disagreement between the two. "You saw it burn down?"

"No," Ahmed said, sheepishly.

"The house caught fire faster than we expected," Karim said. "People were bound to come. The RV was in danger of catching fire."

"So the barn didn't burn down?"

"We used some of the extra fuel and poured it on the ground between the house and the barn. I'm sure it caught fire."

"The fuel cans were yellow," Hakim said.

"What does that matter?" Karim asked.

"It was diesel fuel."

"So?"

"Diesel fuel is combustible, not flammable."

"It still burns."

It did, but not anywhere nearly as easily as gasoline. Hakim didn't have the energy to explain. The fuel had likely soaked into the ground and dissipated before it could give off enough vapor to ignite. "What did you do with the extra provisions?"

"There wasn't time to deal with them," Karim said. "But I am sure they are destroyed."

He really was a pigheaded idiot. "And if they haven't been destroyed, they will find the motorcycles, weapons, ammunition, food, fuel, passports, cash, and the two backpacks that I prepared for each of you." Hakim tried to shake his head, but it hurt too much. "If the FBI isn't already there, they are on their way." He handed Karim the hand-held GPS device. "Head west. Stop at the first gas station you see and then take Highway 54 South. We need to get moving. And remember . . . only diesel fuel. No regular petrol."

CHAPTER 35

WASHINGTON, D.C.

SENATOR Lonsdale wasn't entirely sure why she was going, but as she entered the lobby of the Watergate Complex South apartment building there was no turning back. Harry the doorman had already seen her and was on the move. From the outside she looked put together and ten years younger than her fifty-eight years, but inside she felt fragile, vulnerable, and beat. Even so she continued across the lobby on a course that would carry her toward the elevator bank and Harry, who was now waiting for her with a sad expression on his face.

"Good evening, Senator."

"Evening, Harry," Lonsdale said without much energy.

"Sorry about everything," the doorman said sincerely. "I know you lost quite a few friends."

Lonsdale was on her fourth day in a row of funerals and wakes. The pain of watching families torn apart was difficult, to say the least, but Lonsdale had to carry the additional burden of knowing that it was her hounding of the CIA that had more than likely opened the door for the terrorists. "Thank you, Harry. And my condolences to you as well. I know Senator Safford cared a great deal for you."

"I've been here eighteen years, and he's been here the entire time." Harry choked up a bit. "I'm going to miss him something fierce."

"We all are, Harry. We all are." Lonsdale patted him on the arm. "You take care of yourself."

"You too, ma'am."

Lonsdale took the elevator to the sixth floor, and when the doors opened she stepped out and stopped. She looked to her right and didn't move. She almost got back in the elevator, but the doors closed behind her and then the apartment door to her right opened. Senator Carol Ogden poked her head out and said, "Darling, you weren't thinking of leaving, were you?"

Lonsdale looked at her fellow senator's hot pink velour sweat outfit and put a fake smile on her perfectly lined lips. "Not at all."

"You could have fooled me," the senator from California said. "And you look like you need a drink."

"Twist my arm," Lonsdale said as she entered the apartment. There in the living room were two other women, Fran Burton and Amy Pringle, both United States senators. Together they were the Four Gals. That was the name their sexist colleagues in the Senate had given them sixteen years ago. In that time their ranks had grown to seven seats, but the fifth, sixth, and seventh female senators were all from the other party, so it was decided to keep their little group at four. Schedules were tough, but for sixteen years they got together at least one evening a month.

In the beginning, they played cards, smoked, and drank. Lonsdale figured it was their way of showing the men that they had no problem keeping up with them. Both Burton and Pringle had given up smoking about ten years earlier and that coincided with their starting a book club. That lasted a few years and then petered out after they realized they all liked different kinds of books and none of them were about to change the other's mind. Lately they'd gone back to cards and drinking chardonnay. Mostly, though, they got together to network, to make sure they were watching each other's back and offering support where it was needed.

Ogden handed Lonsdale a glass of chardonnay and in her smoky voice said, "Harry told me you seemed a little down."

Lonsdale took the glass. "I think we all probably are . . . aren't we?"

Burton and Pringle were starting a game of Thirty-one. Burton started dealing cards and said, "I haven't slept more than an hour or two each night. I keep waking up feeling like I can't breathe. Like I'm being suffocated."

Pringle picked up her cards and said, "Me, too. I keep thinking . . . what was it like for them? What did they feel? Were they buried under the rubble and then slowly suffocated, or worse, burned to death?"

"I've wondered the same thing."

Pringle said, "I was supposed to meet Greg Givens from the Sierra Club there for lunch, but canceled at the last minute. He and his wife and their kids all came over this weekend to thank me. We all sat around and cried."

Ogden shot Pringle a look that could kill and then jerked her head toward Lonsdale. Pringle, who wasn't always quick on the uptake, realized what she'd done. While she had canceled lunch and saved a man, Lonsdale had decided to skip lunch and condemned a man by sending her chief of staff to take her place. "I'm sorry, Barb. I wasn't thinking."

Lonsdale nodded, took a massive gulp of chardonnay, and then lost it. She had a full-blown meltdown. Ogden took her wine from her, afraid that she was about to spill it all over the carpeting, and steered her to the nearby couch and had her sit. The other two put their cards down and huddled around their bereaved friend. After a few minutes Lonsdale got her breathing under control and managed to say, "I feel so guilty."

Ogden countered by telling her it was nonsense. "There was nothing you could have done. This was fate and nothing else. You're a survivor. You always have been a survivor."

Through sniffles, Lonsdale said, "And I have survivor's guilt. I sent Ralph to his death. He was my best friend and he tried to . . ." She couldn't finish the sentence and once again began sobbing.

Ogden patted her on the back a bit too roughly. She looked more as if she were trying to get her to spit out a piece of meat than to comfort her. "This is foolish. Ralph, of all people, would not want to see you like this."

"Ralph tried to warn me," Lonsdale said through tear-filled eyes. "He thought it was foolish the way we hounded the CIA and Mitch Rapp. He tried to get me to see who the real enemy was."

Ogden frowned. "Ralph was a prince of a man, but he was . . . shall we say, morally inconsistent."

"He was right," Lonsdale countered.

"Well, I'm not so sure about that." Ogden took a couple of steps back and placed her hands on her ample hips. "What I'm about to say does not leave this room. Do you understand me?" After all three women had nodded, Ogden said, "This whole thing is wrong to me. The timing . . . everything. You were supposed to be at lunch that day, Barbara, and so were you, Amy. You're two of the Senate's most outspoken critics of the CIA. Just minutes after the explosions, Mitch Rapp and this Nash thug just happen to stumble across some immigrant who has the IQ of a Labrador, and then they proceed to beat a confession out of him." She shook her head emphatically. "I'm not buying it."

"What are you trying to say, Carol?" Pringle asked.

"I'm saying this thing stinks, and I wouldn't be surprised if that conniving bitch Irene Kennedy and all of her mercenary pals aren't behind it."

"You're not serious?" Lonsdale asked. "I was there. I was at the National Counterterrorism Center when it was attacked. Rapp and Nash were shot at."

"And neither one of them was scratched, and oh, by the way, all six terrorists who attacked the NCTC were thrown out the window and their bodies were conveniently destroyed by the suicide vests they were wearing. It's all a little much."

Burton, who was sitting on the far side of Lonsdale, looked up at Ogden and with a frown asked, "Have you been visiting those whacky conspiracy sites on the internet again?"

"No," Ogden snapped. "I haven't worked it all out yet. It's complicated, but I'm warning the three of you," she pointed at each of them, "don't fall into this trap and forget the sins of the CIA. They are the reason our friends were killed last week. We need to hold them accountable."

That was the last of the conspiracy talk for the next few hours. Three more bottles of wine were opened and Burton insisted they hold a miniwake of sorts. Pringle then made everyone agree up front that they couldn't say anything negative about their deceased colleagues and friends. Ogden broke the rule twice but each time was shouted down, and Lonsdale only had one more major breakdown and a couple of minor incidents.

All in all, though, it was good for the soul. Especially the laughter. Ogden told the story about her first year in office when they went on a fact-finding mission to Brazil. One night in the bar they were all tanked and everyone was dancing when Senators Safford and Sheldon decided to make an Ogden sandwich at the bar. She was the meat, and they were the bread. Safford got a little too into it and decided to grab the left breast of the new senator from California. Ogden in turn placed Safford's left testicle between her thumb and forefinger and squeezed it like a grape. Safford dropped to his knees and had to be carried to his room. Upon hearing the story for the first time, Amy Pringle nearly wet her pants.

Lonsdale helped clean up. She was glad she had decided to show. Both the laughing and the crying helped. When she finally left, Ogden was saying her good-byes and reminded her about the NARAL Pro-Choice America event they were cohosting on Saturday night. "You're the keynote speaker."

"Oh, God," Lonsdale moaned. "I don't know if I can."

"You can." Ogden rubbed her arm. "I'll write something up for you just in case. Remember, we're honoring the life of Dr. Smith."

Lonsdale nodded.

"And stay tough on this CIA thing. Don't give in to them. Let me do some poking around."

Lonsdale didn't have the energy to fight with her, so she let it go. "Thanks for the laughs. I'll see you tomorrow."

As Lonsdale waited for the elevator she thought about the NARAL event. They were going to honor the work of an abortionist who'd ended more lives than anyone dared count, and Ogden wanted to destroy a man who had devoted his entire career to protecting his country. Lonsdale suddenly felt as if she were trapped in a Lewis Carroll novel. "We're all mad here." Washington was a very strange town.

CHAPTER 36

SOUTHERN MISSOURI

HAKIM drank some orange juice and popped four extra-strength Tylenols. He was propped up in the bed with three pillows behind him, staring at his laptop, trying to figure out what to do. Logistically things were perhaps more straightforward than one might imagine. It was as simple as riding down the Mississippi River in a raft. There were twists and turns, but eventually everything made its way south and dumped into the Gulf of Mexico. They weren't following the river, however, they were working the state highways and county roads of Missouri in a gamble against time.

Looking back on the day it was almost impossible to believe what had happened. A single rash decision had led to a string of them, each one limiting their options and exposing them needlessly to capture. He and Karim could spend the rest of their lives debating the wisdom of deciding to kill the father and son, and they would never agree, but it was undeniable that the act had set in motion a series of bungles. One rushed decision had led to another, and now they were on the run with no idea how close the law was on their trail.

Hakim pecked away at his laptop searching various news sites for most of the evening as they worked their way down Highway 54, through Jefferson City, and then Lake of the Ozarks, and finally the turn for Springfield at Highway 65. Hakim decided not to take Interstate 44 over to Oklahoma. He had labored over that decision for quite a while but eventually decided they might be too exposed on the interstate. He made the decision to head for Branson. It was a major tourist destination that also catered to RV enthusiasts. He determined the smartest move would be to lay up for the night in a big lot with other RVs and wait until morning. Then, depending what they found on the news, they would either dump the RV or fill up on gas and make a sunrise-to-sunset dash to Houston.

Somewhere north of Branson, Hakim wasn't exactly sure where, he felt the RV begin to slow and then sway as they turned off the highway. He pulled back the rear shades an inch and stole a one-eyed glance, half expecting to see the twirling emergency lights of a police car. There was nothing. Not a car in sight. Hakim looked to the front of the RV just as it came to a complete stop. He watched as Karim unbuckled his seat belt and came to the back.

Karim pulled the privacy curtain back completely, hesitated for a long moment, and finally said, "I am worried about something."

"You are always worried about something."

Karim exhaled his frustration and lowered his voice so Ahmed couldn't hear. "For a minute, could you try not to be so difficult?"

Hakim nodded his consent.

"I have been noticing more RVs as we get farther south."

"I know that. Branson is like a Bedouin watering hole for RVs."

"Well . . . they are all old."

"The RVs?" Hakim asked.

"No, the people driving them. Every time I pass one they wave."

"And that bothers you?"

"It doesn't bother me," Karim scowled, "but I have not seen another RV in nearly an hour."

Hakim suddenly saw why he was concerned. "They are stopping for the night."

"I think so. I passed a truck stop a few miles back and there were at least ten of them lined up with the big trucks."

Hakim thought about it for a moment. "Maybe we should go back. Park there for the night."

Karim shook his head vigorously. "There must be a charge of some sort. Someone you must check in with."

Hakim thought he might be right. "What other option do we have?"

"You can get satellite images on your laptop?"

"Yes." Hakim hit the space bar and took the computer out of sleep mode. Google Maps was already up. He moved the cursor and clicked on the satellite tab and then turned the computer so Karim could see the screen.

"Is that our exact location?"

"No, but it is close. You can zoom in and out over here. If you bring me the GPS device I can tell you exactly where we are."

Karim took the laptop and sat down at the kitchen table facing Hakim.

"What are you doing?" Hakim asked.

Without taking his eyes off the screen he said, "Finding a place to stay tonight."

Hakim got a sinking feeling in his stomach. "What kind of place?"

"A house. Preferably one without any neighbors."

CHAPTER 37

DULLES INTERNATIONAL AIRPORT

RAPP landed back in the States feeling a lot better than when he'd left. He'd slept a solid four hours on the flight back. He woke up almost precisely an hour before landing and put on a fresh pot of coffee. While he waited for it to brew, he ate a turkey and bacon sandwich and some chips and drank a bottle of water. With that out of the way he set about drinking some coffee and making a list. Every time he got out one of his yellow legal pads and a pen, Kennedy cringed. She adhered to the old-school ways of guys like Bill Donovan, Bill Casey, and Thomas Stansfield. They liked to say if you needed a pen and paper you were in the wrong business. Rapp didn't have their photographic memory, and they almost certainly couldn't break a man's neck with their bare hands.

So he made his list. He tore off a single sheet at a time and scratched down his thoughts in near-unintelligible handwriting. No names were used, just initials, last and then first. He filled up two and a half sheets with his chicken scratch, jumping from one person or problem to the next and then back as new solutions or concerns came to him. He'd found that if he didn't do this at least twice a week things began to slip through the cracks, and in his line of work that usually meant someone was either going to have his career ruined or end up dead.

By the time the plane landed on the rain-slick Dulles runway Rapp had torn the sheets into quarters and fed them through the shredder. The slivers of paper, like strands of angel hair pasta, were collected in a burn bag. The ground crew would dispose of it later, and if by chance it fell into the wrong hands, Rapp wished the fools luck. Even if they could reconstruct the original pages they wouldn't make much sense.

The plane taxied to the private aviation hangars, where the CIA kept their planes. Rapp looked out the window and was relieved there were no government sedans waiting for him. He gathered his stuff, thanked the pilots, and moved across the tarmac with his garment and duffel bags. As he passed through the gate, he saw someone standing under an umbrella, next to his car. Rapp tensed a bit and draped his garment bag over his right arm. In a smooth, casual motion his left hand tugged at his belt buckle and then slid around to the hilt of his gun. Two steps later he realized it was Coleman and relaxed.

Rapp fished his keys out and unlocked the doors from about twenty feet away. "What's up?"

Coleman looked as if he was in a shitty mood. "We have a problem."

"What kind of problem?"

"I think it'd be better if we talked on the way back into town." Coleman glanced over at the entrance to the private aviation center. A couple of beefy guys who looked like they might be Diplomatic Security were waiting for someone.

Rapp threw his stuff in the backseat and asked, "Can you ride with me?"

"Yes." Coleman pointed a few rows over and said, "I brought Mick with me. He'll follow us back downtown."

"Downtown . . . why are we going downtown?"

"Because I think you're going to want to talk to someone."

Rapp almost asked who, but decided he'd wait until they were on the road.

As they pulled out of the lot, Coleman said, "Your car's clean. I swept it while I was waiting."

"Good." Rapp turned onto the service road and asked, "You sure?"

Coleman glanced over at him and gave him a noncommittal stare. "I checked out Doc's office."

"And?"

"I didn't find shit."

Rapp frowned. "How many guys did you use?"

"Myself plus three."

"Marcus?" Rapp asked, referring to his main computer guy.

"Yeah."

"And you found nothing. Damn it."

"I didn't say nothing. I said I didn't find anything in his office. Across the street in a leased office we found some serious equipment."

"How serious?"

"I've never seen anything like it. All passive stuff. You know how they always taught us to close the drapes so the lasers couldn't pick up the vibrations on the glass?"

"Yeah."

"Supposedly, it doesn't matter with this stuff. Marcus knew about it. He said it's the latest version developed by your boys in S and T."

Coleman was referring to the Science and Technology people at Langley. They were the whiz kids of surveillance equipment and they also happened to work very closely with the men and women in Security at Langley, which meant Johnson would have gotten to know plenty of them over the years. Still, Rapp asked, "If it's brand-new and Johnson no longer works at Langley, what in the hell is he doing with it?"

"That's a question you might want to ask Irene."

"You think she knows?"

"I have no idea. This is your turf, not mine, but if I were you I'd pick up the phone and call her."

"Later," Rapp said as he got on the expressway. He doubted Irene knew anything about Johnson, but it was something he'd have to run down. "What else?"

"The shit's wired to a fiber-optic line. It was being sent out in real time. Marcus thinks the recordings were probably run through a program, cleaned up, and ready for listening in less than a minute."

"Does he think he can trace it?"

"He's working on it right now, but he says fifty-fifty at best."

"So, no hard evidence unless we catch him coming back to retrieve the equipment?"

Coleman considered it for moment and said, "If we brought in the feds, we could start rounding people up and find out who tells the biggest lie. We could probably even put some heat on the S and T guys to find out who gave Johnson the equipment, but . . ." Coleman's voice trailed off. He didn't even like the idea.

"We can't bring in the feds, because we can't tell them how we know the shit even exists."

"Exactly."

"Plus," Rapp checked his side mirror and changed lanes, "I don't feel like airing the CIA's dirty laundry with some overzealous federal prosecutor."

"I thought that's what you'd say."

"So why are we going downtown?"

"Because that's where Johnson is."

Rapp glanced sideways at Coleman. "And why would I want to see him right now?"

"Because he's running with a crowd that should make you nervous."

"Who?"

"Russians. Lots of them."

"Is he working for them?" Rapp asked, more than a little surprised.

"I couldn't prove it in a court of law, at least not yet, but these aren't the kind of guys who hang out with fat, fiftysomething retired CIA security officers because they have a good sense of humor."

"What kind of Russians?"

"The kind with lots of money."

"Shit." Rapp was pissed off. "The worst kind. Former KGB guys?"

Coleman shrugged. "Maybe in his entourage, but the main guy is too young. He's a thirty-six-year-old whiz kid. Peter Sidorov, you ever heard of him?"

"The name rings a bell."

"He's got a Ph.D. in physics from Cambridge."

"What does he do?"

"Uses all that brain power to run a hedge fund. He's made billions the last couple of years. Mostly, and this could be a lot of jealousy talking, by manipulating commodity prices."

"A Russian hedge fund manager, manipulating commodity prices," Rapp said with feigned surprise. "I'm shocked."

"I know . . . but you know how people are with success. Especially with this new crowd out of Russia. Everyone wants to believe they're in bed with either the FSB or the mob."

"Or both."

"Yeah."

"There's also a few of them who play it up so they can act like tough guys."

Rapp was familiar with both types. His preference was clearly for the ones who were acting. "So which is it with this guy?"

"I don't know. This isn't my area. I never operated in that part of the world."

"Well, I have, and I happen to know someone who is probably our top expert on the subject."

"Irene?" Coleman asked, referring to Kennedy.

"Yep, but I think I already know the answer."

"How?"

"If there's one thing I've learned about the Russians over the years it's that rules and laws are nothing more than obstacles. For them, hiring a guy like Max Johnson to rig the game in their favor would be like us hiring an accountant to do our taxes."

"So how does that tell you who they are?"

"If it was the Russian Mafia they'd try to hire someone like you or me. Besides, none of our intel says they're in D.C. Los Angeles, Chicago . . . most of the big cities on the East Coast and a few in the Rust Belt, but not the capital. Irene says Putin doesn't want them screwing things up things for the SVR."

"So what . . . you think this is straight industrial espionage?"

"I don't know, but whatever it is, Max Johnson has decided to hang out with the wrong crowd."

CHAPTER 38

MISSOURI, ARKANSAS BORDER

THEY agreed it was better to travel eleven more miles and cross into Arkansas rather than backtrack north from Branson to a less-populated area. It seemed to them that the more state lines they could put between themselves and the farmhouse, the better off they'd be. Hakim was not in disagreement that it was a good idea to get off the road for the night. He did, however, fear the unknown, and by unknown, he meant what Karim would do to the unfortunate occupants of the house they happened to choose.

Not far across the border, they found a few interesting prospects just off Highway 65 on Old Cricket Road. Karim carried the computer over to Hakim and showed him the two homes he'd zoomed in on. Hakim knew instantly which house they would be visiting. They were adjacent to each other, but more than a quarter mile of woods and pasture separated them. They shared a gravel driveway for several hundred feet and then it split off. To the left the drive led to a series of buildings that, even from space, did not look well cared for, and then a house. Hakim stared closely and identified eight vehicles that were parked randomly in clusters around the main portion of the property. A couple of them could have been farm equipment but it was too difficult to discern. The place had a disorganized feel to it. Hakim imagined a large extended family living on the property, people of all ages coming and going. Lots of dogs. Too many variables at play to go wandering into at this late hour, or any time, for that matter.

The other property was uncannily similar in layout and geography to the farm in Iowa. The gravel road ran for a thousand feet up the side of a gentle rise and then hooked around the top to dump into a gravel courtyard that was situated between the house and a large barn. A thick picket of trees encircled the house on three sides, and then beyond, as the hill fell away, there was pasture. It was precise, immaculately maintained, and by far the better choice.

Karim pointed at the screen and asked, "Does that remind you of anything?"

"The house in Iowa."

"Yes. It is almost the exact same."

Hakim kept his eyes on the screen searching for other clues. "I don't know how old this image is, but there are no livestock trails in the pasture."

"What does that mean?"

"If they had cows or sheep," Hakim pointed at the screen, "you would see lines in the pasture. Like a goat trail in the mountains. The cattle use them to get from the barn to the pasture and back."

"Is this good?"

"Yes. If they have cattle, they have to be taken care of. Especially if it's a dairy operation. The milk has to be picked up daily. That would mean someone showing up tomorrow morning."

"We might be gone by then."

Hakim said, "If we are lucky this might even be what they call a hobby farm."

"What is that?"

"It is no longer used as a farm. People live there and that is it. Some people use them as vacation homes. They live in a bigger city and spend their weekends at a place like this."

"So it might be empty?"

"It's possible." Hakim hoped so.

Karim conferred with Ahmed briefly and explained what they would do. He laid out a precise plan in less than sixty seconds. Hakim had to admit this was where his friend shone. He had a mind for such things. From the moment they had arrived in Afghanistan all those years ago, he proved almost immediately that he was a battlefield commander.

Karim climbed behind the wheel of the RV and pulled back onto the highway. They drove the exact speed limit through Branson and took some comfort in the increased traffic. A few miles later they crossed the border into Arkansas. Two miles after that, they turned onto Old Cricket Road. Karim saw the driveway on the left a short while later and slowed to get a better look. There were two mailboxes, one in perfect shape, the other tilting and looking as if a strong wind might push it over. Karim took note of the name on the nicer box. Ten feet back there was a private driveway sign and a no trespassing sign. Karim checked the odometer and continued. Six-tenths of a mile later he slowed to a near crawl and gave the signal.

Ahmed had changed into black coveralls, a tactical vest, and black floppy hat. Holding a silenced M-4 rifle, he stepped from the RV at a trot and then disappeared into the night. Karim picked up speed and continued down the road at a leisurely pace. Four miles later he pulled into a driveway with a gate. He backed up and went in the direction he'd just come from. The Motorola radio sitting in the cup holder crackled to life with Ahmed's voice.

"No sign of people. One faint light."

Karim picked up the radio and pressed the transmit button. "Any animals?"

"Not that I can see."

"Security system?"

"Not that I can see."

Karim paused. "Dogs?"

"No."

"Are you in position?"

"Yes."

"I will be there in a minute." He placed the radio back in the cup holder and began looking for the turn. A short distance later he found it. Karim wrestled with the big wheel as he made a near 150-degree turn. He stayed to the right and a hundred feet later cruised past the turnoff for the other house at a respectful twenty miles an hour. As they began the slow, steady climb up the driveway, Ahmed announced that he could see the RV and that the situation in the house hadn't changed. Karim was feeling more confident by the minute that they had found the perfect place.

Then, as they swung around the rise and pulled into the courtyard, the place lit up like a shopping mall parking lot. Two floodlights on the barn flickered to life as well as the entire front porch of the house. Karim slowed and grabbed the radio. "What is happening?"

"No movement." Ahmed's voice came back steady. "I think they are motion lights."

Karim slowed to a stop, directing the RV headlight at the front door of the house. He put the vehicle in park and climbed out of the chair. With the radio in one hand and his silenced 9mm Glock in the other, he exited the RV and began to walk across the gravel toward the house. He glanced to his left and right and was careful to keep his gun close to his right thigh. He was forty feet away when the front door opened.

CHAPTER 39

WASHINGTON, D.C.

RAPP turned off H Street and parked the car at a yellow curb. He threw a plastic police placard on the dash and looked down the length of the block at the old warehouse. People were lined up from one end of the street all the way to the near corner, a flock of mostly twenty- and thirtysomethings moving and bobbing to the heavy bass that was rattling the grimy windows of the club. The guys trended a little older, the women probably six years younger. The guys all wore their urban chic uniform; two-hundred-dollar designer jeans, splashy shirts, and snappy shoes. The hair was either really short or really long and there was a lot of stubble on the faces. To Rapp's eye they looked as if they were all going after the eurotrash look that had been all the rage on the French Riviera some ten year earlier.

The women were pure eye candy. Three-inch platform shoes and skimpy dresses of every cut and fabric and lots of heavy makeup and wild hair. They looked more as if they were in line to audition porno than for a night on the town. Every thirty feet or so, a couple of buttoned-up preppy kids from the Hill could be seen trying to fit in. Their efforts consisted of losing their ties and unbuttoning their dress shirts two whole buttons. This had never been Rapp's scene and it sure as hell was no place for a fifty-six-year-old former Agency employee.

Coleman could tell by the way his jaw was set that Rapp was looking for a fight. His brow was slightly knotted and he was looking at the group with a disapproving frown. "I know what you're thinking," Coleman said in an easy tone, "and I don't think it's a good idea."

Rapp kept his eyes on the front door. "What am I thinking?"

"You're thinking of jump-starting this thing. You have other shit you need to take care of and you're really not in the mood to sit around in a car all night doing surveillance."

Rapp's gaze didn't waver. "Anything else?"

"Yeah . . . you're frustrated. You're thinking this Max Johnson should know better and the fact that he doesn't means he deserves a good ass kicking."

"And the Russians?" Rapp asked.

"You don't like that they come over here and break all of our rules."

"Anything else?"

"Yeah . . . I see the way you've been eyeballing those four bouncers at the door."

Rapp grinned.

"You're itching," Coleman said in a not-so-happy voice.

"Sometimes," Rapp said as he unbuckled his seat belt, "the best way to handle these situations is to force the issue."

"These Russians are nasty people, Mitch. They don't play by the rules."

Rapp turned to Coleman and arched his left eye. "And we do?"

"No . . . not exactly," Coleman stammered for a second, "but we're not crazy like they are."

"Well maybe it's time we get a little crazy. Make them feel a little uncomfortable about coming into our backyard and recruiting some jackass like Johnson."

"They don't scare easy."

"We'll see about that."

Coleman sighed. He knew there was no changing Rapp's mind when he got like this. "So what are you going to do?"

"Improvise."

"And if the locals show up?"

Rapp dug into his suit coat pocket and asked, "You said Marcus is monitoring the club's network?"

"Yes."

Rapp pulled out a leather ID case. He opened it, reached behind his CIA ID and pulled out a second laminated piece of paper. This one said HOMELAND SECURITY in dark blue block letters. He slid it between the CIA ID and the clear plastic window. He showed Coleman. "Works like a charm. Who's not for Homeland Security?"

Coleman shook his head. "If the cops show up I'm out of here and I'm taking my guys with me."

"Understood. Tell Marcus that in about two minutes I want him to crash their security cameras and their phone lines and kill the mobile phone traffic."

"Who's going in?"

Rapp thought about it for a second, looked at the four big guys at the door, and assumed there were at least another six or eight inside. "I think you and I can handle it."

Coleman half laughed and said, "Fine, but I'm telling Mick to stay close."

Mick Reavers was Coleman's one-man wrecking crew. He was built like an NFL linebacker, only meaner. "Fine by me." Rapp got out and popped the trunk while Coleman issued instructions to the rest of the team. He dialed in the two three-digit codes on a large black rectangular case and then slid the buttons out. Both hasps popped up with the thud of an old-fashioned briefcase. The inside of the case consisted of a large gray block of foam. Sections of the foam had been cut out in the silhouette of a variety of weapons. Rapp already had his 9mm Glock on his hip. As was almost always the case it was loaded with subsonic hollow-point ammunition. Rapp took his wallet out of his left pocket and set it next to the case. He grabbed the shorter of two silencers and put it where the wallet had been.

Rapp never went anywhere without a gun, and he had all the proper paperwork to carry the thing anywhere he wanted, but even so, the quickest way to land yourself in hot water was to fire your weapon in the District. Whether the action was warranted or not, the District was very sensitive to gunplay. Rapp looked toward the door and considered the crowd. He wasn't going to go in without a gun, but he would have to be in big trouble before he used it. The Glock would be for defensive purposes only. He stared at the cutouts, trying to decide between several other less-than-lethal options. There was the pepper spray, but it wasn't exactly his favorite, especially in a crowded place like a club. If you used enough of it, the next thing you knew, it got sucked into the ventilation system and the entire place would empty as if there were a fire, people coughing and spitting, emergency crews showing up to give medical aid. That was the type of thing that might attract a local TV station.

Rapp didn't want to cause that kind of stir if he could avoid it. He decided on an expandable tactical baton, an ASP F21 in a small belt holster. It was a heavy black piece of steel about eight inches in length with a foam grip. With the proper flick of the wrist the eight inches extended to twenty-one. It was a nasty little weapon that was great to use against bigger people with long reaches. It also worked well if you needed to clear a path through a crowd of people. A couple of flicks and people would start moving like spooked cattle.

Rapp hooked the ASP onto his belt on his right side and then decided on one more thing. He grabbed a Taser X26 and two extra cartridges. It looked pretty much like a gun except parts of it were yellow. He put the two extra cartridges in his front right pocket and stuffed the taser between the small of his back and his pants. Coleman joined him at the back of the car and Rapp asked, "Do you need anything?"

Coleman looked at the case as if he were shopping for watches. "Is that your new M-4 rifle?"

"Yep."

"I'll take it."

"Funny." Rapp handed him the pepper spray and said, "Don't use it unless you really think we need it."

"Got it." Coleman hooked the bottle to his belt and buttoned his suit coat. "So what's your plan?

Rapp shrugged and closed the trunk. "We go in like we own the place . . . which we do. This is Washington, not Moscow."

"And then what?"

"We grab the little prick by the scruff of his neck and we pull him out of there."

Coleman had a worried expression on his face. "And if they try to stop us?"

Rapp thought about it for a second and then said, "A few of them will probably end up in the hospital."

Coleman moaned, "I've got a bad feeling about this."

Rapp shook it off and started walking toward the club and its four massive gatekeepers. "You always say that."

Coleman fell in a half step behind and under his breath mumbled, "And I'm usually right."

CHAPTER 40

NORTHERN ARKANSAS

OTHER than the four years he'd spent in the army, Dan Stewart had worked his entire adult life for the same employer. A Lowell, Arkansas, native, he'd practically fallen into the job when he returned from his second tour of duty in Vietnam. A new low-price retail chain just up the road was hiring. Stewart took a job as an assistant manager and moved to Eureka Springs a few hours east. Within a year he was rewarded for his strong work ethic by being promoted to manager and moved to Branson, Missouri, to open one of the company's new stores.

That was where he'd met his Kelly. She was one of his cashiers and after a courtship of just five months he married the daughter of the local Baptist preacher. Not a big deal for most, but Stewart was a Methodist, and in Lowell, Arkansas, the Methodists were warned to stay away from the Baptists and vice versa. Fifteen years, four kids, nine stores, and six states later, he was transferred to headquarters in Bentonville, Arkansas, and promoted to senior management. The timing was perfect in the sense that it allowed all four kids to put down some roots and attend Bentonville High School. The kids all graduated and three of them went on to college and one joined the army like his dad.

As the years trickled by Stewart took part in the employer stock plan. During all those moves he had promised Kelly they would return to Branson when he finally stopped working. It was during his thirty-ninth year with Wal-Mart that she found out they had accumulated over three hundred thousand shares of preferred stock. With the price hovering around fifty dollars a share at the time the math was not difficult. On his fortieth anniversary with the company his wife forced him into retirement. They bought a cabin on Table Rock Lake where Kelly had spent the summers of her youth. After the first year Stewart bought the hobby farm just down the road. Kelly's relatives seemed to drop by the lake a little too frequently and he was getting way too much crap from his friends for living in Missouri. So he convinced his wife they needed the hobby farm so he could store all of his stuff and avoid paying the outrageous Missouri taxes.

Stewart was sound asleep in his big leather recliner when his German shepherd started to make noise. Her name was Razor the Third. Two and three had lasted ten and eleven years and the Third was going on nine. She was a good dog, perfectly obedient to her master, protective of Kelly, and reasonably tolerant of the grandkids. Stewart was sleeping in the chair because his shoulder was giving him problems. He'd been putting off surgery for years and had finally decided it was time to fix the darn thing. All of his friends were playing golf and hunting and he was in so much pain he could do neither.

He came to hearing the low growl of Razor, and then she let loose two unhappy barks. Stewart was about to shush her when the exterior lights snapped on, and then he could hear the grumble of an engine. Stewart was a motor guy, and he could tell immediately it was not a car. It was something bigger. He pushed forward in the chair, dropping the footrest and springing to his feet. The blanket fell to the floor and he watched as the headlights washed across the opposite wall, above the TV. The first thing he thought of was the meth heads who had been causing all the trouble with local law enforcement over the past few years. There had been a home invasion at the lake just after Christmas. An elderly couple had been beaten, tied up, and robbed at gunpoint.

Stewart had vowed he would never let a couple of hopped-up pieces of white trash get the draw on him. He yanked open the front hall closet and stuck his hand in, shoving the collection of fall, winter, and spring jackets from the right to the left. Without his having to look, his right hand found the back corner and the cold tempered steel of his Remington 870 shotgun. He closed the closet door, threw back the bolt on the main door, and opened it. Stewart stepped into the cool evening air, wearing a pair of maroon Arkansas Razorbacks pajamas his grandkids had given him for his sixty-sixth birthday.

His bare feet hit the white-painted porch. Razor growled at his side, showing her menacing teeth. Stewart saw a man coming at him out of the near-blinding white lights on the front of a big motor home. He racked a shell into the chamber and flipped off the safety with the smooth, practiced motion of a man who had hunted game since he was seven. He kept the muzzle pointed at the intruder's feet and said, "Who's there, and what in the hell do you want?"

The next part happened fast. Somewhere to his right, Stewart heard a slapping noise and then he heard Razor's nails sliding around on the glossy porch floorboards as if she were wearing roller skates, and then she was down. Stewart glanced at her to see what was wrong and right as he noticed the blood pooling against the white backdrop of the porch, something big and heavy smacked him in the upper left chest. There was no time to figure out what it was. He was spinning and falling, his bare feet giving him no traction. He landed hard on his left side, the shotgun clattering away as it bounced down the steps.

Another moment passed and Stewart's brain still wasn't processing what had happened, but as he lay there, a warmth began to spread beneath his left side. Stewart realized he'd been shot. He thought of Razor for a second and then his wife. He heard a scraping noise on the gravel and knew it was the shotgun being picked up. Then there were footfalls on the porch steps, slow and deliberate. Stewart tried to crane his neck around to see who it was, but a stabbing pain in his left shoulder stopped him. The intruder used his foot to roll him onto his back. Stewart winced in pain and clutched his shoulder as he took in the shadowy figure standing above him.

"What do you want?" Stewart asked in a pain-laced voice.

"How many people in the house?"

Stewart had never met a meth head, but this man sounded far too calm, and he had an accent he couldn't place. "It's just my wife and me. Take whatever you need and leave us alone. We haven't hurt anyone." Stewart could see the shotgun in one hand and something else in the other. The man began to point the mystery object at him and Stewart realized a split second before he died that it was a gun.

CHAPTER 41

WASHINGTON, D.C.

RAPP was still wearing his dark suit and white shirt. He didn't bother unbuttoning the shirt an extra button. He was either a three-button or two-button guy. He'd never really put any thought into it, but he knew he wasn't a four-button guy, way too much skin and hair. With his scruffy facial hair, Rapp did not scream cop or fed the way Coleman did. The retired SEAL officer was in a blue sport coat, black polo shirt, pleated khaki dress pants and thick-soled lace-up black dress shoes. Anyone with a decent amount of experience would notice the bulges under their jackets and guess that they were carrying.

Rapp, used to blending in, had to consciously tell himself to act more like a cop, make his fluid movements a touch more robotic, and instead of avoiding eye contact, make sure he made it, kept it, and left no doubt who was in charge. He decided to cross the street directly across from the front door rather than at an angle. As he stepped off the curb, he sized up the four bouncers. Three of them were black and one of them was white, big fellas, with big legs, big arms, big chests, and big necks. They were easy to pick out since they were in black jeans and black polo shirts and they were two to three times larger than anyone else in the vicinity.

When Rapp was five steps from the sidewalk, one of the black guys did a sweep of the area and noticed the two men coming for them. His eyes screwed in on them and his face betrayed a split second of surprise that these two were different from all the other partiers they dealt with. Rapp locked eyes with the man and headed straight for him. No one was wearing any indication of rank, so it was impossible to see who was in charge. Instincts told him, though, that the most alert of the four would be the best place to start.

Rapp stopped just his side of the velvet ropes and glanced over the guy's broad shoulder at the open doorway. Through a crack in the red velvet curtain he could see strobes and silhouettes of bobbing and swaying people. Loud music, with a heavy thrumming bass, rolled out the door and hit them like a strong gusting wind. Rapp put his eyes back on the big man. Rapp was six feet tall and he figured with the pitch of the sidewalk running away from the building to the curb, the guy was probably a few inches shorter than he looked. Rapp guessed he was about six and a half feet tall. The height didn't concern Rapp. The taller the better when it came to a street fight, and if you wanted proof all you had to do was watch an Ultimate Fighting Championship match. The big guys had the reach but their center of gravity was way too high for no-rules fighting.

Rapp opened his suit coat on the left side and reached into the breast pocket. He watched as the bouncer's eyes moved down to his waist. The guy noted the gun on Rapp's left hip and didn't bat an eye. Rapp pulled out the ID case in a smooth one-handed motion and held it open next to his right ear, so the bouncer wouldn't have to work too hard.

The guy's eyes flickered back and forth and then he nodded and said, "What's up?"

"National Security. Nothing to do with the club directly. I just need to get in there and talk to someone."

The bouncer started to answer, but was stopped by another bouncer who had been standing next to the door. This guy was even taller. He had to be six-nine and easily tipped the scales at 350-plus pounds. His white head was clean-shaven and tattoos peeked out from under his shirtsleeves and collar. Rapp noted a hammer-and-sickle tattoo with a sword on the man's forearm. He repeated what he'd already said to the other bouncer and for good measure held up the Homeland Security ID.

The big white bouncer reached out to grab the ID case and Rapp took a step back. In a cool voice Rapp said, "I'm not going to cause you any trouble. I just need to talk to someone."

"No." The man had a foul look on his face. "You have paper?" he asked with a thick Russian accent.

"Paper?" Rapp asked, having no idea what the guy was talking about.

The big Russian snapped his fingers several times while he searched for the right translation. "Warrant," he said, finally coming up with the word. "You must have warrant. No warrant, no come in."

Rapp looked at the big black guy and said, "He's not serious?"

The black guy gave Rapp a shrug that said he was the wrong guy to ask.

Rapp looked back at the Russian and said, "Let me see your passport."

The Russian made a big show of patting himself down as if he were searching for the proper documentation. Then with a smartass smile he said, "Sorry. No passport."

"Then you better let me in, or I'm going to have to arrest you."

The man laughed at Rapp. "Come back with warrant. No warrant . . . piss off."

Rapp watched as he made a shooing gesture with his hands as if he was trying to send a door-to-door salesman on his way. Rapp glanced at Coleman, who was already looking over his shoulder wondering where Reavers was. "Three options," Rapp said in a loud voice. "The first, I ignore the fact that you're a rude son of a bitch and you get out of my way. Second, you decide not to let me in, so I arrest you for obstructing a federal agent, and I have you deported with all the other Russian assholes who were picked up this week."

"And the third?" The Russian asked as he defiantly folded his big arms across his enormous chest.

"Third," Rapp said as he cocked his head to his left, "I kick your ass and leave you bleeding and crying here on the sidewalk. Your choice . . . and to show you I'm not a bad guy, I'll even give you a second to think about it."

While the big Russian stood there like a statue Rapp turned and walked over to Coleman. In a voice that only the two of them could hear, Rapp said, "Call Marcus and tell him to jam everything. There are probably more Russians inside the club. I don't need these guys calling for reinforcements when this guy goes down."

"What are you going to do?" Coleman asked.

"I'm going to drop the asshole before he even knows what hit him." Rapp looked back over his shoulder and gave the big man the once-over from the heavy soles of his black boots to his shiny bald head. There are a lot of ways to take down a man. Every guy is different—different strengths and different weaknesses. Big guys like this all had one weakness in common and Rapp had already scoped it out. This thing would be finished before the guy even knew it'd started. Rapp was sure of that. His only real concern had to do with the other three big locals. Giants like these guys were easy to handle one at a time, but in groups, they could be a problem. All they had to do, after all, was get their arms around you and fall to the ground. If you got caught between them and something really hard like a concrete sidewalk, you were bound to break a few ribs.

Rapp saw Reavers crossing the street and decided it was safe to start. His presence might be enough to give the other three bouncers pause. Rapp turned and marched straight back to the Russian. He stopped one pace away and placed his right hand on his hip and his left hand on the hilt of his gun. "So . . . what's it going to be?"

The Russian kept his arms folded across his chest. Each fist was stuffed under an armpit in a show of immovable defiance. "How do you say in English?" he said again searching for the right word.

"How do I say what in English?" Rapp checked the man's feet again. They were shoulder-width apart, feet planted firmly on the ground, knees barely flexed. This guy was used to intimidating people.

The Russian's face lit up with a smile and he said, "Go fuck yourself. Freedom of speech, right? God bless the U.S.A., and fuck all the cops."

"Fuck all the cops," Rapp repeated in a voice loud enough that it would get the attention of the other bouncers and some of the people in line.

"That is right. You Americans think we Russians are stupid, but we know your laws. You can't do shit. You are a cop. You can't touch me."

Rapp smiled and nodded. He kept nodding and leaned in a little farther. He got up on his toes and lowered his voice so it would stay between the two of them. "I like your theory, but there's only one problem with it. I'm not a cop."

Rapp turned as if he were going to walk away. He took one step with his left foot, and then started to lift his right foot off the ground. Everything looked normal. There wasn't a single sign that would betray what was about to happen. The toe of his right shoe touched the ground for an instant and then he moved. Rapp's left leg flexed and his upper body leaned forward. His head turned to the right, and then in one lightning-fast move, Rapp's right leg shot out like a donkey delivering a kick. The heel of his shoe landed directly on top of the Russian's right kneecap and kept going, driving the knee past the vertical line and folding the leg back in the wrong direction. A healthy knee would not have been able to take the blow, let alone one that had been carrying around an extra 150 pounds for a good decade. The snapping noise of the knee joint breaking was followed by the crunching sound of tendons tearing away from various bones.

Rapp held his strike at maximum extension for only a fraction of a second and then he was away like a lumberjack clearing the area in case the tree kicked back at him. The Russian stayed upright for another second, and it seemed like an eternity. Rapp's right hand slid around his belt, found the heavy black baton, and yanked it free. He watched as the Russian began to teeter to his right. Rapp knew exactly what was about to happen. The brain hadn't registered the catastrophic failure of the right knee. Its internal gyroscope was telling the body that it needed to place weight on the right leg to prevent toppling over. It was something the brain did on autopilot a million times a day, and it always worked, unless some external force got in the way or the right knee had just been shattered.

The Russian didn't even scream. There wasn't time. He just kept tipping to his right, stepped as if he was going to catch himself, and then when the full weight of his 350-plus pounds started to come down on the bad knee it folded in the middle like a cheap card table chair. He hit the sidewalk hard, even though his arms reached out to slow his fall. His right temple bounced off the hard, dirty surface and landed facing the toe of his right boot. That was when the screaming started.

CHAPTER 42

RAPP figured he had five minutes to get in and out before things got heated. Maybe as much as fifteen, but that was pushing it. Shutting down the phones and radios would certainly delay things, but the cops had to patrol this neighborhood on a pretty regular basis. Rapp could handle the cops if he had to, but he didn't feel like spending the night calling in favors and then having to explain himself for the next two days. The whole point of tonight's exercise was to take this particular problem off the burner and put it behind him.

Life would be a lot easier if he simply marched in, grabbed Johnson by the scruff of his neck, and dragged his lame ass out of the joint. Simple and direct. Rapp knew all about momentum. In a situation like this, the best thing was to keep moving. More often than not, if you had the right bearing and you acted as if you were in charge, people followed your lead.

Rapp looked at the first bouncer and flicked his wrist in a hard downward motion. The two extendable sections of the baton snapped out and into a locked position with a hard click. Rapp pointed the stick at the big bouncer and said, "I gave him three choices. You only get two."

The bouncer looked down at the big bald Russian. He was writhing on the cement, swearing in his native tongue and staring in shock at his knee.

Rapp said, "You either take me to Peter Sidorov or you spend the next three days in the D.C. lockup with every other shithead and drug addict in the city. You're a big guy, but they're like hyenas in there. They attack in packs. They might not be able to rape you, but they'll probably cut you and then you can spend the next year wondering if you have AIDS."

The bouncer hesitated for maybe a half second and then undid the velvet rope and gestured for Rapp to follow him. Rapp looked at Coleman and said, "You stay here and keep an eye on things. Mick," Rapp said, looking at Reavers, "come with me."

The big bouncer led them through the front door. Rapp followed two paces behind, and then Reavers. A long bar with a galvanized top ran for a good hundred feet along the left side of the old warehouse. Exposed metal trusses ran from left to right. Rapp paused for half a step to scope out the high ground. Old warehouses like this one often had a catwalk, but this one didn't. With one sweep of the place Rapp noted four more bouncers dressed like the four guys out front. To the right was a dance floor with an elevated DJ booth. The place was packed and their pace slowed as they threaded their way through the crowd.

Rapp saw where they were headed a few steps later. There was a VIP section at the far end. A set of stairs on the left and another one on the right led up maybe six feet to a big area that was probably eighty feet wide by twenty feet deep. There was a steel column every ten feet that acted as a divider between the individual VIP seating areas. Red velvet curtains hung in front of each area, swooping down from the rafters to where they were tied off around the columns. Through the openings in the drapes Rapp could see couches and chairs, revelers standing and sitting and in far dark corners, probably doing things that could get them arrested.

The music was loud, so loud that Rapp figured he wouldn't need to bother with the silencer if he had to start shooting people. They reached the base of the stairs for the VIP area and the big black bouncer slowly climbed four treads and he and another monster began screaming into each other's ears. Rapp noted the tattoos on the man's neck and wondered if his theory was flawed. This guy was a lot like the other Russian he'd just crippled except he had hair. The world of the Russian Mafia and their tattoos was a strange one. Over there, you could get killed for wearing a tattoo that you hadn't earned, but here in the States Rapp wasn't so sure. Were these guys the real thing or a couple o' wannabes trying to intimidate, by putting some ink on their skin?

The new guy finished listening to the big black guy, gave Rapp the universal stop motion with his hand, then disappeared into the dim recesses of the VIP area. Rapp immediately worried there was a back door up there somewhere. If Johnson had half a brain and he found out a federal agent was in the building he would bolt. *Momentum*, he reminded himself. Keep moving forward. Basic battlefield doctrine. Never give your opponent a chance to get his shit together.

Rapp did a quick 360 of the area. He noted two bouncers within sight, but they weren't looking his way. Rapp smiled as he saw them fiddling with their radios. That alone would cause a diversion. With them focused on trying to fix their radios Rapp saw his opening. Looking over his shoulder at Reavers, Rapp waited for the big guy to lean in. Reavers stepped forward and placed his ear near Rapp's mouth.

"I don't want him sneaking out the back door. I'm going to tase this big fella here. Step around to my right and shield me. When I hit him, help me lower him nice and slow."

Reavers nodded.

Rapp looked up at the big black bouncer and started to move his lips. The bouncer couldn't hear so he leaned forward and turned his head away from Rapp, offering his right ear. Rapp's left hand slid inside his jacket and around his waist. He grabbed the taser and kept it close to his body. As he started to ask the bouncer about a back door, he turned his body a shade to the left and with his right hand grabbed the tip of the taser and removed the cartridge. With the two contacts exposed he leaned in real close and placed the contacts on the man's lower back, only a few inches from his spinal column. Rapp squeezed the trigger and instantly fifty thousand volts passed from the plastic gun into the big guy's body. While he went rigid Rapp kept the prongs pressed into him and was careful to make sure their bodies didn't touch. He counted to three in his head and then withdrew the taser.

Reavers was right there. As the big guy started to go down Reavers grabbed him by the shoulders and slowly lowered him so that he was lying on the steps. Rapp snapped the cartridge back into the taser and slid it back into his belt at the small of his back. At this point he didn't bother to look left or right to check on the other bouncers. He went up the stairs. When he hit the landing at the top his eyes swept the area. They were drawn to a space midway down on the left. The Russian bouncer who had gestured for him to wait was talking to two guys in suits. They were both bigger than Rapp but smaller than the mammoth bouncers. These would be the real professionals. Probably former Special Forces, but not necessarily Russian. They might even be local guys, which Rapp would welcome. Beyond the three men Rapp caught a glimpse of Max Johnson sitting on the couch with two women draped over him.

The big Russian saw Rapp, said something to the man in the suit, and marched off with a really pissed-off look on his face to intercept the two unwelcome visitors. Rapp showed his hands, palms out and up, in an effort to sucker the guy into continuing his headlong march toward him. Rapp kept moving as well, closing the distance at a deceptive pace. Rapp lowered his left hand a notch, making his right hand the more presentable target. He watched the six-and-a-half-foot-tall brown-haired Russian take the bait and begin reaching for his target.

Now was the moment of decision for Rapp. At this juncture he had several options. The solar plexus was out because of the guy's girth. There were too many layers of fat to get through to deliver an incapacitating blow. The second option was the chin, but as Rapp took a final good look he noticed the guy had some pretty decent traps. Traps, short for trapeziuses, were the muscles that anchored a guy's head to the rest of the body and the more developed they were the harder it was to knock a guy out.

The last and best option carried a risk with it, but Rapp wasn't too worried. This wasn't exactly some innocent bystander out on the street. At the exact moment the bouncer's beefy fingertips were about to grab Rapp's right wrist, Rapp uncoiled. He sprang off his left foot and transferred about 90 percent of his weight onto his right foot as his hips rotated. The big man never saw it coming. For a move like this, both the closed fist and the open palm were too big to make the precise strike, so Rapp had to use a knuckle strike.

Rapp's first set of knuckles on his left hand folded under so the tips of his fingers were touching the pads of his palm. His left arm formed a battering ram from the elbow down to the jagged second set of knuckles. The target was one of the weakest points on the human body—the Adam's apple. Lots of cartilage and soft tissue. It didn't matter how good or tough you were, if you got hit with a direct strike to the Adam's apple you were going down. There was only one problem with the move. If it was delivered too forcefully you could kill a man. Just as Rapp was throwing the blow an image flashed before his eyes. It was of the big Russian rolling around on the carpet clutching his throat and dying from a crushed windpipe. It was that image that caused Rapp to lay off a touch, and that was his first mistake.

CHAPTER 43

NORTHERN ARKANSAS

HAKIM took a bit of comfort in the fact that the old woman had died in her sleep. He wasn't in the room when it had happened, but he'd heard the mechanical clank of the slide jerk back and then forward and the spit of the 9mm round as the gases were vented through the silencer. He'd watched the old man die on the porch first. He didn't know why, but he wanted to see it with his own eyes. With his broken and bruised body he pulled himself out of bed and hobbled his way to the front of the RV. He watched his friend raise the gun and shoot the old man from a distance of no more than a few feet. There was another brief flash from the muzzle and the body convulsed one last time.

Hakim had killed before, in the mountains of Afghanistan and Pakistan, but never so close—so personal. They were just silhouettes in the distance. He considered how difficult it must be to see every wrinkle and misplaced hair. To know the exact eye color of the person whose life you were extinguishing. Would those eyes come back to haunt your dreams? For Hakim the answer was yes, but for his friend he wondered. Did anything really get to him? Was there a line he would not cross?

Hakim stared through the windscreen and then watched with increasing concern as his friend climbed the porch steps and moved into the house. With great effort, Hakim climbed down the RV steps and moved as quickly as his broken and battered body would allow. He climbed the porch steps no more than five seconds behind Karim. He looked down at the lifeless carcass of the dog and the old man, who had been literally shot between the eyes. He moved with increasing alarm. He didn't know why but he was convinced there were children in the house. No matter what the maniacal clerics said, Allah would never condone the killing of children.

In the foyer Hakim paused. There was a staircase straight ahead and a hallway just to the left. Farther to the left there was a TV room. There was a big leather chair and a matching footstool. A blanket was in a pile on the floor. That must have been where the old man was when they pulled in. That would explain why he was up so fast and was able to intercept Karim outside. He hobbled over to the chair to confirm his theory. He touched the leather chair. It was still warm from the body heat of the man.

That was when he heard the faint yet distinctly mechanical clank and spit of the suppressed Glock firing a round. The sound did not come from the second floor. The headlights of the RV were still spilling through the big picture window on his left. As he looked in the direction of the sound he saw Karim come through a doorway at the back of the house. He raised his weapon and pointed it directly at Hakim. And then something very strange happened. Hakim had thought of death before, but he had never welcomed it. Now it felt like a warm blanket against a cold biting wind. He was ready to wrap himself in it and fade away. Face whatever judgment waited for him in the afterlife. Based on what he had allowed to happen the last few days, he doubted he would see paradise.

"You idiot," Karim's voice cut like a knife through the dark, still house. "I nearly shot you." He moved across the room quickly, his footfalls silent on the carpet. "Stay put while I check upstairs."

As he walked past, Hakim reached out and grabbed his arm. "We do not have to kill every person we encounter."

His friend angrily shook himself free and moved swiftly upstairs. After he had disappeared, Hakim walked to the back of the house. He stood at the bedroom door and hesitated. It was dark inside, but he could easily discern the shape of the bed and the nightstands and lamps. The near side of the bed was flat and undisturbed. The far side had a lump. Hakim sighed and without making a conscious decision his feet were moving. They carried him across the room to the side of the bed where he guessed the man's wife had been lying, doing what billions of people do every night—sleep. How had she offended Islam? Could someone be an infidel if she was asleep in her own house thousands of miles from the heart of Islam, in a largely Christian country?

Hakim stood over the shape and willed himself to look closer, to confront yet another evil perpetrated by his best friend. At first he could only make out a silhouette under the covers and a head on a white pillowcase. He bent farther and the features of the woman's face became clearer. Then he saw it. A dark circle at the woman's temple no bigger than a small coin. Hakim reached out and turned on the bedside lamp. The red pucker mark was surrounded by a circle of gray. Karim had shot her point-blank, the tip of the muzzle no more than a few inches from her skin. He had expected to see an elderly woman, but instead saw someone who looked to be in her early sixties with many years left to live. Until they picked her house.

Hakim felt sickened by the whole thing. He turned off the lamp and walked back into the TV room. He stopped at the fireplace and looked at the photos arrayed on the mantel. Lots of kids. School photos, sports photos, and photos of family vacations. Hakim guessed they were grandchildren. He could barely breathe. He closed his eyes and prayed and listened. Listened for the clank and the spit of Karim's gun. He prayed that the kids were not here. He could not take any more senseless killing. Not tonight. Maybe never again. He asked Allah for guidance, asked him if this was truly what he wanted, and when he didn't hear from him he made a promise to Allah. It was a bargain. He would follow through on his end of the deal, and he hoped that Allah would keep up his end of the bargain.

Shortly after that Karim came downstairs and announced that the upstairs was empty. Then he radioed Ahmed and told him to make a quick sweep of the perimeter before coming in. Hakim breathed a sigh of relief, but he didn't have much time to enjoy it. He felt a slight tickle in his throat and then he began to cough. At first it didn't seem unusual, but then he felt the coppery taste of blood in his mouth. He moved to the chair where the man had been sitting and managed to fall into it just as he blacked out.

CHAPTER 44

WASHINGTON, D.C.

THIS Russian was quicker than he looked. Rapp figured he must have twisted into the blow at the last second, blunting Rapp's strike and causing him to miss by a fraction. The Russian's throat would be a little sore in the morning and he wouldn't be eating any tacos for a few days, but his windpipe was intact and in working condition. That meant he would have no trouble sucking oxygen into those big lungs and in turn providing fresh blood to those big arms, and that was a problem.

Fights tended to follow a pattern, and for Rapp it was usually pretty predictable. It started and five seconds later it was over, Rapp on his feet, and the other guy on the ground clutching some part of his body that would need a doctor to fix. So, when his first strike missed it was like a symphony conductor hearing a poorly played note. The audience might not have caught it, but he knew it, and he knew he had to do something fast or this big guy would get hold of him, and he'd be the one in need of a doctor's attention. The other thing Rapp did was re-evaluate his opponent. Moving into a blow was not the tactic of an amateur. Pros leaned in, rookies leaned back, and if you never learned to move into the blow, you weren't long for this rough-and-tumble world.

As Rapp withdrew his strike he felt the hand of the Russian clamping down on his right wrist. Rapp yanked his right hand down hard and rotated it clockwise. At the same time he delivered a quick rabbit punch to the Russian's nose, not hard enough to break it, but enough to make him bleed and maybe stun him for a second. Rapp made his first retreat. With his right wrist free, he hopped back a step, and that was when he felt more than saw the guy's massive right fist screaming toward the left side of his head. Another move every fighter has to learn is a standing turtle. There's nothing pretty about it, you simply tuck your chin into your chest, bring your shoulders up, and prepare to receive a few blows.

The punch glanced off the top left side of Rapp's head. Rapp registered the stinging pain, but ignored it. When a guy this big throws that big a punch he almost always leaves himself open. Rapp found the opening. He ducked, slid to the left, and delivered a hammer punch just beneath the guy's right armpit, where the ribs are most exposed. The brutal punch stood the big man up as he arched his back and tried to step away from the next blow. Then three things happened in quick succession. Rapp eyed his spot. It was the back of the guy's right knee, just above the top of the calf. Always the knees with these big guys. That was their most vulnerable point. Rapp stomped down hard with his right foot. This time the joint would be working with him. The guy wouldn't go to the hospital, but he would be going down, and for now that was all Rapp cared about. He had other things to do that were more important. As the big Russian started his tumble, Reavers stepped in and hit him with a perfectly placed right hook that snapped the Russian's head a quarter turn to the right.

It was as if someone unplugged the guy. He went down on one knee, his arms dangled, his shoulders slouched, he started to topple forward, and although Rapp couldn't see it, he knew the guy's eyes were rolling back in his head. That was when the third thing happened.

Rapp spun to go after Max Johnson and found himself face-to-face with the muzzle of a Sig Sauer pistol.

"One more fucking move and I blow your head off."

The English was perfect. The accent a slight southern drawl. Most likely Texas or Oklahoma. The face, lined and weathered. Rapp guessed him to be in his midthirties. "You wanna shoot a federal agent in the head you go right ahead. They'll ship you back to Texas and fry your ass!"

The guy blinked, thought about it for a minute, and said, "Show me your ID. Nice and slow."

Rapp carefully reached into his jacket pocket, withdrew his ID, and flipped it open. He watched as the bodyguard glanced back and forth between Rapp's face and the ID. Rapp knew what was going through his mind, so he asked, "Who do you work for?"

"Triple Canopy."

They were good. One of the best, which meant this guy was more than likely pretty level-headed. "I'm OGA . . . attached to Homeland Security, while I'm back here in the States. You guys do a lot of work with us over in Afghanistan and Iraq."

The guy nodded.

Rapp hadn't said a lot but he didn't need to. OGA stood for Other Government Agency, which anyone who worked for Triple Canopy, and had been over to the Sand Box, knew was a polite way of saying CIA. Mentioning all of the work that Triple Canopy did for Langley was a subtle reminder that while Sidorov might be paying a small fortune for protection, the CIA, the State Department, and the DOD were paying a real fortune, to the tune of about a half billion a year, to Triple Canopy and its subsidiaries.

Rapp said, "I just need a word with your employer."

"Not going to happen. He won't talk to anyone who has anything to do with our government. You're supposed to go through his lawyers."

Rapp wondered what kind of trouble Sidorov had gotten himself into. He motioned for the guy to point his gun in a less-threatening direction.

The guy took a step back and pointed his weapon at the floor.

Rapp asked, "You spend any time in Moscow?"

The guy shook his head.

"Well I have, and let me tell you something. They don't use warrants over there. If the FSB wants to talk to you . . . they don't ask for permission. They talk to you, and it's typically not very pleasant. Now, I don't want Sidorov. At least not yet, but if he pisses me off any more than he already has I'm going to take a real hard look at him and it won't be pleasant. The guy I want is sitting right over there." Rapp pointed to the big horseshoe sitting area where Sidorov and his party were set up. There were only four men. The rest were women.

The bodyguard turned. "You mean the older guy in the jeans and loud shirt?"

"And funny glasses. That's him." Rapp shook his head. Johnson was dressed like one of the twenty-five-year-old kids on the dance floor. He hadn't seen him in maybe a year, but he still recognized him. He'd grown his hair out a bit and even in the soft light of the lounge area Rapp could tell he was dyeing it dark brown. It also looked as if he had grown a patch of hair under his bottom lip in an effort to look hip.

The guy holstered his sidearm. "Let me see what Sidorov says. Wait here."

As the first guy retreated to talk to his boss, the second guy filled his place and blocked the path. Rapp frowned and stepped forward to talk to him. "Marines . . . Army . . . Navy?"

"SEALs."

Rapp laughed. The guy was a virtual replica of Reavers. Normally SEALs were of the smaller variety. As Rapp motioned for Reavers to join him, he made eye contact with Johnson, who had finally managed to tear his eyes away from the well-endowed woman sitting on his left. Johnson's face went blank. His lips parted and then he blinked several times as if he wasn't sure what he was looking at.

Rapp's expression was not friendly. He pointed at Johnson and then gestured with two fingers for him to come to him.

Johnson got up, but instead of coming to Rapp he joined the bodyguard and Sidorov. A heated exchange ensued. Rapp couldn't hear a word, but he could tell Johnson was loudly stating his case and Sidorov appeared to be agreeing with him. The clock in Rapp's head told him they were close to the five-minute mark. He needed to wrap it up. The bodyguard left Sidorov and Johnson and came back shaking his head.

"Sorry," he said when he was within a few feet. "He says no go. He wants you guys out of his club right now."

"You don't want to do this," Rapp said ominously. "He's one client and he isn't even an American. In ten seconds I can have Director Kennedy on the phone. Ten seconds after that she'll have the chairman of Triple Canopy's board on the phone and thirty seconds after that your phone will ring and you'll be fired. And for what? Your protection order is for Sidorov. Not some rat bastard who's selling his government's secrets."

"Listen, I don't want to be caught in the middle of this."

"Then don't be. Step aside. Sixty seconds from now I'll be gone and Sidorov can bitch all he wants but it isn't going to get him anywhere. Once your bosses talk to Director Kennedy they'll give you a promotion, and they'll politely tell Sidorov to pound sand."

"I don't know."

"Well, I do. Step aside. This is National Security. Way above your pay grade. I'm doing you a favor."

The guy finally nodded and stepped back.

Rapp wasn't going to wait for him to change his mind. He moved forward quickly and entered the pit where Sidorov and his crew were sprawled out. Johnson was now one woman over from Sidorov. Rapp ignored the Russian and pointed at Johnson. "Get up." He made the same get-over-here motion with his two fingers. "Right now."

Sidorov stood, saying something in Russian before switching to English. "You are not welcome here. I must ask you to leave."

Rapp pulled out the ID case for the last time, flashed it at Sidorov, and said, "National Security. Stay out of it."

"I know who you are, Mr. Rapp. This is not Russia. The CIA has no authority to arrest people."

Rapp turned to look at Sidorov for the first time. He was a handsome man with thick brown hair parted to the side. High cheek bones and deep-set eyes. "Stay out of this. I don't care how much money you have."

"I am not someone you want to pick a fight with, Mr. Rapp."

Rapp put his nose to within a foot of Sidorov's and said, "Let me tell you something. Normally, I'm not one to follow the law, but this little asshole here is in violation of a half dozen national security statutes. Now I don't care how many cabinet members you own or how many senators you play golf with, he's off the reservation and it's my job to bring him back. So you can either get the fuck out of my way or end up in the hospital like that big ugly Russian bouncer you have out front."

Sidorov snorted, looked at Rapp with bemusement, and then took a step back. "I have heard a great many stories about you from my associates in the Russian intelligence services."

"Then you should know I'm serious."

"I see that. You are not to be deterred."

"That's right."

Sidorov looked at Rapp for a long moment and then said, "I would like to make one request of you."

"What's that?"

"A meeting."

"A meeting?" Rapp asked, not quite sure what in hell the Russian was talking about.

"With you, Mr. Rapp. There are certain things I would like to ask you."

Rapp glanced at his watch. He needed to get out of here. A concession that he would never follow through with was harmless. "I'll check my calendar, but don't expect me to roll over for a bunch of cash, like this piece of shit." Rapp pointed at Johnson.

Sidorov offered up a business card. "You are not the type of man who betrays his country, Mr. Rapp. I wouldn't be so stupid as to insult you. We have some mutual areas of interest that I think would be worth exploring."

Rapp took the card and said, "Fair enough. I'll give you a call." He walked over to a terrified Max Johnson, who grabbed the nearest girl and hung on for dear life. "Get up," Rapp ordered.

Johnson shook his head and drew the girl closer.

Rapp reached over the girl and grabbed Johnson's left ear. He gave it a good twist and then yanked Johnson to his feet. Rapp grabbed one arm, Reavers grabbed the other, and they dragged him out of the club.

CHAPTER 45

RAPP stuffed Johnson in the back of his car with Coleman. They started driving east, away from the FBI, the Justice Department, the Supreme Court, and pretty much anything else that might represent legal protection for Johnson. With each passing block the houses fell into increasing disrepair. This seemed to add to Johnson's agitated mental state. Like someone who was afraid of the water being driven farther and farther out to sea, Johnson was not able to keep his cool. He pissed and moaned and begged and pleaded the entire way.

After traveling twelve blocks they pulled into an alley just off the railroad tracks. Rapp had ordered two of Coleman's guys to scope out the place in advance. It was on the fringe of one of D.C.'s more inhospitable neighborhoods. Dilapidated, abandoned, rusted-out warehouses dotted the area around the railroad tracks. It was the perfect place to kill a man and dump his body.

The setting put Johnson over the edge. He took one look at the two tough-looking guys standing next to the van and started sobbing.

Rapp would have laughed at Johnson's less-than-noble performance, but he was experiencing the front end of a nasty headache that was no doubt the result of the punch he'd taken to the side of his head.

The alley was strewn with garbage. An abandoned mattress was leaned up against a wooden utility pole with a shredded tire sitting next to it. The floodlight that hung from the pole had long ago been shot out, probably by some local gang bangers. Coleman dragged Johnson from the backseat and stood him up. The two guys grabbed him and slapped on a pair of plastic flex cuffs. Johnson stood motionless for a moment looking at the cuffs, trying to decide if this was a good or bad development.

With moist eyes and a pleading voice he said, "Mitch, please don't do this. There are things you don't know. You have to give me a chance to explain myself. I haven't done anything for Sidorov. I only—"

Johnson never finished the sentence because Rapp unleashed a backhanded slap that caught him flush on the side of the face. In the relative quiet of the alley it sounded like a thunderclap. "Shut up and listen," Rapp said. "If I hear another fucking lie come out of your mouth I'm going to kill you right here." Rapp pointed at the ground. "Right here in this frickin' alley with ratshit all over the place and God only knows what else."

"But . . . people saw me leave with you. You can't . . ."

Rapp raised his hand again, and it was enough to silence Johnson. "I don't know if you've noticed, but people are a little more concerned about getting hit by another terrorist attack. Nobody gives a shit about you. You're a retired rent-a-cop who was whoring himself out to a Russian billionaire."

"That's not true. I have friends," he stammered, "who I was working with. Important people who will want to know what happened to me."

Rapp wanted to mention Glen Adams, but didn't. "You're a fucking traitor and a liar and you'll say whatever you think will save your miserable ass, but you've got one problem, Max. I don't need a polygraph to figure out if you're bullshitting me. Unlike you, I've spent my entire career in the field. I don't have a support staff and the latest and greatest technology to get the job done."

"I don't have anything against you. I've always admired you."

"See, now that's an interesting example right there," Rapp said to Coleman. "He didn't lie, but he didn't tell the truth. He may not have anything against me specifically, and he probably has a grudging respect for some of the things I've done. But I'll bet you my entire pension that he thinks I'm a cowboy, and that I don't give the other people at Langley enough credit."

"Which is a true statement," Coleman said.

"Exactly, but he's either too afraid to say it because he thinks I'll hurt him or he's a pathological liar, in which case we're all wasting our time. So which is it?" Rapp asked Johnson.

Johnson was confused. "I don't understand."

"Are you too big a coward to tell me the truth, or are you a pathological liar?"

"I . . ." he stammered, "I'm neither. I'm just really, really scared right now. This isn't fair."

"There is no fair in espionage, you asshole. This field shit isn't as fun as it looks, is it? A little easier hanging behind the secure perimeter of Langley where you're the only sheriff in town, isn't it?"

"It's not how it looks. I wasn't doing anything wrong."

Rapp wanted to reach out and choke him. Tell him to hand over the tapes that he'd made from Lewis's office, but he needed to keep that ace buried in the hole for a while. Maybe forever. His voice dripping with sarcasm, Rapp said, "Really? I'm sure a good-looking billionaire like Sidorov is hanging out with you because you're a real hit with the ladies, right?"

Johnson didn't answer.

"Tell me . . . did you bother to inform Langley about your new friend?" Rapp knew he hadn't, but asked anyway.

"I'm not in bed with him."

"Answer my question."

"I told certain people . . . but nothing had been put in writing. I was waiting to see how serious things got."

Rapp glanced at Coleman and then without bothering to make eye contact with Johnson, he unleashed another vicious backhanded slap. Johnson yelped like a kid. Rapp slid his 9mm Glock from his holster and began screwing the black cylindrical silencer onto the end. "Here's how this works. Left foot . . . right foot . . . left knee . . . right knee. Most guys pass out when you get to the first knee. You . . . I don't think you'll make it past the second foot." Rapp pointed the gun at Johnson's left foot and took aim.

"Wait!" Johnson screamed. "I was working for him, all right? But it was all background stuff. Nothing that had anything to do with National Security."

"Again, a half truth," Rapp said. "You were working for him, but don't try to make it sound like you were doing anything remotely legal."

"I never said legal."

Rapp looked down. Took aim and fired the weapon. A small hole appeared on the outside of Jonson's left foot. A second later, blood began oozing out of the puncture and then Johnson started screaming. One of Coleman's guys had a rag ready to go and he shoved it into Johnson's mouth.

Rapp checked his watch. All four men stood there watching Johnson writhe in pain. Fifteen seconds later Rapp pulled the rag out of Johnson's mouth. Before he could ask another question Johnson began blabbing. Rapp listened to a good minute of it. Johnson had been doing nothing even remotely legal for Sidorov, and if the power players in Washington found out what he'd been up to they would gladly pay Rapp every penny in their war chests to have the problem dealt with in a very final way.

Rapp took the rag and shoved it back into Johnson's mouth. He walked to the rear of the van and Coleman followed him. "Take him to the Quarry, put him in a cell, and give him a notepad and a pen. Have him write it all down. Chapter and verse. Everything he's done for Sidorov."

"Can I dangle a carrot?"

"Hell, yeah. Dangle it all you want. Hit him over the head with it. I don't care."

Coleman looked doubtful. "Can I dangle it in good conscience?"

"Hell, yeah. This little snake has some talent. If I can trust him, I'd rather have him working for us than freelancing."

"Shooting him in the foot may not have been the best way of recruiting him."

Rapp shook off the concern. "I shot him through the outside of the foot. No permanent damage. In two weeks he'll be completely healed."

"Still . . ." Coleman gave him a disapproving frown.

"I still might kill him, so don't go all Naval Academy on me."

"A lot of people saw you tonight. If he vanishes, there will be questions."

"It wouldn't be the first time, and once people find out what he was doing, they might not look so hard to find him."

"Should I call Doc?"

"No." Rapp shook his head. "I want to keep him out of it for now. Have Johnson write down everything he can think of. Every single time he's strayed off the reservation."

"You think there's more than just this Sidorov thing and the job he was doing for Adams?"

"Who knows, but this could be a gold mine. Tell the boys to give him a little Vicodin. Just enough to take the edge off, but keep him awake. I'll be back out there a bit before seven and I want him edgy." Rapp leaned back and looked around the corner of the van. Johnson was balancing on one foot and crying. Rapp shook his head in disgust and said, "And if he's dumb enough to hold back on the little dirty op he was running with Adams . . . well, then you're going to have a hard time talking me out of killing him."

CHAPTER 46

FAIRFAX COUNTY, VIRGINIA

RAPP woke up at five-thirty, looked around his Spartan bedroom and thought of his dog. He supposed most therapists would tell him that was progress, since his deceased wife wasn't the first thing on his mind. Time really was the great healer. Not that he was healed, but he was at least coping better. Before Anna, he never remembered waking up and feeling alone. He'd never really been that attached to anyone. Now waking up in an empty house, even one that she had never lived in, didn't feel right. Hence missing Shirley the mutt.

More often than not the border collie mix stayed with the Kennedys where Irene's son Tommy would take care of her. Rapp paid him at first, but after a while Tommy wouldn't let him. He'd grown too attached to Shirley and with Rapp's awkward travel schedule she stayed with Tommy more than she stayed with him. She was a great dog. Smart as hell and very loyal. Rapp wished people were more like her.

Rapp really wasn't one to lie around and wallow in his own misery, and he had a lot to do, so he rolled out of bed and hit the floor. The first ten pushups were always slow. He had to get the blood moving through the shoulders first. This morning he had the added thrill of a throbbing skull. The next forty were done at a precise clip. Every time he lowered his chest and hit the bottom, the pain in his left temple peaked and he was reminded of the big Russian who had almost knocked his head off. Rapp smiled, though, because as bad as he felt, the bouncer would be far worse this morning. That was the way of the competitive mind. As long as you came out on top, all pain was manageable.

After the pushups, Rapp flipped over and rattled off a hundred situps and then he was off to the shower. He stood under the hot water barely moving for five minutes, the day's events cascading through his mind like the water down his back. It was often the clearest five minutes of his day. Oxygenated blood coursing through his brain. Hot water warming his muscles. The sound of the water falling on the tile. No phones, no radios, no TV, no internet, no one around to interrupt his thoughts. It was the perfect way to start any day, and especially this one.

He had stopped by Kennedy's house on the way home. She wasn't much of a sleeper, and he knew she'd be waiting to hear about the meeting with their French and British allies. Rapp realized that was probably why he'd woken up with Shirley on his mind. She'd sat next to him while he filled his boss in on the high points and conveyed George Butler's concerns about his man in Cuba. Kennedy had been in the same spot many times. Countless hours and resources went into recruiting well-placed sources. Once compromised, they were out of the game, never to be used again in a future conflict. Those experiences made her not so willing to share information with agencies that might not treat it with the delicacy it deserved. They agreed to sit on it for a day or two and see if they could come up with a plausible solution. Rapp was already thinking of one, but it was too half-baked to share it with Kennedy. He'd have to let it cook for a while.

Then, when he got up to leave, Shirley ran back into Tommy's room and he remembered standing there for a brief moment feeling jilted. Looking back on it this morning it made him smile. Tommy was a good kid and Shirley was a lucky dog. Now, standing under the hot water, he was trying to punch holes in his own plan. As with anything in his business there were certain risks. The question was, were they worth it? After he'd fleshed it out a bit more he decided to table the idea and get back to it later. He was going to be doing a fair amount of driving today and after he made it through a busy morning he'd have some time later to devote to it. The first item to be checked off, however, was Max Johnson. And if the idiot knew what was good for him, he'd already have filled a notepad with his professional sins.

The rock quarry was situated thirty odd miles west of D.C. Few people knew of its storied history, and for the people who now used it, that was just fine. It was a relic from the Cold War—one of the few places that hadn't been declassified and leaked to the press, and that was due solely to the fact that it had never been on the books to begin with, and no politician in the last thirty years had been informed of its existence. It also helped that even at the height of the Cold War the place was rarely used. Due to poor planning, the site was at the convergence of two underground streams, which meant that it flooded frequently. Some upgrades had been made in recent years. More sump pumps were installed as well as several dehumidifiers and a backup generator, but even so, the place was like a concrete petri dish. The men who worked there liked to joke that they didn't have to worry about Congress blowing the whistle on them, it was OSHA who would shut them down for unhealthy working conditions. Fortunately, the men and the women of the clandestine service were used to working in less than ideal situations.

The place was laid out like an old World War II command bunker, with hallways branching out like a network of arteries. Rapp found Coleman napping in one of the bunkrooms and woke him with a firm shake and a cup of coffee. Coleman swung his feet onto the cold floor and took the mug from Rapp. After a few sips he scratched his blond hair and began to fill Rapp in on what had been an interesting night. One of the guys fetched the notepad and handed it to Rapp, while Coleman hit the high points.

Rapp tried to decipher the chicken scratch. "What about bugging Doc's office?"

Coleman grinned. "I didn't push him on it. I thought you'd want to save it for the shock value."

Rapp nodded. He did.

"He noted it, but it's pretty lame. All he says in there is that he's done a little consulting for Langley's inspector general."

"Is he aware that Adams supposedly left the country?"

"No." Coleman went on to fill him in on a few more things.

Rapp continued to speed-read his way through the notes. After about ten pages, he looked up at Coleman and said, "He's been a busy beaver."

"I'd say so. You gotta hand it to him. He's pretty good at this surveillance game. My guys tell me his equipment is out of this world. Shit they've never seen before."

Rapp thought about that and filed it away. Maybe the idiot was worth saving. He checked his watch and said, "Anything else before I go in there? I'm on a tight schedule."

"I went to bed around five, but up until then it was a full-blown pity party. He definitely sees himself as the victim. He's really upset about being shot. He was in a lot of pain. I think he'd probably crawl out of his own skin for a painkiller right about now."

"Good. Where are they?"

Coleman walked over to a metal file cabinet, yanked it open with a screech, grabbed the red bottle, and handed it to Rapp. Rapp took the pills and a bottle of water and went down the long hallway to the cells. He punched in the code for the cipher lock on the door and pulled it open. There were two cells on the left and two on the right with heavy steel doors that looked as if they might have been salvaged from a battleship. The place was not permanently wired for audio and sound. The humidity wreaked havoc on the a/v equipment, so Rapp carried his own device. It was only a precaution, in case he missed something and needed to play it back later. More than likely, though, he would trash the recording the second the meeting was over.

Rapp stopped at the first door on the left and pulled back the heavy slide on the peephole. Johnson was sitting back with his bandaged foot on the table. In front of him was another yellow legal pad and a pen. Rapp threw the dead bolt on the door and opened it. Coleman's guy left without saying a word. Rapp set the bottle of water on the table and shook the container of painkillers back and forth to get Johnson's attention.

"You ready for another one of these?"

Johnson held out his hand. "Yes."

Rapp looked at the sweat on his upper lip and said, "In a minute."

Johnson started to squirm and looked at his foot with deep concern.

"We just have to go over a few things first."

Johnson moaned and banged his fist on the table. "Come on. Just give me a pill."

Rapp stared him down and asked, "What do you know about me?"

"I know you shot me in the foot last night for no good reason. That's what I know about you."

Rapp could see what Coleman meant now by the pity party thing. "In the broader sense, Max, what is my reputation as you know it?"

He looked around the room nervously and shrugged his shoulders.

Rapp took off his suit jacket and draped it on the back of the chair. He rested his hand on his gun and said. "It's not a trick question, Max. Honesty is what's important this morning. I don't care if you insult me, just tell me the truth. That's the only way I'll let you walk out of here. Do you understand me?"

"I don't know. This is so fucked up."

"There's nothing to think about," Rapp said a bit more forcefully. "The truth is the truth and a fucking lie is a fucking lie, and if I think you're lying to me, we're going to start up that game again."

"What game?" Johnson said in genuine confusion.

Rapp drew his gun for effect and said, "Left foot, right foot, left knee, right knee."

Johnson buried his face in his hands.

"So remember," Rapp said, "the truth. Now for the second time . . . What is my reputation?"

Johnson shrugged his shoulders. "I don't know . . . you've killed a lot of people."

Rapp tried to be objective. "All things considered I guess that would be a true statement."

"And after last night," Johnson added quickly, "I don't doubt it for a moment. I mean what the hell . . . I was at Langley before you were. I put in my twenty-five years. I served. What you did last night was wrong. I mean, that's no way to treat a fellow professional."

Rapp was glad he'd gotten five hours of sack time, because Johnson was a perfect example of what happened to the human mind if deprived of sleep. Add to that the fact that he probably hadn't felt real pain since he was a kid, and you had a very agitated fifty-six-year-old man. "So let's do a quick recap. For the last year, you've been whoring yourself out to whoever will pay you. You've broken dozens of laws. You've illegally spied on officials in your own government—"

"Illegal!" Johnson scoffed. "What would you call this? You don't exactly play by the rules."

"I sure don't, but there's a big difference between what I do and what you do."

"Maybe in your mind."

"Really . . . why don't you tell me how much money I've made breaking the law during the course of my career?"

Johnson squirmed in his seat.

"I'm not into your relativism, Max. I do this job because I think it's important. I do it because narcissistic fucks like you care more about your own ego and making a buck than our national security. What really pisses me off, though, is that you're the same assholes who when the next 9/11 happens, will all sit around pointing your fingers at guys like me and saying I didn't do enough to protect the country. Well, I'm fed up, Max. I'm sick of swimming upstream. I've spent the last two days running around dealing with bullshit like this. Like you. Greedy fucking children, who don't give a shit about anyone or anything other than yourselves."

"That's not true."

"Really?" Rapp folded his arms across his chest. "You call yourself a fellow professional, Max. Well, if you really think you're a professional, then you know damn well that you wandered way off the reservation and I have every right to put a bullet in your head."

"That's not true . . . there are things . . . things you don't know about."

"Bullshit!" Rapp yelled. Adams had tried the same line on him. "It's your choice, Max. Are you going to repent with all your heart and soul, or am I going to put a bullet in your head? Your choice!"

CHAPTER 47

THIS was not Rapp's first séance, as they liked to say in the business. There were a couple of books out there on how to properly interrogate a prisoner, but they were pretty remedial. The more nasty stuff could be found in the CIA's Human Resource Exploitation Training Manual or the KUBARK Counterintelligence Interrogation Manual. This was stuff that the CIA had authored decades earlier when people were either brave enough or crazy enough to put such things in writing. Rapp had read both a long time ago, and found them to be useful in the sense that they offered an outline, but it was all a little bit like reading about a baseball swing. Most people can read and easily understand the swing, but less than one percent of one percent of the population can actually step into the batter's box and hit a ninety-mile-an-hour fastball.

Rapp had no doubt that Johnson was scared to death of him. But was he scared enough to actually tell the truth? With most people, the fear of death or severe pain was all it took, and as long as you could check out the story they would tell you the truth, because if they lied, you went back into the room and pushed whatever button worked.

Johnson looked up at Rapp and in a convincing voice said, "I want to tell the truth."

Now came the sticky part. With Johnson, the crux of the problem was that he had lived by a double standard for so long that he thought lying was his birthright. He was the great inquisitor, charged with making sure Langley's people played by the rules. And if he had to break the rules to catch them, then so be it. He was above it all. The rules were for the little people. It was no wonder he and Glen Adams had become bosom buddies. So Rapp had to come at this one from a slightly different angle.

"I have to be honest with you. I have a long day in front of me. I have to go pick up a friend this morning who's all fucked in the head because he's been working his ass off and he's come within a fraction of losing his life twice in the past year, and his job is made five times harder than it should be because he's got assholes like you running around. And then I have to get up to the Hill and listen to all those blowhards on the Judiciary Committee grill me because I didn't treat some terrorist with kid gloves and then after that I have to get over to the White House and tell the president that I either killed you, like he asked me to do, or I spared your life and went against his orders."

"The president ordered you to kill me?" Johnson's eyes were wide with fear and disbelief.

"After what happened last week, the president has decided this War on Terror is not just a campaign slogan. He's dealing with the aftermath of the attacks, trying to find the guys who are still at large and make those who helped them pay, and in the midst of all of that he finds out that the CIA's inspector general has left the country and flown to fucking Caracas, Venezuela, of all places." Rapp saw the surprise in Johnson's eyes. "That's right. Your old buddy Glen Adams. We've been on to him for about a month now. Someone slipped up, he got spooked, and he bolted. Turns out he's been working for that thug Chavez for the past four years."

"Hugo Chavez?"

"None other. We started going through his stuff and unfortunately your name was all over the place."

Johnson swallowed hard.

"That's how we got on your tail. We didn't know shit about Sidorov and all these other pet projects you had going."

"People saw me last night. A lot of people." Johnson looked up and pointed at Rapp. "And they saw you, too."

"Russians. All of them. They play by a different set of rules. They respect this." Rapp waved his gun around. "They know I'll hunt them down and put a bullet in their head. A guy like Sidorov . . . he has enough problems. The last thing he wants is a guy like me hounding him."

"Those two security guys," Johnson said with a "got you" expression on his face. "They were American. They saw me. They saw you drag me out of the club."

"You mean the two guys from Triple Canopy? The former Special Forces guys? We already talked to them. Gave them the rap sheet on what you've been up to. They wanted to know if they could help with the interrogation. I told them I'd see how things went this morning." Rapp checked his watch. It was six-fifty-six. "You've got thirty minutes to convince me that I should stay your execution."

Johnson was staring off into the distance with a blank expression on his face.

"Do you understand what I just said?"

"I can't believe he was working for Hugo Chavez."

Rapp didn't show it, but he was smiling inside. Maybe there was a bit of a patriot still in the man. "None of us are too pleased about it. Now did you understand what I just said?"

"Yes."

"I'm not sure you did, so I'm going to make it real clear. The president has told me to kill you. He's furious that a guy with Adams's security clearance has defected. Between you and me, he's horrified that little sausage Chavez is going to parade Adams in front of the cameras.

He knows you helped Adams collect a lot of his information." Rapp shrugged. "He can't get his hands on Adams, so you're the next best thing."

"I didn't know he was working for Chavez."

"Max," Rapp said with a heavy sigh, "I'd like to feel some sympathy for you, but it's not like you didn't know you were breaking the law. You climbed into bed with a rat bastard and you were caught. Now . . . the only chance you have of living a minute past seven-thirty is if you put all your cards on the table. I know this won't be easy for you because you're a professional liar. You're going to have to fight your instincts. If I think you're lying, and trust me, I'll know when you are, the gun comes out and we do the left foot, right foot thing. Understand?"

"And if I tell you the truth?"

Rapp grinned. "Let's just say, there are a few people around here who think you're pretty good at what you do."

"What's that supposed to mean?"

"It means, if you are completely honest and you hold nothing back, I might consider letting you live. And if I think I can trust you, I might even give you a job."

There was a genuine glimmer of hope in his eyes. Johnson sat up a little straighter like a dog ready to please. "All right. I think I understand."

"Let's hear it, and remember, no lies."

"All right . . . about six months ago Glen came to me and explained his suspicions about what you and Irene were up to. He said that I was the only one who would understand his situation. That if you were going to catch someone who was breaking the law, you couldn't fight fair. You had to be willing to break the rules yourself."

"And you agreed," Rapp said in a reasonable tone, wanting to help him along.

"Yes." Johnson started to speak but stopped.

"Fight it," Rapp said. "Your only chance is to tell the truth."

"What if it pisses you off?"

"I'll deal with it."

"By shooting me in the foot?"

Rapp shook his head. "Only if you lie to me. So you decided to go to work for him . . ." Rapp made a rolling motion with his hand, telling him to pick up the story.

"It started out pretty simple. He wanted me to bug an office. I didn't even know who the guy was."

Rapp knew immediately that it was a lie. He pointed the gun at Johnson's bandaged foot and said, "Fight it."

"All right," he said quickly, "I knew who he was, but I'd never met him."

"Go on."

"His name is Thomas Lewis. He's a shrink. He's kind of the go-to therapist for the bigwigs on the seventh floor. Has a practice out by Tyson's Corner."

"I'm familiar with him."

"Well . . . we bugged his office."

"That's real classy."

"I wasn't calling the shots. I was merely following orders."

"Like me," Rapp said. "The president wants me to kill you, so who am I to question him. I should probably just kill you right now and get it over with."

"Please let me explain. I thought it was a little underhanded."

"But you also thought it was brilliant."

Johnson hesitated and then said, "Kind of."

"So how'd you do it?" Rapp asked.

"I set up a passive system in a nearby office and started recording. I'd go back to the place every couple of weeks to check on the equipment, but it was pretty much handled off-site. The recordings were uploaded to a server every day. I'd put them on a disk and hand them over."

"Did you ever listen to any?"

Johnson started to say no, but caught himself. "A few, but not many."

"Seriously."

"Yeah. It might sound interesting, but it's boring as hell."

"How many copies?" Rapp asked casually.

"I gave one to Adams and the other one is up on the secure server."

Rapp nodded and picked up the bottle of painkillers. He popped the top and took out two pills. He held them in front of Johnson and said, "You know Marcus Dumond?"

"Yes," Johnson snorted. "He's a disrespectful little shit."

"Not really. Just seems that way because he's so much smarter than the rest of us. At any rate he was telling me the other day that he has a new software program that can tell how many times something has been copied. Now Marcus is at your office right now. If I call him up and ask him to find out how many times this stuff was copied and he comes back with something other than two . . . well . . . let's just say you and I will be finished. So think real hard. How many copies did you make?"

Johnson thought about it for a long moment and then said, "Three. I think there are actually three copies."

Rapp set the pills on the table and slid the bottle of water over. "Good answer." Rapp watched as Johnson popped the pills in his mouth and took a swig of water. "That office you leased?"

Jonson nodded.

"Third floor, directly across the courtyard from Lewis's office. We already have all your equipment." Rapp saw the surprise wash across Johnson's face. "I know more shit about you than you can even begin to imagine, Max. You fucking hold back on me one more time and this will get really ugly. I mean Saddam Hussein, third world, shove a thermometer up your pecker and smack it with a hammer ugly. Shove your head in a bucket full of your own shit ugly. That's what we do to traitors."

"I'm sorry," Johnson said in a shaky voice.

"Sorry doesn't fucking cut it, Max. You need to get it though your head that you have one shot at this."

"I understand."

"Good, because the next time I ask you for a number, you better be damn sure it's the right one."

"I will. I promise."

Rapp wasn't so sure, but maybe with a little reprogramming they could get him back on the right team. He'd never pull a Saddam Hussein on him, but he might show him a few photos just to scare the piss out of him. "All right, now where are these copies?"

CHAPTER 48

MCLEAN, VIRGINIA

THE house was on a nice tree-lined street in North Arlington, not far from where Rapp had grown up. It was upscale, but not obnoxious. Lots of two-story colonials and federal style houses with well-kept lawns. Lawyers, lobbyists, and government contractors lived in the neighborhood. Jobs that fed out of the bottomless trough of federal funds. Very few civil servants lived in the neighborhood, unless, like Nash, their spouse worked in the private sector.

Rapp pulled up in front of the house a few minutes before eight and threw the gearshift into park. He looked up the sidewalk at the white front door and imagined what was going on inside. Kennedy had called Nash before bed and told him he would be traveling with her for most of the day. They had a closed meeting on the Hill with the Judiciary Committee and then a briefing with the president. If Nash had told Kennedy about his problem with Rapp she had failed to pass it along. Rapp undid his seat belt and climbed out of the car. As he started up the walk he wondered if Nash might take a swing at him. Rapp hoped he'd gotten a little sleep and regained some of his senses.

Rapp hit the doorbell and then stepped off the front stoop. If Nash was still pissed it was best to have a little room to maneuver. A few seconds later Maggie answered the door. She had raven-black hair, a button nose, and bright blue eyes, all set against smooth alabaster skin. She was already dolled up for the big day, dressed in a black pencil skirt and white cotton blouse with a shirred waist. Her jet-black hair was slicked back in a perfect high ponytail that both showed off her gorgeous face and gave her a little bit of that corporate dominatrix look that told men to tread carefully. You would never guess by looking at her that she'd given birth to four kids.

Maggie flashed Rapp a nice smile and a conspiratorial wink. "Mitch, what a nice surprise." She offered her cheek.

Rapp kissed it and whispered, "How's he doing?"

"He doesn't have a clue." Then in a louder voice she said, "Come on in." Maggie led him down the hallway. "We're getting the kids ready for school."

"Good, I was hoping I'd catch them."

As Rapp entered the kitchen four faces lit up as if it were Christmas and one face turned so sour you would have guessed his mortal enemy had just walked in the room. Shannon, the fifteen-year-old daughter, jumped up from the kitchen table and threw her arms out. "Uncle Mitch." She gave Rapp a hug and said, "Guess what?" Before Rapp had a chance to answer she said, "I get my permit Saturday!"

It had been a long time since Rapp had gone through that teenage right of passage, but she was obviously extremely excited at the prospect of being able to drive. "Great."

"Will you take me driving?"

"Absolutely." Rapp reached out and rubbed the head of Jack, the ten-year-old brain child, who was simultaneously working on a bowl of cereal and watching *Sports Center*. Maggie was from Boston and the kids were all big Red Sox fans, so Rapp asked, "How are your Yankees doing?"

"Yeah, right," Jack replied. "They're a bunch of overpaid prima donnas."

"Sounds like you're talking about the Red Sox."

Maggie was coming back from the other side of the kitchen with a fresh cup of black coffee. "Don't make me throw this on you." She handed the mug to Rapp, just as Charlie, the one-year-old, started banging on the tray of his high chair.

Rapp took the mug and turned to face Charlie, who was looking up at him with his big brown eyes. He had an expectant smile on his sloppy, food-caked lips. "Sorry, little man. I was getting to you." Rapp bent over and kissed the top of his head. When he straightened up he looked at Rory, who was sitting on the other side of the table. The thirteen-year-old had a plate of Pop Tarts and an open book in front of him. "How'd it go last weekend?"

Rory looked up with a barely concealed grin. "We won all three matches."

Without looking away from the TV, Jack said, "He had fourteen goals. No one could stop him."

"Nice," Rapp said. Rory was a phenomenal athlete. Rapp had been an All-American lacrosse star at Syracuse and took great joy in watching Rory play. The kid was a man child on the pitch and had the potential to play at the highest levels.

"We play again Saturday," Rory said, dropping a hint.

"Great . . . I'll try to make it." Rapp turned his attention away from the kids to Mr. Sourpuss, who was standing on the other side of the kitchen. "Irene wanted me to pick you up." He checked his watch. "She wants us to get there early so we can go over a few things."

"I can drive myself," Nash said gruffly.

"Still pouting, I see."

Maggie cleared her throat extra-loud and said, "Come on, kids. Let's go. It's time to load up." She took a washcloth to Charlie's face and then unhooked and plucked him out of the chair. She handed him off to Rapp and said, "He needs to be dropped off at day care. Make sure Grumpy gets the car seat from the back of the van." She kissed Charlie and Mitch and then walked over to her husband, kissed him, and said, "I love you. Be safe and have a great day. I'll call you later."

Thirty seconds later she was gone with the kids and Rapp was standing in the kitchen with Charlie in one hand and a mug of coffee in the other. Nash was leaning against the far counter looking at Rapp as if he was trying to figure out if he could take a swing at him and not hurt Charlie.

Nash took a sip of coffee and said, "I have a bruise on my chest."

This wasn't Rapp's thing—handling people with kid gloves. He was tempted to put Charlie back in the high chair and kick his dad's ass, but that would be a little shortsighted. The only thing that mattered today was getting Nash to the White House. Rapp swallowed his pride, ignored every code he'd ever learned about leading warriors, and said, "I'm sorry. I wish it hadn't come to that."

"Come to that . . . that's your apology."

Rapp sighed. "Listen . . . let's talk in the car. There are some things I need to say to you, and . . ."

"And what?"

"When was the last time your house was swept?"

"Probably a month ago."

"We'll talk in the car." Rapp's word was final.

They left through the side door. Nash handed Rapp a diaper bag and walked over to the two-car detached garage to grab the car seat. Charlie saw the neighbor's cat and about jumped out of Rapp's arms. He pointed and bounced and yelled and when none of that worked he grabbed a fist full of Rapp's hair and gave it a good yank. Rapp was so amused by the kid's determination that he just laughed.

Once Nash had finished wrestling with the car seat, they strapped Charlie in and were off. Nash didn't speak for the first minute. When they got to Glebe Road, Rapp said, "I know you're mad at me, but you have to tell me where we're going."

"We're going to the Dirksen Senate Office Building. You know where it is."

Rapp thought, *Holy cow, he really is losing his mind.* Then he jerked his head toward the backseat and said, "Charlie's day care."

"Oh, take a left."

Rapp pulled onto Glebe and said, "Listen . . . I'm not the easiest guy to work with, and neither is Stan, but you have to take a little ownership in this."

"In what?" Nash asked, obviously irritated.

"You think I knocked you on your ass yesterday because I'm frustrated with my job?"

"Maybe."

Rapp shook his head. "I've known you for how long . . . and I haven't once laid a hand you . . . other than that time in the Kush when I dragged your shot-up ass out of the line of fire." Rapp looked sideways at Nash. "It'd be nice if you kept that one in mind before you condemned me to hell."

Nash shook his head and looked out the passenger-side window.

Rapp scoffed. "That's it. You've got no reply to that one. I risked my ass to save your ungrateful ass and you've got nothing to say."

"I knew you were going to hold that one over my head for the rest of my life."

"That's usually the way it works when you save someone's life, Mike. To tell you the truth I didn't think about it until yesterday. When you were being so unreasonable."

"Unreasonable . . . me?"

"That's right, Mike. You're a professional. You know better than anyone that in this day and age you can't say shit, because it might get recorded. But that didn't stop you from coming unhinged yesterday. I warned you twice, but you just kept on."

"And then you hit me."

"You're damn right I did, and I'd do it again. This shit is bigger than you and me, and you knew that when you signed up. You were the one who came to me and said you were sick of fighting a war with one hand tied behind your back."

Nash was silent for a few blocks. Charlie hummed away in the backseat and then finally Nash said, "I'm not ungrateful, but I'm not going to throw my conscience out the window. You have no right . . . Stan has no right to—"

"Easy," Rapp said, cutting him off. "Slow down before you make a fool of yourself again. I'm not asking you to sell your soul."

"Well it sure does seem like it."

"Just hear me out for a minute. I spoke with Stan and filled him in on your situation."

"Great," Nash moaned. "I suppose you told him you knocked me on my ass."

"I did."

"Crap. I'm never going to hear the end of this."

"Probably not, but that's not what's important."

Nash stared straight ahead. "What did he say?"

"He said the fact that I was able to knock you on your ass with one palm strike is all the proof he needs that you need to take a sabbatical."

Nash was a state high school wrestling champ in Pennsylvania and had boxed in the Marine Corps. His little altercation with Rapp had been the shortest fight of his life. His sternum hurt like hell, and his ego was ten times worse. "Yeah . . . well, I haven't had a lot of sleep lately."

Rapp could have made any one of a dozen retorts but none of them would have been helpful. This morning wasn't about winning the argument and getting a stubborn friend to do the impossible, which was to admit he'd been wrong. It was about advancing the ball toward the goal line. "All of us have been under a lot of stress lately. You probably more than most of us. Chris was your guy. The way he was taken out really sucked, and then there was Jessica and the rest of the folks you knew in the NCTC. Stan's never set foot in the place, and I don't get in there very often, but you knew those people. I'm not a heartless bastard. I understand why you're a little messed up, but in this line of work, there's no coddling. You need to take a few weeks off . . . take 'em, but you have to honor your promises and keep your mouth shut."

"And if I take a week off and I still disagree with you and Stan, where does that leave us? Do I just ignore my conscience and let you guys do something that I think is a mistake?"

"No," Rapp said. "In fact, I think Stan has a solution."

"Let me guess . . . it involves a Kimber 1911 and a wood chipper."

"No." Rapp shook his head and smiled at the visual. "He's says it's your call."

"What's my call?" Nash asked with a frown.

"Whether that unethical bastard ever sees daylight again."

"Bullshit."

"Nope . . . Stan says he's sick of doing all the heavy lifting. Says he's sick of you bitching about the size of the hole."

"The size of the hole?" Nash asked, not understanding what Hurley meant.

"Yep . . . he says it's your turn to grab a shovel and start digging. He's done. He says it's your call."

"My call about what?"

"On what we're going to do with that rat bastard who leaked our operation. The one that got Chris Johnson killed and quite possibly another 187 Americans."

Nash turned his head slowly and looked out the window. His thoughts turned to Chris Johnson. The retired Army Ranger had been Nash's first recruit. The twenty-nine-year-old had gone completely off the grid, for nearly a year, while he infiltrated one of D.C.'s most radical mosques. He was on the verge of exposing the cell that had pulled off the attacks only a week ago, when a story appeared in the *Post* that accused the CIA of illegally running surveillance on a half dozen East Coast mosques. The day after the article appeared, Johnson was discovered, tortured and killed by the Lion of al Qaeda and his merry band of terrorists.

Without looking at Rapp he asked, "When do you want my decision?"

"Stan says you have a good week before we're done with the debriefing."

A week, Nash thought. Seven lousy days to decide a man's fate. A man whom he hated. What in the hell had he gotten himself into?

CHAPTER 49

CAPITOL HILL

SENATOR Barbara Lonsdale walked down the broad hallway of the Dirksen Senate Office Building and stopped at a nondescript door. She tapped on it once with her dainty hand and then entered. Mitch Rapp was in the corner talking to Irene Kennedy and Mike Nash was in the other corner talking to a couple of Langley's legal eagles. All five stopped and turned their attention to the outgoing chairman of the Judiciary Committee. In one week's time Lonsdale's entire bearing had changed. Rapp likened it to the conversion of a New York limousine liberal who gets mugged and then the next day tears up her ACLU card, buys a gun, and joins the neighborhood watch group.

Lonsdale looked at the two lawyers and said, "Gentlemen, would you please excuse us for a minute?"

The lawyers looked to Kennedy to see if it was okay. The CIA director gave her consent with a nod.

"Why don't you go into the committee room," Lonsdale advised. "We'll be starting any minute."

The two men picked up their briefcases and left through the door opposite the one through which Lonsdale had just entered.

Once they were gone and the door was closed Lonsdale slapped a plain white envelope against her hand and said, "Well . . . this is it."

"Are you sure you want to go through with it?" Kennedy asked. Lonsdale had made a deal to resign her chairmanship of Judiciary in return for control of the Intelligence Committee.

Without hesitation Lonsdale said, "Yes."

Rapp said, "It's not too late." He still wasn't convinced she couldn't do them more good staying right where she was.

"I'll still be on the committee, so I can keep an eye on things."

"But you won't be in control," Rapp said.

Lonsdale smiled. "I'll still have my seniority. I'll be one chair over from the gavel. I know this committee better than anyone. The staff is loyal to me. They all liked Ralph." Her voice trailed off at the mention of her chief of staff, who had been killed in the explosion at the Monocle along with seven senators and a whole bunch of high-level staffers, lawyers, and lobbyists.

"The looneys on the far left are already beating you up," Nash chimed in. "A couple of them have started raising money to challenge you in your next primary."

"It's America. They have every right to do it and I have every right to ignore them. Listening to the idiots is what got me into this mess."

"I'm just saying this isn't going to be easy for you," Nash said. "We could have been a little more subtle about it. Having them think you were still their champion might not have been the worst move."

Lonsdale dismissed his concerns with the wave of a hand. "Those people will never be happy. And besides, playing the game of double agent isn't my style. I'm better out front drawing fire. It's where I shine. If people want to criticize you three, they're going to have to come through me first, or at least expect that I will come back at them fast and furious."

This stuff was difficult to quantify for Rapp. On some level he knew it mattered, but at the end of the day it was all a bunch of words.

He said so, and Lonsdale replied by saying, "Words mean a lot in this town, and don't forget, I'm not the only senator who has undergone this conversion under fire. Others have gravitated to a similar position. I'm not alone. Besides," she said in a more upbeat tone, "I can handle it. Missouri might be a blue state, but we're big on defense. In light of recent developments I think my constituents will understand why I changed my position."

"I think it's a good move, Barb," Kennedy said. "The press will not be able to ignore that one of the CIA's most steadfast critics has now become a champion of the Agency. Thank you."

"You're welcome. Now," she said as she checked her watch, "we're due to start in two minutes. Here's the lay of the land. I've spoken to twelve of the nineteen members." She caught herself. Two of her fellow committee members had been killed in the attack on the Monocle. "Twelve of the seventeen members. Only three that I can think of are planning to make a real stink about this. Maybe five at the most."

Rapp said, "Let me guess . . . Ogden?"

"She's leading the charge," Lonsdale said. Ogden was the senior senator from California. "As you know, this will be a closed meeting, but we all know how that works. This small block of dissenters will begin to selectively leak their side of the story as soon as the meeting is over, so be careful what you say in there. Don't admit to anything that could lead to a referral to the Justice Department. I've already signed an affidavit that backs up your story." With a shrug she added, "If Senator Ogden and her little cabal want to side with a terrorist . . . well that's a fight I don't think they will win in this climate, but we still have to be careful."

Lonsdale covered a few more things and then said, "You should head in. I'll follow shortly." As the group began to move toward the door Lonsdale said, "Mitch, hang back for a second. I want to talk to you about something."

Rapp stopped and waited as Lonsdale walked around the far side of the conference table. As she drew near she took the white envelope she'd been holding and handed it over to Rapp. He took it and asked, "What's this?"

"Call it opposition research."

"On who?"

"Senator Ogden."

Rapp opened the envelope and pulled out three sheets of paper. He scanned the lines. "What's this?"

"Her prepared remarks."

Rapp was impressed. "How the hell did you get these?"

"Senators weren't the only people who were killed in the attack on the Monocle. Nine staffers also died. We're a close-knit group."

"One of her people gave it to you?"

Lonsdale nodded. "You'll have time to read it while we get things started. The first two sheets are her remarks. The third is something I prepared for you. It's something that Ralph used to point out to me on a regular basis. Call it a glaring example of hypocrisy. You might find it useful in taking some of the wind out of Ogden's sails."

Rapp scanned the first and second pages. His name jumped out at him a few times. He had to hand it to the senator from San Francisco. She wasn't going to back down a bit. Even in the wake of the attacks. He scanned the third page with a bit of surprise. "This is all accurate?"

"Yep."

"Interesting."

Lonsdale patted him on the arm. "I'm sure you will put it to good use. Now if you'll excuse me, I need to get things started."

CHAPTER 50

THE seventeen members sat behind the big horseshoe-shaped wooden bench. Since it was a closed meeting only a skeleton crew of staffers were seated behind them. Rapp thought they appeared a little more solemn than normal. Even Ogden looked somewhat mournful. She looked over the top of her reading glasses and made eye contact with Rapp. There was neither joy nor malice in her expression. Just a cold, calculated appraisal. The two had never been fond of each other, and Rapp was in no way delusional enough to think it was solely her fault. He had never given any of them the respect they were used to being accorded. He had managed to stay off the Judiciary Committee's radar for nearly a decade and a half, but then he was involved in a series of high-profile incidents that garnered far too much interest. For the past two years it seemed that the committee had placed a bull's-eye on his back. He had become the white-hot example of everything that was wrong with the War on Terror, at least as far as Senator Ogden was concerned.

Lonsdale gaveled the hearing to order and spent the next few minutes going over the itinerary. Before allowing the first senator to begin with questions, she asked Director Kennedy if she had any statements that she would like to make.

Normally Kennedy would have passed, but this time she took Lonsdale up on the offer. "I would like to offer my condolences to the committee. I know that some of the people we lost last week were far more than just colleagues. They were dear friends and I'm sorry for your loss."

"Thank you, Director," Lonsdale replied, "and on behalf of the committee I would also like to offer our condolences to the CIA and the families who lost loved ones in the attack on the National Counterterrorism Center."

"Thank you, Madam Chairman."

Lonsdale nodded to the ranking member sitting on her right and the questioning began. It started out with more of the same, although the offers of condolences were greatly abbreviated due to the fact that there were no cameras in the room and the transcripts would be sealed for many years to come. Everything was abbreviated, in fact. The senators staked out their turf, but kept things moving. Two members from the minority party and one from the majority voiced their full support of the CIA and didn't even bother bringing up the issue that was at the core of the hearing—had Mitch Rapp and Mike Nash tortured an American citizen?

When it was Senator Ogden's turn, the mood changed drastically. This was where the fireworks were going to start. "Director Kennedy, in your opening remarks you stated that you will not stop until those responsible for the attacks are brought to justice. What exactly do you mean by justice?"

Kennedy leaned forward and was about to answer the question but never got the chance, because Ogden cut her off and said, "In the past your version of justice has been to let men like Mr. Rapp and Mr. Nash here track these people down and play the role of judge, jury, and executioner."

Rapp leaned forward and said, "Madam Senator, you make it sound as if there is something wrong with that."

As Ogden stared down at Rapp the strain became palpable. Rapp returned Ogden's harsh glare as if he was daring her to engage him, which was exactly what he wanted. At the best of times Rapp had found it difficult to follow the decorum and procedure of any committee and especially this one, which was famous for being filled with the Senate's largest egos and biggest blowhards. Considering that he had far more important things to be doing with his time, he really didn't care if he upset Ogden and her little cabal. The senator from California was the quintessential ivory tower politician. She moved in the elite circles of her party, listening to the trial lawyers, academics, and the nuttiest of the crazy special-interest groups. Rapp had never pretended to understand the intricacies of politics, but he felt pretty confident that on this issue Ogden was out of step with the majority of Californians.

"Mr. Rapp," Ogden said in an icy tone, "it is no secret that I have never cared for you, or your methods. I am not alone in my belief that you are out of control, and have been for some time. That your unseemly techniques have been the single greatest recruiting tool for our enemy. That you play to our weaker instincts of vengeance and vigilante justice, and that while this may feel good in the short term, in the long term it is destructive beyond calculation. Your use of extreme measures—and by the way, I hate the way you use that euphemism to describe what you do." She stopped and looked from one end of the dais to the other. "We all know what he does. It's called torture. When you intentionally dislocate someone's arm and then wrench that arm behind that person's back in a way that is specifically designed to cause more pain, it can be described as nothing less than torture.

"While my colleagues may be willing to temporarily forget their oath of office and lose their moral compass, I cannot. You are a black mark, a stain against everything we stand for. You undermine our position on the world stage, and you stand in stark contrast to our national values. Your jackboot tactics and immoral techniques have sullied our reputation beyond repair. The torture that you so wantonly practice is ethically reprehensible and blatantly illegal. It violates our laws. It flies in the face of the international courts and the Geneva Conventions, which we are legally bound to obey and uphold. Your actions have endangered the lives of our service members and inflamed anti-U.S. sentiment around the globe. You have single-handedly eroded our moral authority, and for what? Questionable results, at best. Everyone on this committee who is brave enough to admit it knows that torture doesn't work. Yet here we all sit, most of you hoping we can just wish away this black mark . . . this stain, ignore the fact that we have in our possession an affidavit submitted by a well-known attorney and signed by a respected doctor that an American citizen was tortured by Mr. Rapp and Mr. Nash in the aftermath of last week's attacks."

Rapp waited patiently and respectfully while she built her indictment of him. He ticked off her points one by one and plotted his counterattack. Never in his life would he again have this chance in front of this committee. He stole a quick look from one side of the massive bench all the way around the horn. Seventeen faces, at least half of them scowling at their fellow senator. A few more looked as if they simply wanted to get up and leave, and then there were Ogden's two lone supporters, the senior senators from Vermont and Illinois, Kool-Aid drinkers if there ever were. Out-of-touch party loyalists who had built their careers on trashing the CIA every chance they got.

Ogden shook her head as if she were eyeing a disgusting child rapist and said, "I cannot sit here silently like my colleagues. I must express my absolute outrage at you and Mr. Nash and your brutal, unethical tactics. I think you are both monsters. I think you should be run out of federal service. I think you should be investigated, indicted, put on trial, convicted, and sent to the worst prison we can find in the federal system . . . and I hope it is for a very . . . very long time." She leaned back and glanced to her left and then her right and said, "And I feel that I must express my extreme disappointment in my fellow committee members that they are so willing to turn a blind eye to you and your illegal methods. This is, after all, the Judiciary Committee, where the rule of law is paramount. It is embarrassing that I am the lone voice for justice this morning."

The room remained silent for a few long beats. Rapp was at the far left of the big witness table. Kennedy was in the middle and Nash on her right. The two lawyers were right behind them. Rapp glanced over at Kennedy and gave her a little nod that said he would be handling this one. He looked to the center of the big bench at Lonsdale and said, "Madam Chairman, if I may, I'd like to respond."

"By all means."

Rapp pushed his chair back and stood. He buttoned his charcoal-gray suit coat and stepped around the table.

"Why is the witness standing?" Ogden asked tersely, as she looked sideways at Lonsdale.

Rapp knew this would piss her off. "I stand out of respect, ma'am."

"It's 'Senator,'" Ogden snapped. "I've worked very hard to get where I am and I would appreciate it if you would use my appropriate title and sit back down."

"Senator, why must I automatically defer to you, while you have absolutely no problem calling into question my morals, ethics, and motives?"

"I call them into question, Mr. Rapp, because the people of California have seen fit to elect me four times to the United States Senate, and I would be breaking my oath to uphold the Constitution of the United States if I turned a blind eye to your barbaric behavior. Now sit back down."

"No, thank you. But before I address your points I'd like to ask a fairly simple question. Can you at least acknowledge that Mr. Nash and I have made certain sacrifices? That we have served our country with distinction?"

"Mr. Rapp," Ogden said, her voice dripping with contempt, "there are millions of federal employees, and I would put you both in the lowest percentile of that group."

Rapp felt his anger stir a bit. "Senator, I have been shot on three separate occasions in the service of this country. I received this nice little scar at the ripe old age of twenty-five." Rapp showed her the left side of his face and craned his neck to show her fellow committee members the white mark that ran nearly four inches along his jawbone. "It was delivered by the man who was behind the terrorist attack on Pan Am flight one-oh-three. One hundred seventy-nine Americans were on that flight. Thirty-five of my classmates from Syracuse University perished, including a young woman whom I had dated since high school and planned on marrying. I have been captured and held prisoner by Hamas for nearly a month. I have been detained and beaten in both Syria and Yemen, and this was all before Abu Ghraib and Guantanamo, so please don't sit up there and tell me that myself and Mr. Nash have created this problem. These sadistic bastards existed long before we joined the fight, and unfortunately they will be around long after we've retired."

"Mr. Rapp, this is all fine, but I am not in the mood to—"

"Mood!" Rapp yelled with such intensity that a number of the senators eased back in their seats as if to get out of the way of the coming storm. "You call into question my morals and my service, and cast doubt on whether I have sacrificed for this country, and then when I defend myself, you tell me you are not in the mood to hear it?"

"I will not be spoken to in this manner," Ogden said, trying to regain control.

"Now you want to argue about tone. My insolence offends you," Rapp said in a mocking voice.

"Barbara," Ogden said loudly, "this is unacceptable."

"You're damn right it is!" Rapp shouted. "Our two worlds collided last week and seven of your fellow senators found out the hard way that you can't appease these bigoted, sexist freaks, and now you want to sit here and condemn my actions as immoral."

"Mr. Rapp," Ogden said with force, "I hardly think it's a stretch to condemn torture as an immoral act."

"What about partial-birth abortion?" Rapp asked her.

Ogden frowned as if Rapp had lost his mind. "What are you talking about?"

"You were the one who brought up morals this morning. Not me. You condemned me for dislocating the arm of a terrorist."

"A suspect," she shot back, "who happens to be a U.S. citizen and is innocent until proven guilty."

"Innocent," Rapp replied. "Let me tell you a little something about this piece of human debris you're so strenuously defending. He was born in Saudi Arabia and applied for U.S. citizenship for the sole purpose of helping carry out the attacks that killed 185 of our countrymen last week. You explained to the committee only moments ago that I dislocated this person's arm after the initial three explosions and then failed to mention that while I was in the midst of 'allegedly'—" Rapp held up his hands and made quotation marks with his fingers to emphasize in a contemptuous way the word "—while I was *allegedly* trying to separate the terrorist's arm from his shoulder socket, his fucking friends showed up and gunned down in cold blood eighteen federal employees. And if it wasn't for the brave actions of Mr. Nash here, we would have lost another hundred and probably the entire building. So while you have so kindly placed us in the lowest percentile of federal employees, you do so at the risk of exposing yourself as a very dangerous person who cares more about her political power base than the security of this country."

"I do not have to sit here and take this." Ogden snapped her briefing book shut.

"Tell me, Senator Ogden," Rapp said as he thought of the note he'd received from Lonsdale, "what do you think is more morally reprehensible . . . dislocating the arm of a terrorist who has intentionally lied on his immigration application so he can become an American citizen and help kill innocent people, or sticking a steel spike into the brain of an eight-and-a-half-month-old fetus and then sucking his brains out."

"Nice try, Mr. Rapp . . . you are talking about settled law, and in front of this committee that is a big mistake. You are way out of your depth on this issue."

"Undoubtedly, ma'am, but I don't want you to get me wrong here. I am not condemning your position. I've killed far too many people to begin waving the pro-life banner. I'm merely trying to point out the hypocrisy that you have so perfectly displayed during your twenty-one years in the United States Senate." Rapp recalled the numbers Lonsdale had provided. "You have a one hundred percent voting record when it comes to a woman's reproductive rights. On thirty-eight separate occasions you have voted to protect or expand partial-birth abortions as well as provide federal funding for clinics that perform the procedure."

"The people in this room are well aware of my voting record, and I can assure you that I am not the only senator on this committee who has a hundred percent voting record when it comes to a woman's right to choose."

"I wouldn't know. I don't follow it that closely, and again I'm not in the business of judging why all of you vote the way you do. I'm the one who has been accused by you, Senator, of being a morally bankrupt barbarian, so I'm just trying to figure out where all your outrage comes from."

"You honestly don't understand why I find torture so utterly offensive?"

"You're an intelligent, civilized woman. I would never expect you to openly condone torture. But I'm confused about your outrage. A little over a year ago a Saudi named Abad bin Baaz emigrates to the United States, takes up residence in Washington, D.C., and begins receiving shipments of explosives and providing intelligence for the very same terrorist cell that last week used those explosives to blow up buildings and kill innocent civilians. I catch him red-handed, and in an effort to try to apprehend the terrorists who are still at large, I *allegedly* dislocated his shoulder and slapped him around and got him to spill the beans on his little band of thugs, and you find my behavior reprehensible."

"I think any normal person would," Ogden answered.

"How about sticking a spike through the top of a baby's head, piercing the skull, and then sucking the baby's brains out all because the mother gets a note from two doctors who claim she has depression, or some other mental issue that precludes her from giving birth to a full-term baby?"

"Mr. Rapp, the two issues are completely different, as I said—"

"I know what you said, Senator," Rapp shouted, "and I'm sick of your manufactured outrage."

"Mr. Rapp!" the jowly senator from Vermont jumped in, "You will watch your tongue! This is the United States Senate."

"I'm well aware of where I am, sir. This is where we not only say it's perfectly okay for a doctor to kill a full-term baby, but we think taxpayers should help pay for it." Rapp shot daggers at Ogden. "And you call me a barbarian."

"Mr. Rapp," Ogden said, "for the last time we are not here to discuss abortion."

"I'm well aware of that, Senator. We're here to talk about your moral outrage over what I have allegedly done. And I'm merely trying to point out the hypocrisy that this esteemed body is so famous for." Rapp walked back to the table.

CHAPTER 51

"WHERE the hell did you come up with that?" Nash asked as soon as they were clear of the committee room. Kennedy was still inside having a private word with a few of the senators.

Rapp grinned, thought of Lonsdale's note, and said, "Just popped into my head."

"It was brilliant. I mean frickin' brilliant. I've never seen Ogden that frustrated."

"Yeah, well she opened the door pretty wide for me."

"I think you actually got her to reconsider."

"I doubt it." Rapp shook his head. "She'll make it about me. She'd rather shoot the messenger than confront her hypocrisy."

"Well, there were sixteen other senators in there who all seemed to be agreeing with you."

Rapp laughed. "Maybe fourteen or fifteen at the most. Probably enough to kill this thing before it gets legs, but she'll leak it to the press and all of her buddies at Amnesty International and the ACLU. There's no shortage of attorneys in this town who wouldn't jump at the chance to try to drag our asses into court."

They stopped to wait for Kennedy. "Yeah, but at least we'll get political cover from the committee."

"Probably, and we'll have the president on our side."

Nash waited for a couple of staffers to walk past and then said in a conspiratorial voice, "Wouldn't it be nice if the president would just slip us a couple of blanket pardons?"

Rapp laughed. Nash the martyr appeared to be on break.

"We could tuck them away in Irene's safe for a nice rainy day. No one would have to know."

Rapp thought of their next meeting. "You should ask him when we get to the White House. I jumped on the grenade in there," Rapp jerked his head back toward the committee room, "you handle the next one."

Nash thought about it for a while and said, "Maybe I will."

"Don't hold your breath. I've been waiting to get one for years."

Kennedy joined them in the hallway, and as she pulled up, she shot Rapp a look and said, "That was interesting."

"Sure was," Nash said.

"I think we can count on the committee dropping the issue."

"What about Ogden?" Rapp asked.

"Who cares," Nash said. "You destroyed her."

"She can still make trouble for us," Kennedy warned.

"Yeah . . . she'll be back to fight another day," Rapp said. "She has to. Either that or admit she's wrong, and she's been drinking the Kool-Aid for way too long to admit that."

"You were lucky in there," Kennedy said.

"Lucky?" Nash scoffed.

"I know," Rapp said.

"I don't think luck had anything to do with it. If it was a prize fight they would have called it after the first round."

"What Irene means is that under normal circumstances, they would have never let me get away with that. They would have shouted me down, and if it wasn't for Lonsdale's conversion there's no way in hell I would have gotten away with it."

Kennedy looked at Rapp and said, "I've never seen anything like it in my nearly twenty-five years. They're scared to death." She looked back down the hall at the doors to the committee room and in near-disbelief said, "Your friend from Illinois."

"The one who likes to call us Nazis."

"Yes. He just pulled me aside and told me whatever I want, just ask for it. He told me to take your leash off and turn you loose."

"Unbelievable. The guy's been busting my balls for two years. Thousands of people die in the Towers and the Pentagon, and planes fall out of the sky, and he wants me to Mirandize every piece of crap I come across. Now it hits a little closer to home and all of a sudden we need to take the gloves off and throw away the rule book. God . . . they're the most egocentric fuckers on the planet."

"Yeah . . . well, don't look a gift horse in the mouth," Kennedy said. "Isn't this what you wanted?"

"Yeah," Rapp snarled. "It'd just be nice if they did it for a reason other than self-preservation."

"Well," Kennedy said, "sometimes you have to take what you can get. Just be happy they didn't launch an investigation. You could spend the next year sitting in conference rooms drinking weak coffee and eating stale doughnuts talking to lawyers."

"You're right."

"All right," Kennedy said while checking her watch, "we can't keep the president waiting."

The three of them walked down the hallway. Two of Kennedy's bodyguards fell in, one in front and one in back. Nash asked his boss, "What does the president want?"

Kennedy stole a quick glance at Rapp and then said to Nash, "I have no idea. We'll find out when we get there."

Rapp and Nash parted ways with their boss and went down the back stairs to where Rapp's car was parked. C Street was closed on this side of the building and his car was parked in one of the diagonal spots. He paused at his door with his keys in hand and looked across the boulevard at the teams of special agents combing through the debris of what had been one of Washington's most famous restaurants. The place looked more like an archeological dig than a crime scene. The big parking lot had been divided into more than a dozen sections separated by crime scene tape and orange cones. Agents were sifting through the debris with shovels and by hand. A crane was parked off to the side, just in case, but most of the heavy stuff had already been removed from the pile.

The FBI was looking for clues. Sifting through every pile of debris. This was where they excelled—gathering evidence and building a case. Finding a latent fingerprint on a detonator, tracing the detonator back to the manufacturer, and then following it every step of the way right back to who used it to commit murder. They would spend years building their case, and then as much as a decade trying to convince some foreign government to turn the individuals over. It would be a slow, tedious process.

Rapp shook his head and realized why the president wanted him to expedite things. In this particular situation he wouldn't play the role of judge and jury, but he would gladly play the role of executioner. He got into the car, started it up and backed out. As they drove over the pop-up security barricade and took a right onto Second Street Rapp listened to a voicemail Coleman had left him. At Constitution he took another right.

A block and a half later Rapp was thinking of Coleman's voicemail when he asked Nash, "You ever seen a shrink?" He knew Nash would think the question was a little out of bounds so he quickly added, "Irene's been trying to get me to see one."

"You probably should," Nash answered without giving anything away.

"I did right after Anna was murdered. Didn't go so well."

Nash gave him a sideways glance. "No . . . I imagine it didn't."

"What in the hell is that supposed to mean?" Rapp said with a self-deprecating laugh.

"Guys like us aren't very good at discussing our feelings. I don't have anything against it. I think therapy can do a lot of good, but I also think a lot of people use it as a crutch."

"Yeah . . . I suppose Maggie thinks it's good. Anna used to try to get me to do it. Said it would be a fair way for us to resolve some of our issues."

"Maggie says the same thing. I know she has someone she goes to from time to time. She doesn't say much about it other than she thinks it would be good for me to sit down and talk to someone."

Rapp turned onto Pennsylvania Avenue and added, "Our security clearance doesn't exactly allow us to do that."

"That's what I keep telling her."

Rapp was half tempted to tell him about Coleman's message. Apparently Doc Lewis wasn't the only shrink they had put under surveillance. Max Johnson had told Coleman that Adams had directed him to follow Maggie Nash and see what he could dig up. When he found out she was seeing a therapist twice a month, he ordered Johnson to bug the office. Mitch knew he couldn't tell Nash, though. At least not today. He needed to get him to the White House and let him have his moment. Afterward, he would be sure to tell Nash all the sordid details before he made his decision on Adams's fate.

They entered the White House grounds via the southwest gate and pulled into one of the visitor spots on West Executive Avenue. They handed their guns to the uniformed Secret Service officer who checked them in on the ground floor just around the corner from the Situation Room. He placed them in a locked drawer and handed them claim tickets. Rapp looked at the sign-in sheet and was pleased to see Kennedy was already here. Her security detail would have buzzed over from Capitol Hill without stopping for lights.

They walked down the short hallway and when Nash turned to the right to go to the Situation Room, Rapp grabbed his arm and said, "We're upstairs today."

"Where?" Nash asked in surprise. He didn't do a lot of briefings at the White House, and none so far with this president, but when he did they were always down in the Situation Room.

"Not sure," Rapp lied. He started up the stairs and hoped no one was loitering in the halls. This was all a bit like delivering the honoree to a surprise party. When they got to the main floor they took a U-turn and headed down the hall past the Cabinet Room. Straight ahead two big Secret Service agents in dark suits stood post outside the main door to the Oval Office. Each agent widened his stance a bit and tracked the two visitors with unblinking eyes.

Rapp knew having a couple of guys like him and Nash in the building always put these guys on edge. He locked eyes with the one on the left and said, "Gentlemen."

They nodded, but said nothing. Rapp hung a left just before he got to them and ducked into an outer office where the president's administrative assistant sat. He looked at the woman behind the desk and said, "Good morning, Teresa. I have Mr. Nash here to see the president."

"He's expecting you. Go right in."

"Thanks." Rapp moved to his right and stopped at the door. He stuck his left eye up against the peephole and took in the scene. They were all there—Maggie, Shannon, Rory, Jack, and Charlie, as well as most, if not all, of the president's National Security team and the requisite pool reporters. Rapp smiled to himself, opened the door, motioned for Nash to go in first, and then as soon as Nash had crossed the threshold, Rapp closed the door behind him and put his eye back to the peephole.

CHAPTER 52

MIKE Nash stopped as if he'd just stepped into a foot of thick wet cement and looked at the smiling faces staring back at him. Some he'd never met, but recognized, and a few he knew intimately. He heard the door behind him click shut and he whipped his head around, expecting to share his surprise with Rapp. Instead, he found himself alone, staring at the door, and in that split second he realized he'd been set up. He felt his face flush with embarrassment and for a brief moment considered leaving, but knew he couldn't. As badly as he wanted to, it would be against everything the Marine Corps had taught him about being an officer. Leaders gritted their teeth and took it, while cowards ran. As he slowly turned around, he felt he would rather have taken on an enemy platoon than this crowd.

They were all smiling, and some of them weren't exactly known for having a happy-go-lucky demeanor. There was the secretary of defense, secretary of state, national security advisor, director of national intelligence, FBI director, chairman of the Joint Chiefs, a few people he didn't recognize but was sure were important, his boss, and the biggest surprise of all, his family. They were all assembled in perhaps the world's most famous office, all eyes on him, his wife holding Charlie and blushing almost as much as her husband.

It all started to fall into place. Maggie picking out his suit, shirt, and tie, which she rarely did, making sure the kids were all bathed and in clean uniforms, and Rapp—that Judas—distracting and then delivering him like some suburban Joe to his surprise fortieth birthday party. Despite his discomfort and the bad thoughts coursing through his brain about what he'd like to do to Rapp, Nash was still smiling from ear to ear. He had no idea why, but he felt like a jackass. Everyone else was grinning back at him, nodding to each other in recognition that the surprise had worked. Nash made a promise to himself right on the spot that however long it took he would get even with Rapp.

"Mr. Nash," the president said as he walked across his own office. "I was just informed that this is a bit of a surprise to you."

Nash tried to speak but his mouth was too dry, so he just nodded and took the president's extended hand. Irene Kennedy was suddenly at President Alexander's side.

"I'm sorry, Mike, but we knew you would never have gone along with this if you'd known in advance."

Nash licked his lips and croaked, "What exactly am I going along with?"

"This," the president said, "is a medal ceremony. For your bravery under fire last week."

Nash looked past his boss and the president and smiled awkwardly at his wife and kids. Off to his right someone began snapping photos, which for an intelligence officer was a close second to someone shooting at you with a large-caliber gun. "Is that a reporter?" he asked nervously.

"Yes," the president said.

"But I'm Non-Official Cover," Nash protested. "I can't have my photo taken."

"Don't worry about it," the president continued casually, "you're being promoted."

"Enjoy it, Mike," Kennedy said, "Very few of us get this chance."

"What chance?" Nash asked out of the side of his mouth.

"Receiving an award in the Oval Office." The president stepped aside and placed a hand on Nash's elbow. "Usually, you guys have to die to get something like this. Relax and enjoy it."

"I'm not sure I want it," Nash muttered.

"Nonsense. The CIA could use a little boost in morale . . . Hell after last week, we all could." The president started walking Nash toward his family. "Your wife is lovely, and so are your kids. They're very proud of you."

Kennedy grabbed his other arm. "We're all proud of you, Mike. You deserve a little recognition."

Nash turned to Kennedy and snarled, "What about Mitch?"

Kennedy looked straight ahead and said, "We'll talk about that later. Just try to relax and enjoy."

Nash wanted to talk about it now, but his wife was already moving toward him with the kids. Nash was still trying to figure out how Rapp had gotten out of this when he noticed the tears in his wife's eyes. His anger toward Rapp was shoved aside as Maggie reached up and planted one on his lips. Charlie, the cussed little towhead, managed to wiggle out of his mother's arms and latch on to his dad. The other three kids all came up for a hug, and then it was on to the individual members of the president's National Security team. It took a good five minutes to get through all the handshakes and backslapping. By the time the rounds were done Nash was feeling considerably better.

When they got down to the actual medal ceremony, Nash handed Charlie back to Shannon, his fifteen-year-old, and Maggie took her position on his right side in front of the celebrated fireplace. Things turned serious when Kennedy handed the president the citation and opened the blue velvet box. As the president read the words aloud, Nash felt as if he were having an out-of-body experience.

"On behalf of a grateful nation it is my honor to present to you the highest award achievable by a member of the intelligence community, the Distinguished Intelligence Cross, for a voluntary act of extraordinary heroism involving the acceptance of existing dangers with conspicuous fortitude and exemplary courage." The president paused and looked at Nash and Maggie and smiled. "Thank you for your dedication, service, and sacrifice. Your decisive and brave actions during the terrorist attack on the National Counterterrorism Center saved the lives of countless individuals. You stand before us as a living, breathing example of honor, valor, and heroism. This great nation will forever be in your debt, and we hope that future generations of Americans will look to your actions for inspiration during turbulent times."

Kennedy presented the medal to Maggie, who took it from the silk-lined case as if it were an ancient family heirloom. She gently looped it over her husband's head and kissed him on the cheek. Next came photos. Lots of them. First as a group and then individual shots and then finally the Nash family. When they were all finished Nash was in for one more surprise.

The president approached him and said, "Director Kennedy thinks it would be a good idea if your family stayed in here while we step outside."

Nash wasn't quite following, but he got the sense it wasn't good. "What's outside?"

The president glanced toward the glass door just behind and to the left of his desk. "The press. They're waiting for us."

You would have thought the president had asked him to address the nation. "I don't do press, sir."

Kennedy appeared on cue along with Secretary of State Wicka and Secretary of Defense England. Wicka said, "Nonsense. You're exactly what we need right now. A good-looking hero."

"And a retired Marine officer," England added. "Don't forget that part."

"Don't worry," the president said. "We'll do all the talking. Just stand there and be yourself."

Nash looked at Kennedy for help. Once he walked out that door there would be no turning back. "Irene?"

"Just let it go, Mike. This is bigger than just you. Think of all the people at Langley who get kicked around in the press every day. They'll all be able to go home tonight and hold their heads a little higher knowing there's honor in what we do."

CHAPTER 53

NORTHERN ARKANSAS

WHEN he awoke in the morning, the sun was filtering in through the sheer white shades. Hakim blinked several times before he could focus. There was a DVD player on a shelf under the TV. Four small blue numbers stared back at him. If the device was right, it was nine-forty-one in the morning. Hakim looked down and saw the blood on his shirt. He opened his mouth and felt the dry, caked blood on his lips. He remembered the coughing fit and the blood and the dead man on the porch and the woman in the bedroom and knew he hadn't dreamed any of it. Not with Karim around. He was a living breathing Angel of Death.

Hakim didn't have the strength to get up, so he grabbed the remote sitting on the end table and pressed the power button. A moment later two anchors from a twenty-four-hour news channel were on the screen. Ahmed must have heard the TV. He entered the living room with glass of water and a washcloth.

"How are you feeling?" he asked softly.

Hakim wasn't sure. He was all beat up inside, but his breathing was better than it had been yesterday. "I'm alive." He glanced over Ahmed's shoulder and asked, "Where is Karim?"

A frown came over Ahmed's face and he said, "He is outside."

"Doing what?"

"He is very upset."

"About?"

"You." Ahmed shook his head. "He thinks you are causing us problems."

Hakim told himself not to get angry. He wasn't the one who had gotten them into this predicament. "What kind of problems?"

Ahmed shrugged his big shoulders and tried to remember the exact words. "He said you have become an operational liability."

"Me?" Hakim asked with genuine surprise. In better times he would have laughed, but not now. "He thinks I am the problem. What do you think, Ahmed?"

"It is not my place to think. I am trained to follow orders."

"Are you a monkey? If he orders you to shoot yourself will you do it?"

Ahmed took the washcloth and dabbed Hakim's chin, "You look horrible."

"And you did not answer my question."

Ahmed worked on a crusted piece of blood. "There is enough arguing between the two of you. You don't need me to join in."

"Let me ask it a different way then. You were trained to think tactics. Did you think I had things handled back in Iowa . . . at the house? Did you feel he needed to step outside and shoot them?"

"What if they had been police?"

"If they had been police, we would be dead right now. Shooting them would have solved nothing. The best course was to wait and see. Besides, the police don't use young boys. They were simply a father and son looking to do some hunting."

"But we did not know that at the time," Ahmed said.

"We?" Hakim asked. "You mean you and Karim did not know, and you did not know because you have spent no time in this country. You do not understand America the way I do. So you do not see what is obvious. You blindly follow him, and where does he keep leading you? To another house where he kills a husband and wife. Two people minding their own business, breaking no law, and doing nothing to offend Allah."

Ahmed looked out the window for a moment and said, "These are strange times."

"Tell me . . . why couldn't he have tied them up?"

"I don't know. He has his reasons." Ahmed turned his attention to the TV and a moment later added, "It is not my place to question him."

"You keep saying that, but if you ever want to see Paradise, you had better start thinking for yourself. Allah does not condone this. The people who lived here were not infidels. They had done nothing to provoke his wrath."

"This is different. We are in the land of our enemy, thousands of miles from any support. We must do whatever it takes to survive."

"Whatever?" Hakim questioned Ahmed's choice of words. "Now you sound like him. You know what pleases Allah, and you know what displeases him. Tell me . . . do you think Allah will condone what was done here last night in his name?"

Before Ahmed could answer Karim entered the house through the front door. He stood in the foyer and looked suspiciously at the two men. "What have you been discussing?"

Ahmed quickly said, "I was telling him that the White House has announced a major press conference."

"About what?"

"The media is saying their president is going to discuss what happened in Washington last week."

"What is to discuss?" Kakim holstered his pistol and took off his jean jacket. "We won . . . they lost."

Ahmed flashed Hakim a nervous look and then said, "They are speculating it is about the investigation."

"Who?"

Ahmed was confused. "I do not understand."

"Who is speculating?"

"The reporters. They are citing sources inside the administration."

"Good," Karim said, "we could use some information." With that he moved down the hallway to the kitchen.

Ahmed gave Hakim a worried look and whispered, "Be respectful. Do not upset him."

Hakim watched his Moroccan friend follow Karim into the kitchen. He turned his attention to the TV and wondered how much longer it would be before they had their final confrontation. A minute passed before Karim came back into the room. He was holding Hakim's black backpack. He placed it on the coffee table and opened one of the side pockets.

Karim withdrew three mobile phones and said, "Why did you not tell me about these?"

Hakim looked at the three prepaid phones he had purchased months earlier. "I did."

"You did not."

Hakim eyed him cautiously. His friend was looking to provoke a fight. "I thought I told you while we were at the farmhouse . . . back in Iowa."

"You did not."

Hakim swallowed. "The day after we arrived I made sure they were charged. They were in the kitchen. On the counter." Despite being beaten unconscious he remembered it clearly. Karim had questioned him about the phones.

"I never saw them," Karim said.

He was lying and Hakim knew it. "I purchased them months ago. They are also radios. We can talk to each other by pressing the buttons on the side."

"Where did you buy them and how?" Karim said while shaking the phones.

"In New Orleans and with cash." This had all been covered the previous weekend.

"I do not remember giving you approval."

"There is no way to trace them."

"What about a surveillance tape at the store where you bought them?"

"It is possible, but extremely remote. I wore glasses and a baseball cap and used a British accent when I spoke to the clerk."

Karim paused and considered all of this. He looked at the phones and said, "No more secrets." He tossed one phone to Hakim and the second one to Ahmed, who was standing in the dining room. "Do not turn them on unless I tell you. Are the numbers for all three phones programmed?"

"Yes." Hakim watched Karim stuff the last phone in his pocket and then leave the room without another word. Hakim looked down at the phone in his hands and briefly questioned his own sanity. Was everything that had happened in Iowa a dream? He was almost certain it wasn't. The phones had been discussed. Hakim had specifically told him they had been purchased well in advance as a precaution. He told him they needed the phones in case they were separated. That meant Karim either had a terrible memory or was conveniently forgetting that it had all been discussed. Hakim knew the truth, and he was also beginning to understand the depths of Karim's immaturity. This was all about him and nothing else. It wasn't about Allah, or Muslim pride, or a battle against the colonial powers. It was about the need to feed the Lion of al Qaeda's ego.

CHAPTER 54

WASHINGTON, D.C.

RAPP cruised up Massachusetts Avenue toward Rock Creek. His mind worked geographically. It connected dots like stick pins on a map with strings running between points of interest, linking one location or fact to another. He was listening to Special Agent Art Harris, the FBI's senior guy at the NCTC. Art had just stuck a pin in Rapp's map and it wasn't making a lot of sense. He trusted Harris, though, so he let him work his way through the preamble rather than telling him to cut to the heart of it.

Harris and Rapp had a nice arrangement. Through unofficial channels Art passed along what the FBI knew on various cases that bumped up against things Rapp and his people were dealing with. And he made sure very little was put in writing. Over the last few years, his early warnings had allowed Rapp to get out in front of certain things and deal with them before all the badges and lawyers showed up.

Harris had just told Rapp about an investigation in Iowa. Two bodies had been found in the basement of a torched farmhouse. They were burned beyond recognition, but preliminary reports said they'd been shot. The local sheriff was all but sure they were two hunters who had gone missing the day before. He gave Rapp the backstory on what the sheriff thought had happened. While Rapp found it all about as interesting as a whodunit episode of *Primetime* he knew there had to be more to the story, or Harris wouldn't have bothered to call.

"The sheriff called the JTTF gang over in Chicago," Harris said.

JTTF stood for Joint Terrorism Task Force. They were formed after 9/11 to foster cooperation and preparedness between the myriad local and federal law enforcement agencies in communities across the country. "I'm listening."

"The barn almost caught fire but survived the blaze. Inside, the sheriff found a bunch of supplies . . . the kind of crap the Armageddon types would have. A bunch of MREs, guns, ammunition, and some handy-dandy military grade C-4 plastic explosives complete with detonators. They also found a couple of backpacks that contained maps, cash, credit cards, IDs, and passports."

"Photos?" Rapp asked, already knowing the names would be bullshit.

"Yeah."

"Your boys run them through TIDE?" TIDE stood for Terrorist Information Datamart Environment and was an extensive database run by the NCTC.

"Doing it right now, but it doesn't look promising. They prioritized it and have already blown through all the usual suspects. What's left we wouldn't be interested in. Unless you think one of these guys might be Filipino."

"No . . ." Rapp said as he thought about it. Some weird crap went on in the rural areas across the heartland. It was amazing the type of hardware these militia groups could get their hands on. It was probably nothing, but just in case he said, "Do me a favor and send the photos to my BlackBerry."

"I will, but there's one other thing you might find interesting. The farm was purchased about six months ago by an LLC. It was handled by an attorney out of New York."

"I'm sure people do that all the time." Rapp had done it himself.

"I'm sure they do. The sheriff also said no one has ever seen anyone use the place. Kinda strange when you think of those Hitler-lovin' groups. They tend to turn these places into full-blown communes. People coming and going all day and all night."

"Yeah . . ." Rapp said, "I suppose you're right."

"Well, I just thought I'd pass it along. I wouldn't be surprised if the wonder boys at Justice decided to send us knocking on that New York attorney's door come Monday. If for no other reason than the C-4."

It was late Friday morning. Rapp considered the possibilities. "Did the sheriff by any chance give your boys a copy of the deed and all the title work?"

"Public record. I'm looking at a copy right now."

"Good. Send it to me. And cc Marcus. Are your guys from Chicago on scene?" Rapp asked.

"They got there an hour ago and we have a Rapid Deployment Team on standby."

"Good." Rapp took a half loop around Sheridan Circle and continued one short block before taking a right onto Decatur Place. The place he was looking for was on S Street, but he wanted to drive past the back first to see if there was anything of interest. Up ahead on his left he got his answer. "Hey, Art, I gotta run. Thanks for the info and call me as soon as you hear anything else."

Rapp hit the end button and then hit the speed-dial button for Marcus Dumond. A few seconds later the computer genius was on the line. "Marcus . . . you're gonna get an email from Art in the next few minutes. It's going to have a copy of a deed and title for a farm in Iowa. It was purchased a few months back by an LLC. An attorney out of New York handled it. Do you think you could get into his system and find out where the money came from?"

"To buy the property?"

"Yeah."

"Shouldn't be a problem. Give me an hour or two."

"Thanks. Call me as soon as you find anything." Rapp slowed down and looked through his heavily tinted windows at the back entrance to the big property. A serious man with a dog was on the other side of the gate. At the end of the block Rapp hung a left on Twenty-second and then another left on S Street. A third of the way down he pulled over and dug out the business card. It was a local number, so he skipped the first three digits and punched in the next seven. A woman answered on the second ring.

"Mr. Sidorov's private line, how may I help you?"

"Peter, please."

"May I have your name?"

"No thanks. Just tell him it's his friend from last night. He gave me his business card at the club," Rapp said as he looked through his windshield at the recently purchased $8 million federal style home. "Trust me," he said to the young woman, "he'll take the call."

Rapp didn't have to wait too long. Sidorov's familiar voice came on the line and said, "Mr. Rapp, good to hear from you so soon. Have you decided to come work for me?"

Rapp cringed at the thought that the FBI's counterespionage boys might be listening in. He would have to play things really straight while they were on the phone. "I was actually thinking you could come to work for us."

Sidorov had a good chuckle and then said, "I don't think you can afford me."

"Probably not, but I thought I'd play to your newfound love of freedom and democracy."

"Yes, that would be your only chance. Now listen . . . I had friend in Russian intelligence fill me in on your exploits this morning. You are a very interesting man. A dangerous one as well, according to my source."

"Only if you piss me off."

"Well," he said dramatically, "I hope I have not offended you."

"Not yet."

"You didn't seem too pleased last night."

"I was more upset with your new business associate than you."

"He was only trying to make a little money. I can't begin to imagine trying to live on one of those pensions they give you."

"I don't suppose you could, with your high-flying lifestyle, but that's not really the point. He knew the rules and he broke them."

"And me?" Sidorov said a bit tentatively.

"You didn't break any law that I'm aware of."

"Well." He laughed. "You don't know me yet."

"I know enough. I made some calls as well."

"And?"

Rapp didn't answer for a beat. "I think we should sit down and discuss a few things."

"I would love to. How does your evening look?"

"Not good," Rapp said, looking at the house. "How about right now?"

Sidorov laughed. "I am barely awake, Mr. Rapp. I still haven't adjusted to the time change and we stayed out very late last night."

"That's all right. I didn't get much sleep either. Besides . . . you Russians can all handle your booze." Rapp put the car in drive and pulled across the street into the flat U-shaped drive. "Listen, I'm parked in front of your house right now. Invite me in for a cup of coffee. I'm kind of on a tight schedule this morning." Rapp turned off the engine and got out. He counted to ten and then Sidorov appeared in a second-story window. He was still in a robe.

"You are a resourceful man, Mr. Rapp. How do I know you are not here to kill me?"

Rapp looked up at him and wondered what assurance he could offer. "For starters . . . I don't like to shit in my own yard."

"Meaning?" Sidorov asked.

"This is Washington. I live here. I don't need that kind of exposure. Besides, if I was going to do something like that I wouldn't call you up and ask you to talk. I'd just do it. You'd never see me coming."

Sidorov thought about it for a long moment. "I suppose you are right. I'll tell my people to let you in. Give me a few minutes to get dressed."

CHAPTER 55

NORTHERN ARKANSAS

HAKIM stayed in the overstuffed leather chair and carefully chewed a banana. Between bites he sipped the warm lemon water Ahmed had prepared for him. The tall Moroccan was outside doing a sweep of the property—his punishment for nursing Hakim. Hakim could tell it bothered Karim that Ahmed was trying to take care of him. He had always held the frail in contempt. Even when they were young. He had no time for excuses or kids who claimed to be infirm.

Hakim watched him pace from one end of the house to the other and could tell he was irked to be in the presence of his feeble friend. Never mind that he had caused the injuries. Karim was far too narcissistic to own up to that. In his mind, Hakim had deserved the beating, and he had done nothing more than carry out the punishment. Karim probably thought that if his friend had been in better shape, he would have suffered less from the blows. None of it actually made any sense, but it allowed him to rationalize away his guilt and look down on his injured friend with disgust.

The front door opened and Ahmed entered the room. He leaned his rifle against the wall and took the binoculars from around his neck.

With flushed cheeks he said, "The perimeter is secure. No sign of anyone."

Karim stood with his deliberate military posture and looked out the big window. "I heard a dog."

"Yes," Ahmed said with a slight bow of his head. "From down the hill. The next house. Eight hundred meters away. There are several of them."

"Are they fenced in?"

"No."

"And what should we do if they wander up here?"

Ahmed looked nervously at Hakim for help and then said, "Shoot them?"

"Maybe." Karim slowly turned and looked him in the eye. "I do not like this place."

"Why?" Hakim asked, inserting himself into the conversation.

Karim looked as if he might not answer the question, and then said, "There is too much we do not know."

"Such as?" Hakim asked

"We do not know if someone is expected to show up. They could have deliveries. The phone has already rung twice." He looked to the photos on the mantel. "Family may live nearby."

He was right, but all of that could have been avoided. He gambled and decided to point out the obvious. "Maybe if you weren't so quick to kill everyone we stumble upon, we might be able to answer some of your questions."

Karim looked to Ahmed and shook his head. It was one of those looks that said, *See . . . what I have been telling you.* Turning back to his old friend, Karim said, "What is wrong with you? Why must you argue with everything I say?"

"Why must you kill every person we come across?"

Karim looked with thinly veiled contempt at his friend. He was like a sick dog that needed to be put down, and if he didn't do it quickly, the disease was likely to spread to Ahmed. They were going to have to leave this place. The woman was still in the bed. He'd considered moving her but the pillow, sheets, and mattress were soaked with blood. The old man and the dog were in the corner of the garage under a tarp. He might as well kill Hakim in the leather chair and leave him there. Maybe even make it look like a suicide to confuse the police. That was a good plan. Trash the place, shoot his friend in the side of the head, and put his gun in his hand. Karim was considering how he would move into position without alerting Hakim when Ahmed stepped between them and pointed at the TV.

"It has started," Ahmed said.

They all turned their attention to the TV and watched as the American president stepped up to an outdoor podium. He began reading a prepared speech. Karim scowled at the man and briefly imagined what it would be like to kill the president of the United States. That would surely earn him eternal glory in the eyes of Allah and his fellow Muslims the world over. The president droned on about the hard work, duty, sacrifice, and perseverance of the rescue workers, emergency personnel, and law enforcement over the past week. Karim noticed, not for the first time, that leaders the world over loved to hear themselves speak. It was as if they were a walking thesaurus. Descriptions came in threes, when one adjective would do just fine. He supposed it made them feel smart.

The president went on to talk about the losses they had suffered. He choked up at the mention of some of the friends he'd lost in the explosions and went on to talk briefly about the funerals he'd attended for much of the week. In a more commanding voice he listed half a dozen tragedies that had beset the country over the past eighty years and gave examples of how each time Americans rose to the occasion and persevered. Then he moved onto a topic that grabbed Karim's interest.

"In regard to the cowardly attacks of last week there is an untold chapter that I had decided to keep from you until now. The reasons for not coming forward with this sooner are complicated, but in essence involve issues of national security. In addition to the three restaurants that were bombed last week a federal facility in Virginia was also attacked. There has been no shortage of rumors in regard to the facility itself and the attack on it. I'm here this morning to put those rumors to rest. The facility that was attacked was the National Counterterrorism Center. As the name would suggest, this relatively new building houses elements of the both the FBI's and the CIA's counterterrorism units as well as personnel from over a dozen other agencies and organizations. The building is the nerve center for the battle against terrorism. Just hours after last week's cowardly attacks in Washington, D.C., a . . ."

Karim pointed at the TV and began screaming. "Cowardly! He puts pilotless drones in the air over Pakistan and fires on villages with women and children and he dares call us cowards."

Hakim thought about pointing out the fact that the reason those missiles were fired was that al Qaeda liked to hide behind the skirts of the very women he was describing, but he thought that might finally put his friend over the edge, and all things considered, he wanted to live long enough to hear the president's side of the story.

The president continued, saying, "A black Suburban disguised as an emergency vehicle showed up at the gate of the National Counterterrorism Center. Inside were six heavily armed men masquerading as SWAT personnel. They shot and killed a number of guards and then entered the building, where they proceeded to the top floor of the facility where the Counterterrorism Operations Center is located. The six men forced their way into the operations center and opened fire on the unarmed employees who were so diligently trying to aid the men and women involved in the rescue operations. Fortunately, there were a few employees who were armed. One such individual is with us here today."

The president stopped and looked over his shoulder to a younger man in a dark suit who was wearing a medal around his neck with a tricolor silk ribbon. "I'd like to introduce you to Mike Nash. Mr. Nash is a retired Marine Corps officer, and until very recently an undercover operative for the CIA's clandestine service."

Karim pointed at the TV and yelled, "That is the snake who was sending his agents into our mosques."

The president continued, "Mr. Nash was at the facility last week when it was attacked and watched in horror and confusion as the six armed men moved into the operations center in a single line and began killing his coworkers at near-point-blank range. A combat veteran and expert on tactics, Mr. Nash assessed the situation and acted decisively. Ignoring extreme danger to his own life, Mr. Nash did the last thing the terrorists expected . . . He charged the line of men head-on. His bravery and superb training caught the terrorists by surprise. In a matter of just a few seconds, armed with a single pistol, Mr. Nash shot and killed all six terrorists. If that wasn't enough, Mr. Nash soon realized all six men were wearing suicide vests that were on automatic timers and were set to explode in less than two minutes. Thinking quickly, Mr. Nash and his colleagues managed to get all six bodies out a sixth-floor window. The explosives then detonated without further casualties. Mr. Nash's bravery should serve as a reminder to . . ."

Hakim noticed the object flying through the air a split second before it smashed into the TV screen, punching a hole in the glass and sending a shower of sparks onto the carpet. He turned to see Karim standing with his fists clenched in rage and the tendons on his neck so taut they looked as if they were about to break free from his own skin.

"Lies!" Karim screamed. "All of it lies!"

Hakim stole a glance at Ahmed, who carefully had his eyes focused on the floor, too afraid to look at Karim.

"They speak of honor and courage . . . they know nothing of such things! Did you hear him? He said superb training!" Karim marched from one end of the room to the other and back, angrily stomping his feet and then kicking the leg of the glass coffee table so hard it shattered. "Superb training! I will show them. I will show them what bravery and courage and superb training is!" Like a feral animal he turned and faced his old friend. "And I will show you, too. You doubt my bravery! You said I sent them needlessly to their deaths! That I am too afraid to martyr myself. Well we will *all* martyr ourselves," he shouted. "In fact, some of us sooner rather than later. We will go to Washington and we will show the world that this president is a lying dog. I will show this Mike Nash what it is like to fight a real warrior!"

CHAPTER 56

WASHINGTON, D.C.

WHEN the front door opened, Rapp was confronted with an unwelcome sight. There before him was the big Russian who less than twelve hours ago had come within an inch or two of tearing off his head. Rapp's left temple began to throb just looking at the guy. The bodyguard had a bandage around his throat and a hell of a shiner from where Reavers had tagged him, but here he was at his post, which said a lot about the guy. After having your ass kicked like that, most guys wouldn't be too willing to show up for work the next morning. The guy was either very devoted or extremely stupid. Rapp hoped it was the former, because guys who suffered from the latter were hard to teach a lesson.

This time the guy eyed Rapp a bit more cautiously. He pointed at Rapp's waist and in a really hoarse voice that was English with a Russian tinge said, "Open your jacket."

Rapp popped the one button and pulled open both sides, revealing the gun on his left hip.

"Leave your toys outside," the man ordered.

"No thanks." It was important not to back down. Rapp had no outward physical mark from their last meeting.

"Not a choice."

"Fuck you," Rapp said. "This is my town, not yours."

The big Russian stared him down for ten seconds and finally said, "Wait." Then he closed the door.

Rapp stood there and wondered how he was going to handle this if they came back and told him to hit the road. He'd told Kennedy in very vague terms where he was headed, just to cover his ass in case some other federal agency was running surveillance, but he had no real backup if things went south, and the Russians weren't exactly known for playing by the rules. He'd learned long ago that you could never let down your guard and think you were okay without your gun. He didn't even like handing it over when he went to the White House. He sure as hell wasn't going to go in here without it.

The door finally opened. This time it was Sidorov. He was in bare feet, torn jeans, and a faded blue V-neck T-shirt. He looked more like a hungover rocker than a billionaire financier. The Russian whiz kid smiled and said, "Are you always so difficult?"

Rapp thought about it. "I suppose I am. No offense to you, Peter, but I don't know you that well, and I have no idea who you have in there. I've made a few enemies over the years."

Sidorov pushed the door the rest of the way open. "I can relate to your paranoia. I myself have had three attempts on my life." Sidorov turned and moved across the black-and-white-checkered marble foyer.

Rapp stepped over the threshold and scanned right and then left as he closed the door. A big curved staircase wide enough for four people looped up and around to his right. Sidorov moved ahead down a center gallery that divided the house in half down the middle. Rapp followed him, checking the rooms on the left and right as they went. There was a music room, a library, a sitting room, a dining room and another sitting room. All were empty. Finally, at the back of the house they entered a colossal kitchen that looked as if it had been painstakingly restored to its original 1930s condition. A babushka in a gray house dress was standing on the other side of the kitchen island staring at Rapp.

Sidorov spoke rapidly in Russian to the woman and continued through the kitchen and into a solarium. He took a seat in a white wicker chair and gestured to the one on the other side of the table. Rapp sat and Sidorov offered him his choice between the *Financial Times* and the *Wall Street Journal.* Rapp took neither.

Sidorov began scanning the front page of the *Financial Times* and asked, "So what can I do to help the famous Mitch Rapp?"

"I had a nice talk with your boy Max last night."

"Very talented man," Sidorov said while still reading the paper. "I'm shocked your CIA couldn't find more use for him."

"I suppose there was a time where they would have, but things have changed."

"Yes, they have. That is what I just told my bodyguard, who for obvious reasons doesn't like you."

"For the record, I did not want to tangle with him, but he didn't leave me many choices. I just wanted to collect Johnson and leave."

"Why did you want him so badly? Surely it wasn't my business dealings with him."

This was the part Rapp wasn't sure about. Had Johnson sold any additional information to Sidorov, or anyone else, for that matter? It would take a while to sort all of that out, but for now Rapp wanted to discuss something else. "His dealings with you are not my concern. At least not at the moment. Let's just say he's been involved in some stuff that has a few people upset."

"What kind of stuff?"

"The kind of stuff he should know better than to get involved in."

"Fair enough." The babushka dropped off the service tray of coffee and poured a fresh cup for each of them. Sidorov took his with cream and sugar. Rapp took his black. "So what can I do for you at this early hour?" Sidorov asked.

"Early? It's almost noon."

Sidorov smiled. "I am a young man, Mr. Rapp. Early is relative."

"I suppose so." Rapp took a sip and said, "Max told me about the moves you're making in Cuba."

"He did? I paid him a considerable amount of money. I would think he would at least know how to keep his mouth shut."

"I can be persuasive."

"Yes . . . I suppose." He regarded Rapp for a moment and then asked, "So, why are you here?"

"It involves Cuba."

"Go on."

"You've had some business dealings with General Ramirez?"

"Anyone who wishes to get things approved in Cuba eventually must deal with General Ramirez."

"So I've heard." Rapp nudged his coffee cup and then said, "I need to meet with him."

"I would think that could be arranged."

"In private."

"Of course, but why would you need my help?"

"I don't want him to know he's sitting down with me until it's too late for him to back out. And I would prefer to meet him on neutral ground."

"The general," Sidorov said, "is a very dangerous man."

"And what would you call me, Peter?"

Sidorov exhaled while he thought about it and said, "I have spent three years building my relationships down there. I have significant sums of money invested in my various endeavors. Why would I want to risk all of that on a situation that is so obviously combustible?"

Rapp had anticipated this response. "Because I think you can turn it to your advantage."

"How?"

Rapp smiled. "This is all unofficial, but there's a man who lives not far from here. Big white house. You get the picture. For reasons that

I'm sure you can understand he is not happy with the events of last week." Rapp prepared to exaggerate a bit. "He has directed me to punish anyone who was involved in aiding the terrorists."

"And how does General Ramirez fit into that?"

Rapp told him how the drugs had been stolen and flown to Cuba. How Ramirez had allowed the terrorists to use Cuba as a staging area for their attack and in exchange was given a large cut of the stolen drugs.

Sidorov's face grew pained as the details unfolded. When Rapp was done he said, "I hate the drug trade. I avoid it like the plague. It's all very bad for business, especially my business, but I do not condemn those who choose to make their living that way."

"And I'm not asking you to take a position against Ramirez."

"You just want me to help you kill him."

Rapp didn't answer right away. "I would like to give the general a chance to make amends."

"By doing what?"

"By providing me certain information about the person he was dealing with."

"One of the terrorists?"

"Yes."

"And if he does not want to cooperate with you?"

"Trust me, he'll cooperate."

Sidorov thought about it for a long moment and then said, "This terrorism is bad for business. I do not understand them, but it really isn't my fight. I fail to see a good reason for me to put my neck on the line."

Rapp smiled. Sidorov, like any good businessman, wanted to know what was in it for him. "When Castro finally goes, it will be a free-for-all down there. It doesn't matter what you say you've purchased or leased, it will be challenged by the folks down in Miami—the Cuban expatriates who had their land seized by Castro. They are going to want it back, or at least to be compensated for it. It will be a very nasty and costly fight and you will need every ally you can find. But then again, you already know all of this, and that's why you hired Max Johnson to start digging up dirt on the important senators and congressmen."

It was Sidorov's turn to smile. "Surely you have more to offer than that."

"My services."

"Your services?"

"As is evidenced by your fleet of bodyguards, you have managed to make some enemies during your relatively short career."

"That is true."

"As you know I have a certain reputation . . . certain skills that at times can make people nervous."

"I'm listening."

"I would be willing to offer you a bit of cover. Possibly deal with some of your more unsavory enemies in a way that will tell others to leave you alone."

Sidorov folded his copy of the *Financial Times* and tapped himself on the leg several times before saying, "I think we might be able to work something out."

CHAPTER 57

NORTHERN ARKANSAS

KARIM vented more of his rage by smashing several lamps and knocking all the photos off the fireplace mantel. Hakim sat in the big leather chair and didn't dare twitch a muscle. Under Karim's untucked shirt the bulge of his pistol was obvious. It was best to let the storm pass. It took a few minutes, but Karim eventually composed himself. He announced that they would leave in precisely one hour. He wanted everyone showered and clean-shaven for the trip. He told Ahmed to go through the kitchen and pack any food that he could find, and then he took the big road atlas he'd found on the bookshelf and threw it at Hakim.

"Find the best way to get there."

"Get where?" Hakim asked in as nonthreatening a voice as possible.

"To Washington!"

Hakim got the impression Karim was looking for an excuse to get rid of him, so he nodded and began flipping through the pages.

"And keep an eye out the window," Karim barked.

Hakim watched him leave. He stopped in the kitchen and said

something to Ahmed, and then he went to the owner's room. A moment later the shower came on. Ten seconds after that, Ahmed came around the corner with a nervous look on his face. As he crossed the room he looked over his shoulder twice.

When he got to Hakim he whispered, "Can you move?"

Hakim didn't understand, and then suddenly Ahmed was pulling something from his pocket and handing it to him.

In a hurried whisper he said, "He's going to kill you. He told me. Take these." Hakim pushed the car keys into his hand. "There is a white car in the garage. I put your backpack in the front seat. Go! Go now, before he gets out of the shower." Ahmed pulled him out of the chair and got him to his feet.

Hakim's body was screaming at him from virtually every point. He was in such pain he didn't know if he could move, but somehow he did. They were short steps at first. More like the shuffle of an old man. He reached the front door on his own and looked over his shoulder to thank Ahmed, but he was already gone. Cupboards were being noisily opened and slammed in the kitchen. Hakim opened the door and closed it behind him. He moved across the porch to the steps and then froze. There were only three steps, but they might as well have been a cliff. Hakim grabbed the railing and willed himself down. His torso twisted stiffly with the first step and he instantly felt a white-hot pain. It was as if someone were stabbing him in the ribs with a knife. Having already diagnosed himself, he guessed that was exactly what was happening. One of his broken ribs was tearing into the soft tissue of his left lung with a jagged, serrated edge.

He practically fell down the next two steps and then he was shuffling across the gravel, his right foot first, and then he'd drag his left foot to catch up. The pain was nearly unbearable. He felt that at any moment he would launch into a coughing fit and then it would be over. He would collapse right there in the middle of the gravel courtyard and pass out. Karim would then saunter out with that arrogant, disapproving look on his face, and before killing him he would have something stupid to say. Some phrase that would elevate his act to something noble while decrying the betrayal of his best friend. That more than anything was what drove Hakim toward the garage. The hate that he felt for Karim at the moment was unlike anything he had ever experienced.

Hakim wanted to win. He wanted to survive and he wanted his arrogant friend to feel the sting of betrayal. He wanted the narrow-minded fool to try to make the journey to Washington on his own, and he wanted the Lion of al Qaeda to fail, and feel the sting of death, just like his six brave warriors.

Fortunately, the garage was closer than the big barn where they had stashed the RV. Hakim lurched for the side door, taking shallow breaths as he went. It was the only way to prevent the stabbing pain. He didn't dare look back until he got to the metal service door and then he did so for only a second. There was no sign of anyone leaving the house. Hakim twisted the knob and practically floated over the threshold. The overhead lights were automatically triggered by a motion sensor. Hakim slammed the door closed behind him and was about to open the big garage door and then stopped. He decided he would get into the car first. There had to be an automatic opener inside.

It was a big four-door white Cadillac DTS. The owner had been kind enough to back it in for him. Hakim opened the driver's door and was relieved to see his backpack sitting on the front seat, just as Ahmed had said. Placing one hand on the roof and the other on the door, he carefully lowered himself into the seat. At some point he couldn't bear the pain and just let go, falling the last foot. Holding the steering wheel, he dragged his right leg into the car and then the other, and then he just sat there completely immobile, wondering if he would pass out.

It seemed like an eternity, but it was probably no more than five seconds. A voice seemed to be guiding him. Walking him through each step. It was now telling him to put the key in the ignition. He did and it turned over on the first try. The dashboard lit up with various gauges and lights. Hakim looked for the door opener on the visor but there was none. It took him a moment, his eyes scanning every inch of the dashboard for the button, and then he realized it was on the rearview mirror. He stabbed the button and the door lurched up.

Hakim put his foot on the brake, pulled the gearshift into the drive position, and prepared himself for the worst. If Karim was blocking his path he would have to run him over. The optimistic side of him was hoping he would be greeted by nothing but daylight, but the vengeful side of him hoped the arrogant asshole would be waiting for him. He slid lower in the seat and prepared to duck farther and hit the gas should his friend attempt to block his escape. With each passing foot of open space the conflict deepened until the door was open and he saw that the courtyard sat empty. Hakim stayed low and slid his foot from the brake to the gas.

Back inside the house Ahmed continued to rifle through the kitchen cupboards, making as much noise as possible, all the while silently counting to himself. His biggest fear was that Hakim would not be able to make it to the car. How would Karim react if he found him outside passed out on the gravel? He turned to head into the dining room and look out the window, but stopped himself. He would give him another thirty seconds. He couldn't risk helping him any further or he would be the one facing a one-man firing squad. Ahmed prayed to Allah over and over, harder and harder, begging that he would heal Hakim's wounds and give him the strength to get away.

Ahmed did not understand any of it. He had nothing but respect for Karim. He was an amazing commander and was as good a leader as he had ever seen, but when it came to his childhood friend, he was not himself. There had been times in the past few days where he had felt as if he was watching two eight-year-old kids fight. The constant bickering. The back and forth about every petty thing they could dream up and then the decision back in Iowa to kill the father and son. It was the first time he honestly thought Karim had made a tactical mistake. Everyone made mistakes, but this one was obvious, and Ahmed couldn't help but think it was rooted in the jealousy Karim harbored for Hakim. Karim needed to be the hero, and everyone around him had to offer absolute subservience. That was why he stepped from the house back in Iowa and destroyed all of the careful plans and set them on this dangerous and uncharted course.

Ahmed finished counting to thirty for a second time and then kicked a pan as he walked across the kitchen floor and back into the dining room. He looked past the living room and through the big picture window. His heart leaped as he saw the hood of the white sedan ease out of the garage. He glimpsed Hakim through the windshield and thought he saw blood on his chin.

"Keep going," he said to himself. "Don't pass out. Allah, please give him strength. Please protect him." Ahmed watched the car turn and accelerate past the big barn. It started winding down the driveway, a faint trail of dust kicking up, and then the taillights vanished. Ahmed exhaled a sigh of relief, but it didn't last long. From the bedroom the noise of the running shower suddenly stopped.

CHAPTER 58

CIA HEADQUARTERS, LANGLEY, VIRGINIA

RAPP parked underneath the building and took the elevator up to the first floor. He was grinning with anticipation as he walked past the CIA's gift shop and cafeteria. The wide double doors to the Award Suite were open and he could see a good number of people milling about inside. He crossed the threshold and paused for a brief second, his eyes sweeping the room from right to left, scanning faces just long enough to see if there were any land mines waiting for him, but not so long as to make eye contact with any single individual. Rapp tended to skip these events. Better to come and go from HQ and make as little actual contact as possible. This afternoon, however, was worth the exception.

It was a virtual who's who of the national security community, the top dogs from every agency and department that had a hand in the alphabet soup of counterterrorism. As was standard procedure, there wasn't a single reporter or photographer in the room. There would be plenty of time for that later, but for now, this was the one chance for the men and women of the clandestine service to poke their heads out of their rabbit holes and celebrate the bravery of a colleague. Most of these folks had the security clearance, or at least the connections, to know the full story of what had happened the afternoon of the attacks, and a good number of them were turning to get a look at Rapp—the other man who had risked his life. These professionals would whisper among themselves, but they would honor their oath. They all knew there were valid reasons for a man in Rapp's position to keep his head down. Rapp had to be realistic, though. His role in the affair would be passed from one person to the next, and with each retelling, it was likely the facts would be warped like a rain-soaked piece of wood—impossible to know in advance just how it would turn out.

Rapp heard the squawk of a child to his left and moved in that direction. He figured there couldn't be too many toddlers at the reception, so the odds were the noise was coming from Charlie Nash. He wanted to get in, give his congratulations to the kids and Maggie, and tell them how proud he was of their father and husband, if possible track down Art Harris for a brief update, and then get the hell out of Dodge.

Rapp made it three steps before a smiling Julie Trittin cut him off. Barely five feet tall in her heels, the petite brunette was the hotshot rising star over on the National Security Council. She'd come up through the ranks on the military side, and until a few months ago was helping run a highly sensitive operation at the Defense Intelligence Agency.

Trittin looked up at Rapp and with a mischievous smile said, "Well, well, Mitchell. Just how in the hell did you pull this off?"

Rapp cracked a dry smile and said, "I have no idea what you're talking about, Julie."

Trittin held up her champagne flute and gave him a minisalute. "I thought you would say that." She swung around Rapp's right side and hooked her arm through his. Leading him off to the nearest corner she whispered, "This is good."

Rapp nodded and continued to scan the crowd. "Nice turnout."

"You know what I mean. For morale. And by the way, where's your medal?"

Rapp laughed off the comment.

"My sources tell me the story is a little backward about who shot who last week."

"Your sources?"

"Don't try to play me. I know you were the one who charged that line of men, and I know Mike was up on the catwalk firing down at them."

"You know how some people get confused in the heat of battle. Don't believe everything you hear."

Trittin looked over to where Mike Nash was standing. He was surrounded by a good number of well-wishers. They were all smiling and beaming at the hero of the hour. "Well . . . I'm happy for both of you."

"Both of us?" Rapp asked.

"Yes. The president was a little disappointed that you managed to sneak out of the White House this morning."

Rapp sighed. "You know how it is, Julie . . . I don't do so well around politicians."

"Perfect segue," Trittin said in a more serious tone. "The president wanted me to tell you that he thinks you're an insubordinate little shit, and that your medal is waiting for you on his desk. He'd like you to personally stop by and pick it up, though."

"I get one, too?" Rapp said in mock surprise.

"Yes, you do." Trittin shook her head and smirked. "You really are something."

"Thank you, Julie. I think you're pretty special, too."

Trittin laughed at him before turning serious. "Two more things for you. The FBI now has the lead on the search for Glen Adams."

"Pretty standard, isn't it?"

"Yes, but you can thank Senator Ogden for putting you at the top of the list."

Rapp showed no outward sign of concern, but Trittin had just gotten his attention. "What list would that be?"

"The list of people who may have had something to do with his disappearance."

"The way I heard it . . . he just up and left the country."

Trittin shrugged her small shoulders and gave Rapp a who-knows-what-could-have-happened expression.

Rapp spotted the Nash kids and out of the side of his mouth said, "I also heard he'd been drinking a lot."

"I heard the same thing, but as you know . . . the FBI will follow every lead."

"Even if it comes from a vengeful partisan hack like Ogden?"

"Especially if it comes from a vengeful partisan hack like Ogden."

"Great."

"She might be vulnerable at the moment," Trittin said without looking at him.

"How so?"

"A new friend of ours told me Ogden's been telling those close to her that she thinks the attacks last week were not on the up and up."

Rapp froze for a second and then turned to Trittin. "What in the hell is that supposed to mean?"

Trittin checked to make sure no one was near and then said, "She thinks it may have been a plot by certain people in this building to eliminate their critics and whip up anti-Muslim sentiment."

"Come on." Rapp didn't know if he should be pissed off, concerned, or just laugh. He decided to go with the first one. "And kill a bunch of innocent people in the process. Including a lot of colleagues over at NCTC."

"Like most conspiracy theories, it's heavy on motive and very weak on evidence."

"It's also crazy . . . I mean don't get me wrong, I've thought of plugging a few of those self-serving idiots, but actually doing it is nuts."

"The president agrees, and that is why he's asked me to quietly see if I can leak it to the press."

"Why?" Rapp asked in shock. "That's not the kind of thing you want floating around out there."

"It already is. At least on the internet. It's all the same jokers who think 9/11 was a conspiracy. The bottom line, Mitch, is that the president is willing to make a move against her. He's sick of her antics. He'd never say it publicly but he thinks she's come unhinged."

"Thinks . . . shit, I could have told him that years ago."

"Well . . . I just wanted to let you know we have your back on this one. You stay focused on finding this Lion of al Qaeda, and we'll deal with Ogden and the FBI."

"Thanks, Julie. I appreciate it."

Trittin gave him a quick hug and then moved off. Rapp circled the perimeter until he reached the Nash kids. They'd staked out their own turf near the back wall. Not an adult within fifteen feet. Just the four Nash kids and Tommy Kennedy, Irene's ten-year-old son. When Rapp pulled up they were standing in an informal circle with Charlie the toddler waddling around in the middle looking like a drunken British sailor—his mom had dressed him in a white sport coat and white shorts with white shoes. The other kids, including Tommy Kennedy, were dressed in their prep school uniforms. They all turned to greet Rapp, and Charlie saw his chance. He broke out of the circle and charged his dad's friend. Rapp bent over, snatched him up, and tossed him up in the air. Charlie let out a squeal before landing safely in Rapp's arms.

"Kids," Rapp said, "how's it going?"

Jack Nash stepped forward. "My dad is really mad at you."

"Me . . . come on . . . you can't be serious."

"He was trying to talk all quiet on the way over here, but he's half deaf from that explosion, so he doesn't know we can hear everything he says. He was really mad."

Shannon stepped forward with a smile and said, "My mom was laughing at him, so I don't think he was *that* mad, but he did say some not-very-nice things about you."

"Wouldn't be the first time. Did you kids enjoy meeting the president?"

"Yeah," Jack said excitedly. "We got to take photos and everything."

"Heads up," Rory said, while looking over Rapp's shoulder. "Here he comes."

Rapp turned and saw Nash coming straight for him, his eyes locked on him as if he were a ram-hell bent on knocking something off his ledge. A few people tried to stop him and offer their congratulations, but Nash kept moving. Rapp was suddenly glad he was holding Charlie. He figured the little fella would deter any serious physical confrontation. He turned so Charlie was in the direct line of fire.

Nash pulled up to the group. "You're unbelievable."

"Nice medal," Rapp said, pointing at Nash's chest.

Nash looked down and fingered it. "I've already taken it off twice. My wife and Irene and some PR handler keep making me put it back on."

Rapp laughed over his friend's obvious discomfort.

"You think this is funny? I swear if you weren't holding Charlie I'd take a swing at you."

Rapp tried to turn serious. "You have to admit I got you."

"Yeah . . . and I'm going to get you," Nash said as he leaned in. "This is bullshit and you know it."

Rapp cupped his free hand over Charlie's ear and feigned shock at his friend's choice of words. "Hey!"

"Dad, I heard that," Jack announced as he appeared at Rapp's side.

"I don't know if you've noticed, Jack, but it's my day. When you're thirty-eight and the president of the United States gives you a medal you can swear all you want to. Now take your brother. I need to have a word with Mitch."

Rapp handed Charlie over to Jack and then followed Nash to a nearby open spot.

Nash looked at the people who had gathered on his behalf. "I can't believe you ambushed me like this."

Rapp couldn't stop smiling. "And I can't believe how easy it was to dupe you."

"Yeah, well, I've been a little preoccupied lately."

"You do work for the CIA . . . you know. You're supposed to see shit like this coming."

"I don't want to hear it from you. Not now . . . probably not ever. You had no right to make this shit up."

"Well, you're welcome." Rapp pointed across the room at Nash's wife. "I haven't seen Maggie this happy in years."

Nash looked at his wife. She was talking with Kennedy, Dickerson, and a few other big shots, and Rapp was right. She looked as if the weight of the world had been taken off her shoulders. "That doesn't mean it was okay for you to out me. How the hell would you like it if I did it to you?"

"You'd be breaking the law."

"Why isn't it breaking the law when you do it to me?"

"Because the president didn't say you could. He gave me the go-ahead . . . and besides, I don't have a wife and four kids who depend on me." Rapp looked back at the Nash brood and said, "Trust me . . . you don't want to turn out like me. They need you, and you need them."

The words seemed to at least make Nash stop and think. He considered them for a moment and said, "I would have at least liked to have a say in it."

"And you would have said no."

"You're damn right I would have. I didn't do all those things the president said I did. You did!"

"I did some of them, and don't get all Semper Fi on me. You were a big part of it. If you hadn't zipped that first guy, I'd be dead and so would a hell of a lot of other people, including you." Rapp poked him in the chest. "You deserve that medal."

"What about you?"

"Shit . . . I already have three of them."

"Bullshit."

Rapp shrugged. "See for yourself. Now that you're getting promoted you might be able to read about some of the stuff I've done."

Nash suddenly lit up. "Irene says I'm your boss now. About the only good thing that happened today."

"Quit your pissing and moaning. Look at how happy your wife and kids are. Once you calm down you're going to look back on this day and thank me."

Nash looked over both shoulders and said, "I'm going to ride your ass is what I'm going to do. I'm going to be the worst boss you've ever had."

Rapp laughed. "Good luck. You're not the first guy who's told me that."

Art Harris, the deputy assistant director of the FBI's Counterterrorism Division, ambled over with a huge grin on his face. Rapp matched it and Nash frowned. Harris stuck out his big mitt and said, "Mitch, nice work! You got him good!"

"Thanks, Art, I appreciate it, but it's not the first time someone's duped a jarhead."

"They're like Labs," Harris said, "extremely loyal, but at the end of the day not real smart."

"Boy . . . you two are a regular Rowan and Martin."

"Who?" Harris asked.

"Never mind." Nash turned away from them and saw the CIA's director of public affairs headed their way. "Oh, shit."

Marian Rice approached her new hot commodity and said, "Good news—*60 Minutes* wants an exclusive with you. They're willing to put all their best people on it." When she saw Nash hesitate she said, "This is huge. I know you don't like it, but it's huge, and we have to strike now while you're hot. Come on," she said, grabbing him by the arm. "There are a few more people who would like to meet you."

Nash resisted for a second, and then when he saw the shitass grins on Rapp's and Harris's faces he said, "Keep laughing. Great friends you two turned out to be." He started to walk away and then looked over his shoulder with all the excitement of a man being led to his own execution.

CHAPTER 59

NORTHERN ARKANSAS

HAKIM reached down and adjusted the seat a touch more, leaning it farther back. It seemed as if he was feeling better with each passing mile. He'd almost fainted twice during his escape. The first time was going down the steps of the house and the second was when he had to lower himself into the seat of the car. Each time the pain of his broken ribs tearing into the soft tissue of his lungs was almost too much to take. Looking back on it now he was sure that Allah had given him a helping hand. Nothing else could explain his not blacking out from the pain. As he turned onto Highway 65 and headed south a coughing attack almost became a horrific reality, but he forced himself to take slow, shallow breaths.

Now, nearly two hours later, he was feeling pretty good. The big sedan was comfortable and the owner had fortunately left him a full tank of gas. The wind was howling out of the north and he was headed south so he figured he could get in at least three hundred miles before he had to fill up on gas. He was nearing the outskirts of Little Rock, so everything was back to a two-lane divided highway. He'd already blown through several small towns on the journey south. The speed limit went from 65mph to 30mph and he hadn't even noticed it until some guy standing on the corner motioned for him to slow down. After that mistake he tried to pay more attention. He set the cruise at 68mph and found an AM news station with a strong signal and settled in for the drive. He'd already listened to two local news updates and one national, and there still wasn't a single mention about anything to do with what had happened in Iowa.

There was one big problem that he needed to deal with and one small one that could become a big one. He needed to go to the bathroom, and under any normal circumstances he'd have found the nearest gas station and made it happen, but he was in such bad shape that he didn't dare try to get out of the vehicle. Just the thought of the pain that ripped through his body when he'd gotten into the vehicle brought on a wave of nausea. Hakim thought he had a solution, and he began scanning the billboards on the side of the road for the right place.

Sure enough, within a few miles there was a sign for a McDonald's. Hakim got in line with all the other cars. He checked himself out in the mirror while he waited. He'd found a pair of large sunglasses in the center console, the kind that you saw older people wear over their regular glasses. They were so big they effectively covered most of the bruising around his eyes and also helped age him. He ordered a vanilla shake, large coffee, two bottles of water, a couple of cheeseburgers, some fries, and some extra napkins. He wasn't hungry, but he thought it would be good to have some food in the car just in case. He filled the cup holders with the shake and the coffee and tossed everything else in the passenger seat. As he was leaving the parking lot he saw two signs that told him Allah truly was looking out for him. The first was a drive-through pharmacy and the second was a full-service gas station. If he filled up now he would have no problem getting across the state line without stopping again.

Hakim pulled up to the line of pumps farthest from the building and waited for a man to come out. It turned out to be a young kid, which was all the better. While the kid topped off the Cadillac's big tank, Hakim slowly began sipping his vanilla shake. The total came to $38.50. Hakim gave him two twenty-dollar bills and told him to keep the change. As he crossed the busy street and pulled into the drive-through lane at the pharmacy he began thinking about his decision. Hakim had been up and down the Gulf Coast. From the Florida Keys all the way up and around to Brownsville, Texas. He had contacts in a half-dozen cities, none of them Muslims and most of them involved in the illegal trade of drugs. His most trusted contacts, and the ones who owed him the most, were down in Miami, but that was a long drive. Brownsville was as well. In his condition he could never make it to either city without stopping, and that would complicate things. He would have to dump the car because eventually someone would find the murdered couple and report the car stolen.

No, he decided, *it would be better to drive to New Orleans.* He could make it there in ten hours, arriving well before midnight. He would have to ditch the car and call his contact. There was one other option, and he was tempted to go with it, but he would have to see how things played out first. He picked up some heavy duty aspirin and antibiotic cream at the pharmacy and was back on the highway a few minutes later. Hakim figured when he was done with the shake he'd pee in the cup and then dump it out the window. With his decision to go to New Orleans, though, he needed to make a call. He fished the cell phone out of his pocket and decided to turn it on for the first time.

Hakim set the cruise at sixty-eight miles an hour and held the phone on the steering wheel while he waited for all the various signals to light up. It took about twenty seconds with the phone making some funny noises as it ran through its setup, and then it made a weird chirping noise and the screen told him he had one new message. For a split second, Hakim's heart sank, and then he realized it was probably one of those messages left by the wireless company. He held the message button down for a few seconds and then heard the phone dialing.

He pressed the speaker button and listened as the computerized voice told him what he already knew—that he had one message. A few seconds later a voice from his not-so-distant past sent a chill up his spine.

"You dare call me a coward. What are you? You sneak out of here like some frightened woman while I am in the shower and leave me to fight for myself. Stuck in the middle of America. You will pay!" Karim sounded so angry Hakim wondered if Ahmed had received a beating for not stopping him. "Allah will make you pay. I will tell everyone that you are a traitor. Nothing more than a woman with a man's genitalia. And that I'm not even sure about. When I am done with my mission I will find you. I will hunt you like a dog and I will make you endure unimaginable suffering and humiliation. And trust me, I will not fail. I will find you."

Hakim listened to it again. This time the surprise was gone and with it his fear of Karim. He looked down the highway for a moment and decided to throw caution to the wind. He pressed the callback button on the phone and left it on speaker. It was picked up on the sixth ring.

"I can't believe you are calling me!" Karim's angry voice came over the speaker.

"I can't believe you have your phone turned on. Are you slipping? Are you letting your emotions get the best of all your self-proclaimed military discipline?"

There was an angry laugh and then, "You are running away . . . just like in Afghanistan. You are a coward."

Hakim knew he was trying to bait him with lies. "And you are a psychotic killer of innocent people as well as a delusional liar."

"I speak the truth, as Allah is my witness."

"You are so arrogant. Allah does not condone what you do. You are not important enough for him to care about you."

"And you have lost the way. You spent too many days in the West and have been weakened. You are soft. That is why I beat you so easily."

"We will see who beats who in the end."

"I am not running. Like Jonah, I am heading into the belly of the beast while you run off to your drug-dealing friends."

"You mean you are going to kill more innocent people . . . or will you have Ahmed do it for you like you did the others?" Hakim paused and then answered his own question. "I think you will have Ahmed do it. You love yourself too much to risk being killed."

"Why don't you meet me in Washington and find out."

"I think not. It is my duty to tell the world the true story of the Lion of al Qaeda."

There was a long pause and then Karim asked, "And what would that be?"

"Why do you not like women?"

"What are you talking about?"

"I think I will tell everyone that the Lion of al Qaeda likes little boys and is afraid to kill real men with guns. He must kill old men and women in the middle of the night like a common criminal."

There was a long silence. Hakim could hear his friend breathing heavily on the other end. He knew he had him near his breaking point. Hakim smiled to himself and laughed at the phone. "I will tell them how you send other men to their death while you take all the credit and then shoot unarmed boys. I will tell the world that you are an evil little man."

In a voice seething with anger, Karim said, "I will kill you if it is the last thing I ever do."

"You will have to find me first, and since you are not very smart that will prove impossible."

"Maybe I will tell the police about the car you are in. Report it stolen."

Hakim laughed out loud this time. "Have you ever heard the phrase, it is better to keep your mouth closed and have people wonder if you are stupid than open it and remove all doubt? If you report the car I am driving stolen, and I am arrested, I will simply tell them everything I know about you. I even have a nice photo I could give them."

Hakim laughed again and then, knowing it would drive Karim insane, he rushed to get in the last word. "I have to catch a plane. Maybe I will call you later. Try not to kill any more innocent people. Good-bye."

Hakim hadn't felt this good in weeks. He flipped over the phone and pulled out the battery. Several hundred miles to the north, he imagined Karim breaking more things and throwing another fit. After a moment he thought of Ahmed and hoped his petulant friend did not take out his anger on the Moroccan. Hakim looked down the long, smooth highway and said, "I am free. Free from the torment and stupidity of a man who never should have been my friend."

CHAPTER 60

CIA, LANGLEY, VIRGINIA

AFTER they had managed to collect themselves and stop laughing at their friend's misery, Harris asked Rapp, "Did you get the photos?"

Rapp had forgotten all about them. He pulled out his BlackBerry and found the email Harris had sent him several hours earlier. He waited for the photos to come up on the screen and then scrolled down. The first man he didn't recognize, but the second one looked an awful lot like a certain Moroccan he'd seen in a photograph provided by Catherine Cheval. Rapp scrolled back up to the first photo and wondered if it was possible. Could this be the Lion of al Qaeda? He felt as if he were holding the winning lottery ticket.

Harris saw the change in Rapp's expression and asked, "What is it?"

Rapp lowered his BlackBerry and tried to figure out how much he could reveal. There was no way he could sit on this information. *Iowa,* he thought to himself. *The bastards had gone to the middle of the country to hide out.*

"What do you know?" Harris asked impatiently.

"Let me check with a few of my sources."

Harris studied him with the eyes of a career lawman. "You're holding back."

Rapp hesitated. That he was holding back was obvious. Here they were at the tangled and mangled intersection of politics, law enforcement, and international espionage. He could trust Harris, but the FBI did everything with one eye on a possible prosecution and court date and right behind them were all the lawyers over at Justice. They would be obsessed with following the trail of evidence, knowing that any defense attorney would do the same in an attempt to punch holes in the government's case.

This was exactly what the president and Dickerson were afraid of. He was screwed both ways. If he brought them in and told them everything, it would eventually blow up in the face of the French and further damage their coöperation. Rapp would lie through his teeth before he'd let that happen. But he needed the FBI's help. He simply didn't have the manpower to do what needed to be done. At some point they were going to need a lucky break, or they would have to go public with these photos. Rapp suddenly thought of something else and it turned his mood foul. If it came out after the fact that he had sat on this information, even if it was just for a day or two, he and the CIA would be crucified.

Rapp eyed Harris and thought of the FBI's rapid deployment teams. He couldn't remember how many they had, but he thought there were at least six. "You still have that rapid deployment team in Chicago on standby?"

"Yeah."

Rapp wavered for a minute. "I think you should deploy them."

"I need a reason to deploy them," Harris said, pushing for information.

"Twenty-plus years of experience. You're not a janitor. Tell everyone to snap to and make it happen."

Harris resisted. "New development since we last talked. The director sent out an edict this morning. We've been getting false leads for a week, Mitch. These teams have been flying all over the country. They're at their breaking point. The director told us no more chasing ghosts. Keep the teams home until we have some hard evidence."

"I'd say two dead bodies, a bunch of military-grade C-4, and two sets of fake IDs with photos of two men of possible Middle Eastern persuasion is a decent start."

"What aren't you telling me, Mitch?" Harris asked.

"Art, you know how this works. I can't tell you what I know right now, because you guys are going to make me sit down in front of a bunch of lawyers and put me under oath and ask me how I know what I know." Rapp shook his head. "That can't happen."

"But, Mitch . . ."

"But nothing. Leave me out of this. Get your team there, put these photos up on the wire, and list them as possible suspects in a double homicide and let your guys piece it all together."

"Are you trying to tell me you think these are two of the three terrorists we're looking for?"

"I'm not telling you anything, Art." Rapp winked. "The only thing I'm saying is that my brain tells me these two guys are Middle Eastern, not Mexican as their names would suggest." Rapp looked at his BlackBerry and said, "My gut tells me there's a chance these might be two of the three guys we're looking for and your gut should be telling you the same thing."

"That's all you're going to give me . . . your gut?"

"For now . . . yes. I gotta run, Art. Deploy the team and see what they dig up." Rapp turned to look for Kennedy.

"Where are you going?" Harris asked.

Rapp ignored him and threaded his way through the crowd toward Kennedy. She was surrounded by too many people Rapp didn't want to talk to, so he maneuvered into a position where he could catch her eye. It took a few seconds, but Kennedy eventually saw him.

He pointed his finger straight up and mouthed the word *Now.*

Rapp left the room and pulled up Marcus Dumond's phone number. He listened to it ring in the hallway across from the gift shop while he waited for Kennedy. The computer genius answered on the fourth ring.

"What's up?"

"Are you in the building?" Rapp asked.

"Which building?"

"Old HQ."

"Yeah. I'm down in the basement working on—"

Rapp cut him off. "Drop whatever it is and get your butt up to Irene's office on the pronto."

"Am I in trouble?"

"Only if you're late." Rapp ended the call and put the phone back in his pocket, just as Kennedy joined him in the hall. Two of her bodyguards hovered nearby.

"What's wrong?"

Rapp started walking. "I'll save the good stuff for your office."

They moved quickly down the wide hallway, while Rapp filled her in on the developments in Iowa. They turned a few times until they got to a door that led to Kennedy's private elevator. No one spoke on the ride up to the seventh floor. When the door opened the two bodyguards stepped aside and Rapp followed Kennedy to the left and into her office.

"I asked Marcus to join us," Rapp said. "He should be here any second."

Kennedy leaned against the front of her desk, placed her hands on the edge, and crossed her legs at the ankles. She was dressed to the nines for the cameras. Dark blue skirt and jacket with black nylons, black pumps, and an ivory blouse. "I'm not sure I understand why you're so concerned."

"Yesterday, when you sent me on that little hop to go meet with Catherine and George?"

"Yes."

"Well, I told you last night they gave me some pretty good intel."

Kennedy could tell by his sour expression that there was a catch. "And?"

"Let's just say your friends up on the Hill wouldn't approve of their methods."

Kennedy noticed how he referred to them as her friends. "So you're nervous about sharing the intel with the FBI?"

"Yes . . . and I promised George up front that I would be really careful with the stuff he gave me. Between the two of us, I'm about 99 percent sure it came from his top source inside the Cuban government."

Kennedy nodded and considered how nervous she would be if she had to share one of her top sources. "Understandable."

"I told you they IDed two of the three, and they have a line on the third."

"I remember."

"Well . . . you're not going to believe this." Rapp pulled out his phone and showed her the photos. "Art just sent me these. This is why I asked you to come up here. They found these fake IDs at the crime scene in Iowa. One of these—" Rapp checked the small screen. "This one right here, I'm almost certain, is a Moroccan named Ahmed Abdel Lah, who Catherine tells me is one of the three men we are looking for."

"And just how does she know that?"

"Unofficially, and I mean really unofficially, someone Catherine trusts picked up Ahmed's brother and had a long talk with him. I don't know all the details, but it sounded pretty solid to me."

"And?"

"You know Catherine as well as I do. She wouldn't dump something like this on me if it was bullshit."

"What about the other photo?"

"I don't know. When Marcus gets up here I'll have him send it to George and Catherine. I don't want it to come directly from either of us. Better to make it look like it was part of an information dump."

Kennedy thought about it for a second and said, "So Ahmed's brother was more than likely tortured."

Rapp shrugged as if to say of course he was.

"And if we share this information with the FBI, they will want to know where we got it?"

"Exactly."

"And then at some point in the not-so-distant future they'll send a couple dozen agents and attorneys over there to question Ahmed's brother and Catherine's man."

"And we can't let that happen," Rapp said.

"No, we can't." Kennedy stared out the window.

"What I need you to do is come up with a plausible explanation for why we think this double homicide is linked to the attacks of last week, and do it in a way that doesn't compromise George and Catherine or their people."

"We could alter those photos and dump them into the database."

"Not a bad idea, but Art already ran them through TIDE and came up with nothing. This has to come from overseas." Rapp looked toward the door, hoping to see Dumond. "As soon as Marcus gets up here he'll know how to handle it without leaving any fingerprints. I also have him looking into an issue in New York."

"New York?"

Rapp was getting ahead of himself. "The farm in Iowa was purchased through an LLC . . . I don't know . . . six . . . eight months back. The lawyer who handled it was out of New York. I wanted to get a look at his files before all the Dudley Do-Rights show up on Monday."

"Follow the money?"

"You got it. I'm half tempted to fly up there myself and slap the guy around a little bit. Make sure I get the whole story out of him."

Kennedy shook her head. "I don't like that idea."

Rapp knew she wouldn't, but asked anyway. "Why?"

"If this adds up like you say, the FBI will most certainly be all over this attorney on Monday. I know you can be persuasive, but there is no guarantee the attorney won't file a complaint . . . in fact, once he's surrounded by a bunch of federal agents I can almost guarantee he'll file charges, and then I'll have to explain to a lot of upset people what one of my top operatives was doing beating an American citizen and subject in a major criminal investigation."

Before Rapp could answer, there was a knock on the door. Dumond entered the office and ambled over. He was wearing khaki flat-front pants, a short-sleeved blue button-down shirt, and an old black knit, square-bottom tie. With his afro he looked like a reject from the seventies. "What's up?"

"We need your expertise," Rapp said. He showed Dumond the two photos. "I need you to pull these off here and send them over to Charles and Catherine. Can you make it look like an information dump? Send it to them first and then send the photos to all our allies asking for help in identifying them."

"No problem."

"How's it going with the lawyer in New York?"

"James Gordan," Dumond said.

Rapp could tell by his tone that he wasn't impressed. "Did you find the money trail?"

"The start of it. Chase Manhattan provided the funds for closing here in the States."

"Where'd the money come from before it got to Chase?"

"Nassau, and that's going to take a little longer to crack."

"Why?"

"Royal Bank of Nassau . . . very good security. I'll crack it eventually, but it's going to take the better part of a day if not the weekend."

"Shit." All this international banking secrecy drove Rapp nuts.

"Give me a few hours. I'll see what I can dig up."

"Good. Get to it. I'll be down to grab the phone in a few." Rapp looked back at Kennedy and said, "I think you should call George and Catherine. Try to explain our predicament."

Kennedy looked at the clocks on the wall behind her desk and then hit the intercom button and asked her assistant to get Butler and Cheval on the phone. "Tell them it's urgent, please."

"Any ideas?" Rapp asked.

"A few. Nothing great, though."

"I think I might be able to thread the needle."

Thirty seconds later Butler and Cheval were on the line. "I've got Mitch here with me," Kennedy said into the speakerphone as Rapp joined her at the edge of the desk.

"Hello, Mitch," Cheval said, "you were going to send me those DNA samples from the six terrorists."

"Sorry, Catherine, but I might have something better." Rapp filled them in on the double homicide in Iowa, the explosives, and the fake IDs. "One of these guys looks vaguely familiar to me. I could swear I've seen a photo of him recently." Rapp shared a look with Kennedy and added, "He looks Moroccan."

There was a prolonged silence and then Cheval asked, "Why don't you send me the photo?"

"On its way shortly. When you get it . . . maybe you could run it by your people in North Africa and see if they get a hit. Maybe it matches a passport on file."

"I will do that."

Butler cleared his throat and asked, "What about the other photo?"

"He looks Saudi to me," Rapp replied.

"I see," Butler said. "What exactly are you looking for, Irene?"

"Just trying to be careful, George. You know how this works. If we put these guys on our watch list and tip off the FBI, they're going to want to know how we figured out who they were. So far, Mitch is running with the idea that they don't look Hispanic like their names would suggest."

"Yeah," Rapp said, "I'm thinking Moroccan and Saudi."

"I just received the photos," Cheval said. "The one man is definitely Moroccan. I think I can get independent confirmation for you within the hour."

"By independent, do you mean something the FBI could use in court?"

"Yes. I would be careful with this other photo, though. I'm not sure the Saudis will be much help. They might even begin to destroy evidence."

"I'm not sure we need confirmation on both photos at the moment," Kennedy said. "The Moroccan should be good enough to pass the entire thing off to the FBI nice and clean."

"Anything from my end?" Butler asked.

Rapp leaned in. "If you could show the second photo to the right people, George, that would be great."

"Will do."

"And one other thing," Rapp said. "You're not by chance heading to the Bahamas this weekend, are you?"

Butler laughed. "I wasn't planning on it."

"Well, I'm flying over to Nassau in the morning."

"What on earth for?"

"I need to talk to someone about a shipment of stolen drugs. And while I'm there I might visit one of your banks."

"Oh," Butler said, showing a bit of concern.

"If you're interested, meet me at the Graycliff. Say around eleven. If not . . . send someone you trust. Someone who might help expedite things."

"Let me see what I can do."

"Fair enough. Just shoot me an email and let me know if you can make it."

Kennedy covered a few more things with them, thanked them for their time, and then disconnected the call. She looked up at Rapp with a pensive stare and said, "The Bahamas."

"Yes."

"And when were you going to tell me about this?"

"I thought I'd send you a postcard from the beach."

"Really . . . and just how do you plan on getting there?"

"Actually, I need to borrow one of your planes. The guy I'm going with is sending his plane to Cuba to pick up the man I need to talk to."

"Cuba . . ." Kennedy frowned. "Who?"

"I think it would be better for both of us if I spared you the details."

"You're unbelievable," Kennedy said with a shake of her head and a sigh.

CHAPTER 61

NEW ORLEANS

HIS watch woke him up with a steady beep . . . beep. Hakim turned off the alarm and looked over at the dashboard clock. It was four-thirty in the morning. He reached down with his left hand and searched for the seat controls. After he found the big vertical knob he pulled up and the driver's seat began to raise itself out of the fully reclined position. He looked over the steering wheel, half expecting to see a cordon of police officers. There were none. He smiled at the cars opposite him. There wasn't a person in sight and beyond the edge of the concrete parking ramp he could see the sky in the east turning gray with the first hints of dawn. The relief felt good. So far his plan had worked.

On the drive into New Orleans he'd weighed his options and decided it was time to press his luck, before his window of opportunity closed. It was time for a bold move. He had a brief conversation with his Cajun associate, Timmy the Bayou Coke King. The Coke King told him he was running a boat in five days. The thought was Hakim could ride out for the transfer and then ask for passage on the other boat. The plan might work, but Hakim had other concerns. The first involved staying at the Cajun's swamp shack for five days. The place was filthy. In his current state he was likely to catch a debilitating infection. His second concern was the vision of himself attempting to climb from one boat to the other in the inevitable swells. And that would be after pounding through who knew what kind of seas, at close to fifty knots. If it had been his only option, he still would have wavered, but he supposed in the end he would have simply dealt with the pain.

Fortunately, there was an alternative. There was a great deal of risk in the sense that he would be trapped as soon as he entered an airport, but sometimes the best course of action really was the simplest. He had an American passport and a matching credit card with a ten-thousand-dollar limit. On the way down the night before he'd pulled into a Wal-Mart parking lot outside Vicksburg and turned on his laptop. There were no direct flights, but in a way that was better. He had his choice of ten or more flights that would work, but the best combination was the 6:00 A.M. out of New Orleans with a connecting flight through Miami. He was very familiar with both airports. The security people at New Orleans International Airport weren't exactly the cream of the crop, and the people at the Miami Airport weren't much better. Miami was also one of the busiest airports in the world, and they were far more worried about who was entering the country than who was leaving it.

So Hakim said a quick prayer and booked the tickets through an online travel site. He then very carefully eased himself out of the car and slowly walked into Wal-Mart so he could use the bathroom and purchase what he would need for the next leg of his journey. Back in the parking lot he took all of his purchases out of the packaging and neatly placed them in the new carry-on bag he'd purchased. He was back on the road in less than thirty minutes and headed over to Jackson, Mississippi, where he pulled in to a truck stop. He hobbled in with his new roller suitcase and found the pay showers that the truckers used. He fed dollar bills into the slot and then entered the cramped space. Slowly and carefully he peeled off his clothes and rolled them into a neat ball before stuffing them into one of the two plastic Wal-Mart bags he'd saved.

Hakim stood in front of the streaked and scratched mirror and inspected the full extent of his injuries. The left side of his body from under his armpit to nearly his waist was one marbleized slab of purple. Both eyes were bruised, his nose was broken, and his lip was split. Even when confronted with the severity of his injuries, he had a hard time believing his friend had done this to him. He plugged in the electric clipper, set it to one, placed his head over the sink, and began to buzz off his medium-length black hair. In a few minutes he was done. All of his hair was buzzed to a uniform quarter inch. He then took the electric razor and took off the two days of stubble on his cheeks and neck, leaving the thick black hair on his upper lip and chin. It was exactly the way he had worn it for the photo he used on his fake passport.

After a quick shower, Hakim placed the electric razor in his suitcase and put the clipper in the second bag with his shoes. He then put on his baggy khaki cargo shorts, a striped light blue and white polo shirt, flip-flops and a Budweiser hat. On the way back to the car he tossed the two Wal-Mart bags into a garbage can, then drove down to New Orleans and the Louis Armstrong International Airport.

He arrived a few minutes past eleven and pulled up to the short-term parking kiosk, where he grabbed his ticket and entered the large multilevel parking structure. He found the perfect open spot on the fourth floor. It was dark and the space was bracketed by a large SUV and a pickup truck. He carefully backed the vehicle into a tight space. There was barely a foot to spare on each side, which was good. If any security guards were on patrol this was the last row they would pick to cut through. Hakim set the alarm on his watch, reclined his seat, turned it all over to Allah, and went to sleep.

Now he had a flight to catch. He was about to open his door when he realized he needed more room. He started the car and pulled out of the spot. Near the end of the row he found two open spaces and pulled in. He popped the trunk and took the keys with him. He stuffed the keys in the pocket of the hoodie sweatshirt he had on over the polo shirt and then very carefully slid the carry-on over the edge and let it slide off the bumper to the ground. After extending the handle he grabbed the bag of cotton balls and tore it open. He took three and stuffed them in his mouth on the left side between his teeth and his cheek. He tapped his cheek with the palm of his hand and decided he could use a few more. After that he put just two on the right side and stuffed some extra ones in his jacket pocket. He then grabbed the dull metal cane he'd picked up at Wal-Mart and closed the trunk. With the left hand on the cane and his right hand on top of the wheeled carry-on he began hobbling toward the terminal.

Just before he got to the double glass doors he stopped and dumped his other forms of ID in the garbage can. It wouldn't look good if he was searched and they were discovered. He took the elevator down a couple of floors and then took the skyway over to the main terminal. So far he'd seen just one person, a flight attendant who walked briskly past him. Inside the terminal there were more people but it didn't look like much in the big space. Hakim looked carefully both ways and saw only one police officer. Overweight and barely awake, he didn't look like much of a threat. If they knew he was coming they were doing a wonderful job concealing themselves.

American Airlines had the busiest counter. Hakim wrote it off to the six-o'clock flight to Miami. He got in the coach line and waited a few minutes before it was his turn. The woman behind the counter looked at him with a combination of shock and concern.

"Oh, you poor dear," she proclaimed. "What happened to you?"

"Carrr assssident," Hakim mumbled through his cotton-stuffed mouth. He handed over his passport.

"I'm so sorry," the woman said as she took his passport and punched his name into the computer. "I have your reservation right here, Mr. Andros. You're on the six o'clock to Miami." She tapped a series of keys and looked at the screen for a moment. "You know what I'm going to do for you. First class is wide open. I think you'll be more comfortable up there. Now once you get to Miami you'll have to check with the gate agent. The computer isn't showing what aircraft you have for the next leg of your trip, so I can't assign those seats. Would you like to check your bag?"

Hakim smiled and said, "Pweeeze."

The woman took the bag and handed him his boarding pass. After he was done thanking her, Hakim hobbled over to the security line. Only one metal detector was open and again the security people looked about as alert as the cop by the front door. *No sense in turning back now*, he thought to himself. He showed the TSA agent his passport and boarding pass. The agent, a fifty-some-year-old man with bloodshot eyes, made sure the name on the passport and the boarding pass matched and that was about it. Hakim kicked off his flip-flops and very slowly bent down to pick them up. He placed them on the conveyor belt and tossed his money, watch, phone, and car keys in a dish. A female TSA agent standing on the other side of the metal detector asked him if he could walk without the cane and he nodded that he could. He placed the cane and his zip-up hoodie on the belt as well and slowly made his way through the detector. On the other end he picked all of his stuff up without a problem.

He felt so good after clearing security that he had to remind himself to slow down. Using the cane, he made his way over to the closest coffee shop and was about to get in line when he remembered the cotton balls. He picked up two newspapers instead and then headed down to the gate. On the way he extracted a few of the cotton balls and placed them in his left pocket with the others. A twenty-four-hour news channel was on an overhead TV near the gate. He stopped and watched for about five minutes. There was nothing new except that the director of the FBI had announced a press conference for 11:00 A.M. Eastern.

Hakim boarded early with the only other first-class passenger and settled into his seat. When the flight attendant came by with a glass of champagne and orange juice, he decided things were indeed looking good and he took her up on the offer. That was when he decided to call

Karim. He removed a few more cotton balls, turned on the phone, and then hit send twice. Surprisingly, the phone went straight into voicemail. At the beep, Hakim turned toward the window and in a quiet voice said, "It's too bad you didn't trust me. I'm already on my way out of the country. I suppose you're stuck somewhere in the middle of America getting ready to kill another innocent woman. The Lion of al Qaeda." He laughed. "It should be the Lamb of al Qaeda. It's too bad you don't have the genitalia to fight a real man face to face."

Hakim ended the call and removed the battery as a precaution. He couldn't help but smile at the thought of what the message would do to the thin-skinned Karim. He sincerely hoped the idiot would meet his death in a hail of bullets. Hakim hoped he could read about it on a beach somewhere. He would put the madness of al Qaeda behind him and start a new life.

CHAPTER 62

NASSAU, BAHAMAS

RAPP was wearing a black Nat Nast bowling shirt with a couple of vertical cream stripes, linen pants, and black loafers. His face was clean-shaven and his eyes were concealed behind a pair of dark aviator sunglasses. He saw them sitting at the outdoor café as he ambled down the street, glancing in the windows of the high-end shops as he went. Sidorov's detail knew who he was and expected him, but the general had brought along two men of his own. Rapp had no idea if they were armed or not. It was highly possible that they had carried their weapons through customs in a diplomatic pouch just as he had. Gunplay was to be avoided. If the Cubans got rough, Coleman, Reavers, and Wicker were just up the street in a minivan and Butler and his men were at the other end of the block sitting at an outdoor café.

So Rapp moved down the street with relative calm, casually taking in the surroundings. There were banks on all four corners of the block and between them a spattering of jewelry stores, cafés, art galleries, and French and Italian designer labels. There wasn't a cobblestone out of place or a speck of garbage to be seen. Rapp had walked down streets just like this in dozens of cities the world over. The ultrarich who wanted to avoid taxes flocked to cities like Nassau with their strong banking-privacy laws. Along with them came a smaller percentage of men who made their money in the illicit trades of guns, drugs, and organized crime. Rapp had spent a great deal of his career tracking these modern-day pirates, and the trail often led to these tiny island nations.

Rapp stopped next to the outdoor café and pretended to check out the display of Panerai watches in the window of a jewelry store. Through the reflection in the large plate-glass window he could see five bodyguards, three for Sidorov and two for the general. He was close enough to smell the smoke from the general's cigar and could faintly hear him talking to Sidorov in English. Rapp nonchalantly stepped over the rope that divided the outdoor seating for the café from the rest of the sidewalk. He kept his right shoulder to the building and his eyes on the bodyguards. If they reached for a weapon, Rapp would raise his hands and let Coleman and the Brits come riding in. With the bodyguards out of the way, Rapp could focus on Ramirez.

Not a single bodyguard reacted until Rapp was next to the table. Sidorov and Ramirez were sitting across from each other. There were two more chairs and Rapp stepped behind the one that had its back to the building. "Peter," Rapp said in a friendly voice, "good to see you."

Sidorov stood and offered his hand. "Mitch, very nice to see you. Please join us. I'd like you to meet General Manuel Ramirez."

The general stayed seated. He looked up at Rapp from behind his reflective glasses, his upper lip pushed out while he sized up this new person. After an awkward moment, he offered his hand.

Rapp clamped down on the general's thin hand and squeezed hard. "General, I've been looking forward to this for some time."

The general just stared. "I'm afraid I don't know who you are."

Rapp shook his head while he pulled back the chair and sat. "No reason for you to know me. Peter was kind enough to set up this meeting."

"What are you talking about?" He removed his sunglasses and gave Sidorov a disapproving glare. "I do not like surprises."

"Then you're going to hate this," Rapp said, not wanting to give Ramirez a chance to get rolling. "As you've probably already guessed, I'm an American, and while that might not interest you too much I think this will . . . I'm a counterterrorism operative for the CIA, which is a nice way of saying I kill terrorists and the scumbags who help them."

If Ramirez was impressed, he didn't show it.

Rapp pressed on. "I'm going to assume you're familiar with the terrorist attacks in Washington last week. A lot of Americans were killed, and my president isn't very happy about that. He has given me the green light to kill anyone who had anything to do with the attacks."

Ramirez remained stoic. "And just how would this concern me?"

"Well . . . as it turns out, the terrorist cell that hit Washington used your island as a staging area for their attacks."

"I don't believe you," the general said, glancing over his shoulder at one of his bodyguards.

Rapp ignored the denial and said, "Last week a plane landed on your island and you ordered your men to help off-load a large amount of cocaine onto two speedboats and one truck."

"I don't know what you are talking about."

Rapp's eyes stayed locked on the general. "We can handle this one of three ways. The first way is the best. You tell me everything you know about Hakim al Harbi."

"I have never heard of this man."

"That's the real name of the smuggler you were dealing with. He's a Saudi who spent a little time fighting in Afghanistan and then left as an advance scout for the al Qaeda cell that hit Washington last week." Rapp pulled an envelope from his pocket and extracted three photos that had been lifted from al Harbi's driver's license, college student ID, and passport. Dumond had hacked into the various databases and snatched the photos without alerting the Saudis. Rapp watched the general closely. "This is the guy you made the deal with. He passed himself off as an intermediary who was helping the Taliban smuggle opium."

The general exhaled nervously and again looked over his shoulder to the closest bodyguard.

"He can't help you, General. You need to tell me everything you know, and I mean everything. Email accounts, hotels, airlines he traveled on, any contacts you know of . . . and most important, the banks he dealt with." Dumond had had his team scouring the international banking community for close to twenty-four hours and so far they had come up with nothing.

"I don't know this man."

"I'll make a deal with you, General. You don't insult me, and I won't insult you."

"You bring me here under false pretenses and then complain that I am insulting you." The general angrily shook his head. "The arrogance of you Americans."

"I know more about you than you can possibly imagine, General. I know, for instance, that before you will do business with anyone, you require an up-front deposit. You used to take it in cash, but with Fidel's recent decline in health, you've begun to have that money deposited in offshore accounts. In fact I've been told you prefer it in gold . . . one hundred thousand dollars."

"Lies."

Rapp's patience was waning. He figured he'd give it one more shot before he dropped the bomb. "General, this doesn't have to be difficult. I really don't give a shit about these drugs. I just want the information."

General Ramirez looked at the nearest bank for a long moment, and then turned back to Rapp and said, "For one million dollars, I will give you the information you ask for. And I want it in gold," he added with wry smile. "The American dollar isn't worth shit these days."

Rapp's entire impression of the man changed in that instant. He was either incredibly greedy or extremely stupid. "Let's get one thing straight. I'm here because Peter convinced me to at least sit down and talk to you. I have been ordered to kill every last piece of scum-sucking shit who had anything to do with this mess. I don't know you, and going into this meeting I guess I somehow got it in my head that you would be a reasonable man. You'd recognize that you were on the wrong side of a really nasty situation and you would gladly help make amends."

"You will have to excuse me, Mr. whatever your name is, if I do not feel like kneeling at the American altar. Your country is not without sin. You cannot lure me here under false pretenses and threaten me. What are you going to do—kill me? Right here?" Ramirez held out his hands and looked around. "You think me a petty thug and you are sorely mistaken. You are a wealthy country. A million dollars is nothing to you. You can threaten all you want, but at the end of the day I know you will pay. It is much easier to do things that way. So get on your phone," he made a move-along gesture with his right hand, "and get the approval to have the money transferred. When you have it, I will consider providing you with the information you seek."

Rapp's brow furrowed in disapproval as he sized up the general. He knew Butler and his men were nearby listening to the conversation, and right about now his British friend was hoping he would give the crass general a million dollars and move on. That wasn't going to happen, though.

Rapp cleared his throat and placed both elbows on the table. "You don't know me, so I suppose I'll have to give this one more try. I came to this meeting with a few contingency plans. When you've dealt with as many scumbags as I have, you learn that you have to be prepared for the worst. My initial thought was that I'd just shoot you right here and send a clear message to all the other greedy third-world dickheads who want to make deals with terrorists. My second thought was that I'd have one of my guys pop you in the back of the head at the airport. Pretty easy shot, really. We've done it before. Everything is set up in advance. You start climbing the stairs to get in the plane and when you hit the top step, bam! A nice heavy-grain, soft-tip bullet right in the back of the head from about three hundred yards. You fall into the plane, door closes, plane takes off, and your dead body gets tossed out the back door in the middle of the big blue ocean never to be found."

"You don't scare me, Mr. Rapp. Give me the money and we will talk. Until then I am done with you." Ramirez started to stand.

Sidorov put his head in his hand and began mumbling to himself. After a moment the Russian looked up and said, "General, this is not the wise approach."

"Don't lecture me," Ramirez snapped.

Rapp reached out and clamped onto the general's wrist. "Sit." He pulled him back into his seat.

"Don't touch me! You Russians and Americans are the same. Your condescending ways have grown old. Neither of you scare me. One word from me to my bodyguards and you will both be dead. Like that!" Ramirez snapped the fingers on his free hand.

Rapp regarded him for a moment and then decided it was time to hit him with option number three. "General, you think that because I'm American I won't actually follow through with my threats."

Ramirez snorted. "That is correct. Every time you have tried subterfuge with Cuba you have failed. Just as you will fail to intimidate me."

"We'll see about that. That planeload of drugs you and your men helped off-load last week . . . any idea where it came from?"

"I do not know what you are talking about," the general said in a haughty voice.

Rapp ignored his denial. "Your new friend al Harbi—the guy you set up the drug deal with—he stole it from the Red Command Cartel." Rapp let the words hang in the air for a beat and saw a flicker of recognition in the general's eyes.

"I don't believe you."

"I really don't give a shit if you believe me or not. The important thing is that they will believe me, because I have the intel to prove it. Satellite photos of your men off-loading the plane. My source told me you've already sold half your take. Phone intercepts of you talking about a new lucrative business partner." Rapp made some of it up, but he knew the general was too focused on the Red Command Cartel to doubt him. Of all the South American drug cartels the Red Command was by far the most violent. "I figure you have two problems. I tell the Red Command that you helped orchestrate the theft and then I tell the Brits what you did. They'll come swooping in and seize every offshore account with your name on it. All of those dollars you've squirreled away will be locked up in a legal fight for years to come. The families who lost people last week will line up by the hundreds to sue you, and they'll take every last penny."

Ramirez turned to Sidorov and said, "You will pay for this."

"For what?" Sidorov asked. "Trying to save your life?"

"Consider everything you have invested in my country gone. All of it."

Rapp laughed and said, "What an asshole. Here Peter is trying to help you, and this is how you repay him."

"He is not trying to help me."

"Trust me . . . If it wasn't for him you'd already be dead." Rapp shook his head at the stubborn prick and said, "You know, before meeting you, I thought I would make this clean and easy. You either tell me everything you know about this Hakim guy, especially any financial transactions, or I kill you."

"Please, enough of your false threats and theatrics. Pay me a million dollars or I will walk away."

"How about I tell you to go fuck yourself and call the Red Command Cartel and tell them that you helped plot the raid that killed seven of their men and looted one of their distribution facilities of approximately twenty million dollars in cocaine."

"You are bluffing."

"I doubt they will be so kind as to fly you to the Bahamas on their private plane. In fact, you will never see them coming. They'll show up at your house one night and slit everyone's throat. They'll kill your grandchildren, your servants, anyone and everyone they find, and they will probably keep you alive just to watch." Rapp watched him squirm for the first time. He stood, pushing his chair back and eyeing the Cuban bodyguards. "So what's it going to be, General? Do you want to live and keep your money, or do you want to die?"

Rapp waited five seconds. He watched the greedy general try to figure out what he would do. Five seconds after that Rapp decided he was done dealing with the idiot. "Fuck you, General." Rapp started to walk away.

"Wait."

Looking over his shoulder, Rapp saw the general reaching into his pocket. He pulled out a pen and a small notebook.

"He told me he was Lebanese." The general began writing down a name. "Adam Farhat." He wrote a few more lines on the paper and then tore it off and gave it to Rapp. "That is the bank he used. He specifically directed me to contact a banker, Christian something . . . I can't remember the last name. The deposit was to be held in escrow until our deal was completed."

"Account numbers?"

"I do not have the account numbers, but I would imagine a man of your resources can figure that out."

You're damn right, Rapp thought to himself. He looked at Sidorov and said, "We'll talk later." Then turning to the general he said, "For your sake, I hope we never cross paths again."

CHAPTER 63

NASSAU, BAHAMAS

THE transfer in Miami was easy. Hakim got in line at the gate and was given his seat assignment for the flight over to the island. He didn't get first class this time because there was no first class. The plane was a turboprop operated by American Eagle. The only real moment of stress came on the other end when they landed at Lynden Pindling International Airport. When clearing customs he lied on his form and said that he would be staying at the megaresort Atlantis. He planned on going nowhere near the place and grew worried as the customs agent punched in his name and allowed his eyes to linger on his computer screen for what seemed an unusual amount of time. He had used the passport on other occasions, but this would be his last. When Michael Andros didn't show up for his return flight on Monday morning the passport would be flagged, but by then Hakim planned on being at least a few hundred miles south of the current location.

The man gave him the proper stamps, and he went out front to catch a taxi. He was hyperalert now. Too alert. Behind every pair of sunglasses he saw a potential spy watching his every move. He decided he needed a good long sleep in a warm bed. Hakim directed the driver to take him to Princess Margaret Hospital. The drive through town was uneventful, but then again he couldn't turn around to see if anyone was following them. The driver asked him if he wanted to go to the emergency room or the main entrance. Hakim told him the main door.

He paid the man in American dollars and gave him a five-dollar tip. He spent five minutes walking through the hospital, his suitcase trailing behind him. At the first garbage can he found he ditched the cotton balls. When he got to the emergency area he leaned his cane against a chair and exited the building. Across the street he found a string of cabs. He carefully slid into the backseat of the first one and asked the driver to take him to the Towne Hotel. Hakim had stayed there before. It was nothing special, in fact it was pretty down-market, but it would do for one afternoon. The drive took just a few minutes. When Hakim got out he looked across the street and laughed at the irony. The entire block was dominated by the American Embassy.

The clerk behind the desk was a young man. Hakim pulled out a wad of cash and said, "A room for one night, please."

"Just you, Mr. . . . ? "

"Smith," Hakim said pleasantly as he slid a hundred-dollar bill across the counter.

The clerk glanced toward the restaurant to see if anyone was watching and then casually pulled the bill toward him and placed a stack of envelopes on top of it. "Will you be paying cash, Mr. Smith?"

"Yes."

The clerk quoted him the rate and then added the taxes. All told it came to a little less than ninety dollars per night. Hakim gave him another hundred and told him to keep it. He took the key and moved down the hall toward his room, smiling to himself. He couldn't wait to feel the sand on his feet, but first he had to make a phone call and ask for a favor. When he reached the room he left the suitcase by the door and sat on the edge of the bed. He stared at the phone for a second and made sure he remembered the number. His eyes danced over the keys and then he picked up the handset and dialed his friend's number.

"Hello," the male voice on the other end said.

"Christian," Hakim said in a happy voice that concealed his nerves. "It's Adam. How are you?" He listened intently for even the slightest sign of nerves from the other man.

"Adam! I was wondering when you would pop up. I received some very nice deposits for your account this week. Quite a bit more than you told me."

"Yes," Hakim said, thinking of the two pallets of drugs. "My importer decided to double their order at the last minute."

"That's a lot of coffee."

"Yes." Hakim thought he sounded normal and was apparently still buying his story that he was a coffee bean importer. "Even during a recession people need their caffeine."

"I know. I couldn't live without it. At any rate, I must thank you. My boss is very happy with your deposits. You are making me look very good. Now I suppose you will want to move it."

"Not before I give you the chance to try to sell me some investments."

"Good. Are you free for dinner?"

"Possibly . . ." Hakim honestly wasn't sure. He needed to put something on the table so he didn't surprise Christian too much when they met. "I was in a car accident and am not feeling 100 percent."

"Oh, my gosh . . . I'm sorry to hear that. How serious?"

"Some broken ribs, but mostly bruises."

"Can I help? Are you on the island? Do you need to stay at my place?"

"I am. I just arrived. I planned on getting here yesterday, but wasn't well enough to travel."

"What can I do to help?"

"Well . . . I need to get something out of my safety deposit box. I'm leaving tomorrow, and I remember when I purchased the box you told me that for special clients access to the box could be arranged on weekends as well."

"Absolutely! You are one of my best clients. When would you like to access your deposit box?"

"Would an hour from now work?"

"Absolutely! And I hope you will allow me to buy you a drink. And we need to get our fishing trip planned. Remember . . . you promised me."

"We will," Hakim said with a laugh. "Don't worry. I will see you in an hour." Hakim hung up the phone with the confidence that his cover was secure. He picked up the remote and turned on the TV. He flipped through the channels until he found CNN and then he froze. Plastered across the screen were two passport photos that Hakim instantly recognized. They were headshots that he had had Karim take while he was training the men in the jungle near Ciudad del Este. Karim then emailed him the photos and Hakim used them to purchase two fake passports, one for Karim and the other for Ahmed. They were the passports that he had placed in the backpacks and had stashed in the barn back in Iowa. The same barn that Karim was convinced had been burned to the ground.

CHAPTER 64

WASHINGTON, D.C.

THEY passed through Centerville on Interstate 66 just before noon. The plan had been to reach the outer-ring suburb at 8:00 A.M., but they had taken a wrong turn in Tennessee. The quickest route to Washington would have brought them back up through St. Louis, and Karim reasoned the last thing they wanted to do was head back in the same direction they had come, so they swung down south and took a very confusing route. That's what Karim kept telling himself, because the alternative was to take the blame, and that simply wasn't going to happen. He had been at the wheel when the mistake was made, while Ahmed was in back sleeping.

Karim was tired and irritable, but with Washington on the horizon the prospect of revenge helped lift his spirits. He was a man of action. Cowering in a farmhouse did not suit him, although the betrayal of his closest friend was weighing heavily on him. He knew that was the real reason he had missed the turn. He had been absorbed in his own self-pity. For the benefit of Ahmed, he was trying to act as if none of it bothered him, but it did, and in ways he could have never imagined. The betrayal, the words, the deeds of someone so selfish. He had given

Hakim so much and this was how he repaid him. How could he not have seen it earlier?

All of his careful planning, his bold moves, his bravery, all of it was on the verge of being destroyed, by one man, a man who was supposed to be his friend. Looking back on it now, though, the signs were obvious. Hakim had never been a true Muslim. He had always questioned their teachers and their clerics. He had been poisoned by all of his time in the West. His obsession with American literature and sport fishing. All of it should have been a warning to him, but he wanted to believe his friend did it only for show, so he could blend in and pave the way for his elite group to strike Washington. It had been Hakim's idea to flee to Iowa and wait for the storm to blow over. He had named him the Lion of al Qaeda. He had planted the seeds of doubt in regard to the al Qaeda leadership. Hakim had whispered in his ear not to trust them. That they could finance the operation on their own. Karim could not believe he had been so naïve as to not see the true selfish motives of his friend.

And now the coward had run away and was threatening to spread lies, complete fabrications that would make him the laughingstock of the Muslim world. Karim had spent much of the night behind the wheel of the RV telling himself that Hakim either would not go through with it or was not capable of pulling it off. As the miles ticked by, though, he knew that he was wrong on both counts. Hakim had helped create the Lion of al Qaeda, and he was surely capable of destroying the carefully constructed legend. At one point, when Karim was sure Ahmed was asleep, he actually wept. It had been the first time in years. The tears flowed over the injustice. How could a fellow Muslim do such a thing? When the tears finally stopped, Karim turned the anger on himself. He had allowed his friendship and affection for Hakim to blind him. For too many years he had allowed Hakim to get away with things he would have never tolerated from another warrior.

Early in the morning, as they passed over an unknown mountain range, Karim was greeted with perhaps the most beautiful sunrise he had ever seen, more beautiful than all the sunrises combined that he had witnessed before going into battle against the Americans in Afghanistan. Fog clung to the valley below and it looked as if they were in paradise looking back down on earth. It was in that dazzling, beautiful moment that Karim felt Allah calling for him. Hakim had deceived him and distracted him from his destiny. He had robbed him of his deserved glory, of the honorable death of a commander leading his warriors in battle, standing by their side and dying with them. The tears came again, but this time they were tears of anger, not self-pity. He thought of his brave, beautiful warriors charging into the teeth of Satan himself. Not a single one of them hesitated or even looked back. It was the bravest thing he had ever seen.

And the American president called them cowards. Karim gripped the steering wheel so tightly he thought he might break it. He had lied to the world and flaunted the inflated tactics of his own people—this Mike Nash and his meaningless medal. Every time he recalled the orchestrated press conference he wanted to scream. The American president couldn't open his mouth without spewing lies, yet there was the press, complicit in every way, repeating and amplifying the lies. Karim would wake them up. He would give them something to remember him by. He would make his men proud, and he would show the world that America's president was a liar.

Karim had the address as well as the phone number memorized. It had been emblazoned on his subconscious nearly a year earlier. It was part of the original plan orchestrated by al Qaeda's senior leadership. They were not far from the safe house, but first he needed to get rid of the RV. Karim called for Ahmed to join him up front.

"Two more exits. Are you ready?"

"Yes."

Karim stayed in the right lane, slowing with the merging and exiting cars. At the Fairfax County Parkway exit he looped around and headed north. He took his second right turn at Fair Lakes Parkway and then followed it straight to the big mall. The place was huge, with rows and rows of cars to choose from. Karim pointed out several cameras as well as a mall security vehicle parked close to one of the main entrances.

"Remember," Karim said, holding up the phone. "Turn yours on and we will use the talk button on the side."

"I remember."

Next to a grassy boulevard with a row of trees, Karim brought the big RV to a stop. Ahmed exited the vehicle and crossed the boulevard. Ten seconds later he was wading through a sea of cars, working his way toward the Macy's entrance just like the thousands of shoppers who would attend the mall on this sunny Saturday afternoon. Karim drove a hundred meters and parked in the area farthest from the mall. The parking lot was about 70 percent full. He glanced down at his digital watch. Every man on his team had been taught how to steal a car. They focused on the most common makes and models and knew exactly what wires to clip and how to disengage the steering lock. Even so, Karim's heart was racing.

His phone beeped and for an instant Karim thought Ahmed was trying to talk to him. He looked at the screen and saw that the message light was blinking. He stared at the phone, wondering if he could listen to the message and still receive a call from Ahmed. He knew the message was from Hakim, and the pull to find out what he had said was too much. Karim pressed the message button and waited for voice prompts.

Karim's eyes scanned the parking lot while the quiet voice of Hakim played over the tiny speaker. "It's too bad you didn't trust me. I'm already on my way out of the country. I suppose you're stuck somewhere in the middle of America getting ready to kill another innocent woman. The Lion of al Qaeda . . ." the words were followed by mocking laughter. "It should be the Lamb of al Qaeda." Karim's jaw clenched. "It's too bad you don't have the genitalia to fight a real man face to face."

Karim let loose an unbridled scream of anger that echoed through the RV, while he smashed his fist repeatedly down on the dashboard. When he was done he looked around to see if anyone was close enough to hear and then repeated the process. He didn't think he had ever wanted to kill anyone more in his life. Karim replayed the message one more time and then pressed the button to reply. At the beep, he said, "You are a coward and you have always been a coward. You have proved it once again by running away and leaving me to fight. I will prove to the world that I am the lion and you are the lamb. My only regret is that I will not be able to kill you with my own hands, but do not worry . . . I will make sure that you are marked as a traitor to Islam and hunted to the ends of the earth."

Moments after he left the message the phone crackled with the voice of Ahmed. "I am pulling up behind you."

Karim checked his side mirror and saw a dark blue pickup. He pressed the button on the side of the phone and said, "Follow me."

They left the mall lot and went back down Fair Lakes Parkway. Karim remembered seeing an office park not far away. It would be mostly empty on a Saturday afternoon. He took a right at Fair Lakes Court and pulled into the tree-lined lot a few hundred meters ahead on his left. He was pleased by the absence of security cameras. Karim parked the RV, climbed out of the driver's seat, and went back to the kitchen area where two bags were packed and waiting by the door. He went out the side door and locked and closed it behind him. Ahmed had already opened the rear-side storage compartment. He took two bags from the compartment and placed them in the back of the pickup before going back for a third.

Ahmed then climbed back behind the wheel of the Ford F-150 while Karim jumped in the passenger seat. Karim pulled the map from his pocket and checked their location one more time before telling Ahmed where to go. He led him back toward the mall and had him take a left on Ox Road. They wound through some plush residential neighborhoods until they found themselves on Stuart Mill Road. The rolling tree-lined street held some of the county's most expensive homes. Karim, however, was not impressed.

The house was ahead on the right. Karim instantly recognized the gate even though it had been nearly a year since he'd looked at the photos. Before leaving Pakistan they had spent weeks going over every detail of the plan. Originally this place was to serve as the staging area for the attacks. The hilltop estate was shrouded in trees and was big enough to house a battalion of men. Over thirty-thousand square feet of opulence owned by Saudi Aramco. It was used to entertain and house the man who ran the Saudi-owned national oil company's Washington office. Karim had been assured the executive would be out of the country for the week before the attack and the week after. The staff would also be given time off.

They pulled up to the gate and stopped. Both men looked up the long, paved driveway. From their vantage they could glimpse just a portion of the house. Karim glanced over at the keypad and remembered the code. It was simple enough. "The four corners," he said to Ahmed. "One, three, nine, seven."

Ahmed pressed the numbers and the gate slid open. They drove slowly up the driveway, continued past the circle that led to the front door, and went around the right side of the house where the garage doors were located. Karim drew his gun and spun the silencer into place before jumping out of the vehicle. He found the keypad on the first of four doors, punched in the same code they used for the gate, and then hit enter. The door began sliding smoothly up. Karim moved off to his right and looked around the corner of the house to the backyard. It was landscaped in such a way that his view was blocked. He moved back to the edge of the garage and bent to look under the rising door. The space straight ahead was open, but the other three were occupied. Karim was pleased. He ducked under the door and moved across the gray floor. Ahmed put the truck in drive and followed him.

When the vehicle was clear of the door Karim pressed the button and lowered it. Ahmed turned the truck off and jumped out. Before Karim had to tell him, the Moroccan drew his pistol and quickly spun a silencer onto the end of it. Karim placed his hand on the doorknob. He'd been told it would likely be unlocked, but if it wasn't there was a key hidden behind the garbage can. He tried the handle and it moved. Both men stepped into a back hallway and turned their attention to the buzzing keypad on the wall. Karim punched in the code, but in reverse this time. The buzzing stopped a split second later and they both breathed a sigh of relief that did not last long.

Footsteps could be heard down the hallway and then the voice of a man called out. Karim leveled his gun and glided down the hall in near silence. Ahmed trailed two steps behind. The wide hallway had doorways on the left and the right. Karim bypassed both of them, leaving them to Ahmed. A modern oil painting hung on the wall straight ahead and there were open archways to the left and the right. Karim moved to the right side and took a quick look into the room on the left before springing back to his left so he could get a better angle on the room where he thought he had heard the voice. There was movement. At least one person. Karim charged ahead, his gun ready to dispatch any threat. A man was seated at the kitchen table in a white robe and a woman was standing in the middle of the kitchen, also in a white robe, frozen like a statue with a coffee cup in one hand and a saucer in the other.

Karim would never know if it was the dropping of the cup and saucer and the way they shattered on the stone floor or the woman's earsplitting scream that caused him to squeeze the trigger, but he did know that it happened without any forethought. The bullet sailed clear through her open mouth and blew out a good portion of the back of her head. An instant later she was on the floor twitching among the broken white ceramic shards of her coffee cup and saucer. Karim glanced at her and then his eyes traveled back to the white cupboards that had been behind her. They were covered with brain matter and blood and looked amazingly similar to the modern painting he had just passed in the hall. His eyes traveled next to the silent man at the table. He was in his fifties and was undoubtedly Arab. The woman could have been his daughter.

The man swallowed hard and then with a quivering lip said, "Please don't kill me."

Karim nodded and asked, "What is your name?"

"Khalid," he said. "Khalid al Saeed."

"You run the Aramco office in Washington."

"Yes."

"You are supposed to be out of the country."

He nodded. "You are the Lion of al Qaeda."

Karim was caught off guard. "How would you know such a thing?"

"Your photo is on TV. Both of you." He pointed over Karim's shoulder to Ahmed.

Karim felt his gut twist. He tried to stay focused and asked, "Why are you here? You were supposed to be gone."

"I decided to return early."

"Your family?" Karim asked.

"They are still in the Kingdom."

Karim looked to the woman on the floor. Her robe had spilled partially open and he could see that she was not wearing any underwear. "Who is she?"

"A friend."

Karim nodded, ran a few scenarios through his head, and made a quick decision. He looked at the man's nervous eyes and said, "*Allahu Akbar.*"

"No," the man pleaded. "I am a Saudi. I am a believer. I have contacts . . . very well-placed contacts. I . . ."

Karim raised his pistol and shot the man twice in the heart.

CHAPTER 65

NASSAU, BAHAMAS

GEORGE Butler looked across the table and said, "You could have just paid him the million dollars."

Rapp smiled, shrugged his shoulders, and said, "I suppose."

"I'm glad you didn't," Dumond said as he pecked away at his laptop. "The guy was a world-class prick."

Rapp laughed. It wasn't like Dumond to offer such a harsh opinion. They were sitting in the Chairman's Club at Graycliff, the eighteenth-century plantation house turned hotel and restaurant. The place was very private and very British. Rapp had suggested it knowing that Butler had a discreet agreement with the manager. A waiter came into the room with a large tray. He set down three plates and refilled the water and iced tea glasses.

When he was gone, Butler said to Rapp, "You almost lost him. Wouldn't it have been easier to just pay him?"

Rapp shook his head. "Maybe, but I think a guy like that is just as likely to take your money and lie to you. He's a thug. He gets his way by threatening people with violence."

Butler set down his iced tea. "So you hit him with the only thing he really understands."

"I suppose. It worked, didn't it?"

"Yes, but you do know I would never have let you lay a finger on him. At least not while he was here."

"I know," Rapp said with a slight grin. "I would never put you in that position."

"Yes you would," Butler said with dry sincerity.

"Well . . . at least not intentionally."

"That has always been your Achilles' heel."

"What?"

"Some people have the Midas touch . . . you, on the other hand . . . have all the grace of one of those American footballers who bashes the quarterback into submission."

"Thank you," Rapp said with a smile.

Butler's phone vibrated. He didn't bother to pick it up. He simply looked down at the screen, read the message, and said, "We have located our banker."

"Christian?" Rapp said.

"Yes, his last name is Nelson. He has a flat over in the Grove not far from here."

"Do your boys have eyes on him?" Rapp asked.

"Not yet. A car is on its way, but we have his mobile, work number, and email account all monitored."

Rapp smiled. When it came to national security and secrecy the Brits could move five times faster than the Americans. "Do we know if he's on the island?"

"According to customs . . . yes."

"I'm in," Dumond announced, raising his hands in the air as if he'd just won an Olympic medal.

"Where?" Butler asked.

"First Caribbean Bank."

"Impossible." Butler looked nervously back toward the door. "How did you do that so fast?"

Rapp leaned in and waved off Butler's question. "If you really want to know, maybe you guys could take a walk on the beach later."

"But . . ." Butler tried to press the question.

"No," Rapp said, knowing where it would lead them. Butler was a techie at heart. "You two will start talking about all of your trapdoors and back doors and portals and hashes and injections and my eyes will glaze over and then I'll get a headache. So you guys can go over all that later. For now," Rapp said, turning all of his attention back to Dumond, "I want to hear about the financials of Adam Farhat."

Dumond was the ultimate multitasker and had never stopped typing. "Sweet mother of Jesus!" he announced with his eyes still fixed on his laptop.

"What?" Rapp asked.

"He has over thirteen million dollars in this account. Almost ten of it deposited this week alone."

"That would make sense," Butler said. "Payments for the drugs."

"What else?" Rapp asked.

"Looks like he runs some kind of coffee import company."

"What about payments? Where has he been sending money?"

"Other than this hundred thousand dollar debit, which was probably to General Scumbag, there's nothing. Only deposits." Dumond squinted at the screen and pecked at a few keys. "He also has a safety deposit box."

Butler's phone started ringing. He glanced at the caller ID and then answered. "Hello." He listened ten seconds, his eyes growing a touch more alert by the second. "And we have people in place?" He listened again for a few seconds and nodded enthusiastically. "Good. I'll be back to you shortly." Butler set the phone down and said, "Apparently Mr. Nelson just got off the phone with his superior at the bank."

"And?" Rapp asked.

"One of his more important clients would like to access his safety deposit box this afternoon."

"Is that normal for a Saturday?" Rapp asked.

Butler shrugged as if to say who knows. "These banks all make exceptions for their better clients."

"Where's Nelson right now?"

"Leaving his flat. We assume on his way to the bank."

Rapp looked at Butler for a long moment and then without saying a word both men stood.

Dumond looked up. "Where are you guys going? Our sandwiches just got here."

"Bring it with," Rapp said. "You can eat in the car."

CHAPTER 66

LANGLEY, VIRGINIA

THE match was a blowout. McLean was up 14–1 over their hated rivals the Langley Saxons. The difference this year was Rory Nash and everyone knew it. The thirteen-year-old had eight of his team's points. Nash watched intently as Rory sliced through the Saxons' defense. Any other game he'd be on the bench at this point, but McLean's coach wanted retribution for last year's blowout. Langley had one big defender whom Nash had been watching all game. He had reminded his son before the game to keep an eye out for him. The kid was a head taller than every other player on the field and was known to lay out at least one opponent per game. As Nash looked out on the field Rory was moving from right to left cradling the ball. He sliced between two defenders and it looked as if the big kid from Langley was finally going to get his shot at Rory. At the last second, though, Rory slammed on the brakes and pulled off a perfect roll dodge. The big kid sailed past Rory with an angry grunt as he tried to command his large frame to do the impossible. Rory closed on the goal, moving to his left as he went. He faked once and froze the goalie and then again as he closed the gap. His feet were dancing along the edge of the crease. He faked low to get the goalie to bite and then the stick snapped around the back of his head, the ball arching softly through the air to the opposite side of the crease, where one of his teammates snatched it and snapped it into the open net.

"Sweet!" Jack yelled.

"Yeah," Nash agreed with some relief. "Your brother shouldn't even be in there right now." Nash looked farther down the sideline in search of his wife. She was standing about twenty yards away talking to two of the other mothers. She smiled at her husband and pointed at him. The other two mothers turned and waved at Nash. They were smiling and nodding as Maggie whispered something to them. Nash cringed. He was not used to all this attention. From the moment he had arrived at the field, people had been talking and pointing.

"Dad," Jack said, as he looked up, "are you famous?"

The comment hit Nash like a slap in the face. He felt himself getting angry, but told himself to take a deep breath. It wasn't Jack's fault. He was only ten. "No, Jack, I'm not famous."

"Well . . . you kind of are. Your photo was on the front page of the paper this morning and you were all over the news last night."

"Just because you get your picture in the paper doesn't mean you're famous."

"That's not what my friend Scott said."

"I really don't want to talk about it, Jack. I'm not famous, all right?"

Maggie walked up just in time. She slid her arms around his waist and gave him a big hug. "You're quite the topic around here."

"Oh . . . God . . ." he moaned.

"Why can't you just relax and enjoy it?"

"Because it's not who I am. I haven't changed. I'm the same guy who's been going to these games for I don't even know how many years. The only thing that's changed is everyone's perception of me."

"A perception that's based on the truth. These people now know who you work for and what you've been doing, and I have to tell you," Maggie said as she lowered her voice, "some of these ladies, like Stacy and Claudia, it's a huge turn-on for them. Very sexy that I'm married to a spy."

"I heard that," Jack said without taking his eyes off the field. "Gross."

Maggie grabbed him and pulled him in for a group hug. A second later the whistle blew and the game was over. As the two teams lined up to shake hands, Nash began looking around the park for his daughter.

"Where's Shannon?"

"Not sure." Maggie looked toward the playground. "There she is—pushing Charlie in the swing."

Nash watched her push the green bucket that her baby brother was in. He felt a pang of anxiety and asked, "Do I have to let her drive home?"

"Yes," Maggie said.

"She's not very good. I mean, don't get me wrong . . . she's a great kid, but she can't drive."

"Michael, she just got her permit this morning. Do you expect her to be a great driver on her first day?"

"I don't expect her to be perfect, but . . ."

"But what?"

"She sucks, Mom," Jack said.

Maggie grabbed his cheeks. "Oh . . . Jack, sometimes, I swear."

"Mom," Jack said while shaking free of her grip, "I'm not saying she's stupid or a bad person. I'm just telling you the truth. She's a bad driver."

"Well, maybe you and your father can walk home."

Jack took a step back to get out of his mom's range and said, "Can we, Dad? Do you know how funny that would be . . ."

"Jack Nash." Maggie reached for him, but he was too quick. He scampered onto the field in search of his brother. "He takes after you," she said to her husband.

"I think he has more than a little of his mother in him."

"The smartass part comes from you."

"And the psycho stubborn part . . . who do you suppose he gets that from, you?"

Maggie was on the verge of upping the ante when an elderly couple approached them. "Excuse me," the man said, "Mike and Maggie Nash?"

The Nashes nodded.

"I'm Charlie Kelly. This is my wife, Mary."

"Nice to meet you," Nash said as he shook the man's hand.

"My grandson plays for Langley."

"Ohh . . . great," Maggie said.

"Not today. Your boy pounded us. Pretty damn good player," he added gruffly.

"Thank you," Nash said.

Kelly looked across the field, his cloudy blue eyes unfocused, his bottom lip trembling ever so slightly. "I just wanted to say hello." He couldn't look at Nash. His wife hung close to his side. "And thank you. I was in the Navy and then I put in forty years at Langley. Clandestine service . . . operations . . . spent most of my time in Europe. What you did," he finally looked at Nash, "it made a lot of us proud . . . and there's not many of us left." He shook his head and then said, "I just thought you should know that."

Nash was caught off guard. He stammered for a second and then said, "Thank you, sir."

"Charlie," the old man said, "please call me Charlie."

"I will. Thank you, Charlie."

"Well . . ." he said as he looked toward the cars. "We'll see you around."

"Sure," Nash said.

"Very nice to meet you," Maggie said. As the older couple moved toward the parking lot, Maggie said, "That was nice."

"Yeah. We don't do enough to celebrate those guys."

Jack returned from the middle of the field with Rory and a couple of his teammates. "Mom," Jack said as he came speeding up, "are you really going to let Shannon drive?"

"I don't think it's any of your business, young man."

"Well, if she is," Jack suddenly produced Rory's lacrosse helmet, "I'm wearing this."

"Okay, that's it . . ." Maggie took a step and reached out to grab the sleeve of his sweatshirt but again he was too quick. He darted off across the field. Maggie composed herself as she came face to face with Rory and his two friends. "Nice game, honey."

"Thanks," Rory said. "Can Will and Ben sleep over?"

"Well," Maggie said, caught a little off guard, "your father and I are going to dinner, so Shannon is going to be in charge . . ." Her voice trailed off and she turned to her husband to see if it was okay.

"Nice game, boys," Nash said.

"Thanks, Mr. Nash," the two boys said in unison.

"I'm fine with you guys staying over. Have you asked your parents?"

Both boys said they would and ran off to find their parents.

"We're going to dinner tonight?" Nash asked his wife.

"Yes," she said with a big smile. "I haven't spent five minutes alone with you in the past week. Do you have a problem with that?"

"Not at all." He put his arm around her shoulder. "We'll eat some-place close by."

"Wherever you want, honey."

"Italian?" They started walking toward the cars. Rory ran ahead to see what Charlie and Shannon were doing.

"Sure."

"And then when we get home?" Nash asked with a hopeful tone.

"We can play spy and you can show me your gun."

Nash laughed. He looked at Shannon pushing Charlie in the swing. Watched him scream as his brother ran up with his arms out as if he were Frankenstein. Charlie cut loose an earsplitting shriek of terror and then began laughing. Nash smiled and thought to himself, *This is the way it's supposed to be.*

CHAPTER 67

NASSAU, BAHAMAS

HAKIM decided to walk to the bank. It wasn't far and he needed the time to think. Just as he feared, the barn had not burned down. Karim was an idiot, all the more so because he actually thought himself smart. He was an intolerable ass. Hakim kept asking himself if there had been anything else in the barn that could put the FBI on his trail. He had been lucky that he had packed his bag in the RV's storage compartment months earlier. Karim's and Ahmed's packs were hidden under a tarp in the barn just as Karim had ordered. Something about wanting to personally inspect them. It served the fool right that his need to control every detail had led to his own downfall.

As he exited the hotel into the sunny afternoon he was positive that his only link to Iowa was the conservancy trust that he'd set up to purchase the farm itself. He would have time, though, before they could get to the bottom of that tangled web, and when they did they would find nothing more than a dead-end. The Royal Bank of Nassau was nearly a mile away and he had never set foot in the place. Everything had been handled over the phone. There was approximately twenty thousand dollars in the account to handle expenses and taxes, pocket change compared to his deposits at First Caribbean. They could have it all. Hakim moved up the sidewalk, confident that he was out in front of the coming storm. Besides, Christian was not a good actor. That was one of the reasons he had chosen him to be his personal banker.

A block before the bank he stopped and checked his watch. He had ten minutes before he was to meet Christian. The wise thing to do would be to spend that time checking for any surveillance, so he crossed the street and casually strolled down the block. Every so often he would stop and pretend to look in a window. He was actually looking in the reflection to see if anyone was watching him. No one was, and he was getting a little giddy at the new life that awaited him. He would go to Brazil. Over 200 million people and a landscape as diverse as that of any country on the planet. The population spoke Portuguese, English, and a little Spanish, and most important, accents were very hard to detect. Bloodlines from all over the Mediterranean, Spain, and Portugal had been mixing together with the natives for several hundred years. His naturally dark skin would be no more out of place than it would be in his native Saudi Arabia.

Hakim had traveled the coast and found dozens of places where he could simply disappear and start a new life. His only requirement was that he be on the water. He would buy a boat and live on it for the first year, moving from port to port, establishing an identity and making friends. Maybe someday in the not-so-distant future he would settle down and start a family. He wondered about his faith, though. Brazil was not exactly a place where a Muslim could still practice his beliefs and not stand out. For now he would have to keep that part of his life very private.

Hakim was so immersed in thought that he didn't hear his name being called until Christian was crossing the street. He glanced up to see the look of deep concern on his banker's face.

"Oh, my gosh . . . look at you! What happened?"

"A bad car accident."

"Did the airbag do that to your face? I've heard they can really screw your face up."

"Yes, but it saved my life."

Christian stood there for a moment, looking him over. "Other than that, how do you feel?"

"Okay . . . Some broken ribs, but I'll survive."

"Well, I'm sorry you had to go through that. Let's get you inside and get you taken care of."

Christian led Hakim across the street to the front door of the bank, where a security guard was waiting on the other side of the glass doors. The guard waved to Christian, inserted a key in the door, and opened it. Once inside, the banker thanked the guard and led Hakim through the lobby to his office, where he stopped to grab his own set of keys and pull up his client's safety deposit box information on the computer.

"Before we head down, can I get you anything to drink . . . tea, water?"

"No, thank you. I'm fine."

"Do you have your key?"

"Yes." Hakim couldn't believe how calm he was. He supposed it had to do with his familiarity with Christian. Still, it would be a huge relief once he got what he needed from the box and disappeared.

They took the elevator to the basement. Christian put him into one of the private rooms with two chairs and a desk and left to get the box itself. Less than a minute later he returned, placed the box on top of the desk, and left. Hakim pulled out his key, inserted it into the lock, and turned it 180 degrees to the left. The lock disengaged and he lifted up the long-hinged cover. Inside were a fresh set of documents, including a credit card with a $25,000 limit, a money belt containing $100,000, and sheaf of corporate bearer bonds totaling $1 million in value. Hakim lifted his shirt and strapped the money belt around his waist. He placed the new credit card and passport in his front right pocket, and then glanced in the large manila envelope to verify that the bearer bonds were in fact inside.

He closed the box, put the key back in his pocket, and told Christian he was done. After the banker put the box away they took the elevator back up to the first floor and then exited the building. Back out on the street, Christian insisted that they get a drink, but Hakim told him he wasn't feeling up to it. The banker then suggested that he give him a ride back to his hotel, but Hakim got out of it by telling him he needed the air, promising that he would meet him for dinner later, even though that was highly unlikely. They parted ways with a set time and location for dinner. Hakim walked back to his hotel with a bounce in his step that he hadn't had in some time. He was already thinking about the sailboat he would buy. He knew the exact length and make and knew where he could buy a nice used one. That was if it hadn't sold in the last couple months.

As he walked down the sidewalk Hakim began to refine the next part of his plan, mainly, how he would island-hop his way to his destination. The boat was in Farmer's Hill, a little over a hundred miles to the south. There was no direct ferry and he desperately wanted to avoid airports for a while and maybe forever. He was so fixated on solving this problem and leaving tonight if possible that he didn't notice the car slowing next to him. Suddenly the side door of the minivan opened and then he felt a jabbing pain in the back of his neck and a strong pair of hands grabbing him from behind. He was both lifted and shoved at the same time. He felt completely out of control and overpowered as he was folded and stuffed into the bench seat and the waiting arms of a man he did not recognize. He noted the pain from his ribs, but it was somehow muted. He thought of screaming but couldn't. Nothing was responding. Not his mouth, not his arms, not his legs. Even his eyes were closing against his will, and then everything went black.

CHAPTER 68

NASSAU, BAHAMAS

RAPP and Butler saw the two men enter the bank and even then they weren't sure it was them. A few minutes later, though, Dumond sounded the alarm. He was inside the bank's network and saw whose safety deposit box it was that Nelson was accessing. Butler let Rapp make the call. Did he want to grab both of them right now and see what was in that safety deposit box, or did he want to wait and follow them when they were done? Rapp knew what Butler would prefer. As far as they knew, Nelson hadn't done anything illegal at this point. Storming into the bank would eventually involve the police and Nelson's superiors. As long as he wasn't a flight risk, it was better to leave him out of it for the moment. Butler's people could keep close tabs on him, and if they found something out in a day or two they could deal with him then.

Rapp decided on a snatch and grab. Coleman had the kit with tranquilizer, flex cuffs, and hood. The minivan with Coleman, Wicker, and Reavers did a dry run while they were in the bank and looked for likely spots on two streets. Rapp wandered into a gift shop across and just down the street from the bank. He greeted the woman behind the counter and asked her if she had any laminated tourist maps. He purchased one and then stood near the front of the store pretending to look at it. They were in the bank for just under fifteen minutes. Rapp was looking in the opposite direction when the target exited the bank. Five of Butler's men were doing the same thing. They had no idea if the target was alone and they didn't want to get caught with tunnel vision.

"They're out."

Rapp heard Butler call it over his tiny flesh-colored earpiece. Rapp slowly turned his head back in the direction of the bank. Al Harbi and Nelson were standing on the sidewalk talking. After half a minute or so, they shook hands and parted ways. Rapp raised the map an inch and lowered his eyes as the target crossed the street and came almost directly at him. When they'd seen him approach the bank he'd come from the same direction. Rapp wasn't sure if he was being lazy or bold. It might have had something to do with the condition he was in. The guy looked as if he'd been in one hell of a fight.

He crossed in front of Rapp's position and continued down the street. Rapp counted to ten and then left the store. He spotted him almost immediately half a block ahead of him. He was wearing a red Budweiser hat that made him easy to find. Rapp held the map in both hands and tilted his head so it looked as if he was trying to read it. Behind his sunglasses, though, his eyes were following the red hat. One of Butler's guys was supposed to be checking his six right now, but Rapp wasn't going to leave that kind of thing to someone he didn't know. Getting too focused on the target was a great way to get a bullet in the back of the head. Rapp spun and walked backward for a few steps, pretending to consult the map to figure out where he was. The pedestrian traffic was moderate, which helped. Rapp noted who had been behind him and then spun back around. He noticed a few security cameras that would have to be dealt with later and noted their position just in case the others missed them.

The bus stop was up ahead. Forty feet of empty curb space. Perfect for what they had planned. Rapp lengthened his stride and picked up the pace a bit. Still acting as if he was consulting the map he said, "It looks good."

When he closed to within thirty feet he gave the signal by putting the map in his back pocket. There was no gunning of an engine. No squealing tires. Nothing that would alert the target. The minivan slowly pulled into the open space fifteen feet ahead of the target. Rapp smiled and moved over for a young couple who looked as if they were on their honeymoon. Rapp closed fast and quietly. His left hand slid into his front pocket and pulled out the short epipen. It was filled with enough tranquilizers to take down a 190-pound man in less than five seconds. Rapp guessed the target was no more than 175 pounds. He pulled the cap off and stuffed it in his right pocket.

The big side door of the van slid open. Rapp focused on the target's head and watched it begin to turn in the direction of the van. He moved as if he was going to pass the target on the left, brought up the epipen, and punched it down on the back left side of the man's neck. His right hand clamped down firmly on the target's shoulder and he half-pushed, half-spun him toward the open door. The guy moved like a rag doll. Rapp tossed him into Reavers's waiting arms and followed right behind him. Coleman was already pulling back into traffic as Rapp was yanking the door closed.

Rapp patted down the target's pockets. He found two sets of identification, one of which was for Adam Farhat. The photo matched the sketch. "We got the right guy. Nice work, guys."

Rapp continued rifling through the man's pockets. He found a phone, a battery for the phone, a room key for a hotel, a money belt stuffed with cash, and a manila envelope stuffed in the back waistband of the guy's shorts. He put it all in a small duffel bag and then began to go through the contents more closely. He was in the middle of opening the big envelope when Butler came over his earpiece.

"We might have a problem. One of the shop owners is on the street. We think he wrote down your tag and he's now on his phone. We think he might be talking to the police."

"Shit." Rapp looked at Coleman's reflection in the rearview mirror and said, "Start making your way out to Paradise Island. Just in case."

Coleman did so without having to ask why.

Rapp pulled out his mobile phone and called the pilots. He told them they might have to make a hasty departure. It was standard procedure to have the plane fueled and ready for this very reason. Rapp tore open the envelope and pulled out a stack of papers. He fanned his way through the heavy stock and fancy seals. "Bearer bonds. Holy shit. A lot of them."

He stuffed them back in the bag, grabbed the phone, and placed the battery back in its place. It took a while for the phone to power up. Rapp wanted to see if he'd made any calls recently. The message light was on, so he decided to start there. He hit the button and held the phone to his ear. "*You dare call me a coward.*" The voice had an Arab accent and Rapp thought the man sounded very angry. "*What are you? You sneak out of here like some frightened woman while I am in the shower and leave me to fight for myself. Stuck in the middle of America. You will pay! Allah will make you pay. I will tell everyone that you are a traitor. Nothing more than a woman with a man's genitalia. And that I'm not even sure about. When I am done with my mission I will find you. I will hunt you like a dog and I will make you endure unimaginable suffering and humiliation. And trust me, I will not fail. I will find you.*"

"Stuck in the middle of America," Rapp mumbled to himself. He looked over at the body of al Harbi. His sunglasses had fallen off and his face looked as if someone had beaten the piss out of him. Rapp was trying to make sense of it all when Butler came back over the radio, his voice more urgent than before.

"The police are now on the scene."

Rapp thought about the message he'd just listened to and made a decision, "Got it. We're out of here."

"What about your computer friend here?" Butler asked.

Rapp had almost forgot about Dumond. "I'll send another plane.

And another thing . . . I have a room key here for the Towne Hotel. Number twelve."

"I'll have it gone over."

Coleman hit the gas and Rapp ordered Reavers and Wicker to stuff al Harbi into the canvas bag they'd brought along. While they wrestled with the limp body, Rapp called the pilots back and told them they were inbound and he wanted to be wheels up as soon as they arrived. The customs stamps and paperwork had already been taken care of. Rapp cringed at the thought of the police catching a CIA black ops team with a heavily medicated terrorist, one they'd abducted in broad daylight in the middle of one of the world's most well-known tourist destinations. Whether al Harbi was guilty or not, this was the type of thing that could set off an international incident. Coleman went straight to the private aviation section of the airport.

By the time they pulled onto the tarmac the duffel bag was zipped up and the engines on the G550 were spooling up. Coleman wheeled the van around to the rear cargo door. Rapp jumped out with the small duffel bag and headed straight for the ground-crew guy who worked for the local aviation company. Rapp slid him a hundred-dollar bill and made small talk while Wicker and Reavers wrestled the big duffel bag into the rear cargo compartment. Coleman dumped the van in the lot and trotted back to the jet while the cargo door was secured. Rapp followed him up the steps and hit the button to raise the stairs. There was a moment of hesitation while he wondered if they should retrieve Dumond, and then he decided he could do without him for a few hours. What they didn't want right now was for the tower to lay down a ground stop.

All four men took their seats and buckled in as the plane taxied. Rapp tapped his earpiece and said, "George?"

"Yes."

"Don't forget the tags on the van."

"I won't." There was a pause and then Butler asked, "Do we have confirmation?"

Rapp looked down at the small leather duffel bag and grabbed both passports. The photos matched the sketch Butler's man had provided. "It's him," Rapp said. "Nice work, George. We owe you big."

"Maybe you could get me one of those medals like Mike got yesterday."

Rapp laughed at Butler's dry attempt at humor. "I'll do one better. I'll make sure you get knighted."

"That would be much better." Butler laughed. "I'll talk to you in a few hours. Nice work."

"Thanks." Rapp pulled out the earpiece, took the small radio from his belt, and set it on the table in front of him.

Coleman looked at him and smiled. "Is there any feeling better than this?"

Rapp returned the smile. "Not in our line of work." The plane reached the end of the runway and didn't even pause. It spun around, put its nose into the wind, and kept going, the two Rolls Royce turbofan engines propelling the plane forward like a rocket. Seconds later they were airborne and banking to port over the water. Rapp looked across at Coleman and said, "One down and two to go."

"Yeah. We'd better wake him up and see what he knows."

Rapp looked over his shoulder at the rear pressurized cargo door. "In a minute. I wanna go through this stuff first and then I should call Irene."

CHAPTER 69

OAKTON, VIRGINIA

THE bodies were dragged to a basement closet and Ahmed sopped up the blood with some towels while Karim quickly searched the house to make sure they were alone and checked to make sure all the doors were locked. Then they set about researching their opponent. The internet was an amazing thing. Computers were sparse where Karim had grown up and the internet was strictly forbidden. His spiritual leader, Imam bin Abdullah, had warned them all that the internet was Satan's invention to corrupt the world. Ahmed, however, had spent much of his youth surfing the world wide web and knew his way around. They started out with the two newspapers that they found on the kitchen table. They were filled with propaganda about Mike Nash and his career.

They settled in the Saudi's opulent office. He had two computer screens on his desk and a bank of large flat-screen TVs on the far wall. There was not a single mention of them or the bodies in Iowa, but the TV and internet were abuzz with speculation. The two photos were everywhere. You couldn't watch five minutes of a cable news program without their images being splashed across the screen. They were the lead story of every online newspaper Ahmed checked. They had already figured out Ahmed's name and there was significant speculation that the other photo was none other than the Lion of al Qaeda. Karim had been alarmed at first, but now he saw the benefit.

He had successfully pushed Mike Nash off the front page. He was the story and they were only in the early stages of this match. After tonight, he would be the story for years to come. He would prove to the world the audacity and bravery of the Lion of al Qaeda. Hakim would be shamed and hunted to the far corners of the world. After tonight no one would believe his lies.

Ahmed showed him how they could access public records to get the information they needed. Karim was shocked what they could find out with just a name. Where people lived, how much they paid in property taxes, when they purchased their home and for how much, phone numbers, where they went to school, it was all there. There was no privacy. There was even an online encyclopedia that had a brand-new page devoted to Mike Nash. It gave his full bio. Where he was born, his athletic accomplishments, when he joined the Marine Corps, when he got married and to whom. It listed his four kids by name and age. Karim was dumbfounded that such things could be so easily unearthed.

They were able to pull up some clippings from local and school newspapers about the two oldest kids. The daughter, Shannon, had been in several plays and was part of a dance troupe that had won a big competition, and the older son, Rory, was a football and lacrosse standout. They found two of the son's team photos online. It was hard to say for sure, but from the shot he seemed to look a lot like his father. There was one good photo of the daughter that showed her performing during her school's performance of *Macbeth,* and then they came across her MySpace page and hit the jackpot. American teenagers were very busy. Karim could not believe they would allow their daughter to do so much unsupervised. They had even better luck with the wife. There were a couple of photos in the paper where she had been standing in the background, but online they found more than a dozen shots. Her company's website offered a full bio and headshot. A search of her name pulled up another half dozen society photos from various charities she'd been involved in. Ahmed printed everything they found and put it into a file for Karim to read.

At five o'clock Karim gave Ahmed the first glimpse of what he wanted to do. The Moroccan didn't ask a single question. He knew better. Part of the plan, the last part, if it worked perfectly, involved something Ahmed had already trained for. It was a contingency plan that Karim had put into place months ago. It was not difficult to prepare for. Not for a trained sniper like Ahmed. The first part of the plan was an entirely different story, though. Ahmed could tell by the passion in Karim's voice that he would not be dissuaded. He had seen him like this many times before and had seen what happened to anyone foolish enough to ask a question, or worse, point out a potential flaw. All he could do was pay attention, nod, and remind himself that it was not his place to doubt his commander. Doubt created hesitation and hesitation gave the enemy the advantage.

The briefing took nearly an hour. Maps were checked and rechecked. If they made it to the second part of the plan, they would use the radios on their phones to communicate. They checked their rifles and pistols to make sure they were in optimal working condition and then they composed the brief letter that Karim wanted sent to the media. It was short. Karim wanted it that way. He would not stoop to the level of the snake-tongued American president. He composed it with one eye on the American audience and the other on the Muslim world. It read: *I am the Lion of al Qaeda. A son of Mohammad. I do not run. I stand and fight. I have killed your hero and sacrificed my life for Islam, knowing that an army of brave Muslim warriors will pick up my banner and fight in my place. Allahu Akbar!*

Karim eyed the words and knew what they would produce. No amount of deceit from Hakim could undo this. He would be venerated in every Muslim home the world over. A modern-day Saladin. In death he would finally achieve the greatness he so richly deserved. There would never be enough time to fully prepare for this plan. Karim did not want to wait. Not even a day. Someone could return to this house at any moment. Every law enforcement expert on TV claimed they were on their way to either Mexico or Canada. A few thought that they might have fled farther West, but no one thought they had doubled back to Washington. The element of surprise was on their side, and this Nash would be so full of himself that he would never see it coming. Now was the time to strike. With everything prepared, they took a moment to pray together. Karim had never felt closer to his creator. Even in the fading light he could feel the warmth of Allah looking down on him. He was enveloped in pride and a righteousness of purpose. Karim knew he would not fail.

There were three vehicles in the garage in addition to the stolen pickup—a bright-red Ferrari, a silver Mercedes Maybach, and a black Suburban. It was not a difficult choice, although Karim at one point considered the benefits of the big silver sedan. In the end, though, one vehicle was clearly best suited for the job. They loaded their gear into the Suburban and then went upstairs to see what clothes they could find. Karim found a dark-gray suit in al Saeed's gigantic closet. It fit reasonably well, although he had to cinch the belt a few notches. The black loafers fit nearly perfectly. Ahmed had a much harder time trying to find something that worked. He moved on to the other rooms and eventually found a blue sport coat that was a little short in the sleeves, but otherwise fit.

In the kitchen pantry they found a box of power bars and grabbed some water. Ahmed climbed behind the wheel and punched the address into the navigation system. The computer plotted the course and told them their destination was 15.3 miles away, travel time, twenty-three minutes. Karim gave the okay and they pulled out of the garage. They waited for a minute to make sure the door closed and then started down the driveway and into the darkening night.

CHAPTER 70

MCLEAN, VIRGINIA

NASH opened the front door and stepped outside. He was wearing a white dress shirt and black slacks. Charlie was on his left hip, already bathed and in his pajamas. Rory was out in the middle of the street with his two friends and Jack was playing whiffle ball. Nash checked his watch. The reservations were for eight, and they hadn't been easy to get. The manager told Nash that they were full, but he could wait in the bar and see what opened up. Nash gave him his name to put on the waiting list and the man practically lost it. "Is this *the* Mike Nash? The one who was given the medal by the president?"

Nash reluctantly confirmed that he in fact was that Mike Nash, and then the man went berserk. He offered the best table in the house, any time he wanted, and insisted on paying. It was about the only good thing that had come out of his public outing so far. Maggie came down the stairs in a little black cocktail dress and a wrap. She joined her husband and Charlie on the front stoop. She was all done up for the evening and she looked great.

"You look fabulous, honey," Nash said.

"Thanks, so do you."

Charlie smiled at his mom. Nash yelled, "Come on, boys! Everyone inside!"

"But, Dad," Jack protested, "we only have one more inning. It's not even dark yet."

Nash looked to the west. "I don't see the sun, do you?"

"It's still light out."

Nash handed Charlie to his wife. "Why don't you give him to Shannon and tell her to put him down. I'll get these clowns rounded up." Nash made the exchange with his wife and then marched down the sidewalk.

Jack whacked the yellow plastic bat on the ground. "Not fair, Dad!"

"Life isn't fair. Get your butt inside." Jack tried to protest again, but Nash cut him off. "Jack, I'm not going to tell you again. I didn't say you couldn't have fun. You guys have a Ping-Pong table in the basement, hundreds of movies, and an Xbox. Get your little butt inside, and I'm not going to tell you again."

Rory stepped forward. "Come on, guys. We'll play you in Madden 360."

Nash and all four kids walked in the house. When they got to the kitchen, Jack plopped down in a chair and ran a hand over his freckled face. "Can we at least have a can of pop?"

Nash nodded. "You can each have one can. And if you decide to microwave some popcorn, hit the popcorn button on the microwave. That's all you have to do. One of you two keeps burning it and it stinks up the whole house."

"How do you know it's not Shannon?" Jack asked.

"Because she's the only person who picks up after herself around here, and I've seen her make popcorn."

Maggie entered the kitchen. "I'm ready."

"One last thing, boys. No one leaves this house. No one answers the door. When your mom and I leave I'm going to turn the alarm on. If you guys turn it off, my phone will beep and I will paddle some major ass. Do you understand?"

All four boys nodded.

"Good." Nash looked toward the staircase and in a louder voice said, "Shannon, we're taking off."

She bounded down the steps a few seconds later and came cruising into the kitchen. "Have a great time." She kissed her dad on the cheek.

"No one leaves the house. Understand?"

"Yes!" she said in a dramatic voice. "I heard you the first four times. You two go and have a good time. We'll be fine."

"Come on," Maggie said, grabbing his arm. "The restaurant is only a mile from here.

Nash followed his wife into the mudroom. He stopped at his locker and opened his gun safe. There were several options. For tonight he grabbed the subcompact .40 caliber G27 and its small leather holster. At the back door he armed the security system and then left and locked the door. Back in the kitchen Shannon and her brothers shared a conspiratorial look and then darted to the front of the house. They dropped to the floor and crawled into the dining room. From the big window they watched their mom and dad back down the driveway and leave. None of them moved for close to a minute and then they sprang to life.

Jack announced, "All right . . . Let's go. We were up two runs going into the top of the seventh."

"But the security system?" Rory's blond friend asked.

"He's been saying that for years," Jack scoffed. "I've already tested it. He has no idea if we turn it off or leave it on." Jack punched in the code at the front door and disarmed the system.

Shannon came back from the kitchen and handed Rory the baby monitor. "Here."

Rory took it without protest. "Be careful."

"Be careful with what?" Jack asked.

"I'm just going to drive around the block a few times."

Jack shook his head. "You're crazy. If Dad catches you, he'll kill you."

"Jack, I'm only driving around the block! It's not a big deal."

"They why did you wait for them to leave?"

"Why did *you* wait for them to leave?"

Jack thought about it for a second. As much as he hated to admit it, she was right, although playing whiffle ball after dark was not a crime. "You're not a good driver. What if you hit something?"

"Come on, Jack, she's just going around the block. Stop arguing and let's get out there or we really will be out of light."

"What if he calls?"

Shannon held up her cell phone. "He always calls my cell."

"Fine, let's go."

The four boys headed out the front door with the baby monitor and the bat and balls and Shannon went out the back door with the keys for the minivan. It took her three attempts to get it out of the garage, and she only backed over one small shrub on her way down the driveway. The boys stopped play to watch her as she inched her way into the street and then put it in drive and moved off at a snail's pace. At the end of the block she hit her blinker and took a right turn. The boys resumed play. Six pitches and two hits later she appeared at the other end of the block. The boys all moved to the side and shook their heads at her as she did another slow pass-by. Then they started to play again and forgot all about her.

CHAPTER 71

FAIRFAX COUNTY, VIRGINIA

RAPP sat across the table from Hakim al Harbi and tried to make sense of it all. He'd seen a lot of strange stuff in the nearly two decades that he had been doing this, but this was a first. They'd flipped guys before, but always after exercising either pressure or incentive. They all broke eventually, but most of these militant types had to be threatened to within an inch of their lives before they would give any good information. There were others, not the front-line troops, but the support people, who helped purchase weapons and other supplies. The moneymen and the deal makers who traveled around the Middle East raising capital and recruiting new bodies for the cause, they could be turned with nothing more than the hint of violence on one hand and the possibility of hard cash on the other if they cooperated. That in itself told him that maybe this Hakim fellow was nothing more than a logistics guy, but then again he had freely admitted to killing American and coalition soldiers in Afghanistan.

On the flight up they'd pulled him out of the bag and given him a drug to counteract the tranquilizer. He woke up groggy, but in obvious pain and discomfort. After a brief inspection they found out that in addition to a bruised and battered face, he had at least two broken ribs and one lung on the verge of collapsing. Wicker was a trained medic. He pulled Rapp aside and told him to be careful. If the other lung collapsed the man could die. Rapp didn't care so much if the man died, he just wanted to get the information out of him first. Until he was in better condition they would have to hold off on the rough stuff.

To Rapp's surprise, though, al Harbi spoke openly and without any preconditions. Rapp handled the questions while Coleman observed and recorded everything that was said. By the time they landed back at Dulles, Rapp was convinced that al Harbi was either telling the truth or the greatest liar he had ever met in his life. On the advice of Wicker they pulled the jet into the hangar and closed the doors. Stuffing him back into the bag was not a good idea. When they arrived at the Quarry, Dr. Lewis was waiting for them. He gave al Harbi a sedative to help with the pain and started him on some heavy-duty antibiotics. After that was out of the way, Lewis hooked him up to a lie detector and led him through a series of questions to establish a baseline. Rapp stayed in the room and looked for any signs that al Harbi was trying to fool the machines. He didn't notice any, but that didn't mean that he hadn't.

Unbeknownst to Rapp, Coleman had gone into Max Johnson's cell and asked him about his contacts in the telecommunications industry. Johnson began babbling through a list of companies and his contacts at each place. Coleman asked him, if he gave him a phone number, would he be able to tell him where the phone was located when it made a call. Johnson explained that he could tell him what tower it used to connect to the network, but that was it. Then he babbled on about some surveillance equipment he'd developed that could pinpoint the whereabouts of a phone down to the nearest foot. Coleman explained that for now he only wanted to verify the location of the one phone call. He went on to tell Johnson that his cooperation would go a long way toward convincing Rapp that he could be trusted. Johnson eagerly leaped at the chance. He told Coleman all he needed was a computer with internet access, and he'd have the info for him in less than five minutes.

True to his word, he had everything verified in only three minutes. Coleman asked him if he had a back door into customs and Johnson said yes. He had him check if al Harbi had in fact traveled under the alias of Michael Andros through New Orleans and Miami on his way to Nassau earlier in the day. He verified that information as well. Coleman told Reavers to keep an eye on Johnson while he went and talked to Mitch.

Rapp was in the middle of interrogating al Harbi with Dr. Lewis when Coleman knocked on the door and asked Rapp to step outside.

Rapp closed the door behind him and asked, "What's up?"

"I thought you'd want to see this. That phone number . . . the one that he says belongs to Karim. I had it checked out."

"Is Marcus back?" Rapp asked hopefully.

"No, I had Johnson do it."

Rapp showed his surprise. "You gave him access to a computer?"

"Relax . . . I watched him."

"Can I trust the prick?"

"He wants to live, so I think we can." Coleman handed over the map he'd printed. "Two things. The first . . . that phone pinged this tower right here south of Branson, Missouri, and it matches the time stamp on the voicemail that was left on Hakim's phone."

"So at a bare minimum he wasn't lying about where they were."

"Correct. I also had Johnson check the ICE database. Michael Andros left New Orleans at six this morning and connected through Miami on his way to Nassau. He was traveling alone and his ticket was purchased online."

"What about the other message?"

"What other message?" Coleman asked.

"Karim left two messages."

"I only heard one."

"Check the phone. There's another one. It starts out very similar to the first. He calls him a coward . . . all that bullshit. See if Johnson can find out what tower he used when he left the second one."

"And what do you wanna do with the FBI?"

It was the million-dollar question and the eight-hundred-pound gorilla all rolled into one. Rapp grabbed the back of his neck and squeezed while he tried to sort it out. "This isn't going to be easy. We give them the phone numbers and they're going to want to know where we got them."

"There are two dead bodies in northern Arkansas, and from everything he's been telling us," Coleman pointed toward the cell door, "this Karim whack job probably isn't done killing people. We have to share this information. The feds are all still up in Iowa trying to piece things together and these guys are hundreds of miles away killing grandparents and God only knows who else."

"I know. I've already talked to Irene and she's trying to figure out a way to source it."

Coleman stepped back and shook his head.

"Scott, I don't like it any more than you do, but come on . . . you got any better ideas? I mean we're not exactly sitting on it. We just found most of this shit out ourselves."

"And if we gave the feds these phone numbers they'd have them pinged in ten minutes."

"Bullshit . . . they'd bring in the lawyers, ask for a fucking warrant, and fill out ten forms in fucking triplicate, and then and only then would they ask the phone companies for their records."

"I don't know." Coleman shook his head.

"Listen . . . Irene's on her way to the White House right now. She'll figure it out. In the meantime, ask our new friend Max Johnson if he would please hack back into the phone company database and find out where Karim was when he left that second message. And see if there's any other activity on the phone."

Coleman nodded and headed back down the hallway. Rapp collected his thoughts and went back into the cell. Lewis and Hakim were talking. Rapp stood behind his chair and placed his hands on the back. They were discussing Karim's temper. Rapp was only half listening to what Hakim was saying. At the moment he was more concerned with how they were going to bring this sordid mess out of the dark covert world and into the transparent world of law enforcement. He didn't doubt for a minute that it had to be done. It was just a question of how. Rapp was trying to figure that out when Hakim said something that caught his attention.

"What did you just say?" Rapp asked Hakim.

"He was very proud of his men. The six that were killed in the attack on your terrorism facility."

"No . . . just before that. You said something else."

"He was upset with me for doubting his bravery. He was very upset with your president for calling his men cowards. He said we were going to go to Washington and show the world that your president is a liar. Show—"

"Washington?" Rapp asked. "Are you sure he said Washington?"

"Yes, but I'm not sure I believe him. I mean . . . he might send Ahmed. That was part of his original plan. To turn Ahmed loose in downtown Washington and let him kill as many people as he could before you managed to stop him."

"Ahmed is a trained sniper?"

"Yes. And he's very good. I saw him work in Afghanistan."

"But he said you were all going to Washington?"

"Yes. To martyr ourselves." Hakim shook his head. "But I do not think Karim will do it. He is too vain."

There was a knock on the door and then it was yanked open. This time Coleman didn't wait for Rapp to come out. "The second message was left at twelve-oh-four this afternoon. It pinged a tower just off Sixty-six and Jackson Lee."

"Shit." Rapp started pacing. His hand was forced. They had to bust this thing wide open. He grabbed his BlackBerry from his pocket and was about to call Kennedy when he saw Nash's name pop up on the caller ID. Rapp thought he might be with Kennedy so he answered the call. He listened for a few seconds and then said, "Mike, slow down. Are you sure?" Rapp listened for another few beats and as he listened to Nash explain himself he felt his stomach begin to twist into knots. "We'll be right there. Don't do anything crazy . . . just wait for us to get there."

CHAPTER 72

MCLEAN, VIRGINIA

NASH came speeding down his street at close to seventy miles an hour. He slammed on the brakes and came to a stop directly in front of his house. Maggie was out the door and up the walk like a shot. He'd already told her what he wanted her to do and explained it in a voice that made it clear there was no room for debate. They weren't even halfway through their first glass of wine when he decided to call home and check on the kids. He tried the home number first and then Shannon's mobile number and got nothing. His tension began to rise, and Maggie did her spousal duty and told him to relax. Five minutes later he got the same result, and his blood began to boil. Maggie tried to reassure him by offering what she thought were plausible explanations. He didn't buy any of them and started dialing the phone every sixty seconds until finally on the fifth try Jack answered.

The ten-year-old's weak attempt at a cover story crumbled in the face of his father's anger, and he spilled the beans. Nash threw two twenties on the table and grabbed his wife by the wrist. Nash offered his apologies to the poor manager who had so proudly set aside his best table. Maggie mumbled something about one of the kids' being sick. They ran two red lights and were home in less than two minutes. During the brief car ride Nash explained that she was to go into the house, lock the door, turn on the alarm, and grab one of his guns from the safe in the mudroom. When Maggie tried to tell him he was overreacting, he ignored her and hoped she was right.

Nash made sure Maggie was in the house and then sped off. He stopped at the end of the block and looked both ways. There was nothing but a few parked cars. He wondered which way she would have turned and guessed right. He sped off and stopped in the middle of the next intersection. He looked left and then right. Two blocks down he saw the lights of a police cruiser. Nash spun the wheel and floored it. As he drew closer he saw the minivan just beyond the police car parked in the middle of the street. The driver's door was open. Nash threw the car into park and breathed a sigh of relief. She'd been stopped for driving without an adult in the car. His worst fears behind him, he got out and approached the police officer, who was standing on the boulevard talking with a woman who looked to be in her late forties.

"The other vehicle sped around the van and stopped in front of it. Blocking the road."

Nash froze. He looked past the van. There was no other vehicle. He turned to look in the back of the police car, expecting to see his daughter. It was empty. Nash's heart began to race.

"Two men," he heard the woman say. "They were in a big black Suburban. Both of them dressed like those FBI guys in all black. They cut her off and then pulled her from the van. They threw her in the backseat of the Suburban and took off that way, toward Glebe Road."

Nash joined them on the boulevard. He checked his emotions and looked at the police officer. "My name is Mike Nash. I work counterterrorism for the CIA. That is my van and that was my daughter who was taken. I need you to get on your radio and put out an Amber alert on that truck and those men and my fifteen-year-old daughter. Her name is Shannon Nash." Nash stared at the dumbfounded officer for a few seconds and then said, "I'd appreciate it if you'd step on it, officer. Before I lose my cool and start screaming."

The officer nodded. "I recognize you from your photo."

"Yes," said Nash, "I'm going to call the FBI right now. Please," Nash said urgently, "get that Amber alert out right now."

The officer grabbed his shoulder-mounted radio and called in to his dispatcher. Nash called Art Harris from the FBI and filled him in as best he could. Harris said he would dispatch agents to the scene immediately, as well as to the house, and that he would make sure that the Amber alert was in place. He was about to call Rapp when his phone rang. He looked down and saw Shannon's face smiling back at him. The call was from her.

Nash swallowed hard and answered his phone. "Hello."

No one spoke for a second, and then a man with a slight accent said, "I have your daughter."

"Prove it."

"Daddy!" The voice was cut short.

"Is that proof enough?"

Nash closed his eyes and told himself to keep it together. "What do you want?"

"I want you."

"All right."

"I will trade your life for hers."

Nash was nodding without knowing it. "All right. Where do you want to meet?"

"You will know soon enough."

"I'm right here. I'm standing in the exact spot where you pulled her from the van. Come back. I'll put my gun in the middle of the street and we'll make the exchange."

There was laughter. "We will see who is the real coward. The world will see who is the real coward. In one hour you will know where we will make the exchange."

"How?"

"Turn on your TV."

The line went dead. Nash stared at his phone, his hand beginning to shake. He was about to call Maggie, but stopped. He had no idea what he would say to her. He decided to call Rapp instead. If anyone could figure a way out of this it would be him.

CHAPTER 73

WASHINGTON, D.C.

AHMED drove down Constitution Avenue and took a right onto Twenty-second Street. The service entrance for the building was up ahead on the left halfway down the block. It was Saturday evening, so the only person they expected to deal with was a night watchman. Karim had the young girl gagged and tied in the backseat. Ahmed pulled over and got out. He walked around the back of the truck and opened the big double doors. He grabbed his long black rifle bag and closed the doors. Karim met him on the sidewalk and held up the phone.

"Remember . . . we'll use the radio feature to communicate."

Ahmed nodded. "Yes."

"And when you see me parked in front and you are ready you will begin calling the TV stations. And then you will radio me."

"I have all the numbers programmed."

"Good." Karim held out his arms and embraced Ahmed. It was the first time he had ever hugged the man. "I am very proud of you. This is what we should have done a week ago. I should have never allowed that snake Hakim to talk me out of it."

Ahmed nodded even though he wasn't sure he believed him. "*Allahu Akbar.*"

"*Allahu Akbar.*"

Ahmed moved up the walk and found the back door. There was a buzzer to the left. He pressed it twice and a few seconds later a voice asked him what he wanted. "FBI," he said in near perfect English.

"I'll be right there."

Ahmed looked at his pistol and thought about the plan. An old man in a security uniform appeared on the other side of the glass door and opened it for him.

"What can I help you with?"

Ahmed stayed with the plan even though he wasn't sure his heart was in it. "We have a possible hostage situation in the park. I need to set up a position on your roof so I can observe."

"Sure. Come on in. Let me show you how to get up there." The man led him to an elevator that they took to the top floor. From there they made their way down the hall to a back staircase and up another flight. They stepped into the dark night, and the security guard led the way to the southern edge of the building.

Two hundred yards away the massive columns of the Lincoln Memorial were bathed in bright light. Ahmed had to hand it to Karim. It was quite the setting to send a message. He slowly drew his gun while the old man was occupied with the view.

"I like to come up here on breaks sometimes. You look around and realize there's a God out there. How else could all of this have happened? Through chaos . . . I don't think so."

Ahmed slowly slid the gun back into the holster. Karim had ordered him to kill the man, but he couldn't do it. There was no honor in killing unarmed people. He wrapped his big arms around the man's neck and head and pinched off the main artery in the neck. He kept the pressure on until he felt the man go limp. Then he dragged him out of the way and tied him up. It took less than a minute. Back at the building's edge he rolled out his mat and set up his M-40 sniper rifle.

He took a quick peek through the scope and acquired the Suburban. It was parked on the street in front of the Lincoln Memorial. Ahmed pulled out the phone and began calling the various TV stations and asking for the news director at each one. There were five in all.

After the last one, he pressed the button on the side of the radio and said, "It is done." Ahmed turned his attention to the Suburban and watched it drive up on the grass and then begin its climb up the steps. Rifle fire began cracking through the still night. Ahmed brought his field binoculars up to his eyes and watched the Suburban lurch forward. Beyond the vehicle he saw people crumple to the ground as they were shot by Karim. He shook his head at the senseless carnage and began to pray.

CHAPTER 74

LINCOLN MEMORIAL

BY the time Rapp and Nash got to the Lincoln Memorial the Park Police and the D.C. Metro Police had the place cordoned off. TV crews were both northeast and southeast of the barricades and the police were trying unsuccessfully to move them back. Both departments had big fire-truck-sized command vehicles parked out front. Rapp displayed his Homeland Security credentials at the checkpoint and told the officer to allow the next vehicle to follow as well. He had Nash in the front seat next to him. Reavers was in the backseat directly behind Nash. Rapp had quietly given the retired SEAL orders to shadow Nash wherever he went.

Dr. Lewis was in the Suburban behind them with some of Coleman's other men and Hakim al Harbi. Lewis had convinced Rapp that they should bring Hakim along. Based on the voicemail messages they had reviewed and his cooperation so far, Lewis felt Hakim might be able to offer some insight into Karim's mind. Rapp had some other possible uses in mind, but so far wasn't willing to share them with the group. Coleman and Wicker were on their way with Max Johnson and his surveillance van. They were going to try to get a fix on the third cell phone that Hakim had given to Ahmed. For now they were assuming that Karim was inside the monument with at least one very important hostage. Rapp parked as close to the command posts as he could get, and then jumped out and raced to cut off Nash.

"Slow down, Mike," Rapp said as he grabbed him by the left arm. He had barely said a word on the twelve-minute drive in from his house. For obvious reasons Rapp was concerned that he might do something stupid.

Nash turned and took a big swing at Rapp, his right fist sailing in a wild roundhouse punch.

Rapp ducked just in time and felt the punch brush the top of his head. He brought his fists up to block his face and took a quick step back.

"Fuck you!" Nash screamed. His eyes were filled with tears and his face was flushed with anger. "This is all your fault! If you hadn't fucking outed me none of this would have happened. You put me and my family at risk and I will never forgive you. So fuck off and get the hell away from me." Nash turned and stalked off toward the command vehicles.

Rapp had been waiting for it. He'd been feeling it himself. He just hadn't expected it to come this soon. He looked at Reavers and jerked his head in the direction Nash had just gone. "Follow him. Stay close."

Dr. Lewis came up. Hakim was a few steps behind him with a guy on each arm. His wrists were bound with flex cuffs but no other restraints. Lewis looked at Rapp and said, "That was unfortunate, but I think understandable considering the circumstances."

"Yeah, I suppose," Rapp said. He was already trying to figure out a way to make things right. He knew what he'd do if he had a daughter. He started moving toward the command vehicles. He tapped his earpiece and said, "Scott, give me a sitrep."

"We're close. Just passing Watergate. Should be there in sixty seconds."

"Anything so far?"

"He has both signals, but we won't be able to pinpoint until we get a little closer and stop."

"Roger that." Rapp did a 360 and looked at the terrain. "My money's on the north side if he's not in there with him."

"Got it."

Rapp looked at Hakim and asked, "What's his endgame?"

"I'm not sure."

"Are you holding back on me?"

"No. I would have never thought he'd paint himself into a corner like this."

Rapp looked at all the police, the camera crews, and the spectators.

Lewis seemed to be reading his mind and said, "He's created a stage for himself. You provoked him," Lewis said to Hakim, "by telling him you would tell the world that he was a coward. He's so narcissistic that his reputation means everything to him. He can't bear the thought of people saying those things about him, so he's going to make sure no one ever doubts his bravery."

"But he kidnapped a fifteen-year-old girl," Hakim said.

Lewis pointed at Nash, who was talking to the police. "That's who he's after. You said it yourself . . . that he flew into a rage during the press conference after the medal ceremony. He thinks that he will kill an American hero on this grand stage and that he will be revered and celebrated by millions of Muslims the world over."

"Not if I have anything to say about it." Rapp turned and walked over to where Nash was talking to all the police brass. Fortunately, Art Harris was approaching the same point from the opposite side of the circle. Nash was already arguing with the two officers in charge.

"I'm not going to say it again. That's my daughter in there. He wants me. When he calls, I'm going in, and she's coming out. It's as simple as that."

Harris was wearing his FBI tactical vest. He introduced himself to the two on-scene commanders and told them that the FBI's Hostage Rescue Team was inbound from Quantico. "And no one," he said to the group, "is doing anything until they get here. Federal property," he said as he pointed to the statue of Lincoln, "and they kidnapped her in Virginia and brought her into the District. It's the FBI's jurisdiction."

"I don't give a shit whose jurisdiction it is. That's my daughter in there. When he calls back I'm going in. And I don't want HRT fucking this thing up."

"Mike, I understand your situation here, but you're not in charge."

"Fuck you, Art." Nash pointed at the building and screamed, "That's my daughter in there! Shannon! You've known her since she was a little kid. What would you do if that was Shelly? Would you trust HRT, or would you go in there and trade your life for your daughter's?"

Rapp heard Coleman's voice come over his earpiece and stepped away from the group. "Say again."

"Max thinks he has a fix on the sniper. Says he's due north of your position. Constitution and Twenty-third."

Rapp stepped out from behind the command vehicle and looked north. The building's roof was in plain view above the trees. Rapp's eyes swept left. There was nothing. He moved them right along the tree line. The buildings on this part of Constitution Avenue occupied entire city blocks. The next block had a peaked roof, but the next block after that housed the Federal Reserve. It was a big, flat-roofed monster. "Slick," Rapp said, using Wicker's nickname.

"Yeah, Mitch."

"Get over to the Federal Reserve and settle in at the southwest corner of the roof. Let me know when you have this guy in your sights."

"Mitch, what do you want me to do?" Coleman asked.

"Drop him off and make sure he gets in. I don't care if you have to shoot your way in. Can Max jam these signals if I need him to?"

It took a moment while Coleman relayed the question. "He says no problem, but he wants to know if you want him to block all signals or just these two."

"For now just these two, but let me think about that. Hurry up and get Slick on that roof!"

"We're already in front of the building and there's a guard out front."

"Show him your DHS creds and call me if you have a problem. I've got Art here."

As Rapp turned to go back to the group he heard some choppers coming in. He craned his head skyward as three Blackhawks came in and landed a few hundred yards away, just south of the Reflecting Pool.

"That's HRT," Harris announced, as Rapp walked up to the group.

Harris gave him a nervous looked and mouthed the words, *Do something!*

Nash was now arguing with one of the on-site commanders. Rapp listened for a good ten seconds and then stepped in. He looked at the two on-site commanders and asked, "Does he have any other hostages?" As Rapp finished asking the question, Wicker's voice came over the net telling him he was in the building and on the way to the roof.

"We don't think so, but we think he killed at least eight people. There are five up there on the steps and three more just inside."

"Any idea where he is in there?"

"We're pretty sure he's around that inside corner on the north side of the building."

"Pretty sure?"

"Three people told us he was on the north side. None of the eyewitnesses said he was on the south side."

"Who cares?" Nash said impatiently. "It doesn't matter. I'm going in there."

Rapp placed a hand on his shoulder and said, "Let's talk about this."

Nash knocked his hand away and made a fist. "Get the hell away from me."

Rapp backed up and put his hands up, palms out. "Don't you even want to try?"

"No. If I go in there, he lets her go."

"Or he blows her head off right in front of you."

"Shut up, Mitch. I've spent too many years doing things your way. Not tonight. That's my daughter in there. I'm calling the shots."

Wicker's welcome voice came over Rapp's earpiece, "Got him. Range 310 yards. No wind. Give me twenty seconds."

Rapp was thinking of Wicker when he looked at Coleman and said, "Fine . . . but if we're going to do this your way, you're gonna call Maggie first. You tell her you love her, you tell those boys you love them, and then you go in there and make the exchange."

The words got to Nash. He slowly started to nod in recognition that it was the right thing to do. He pulled out his phone, stared blankly at it for a moment, and then started to walk away from the group while he dialed the number.

Rapp followed him and when Nash put the phone to his ear, Rapp pulled an epipen from his pocket, flicked off the protective cap, and jabbed Nash in the back of the neck. Rapp held the pen in place for a second and then dropped it and reached for Nash's phone. Reavers stepped in and caught Nash as he collapsed to the pavement.

Art Harris pulled up next to Rapp with a worried look on his face and asked, "What in the hell are we going to do now?"

"That depends on how much time we have, Art." To Reavers he said, "Leave him. Let's go." Rapp broke into a sprint for his vehicle. "Slick, give me updates. If you hear me say Bingo, you take the shot."

"Roger that."

When they got to the car Rapp told Reavers to grab his shit out of the backseat. Rapp popped the trunk and stripped off his suit coat. He slid on his bulletproof vest and Velcroed the sides before putting on his tactical vest. He grabbed his M-4 rifle from its hard case and snatched up a thick silencer. Reavers trotted behind him with an identical rifle and vest.

When they got back to the command post, Harris was waiting for them with his arms across his chest. "Just what in the Lord's name do you cowboys think you're doing?"

"Don't start, Art. Get out of my way."

"I can't do that. This is an FBI op. You guys can't operate around here. Look at all the media."

Rapp stopped and took note of all the cameras. "Good point." Turning to Reavers, Rapp asked, "You got a balaclava?" referring to the black ski masks they sometimes wore on operations. Reavers produced one from his tactical vest at about the same time Rapp did. They put them on but left them up on their foreheads like watch caps.

"Oh, shit," Harris said with genuine concern. "You guys can't do this. Just wait for HRT."

The phone Rapp took from Nash started ringing. Rapp looked down at the smiling photo of Shannon. He glanced at Harris and said, "No time." Rapp pressed the answer button and held the phone to his ear. "Hello."

There was a long pause and then, "Who is this?"

"I'm one of Mike's friends."

"Where is he?" Karim asked angrily.

Rapp looked around said, "Ahhh . . . He just started vomiting."

"Coward," Karim scoffed. "I will make sure the media knows that your hero vomited before facing me."

"Yeah . . . well not everyone can be a tough guy, right?"

"Who is this?"

Rapp looked up and saw Lewis and Hakim. "Dr. Lewis! I'm monitoring the situation here. Mr. Nash is obviously very traumatized by this." Rapp tried to think of the words Lewis would choose. "He just got off the phone with his wife and boys. He wanted to say good-bye to them. He wanted them to have some closure."

"Well, put him on the phone. It is time to make the exchange."

"Hold on." Rapp looked down and hit the mute key. He marched straight over to Hakim and said, "Are you honestly sick of seeing innocent people killed?"

Hakim looked up at the building bathed in lights and said, "Yes."

Rapp thought it through one more time. "All right . . . then you're going to get your chance to prove it. I'm going to hand you this phone and I want you to bait him like you've never baited him before. I want you to work him into an absolute fury."

Hakim nodded. "I know just what to say."

"Mitch," Lewis said, "I'm not sure that's such a good idea."

"No time to argue," Rapp snapped. "Slick, are you good to go?"

"Affirmative."

Rapp grabbed Hakim and dragged him through the police and up the edge of the steps. Harris followed. "Art," Rapp said, "take the phone from him if he tries to warn him."

Harris pulled out his gun.

Rapp looked at the keypad, took a deep breath, and took it off mute. "Are you still there?"

"Yes, and I must warn you I am not alone. If anyone other than Mr. Nash approaches the building I will kill the girl."

"Understood." Rapp handed the phone to Hakim and pulled the black mask down over his face.

"Karim, this is your old friend. I see you are still hiding behind the skirts of little girls."

Rapp turned away from Hakim and said, "Bingo! I repeat . . . Bingo!"

Rapp took the steps three at a time. Reavers was right at his side. "You've got my six. We go in on the right side."

"Tango is down." Wicker's voice came over the net. "I repeat, tango is down."

Wicker's words were welcome but Rapp didn't have time to celebrate. There was one bad guy down, but still one to go. They pushed up the last flight of stairs, their footfalls nearly silent. As they neared the big columns, Rapp could hear someone shouting from inside the immense space. He had a moment of indecision. Should he stop and assess the situation or rush headlong into it and keep surprise on his side? He decided on the latter and already had a picture in his mind's eye. They reached the threshold and Rapp sliced through the farthest opening on the right. His left eye was perched behind his Eotech holographic sight. The red bull's-eye glowed in the middle of the square aperture.

The picture Rapp had in his mind's eye was nothing like the one he was confronted with. Standing no more than twenty feet in front of him, Karim had his phone to his ear and was screaming. His gun was in his right hand, and there was no sign of Shannon. They made eye contact and Rapp saw the gun start to come up. He continued to close, and did three quick double taps, all high center mass. All suppressed. Karim tumbled backward, the pistol falling from his hand. Rapp stopped two feet short and kept the gun trained on Karim, who was now sprawled out on his back.

"Shannon?" Rapp yelled.

Off to his left he saw something in the shadows shift. He glanced over and saw Shannon tied up with her back to him, but moving. Rapp looked back down at Karim, who was clutching at his tactical vest. There was no sign of blood. Rapp figured he was wearing a bulletproof vest. Rapp thought about the president and Dickerson and the bullshit show trial that the country would be dragged through. He elevated the thick silencer a few degrees and put Karim's face in the center of the sight. He was trying to say something, but Rapp didn't really care. He squeezed the trigger one more time and ended it.

CHAPTER 75

LAKE ANNA, VIRGINIA

THE Bell 430 helicopter floated down out of the night sky. Its front spotlight lit up the grassy field north of the house. In the shadows, just beyond the light, Stan Hurley waited at the edge of the field along with Rapp and a slightly groggy Mike Nash. Dr. Lewis was in the house keeping an eye on Shannon. He'd given her a mild sedative and was making sure there wasn't something she was afraid to talk about while her dad was in the room.

Rapp turned his back to the rotor wash, while Hurley and Nash simply closed their eyes and lowered the heads. The CIA helicopter set down softly on its three wheels and its rotors began to slow. The port-side door opened and Scott Coleman jumped to the ground. He held Jack Nash under the arms and pulled him from the chopper and set him on the ground. Rory followed on his own, jumping from the chopper and landing on both feet. He and Jack saw their dad and broke into a sprint. Maggie was next. Charlie was in her arms wrapped in a blanket and somehow still asleep. Coleman helped her step down and finally Kennedy appeared in the doorway. She said something to the pilots and then exited the bird.

Rapp and Hurley stood by smiling as Nash hugged Rory and Jack. Maggie joined the group and buried her head in her husband's chest. Nash wrapped his left arm around his wife's back and placed his right hand on Charlie's head. They stood there for a long moment and said nothing.

Finally Maggie wiped tears from her eyes and asked, "Where's Shannon?"

"She's in the house with Doc," Nash said. "She's fine. Minor concussion and a few scratches, but other than that Doc says she's in good shape."

"I want to see her." Maggie turned and saw Hurley. She stepped toward him and gave him a peck on the cheek. "Thanks for taking care of us, Stan. I had to get out of that house."

The media had descended on the Nash house. The normally quiet suburban street looked more like a carnival midway, all lit up with news vans, reporters, and cameramen trying to get a piece of the story. When Kennedy got wind of it she sent two Suburbans and a full security detail to the house to extract the family and bring them back to Langley. Knowing they would want to be together, she had the helicopter waiting.

Maggie finally noticed Rapp. She stepped toward him. There was a quizzical look on her face, and for a moment Rapp thought she might slap him. He was prepared to take it. He felt like crap for endangering her family.

Maggie reached up and wrapped her arm around Rapp's neck, pulling him in for a big hug. "Thank you. Irene told me what you did."

Rapp kissed the top of her head. "I'm sorry I put your family in danger."

She shook her head bravely and wiped more tears from her eyes.

"That's nonsense. You've given me my husband back. That man tried to take him from me and you stopped him."

"But . . ."

"But nothing," she said. "If you hadn't intervened, he'd be dead right now, and probably Shannon as well." She kissed him again on the cheek and said, "Thank you."

The family shuffled off toward the house. They wanted to be with Shannon. Hurley, Rapp, Coleman, and Kennedy watched them go. When they were far enough away, Kennedy exhaled and said, "I had a nice talk with her on the ride down. She's a pretty strong woman."

The three men nodded, not knowing what to say.

Kennedy glanced back at her helicopter. "I have to get back to D.C. The FBI is a little concerned about how this is going to play in the press."

Rapp shrugged his shoulders. "Let 'em take all the credit. Nobody needs to know it was us."

"There were a number of witnesses who saw you and Mike. The rumors are flying fast and furious. Art Harris called and said the FBI press office is swamped with calls from reporters wanting to confirm or deny that the two men involved in the takedown were CIA counter-terrorism operatives."

"I don't understand the problem," Rapp said. "The military does this all the time. Delta runs an op and they give the credit to the Rangers or some other outfit."

"That's a little different," Kennedy responded. "They don't have dozens of cameras and live footage of it."

"All they have is footage of two men in black hoods and tactical vests. FBI, D.C. Park Police . . . I don't care who gets the credit."

"I think we'll be able to work something out."

"You can't do anything about the rumors," Hurley announced as he lit a cigarette. "People are going to believe what they want to believe. Besides, it's not the worst thing to have floating around out there. It's a nice message. You fuck with us and guys in black masks show up and put a bullet in your head. It'll make the next guy think twice before he volunteers for one of these one-way trips."

Kennedy thought about it for a moment and said, "Stan, you always have an interesting take on things." She kissed him on the cheek and said, "I need to get back. Thanks for taking care of them." She pointed at Rapp and Coleman. "Be available tomorrow. I think some people are going to want to talk to you."

Kennedy headed for the chopper and the pilots started the engines.

Rapp turned back toward the house and said, "Stan, I think I need a drink."

"I like the sound of that."

They started walking back toward the house. "Scott, what's your poison?"

"Just a beer, Stan."

"Mitch?"

"Whiskey and beer, please."

"Cigars?"

"Why not," Rapp said.

Coleman went with Hurley to help and Rapp headed down to the fire by the lake. There wasn't a cloud in the sky and stars were out. Rapp looked up, found the Big Dipper and the North Star and then Orion, the hunter. Coleman and Hurley returned and they all grabbed a chair. Hurley wanted the full debriefing and Rapp gave it to him in an emotionless voice. Hurley only had a few questions, most of them to do with Max Johnson and Hakim al Harbi.

Coleman argued vehemently that Johnson be not only spared but brought on board as a member of the unit. Rapp and Hurley weren't so sure about the second part, but they were in agreement that he'd done enough to earn a stay of execution and more than likely an outright pardon. Hakim al Harbi was more complicated. Rapp told Hurley outright that he had no stomach for killing the guy. Coleman had no opinion on the matter.

Hurley looked into the fire and took a sip of his drink. "I need to talk to Doc about him. We need to find out what makes him tick. And we need to catalog his sins. Figure out just what role he played in all this."

They heard the screen door slam, and a short while later Nash came out of the shadows with more beers. He passed them around and took a chair.

"How's Shannon?" Hurley asked.

Nash stared blankly into the fire. "I'm not sure. She just fell asleep, but I think Doc slipped her some pills."

"She'll be fine," Hurley announced.

Nash shook his head. "Who knows. I gotta think something like this can really fuck a kid up."

Rapp, Coleman, and Hurley all looked at each other. Hurley spoke for the group. "Kids are resilient. We're the ones who don't do too well with this shit."

Nash nodded but kept staring into the fire. "I can't believe I almost lost her." And with that he suddenly started bawling. He tried to stop it but he couldn't. The three men didn't move.

After a minute of it, Hurley announced, "Get it all out. Now's the time." He watched him for ten seconds and then said, "And don't forget it could have been a hell of a lot worse. All things considered . . . you were pretty damn lucky."

Nash got control of himself and nodded. "You're right." He finally looked over at Rapp, who was puffing silently on a cigar. "I'm sorry," Nash said. "Maggie's right. If it wasn't for you, I'd be dead, and Shannon might be dead as well."

"Well," Rapp said, "I'm just glad we could save her. As for your dumb ass . . . I'm not sure it was worth the effort."

Nash started laughing and then they all started laughing. Nash lit

Rapp up with a string of curse words and then said, "Next time you decide to turn me into a poster boy maybe you could check with me."

"You're my boss now. I can't take a piss without consulting you first." Rapp gave Nash a sarcastic wink.

"Oh . . . God," Hurley moaned. "I was his boss once. A long time ago. Worst fucking two years of my life."

"Yeah . . ." Rapp said, "I saved your ungrateful ass one time, too."

Hurley started spewing insults across the fire at Rapp. The group fell right back into their normal stride. It was as if the pressure of the last week was suddenly behind them and everything was back to normal. They told stories and insulted each other and they all took it for what it was—a sign of acceptance and camaraderie.

Hurley announced that it was getting late. There was one more issue that he wanted to cover, though—Glen Adams and what they were going to do with him. He looked at Nash and said, "Mitch tells me you're still not certain about a certain traitorous bastard." Hurley looked over at his barn just in case there was any question about which traitorous bastard he was referring to.

Nash wavered and then said, "I'm not sure. I don't think I'm exactly a paragon of mental stability at the moment."

"Well . . . all things considered I'd like to make the call."

"You want me to pass the buck." Nash shook his head. "Not very noble."

"Mike," Rapp said, "you have a great family. For their sake, and yours, I tried to put you on a different path this week. The honorable one. You can't do both. You can't be a great father and husband and do the shit we do. Something has to give."

Nash stared into the fire and thought about the conflict.

Rapp leaned forward and said, "Let us slosh around in the gutter with these guys. You go take care of your family."

Nash didn't say anything for a long while and then he nodded as if he'd made up his mind. He stood and tossed his empty beer can in the fire. He watched it turn red hot and begin to crumble. He turned to Rapp and said, "Thanks."

They watched him walk away into the darkness between the fire and the house.

Rapp looked at Coleman and Hurley, a look of disappointment on his face, and then he heard Nash say, "I'm going to go take care of my family. Good night, guys."